# BLACK BILE

SAMANTHA DEVIN

# BLACK BILE

Translated by

Peter Bush and Thomas Bunstead

ARISTEIA PRESS

Originaly published in Spanish under the title Bilis Negra
First published in Spanish by Editorial Planeta S.A. Barcelona
© Samantha Devin 2004


Also available in eBook

Copyright for the first edition in English © Peter Bush and © Thomas Bunstead, 2019
All rights reserved

©Samantha Devin 2019
ISBN: 978-1-913209-15-5

Aristeia Press 2019
London, UK
www.Aristeia-Press.com

For Francisco

# I

> What I here make public has, after a long
> and scrupulous inquiry, seemed to me evidently
> true... I do not think myself any farther
> concerned for the success of what I have written
> than as it is agreeable to truth. But, to the end
> this may not suffer, I make it my request that the
> reader suspend his judgment till he has once at
> least read the whole through with that degree of
> attention and thought which the subject-matter
> shall seem to deserve.
> A Treatise Concerning the Principles of
> Human Knowledge
> George Berkeley

Darkness fell slowly over the line of the horizon. In the mountains, dark clouds banked up around a solitary purple wisp and seconds later the last glimmer of daylight was gone. Farther off, lightning bolts fractured the sky and the air shook with thunder. The road was now little more than a narrow earth track. Trees rose high on either side, steep enclosing walls of green. Max stepped on the accelerator. It was imperative he get away before the rain came and washed all the dead leaves, rocks and mud from the roadsides, and the whole place became a swamp.

The roads had deteriorated the moment he left behind the busier towns. Almost imperceptibly, rough paved surfaces had given way to winding tracks, barely wide enough for two vehicles abreast except for small bays where the rock had been dynamited. At least, thought Max, he didn't have to bother keeping to the left any longer.

He glanced at the petrol gauge: close to empty. He groaned remembering the dilapidated petrol station he had failed to stop at some thirty miles before and the small, poorly lit restaurant with the makeshift sign offering home-made food and hot drinks.

It was five o'clock and dark already: at least there was that. Night had cloaked the soaring grandeur of the mountains. It had been beautiful driving, but the immensity of the landscape eventually became oppressive too. He had left London and headed north on the M40, and until reaching the Scottish Borders had a sense of being among people, and therefore safe. Until that point the roadsides were dotted with towns and cities much of the time. The junctions, the signage, the motorway itself, all bespoke civilization. But after Stirling, stopping briefly to stretch his legs and take a few breaths of the cold air – a view of the unnerving monument to William Wallace in the distance – he sensed he was penetrating a zone beyond the control of modernity, a feeling of true wilderness. He advanced along tree-lined roads, dark tunnels which, the further he went, made him feel he was losing his bearings, was gradually diminishing. Skirting a silent, forested mountain, he came upon Loch Ness, one of the many lakes strewn across northern Scotland. Driving along its edge, an unexpected sensation of vertigo came over him. He saw himself from above, as though on the wing and looking down at the red streak inside which he pushed on, bisecting a landscape whose enormity filled him with awe. He had covered a further seventy miles since then. The night had swallowed up distances and dimensions; all spaces had gone, making him feel secure.

Inverness and Strathpeffer were behind him now, and having crossed Loch Shin and turned off the A384, he made his way down roads entirely enclosed by trees, rising eternally all around, and smelling of moss and dank, rotting leaves. He had reached this rocky canyon with all the timing of men destined for disaster, destined always to be in the wrong place at the wrong time. Although, in Max's case – just as in mine and that of every person marked with this particular sign – his fate was beyond him to discern.

It was raining heavily now and, as he had foreseen, the dead vegetation washing down from the verge threatened to block the road. His chest felt tight, and he decided to put on some soothing music. But he'd opted for a car with fully comprehensive insurance, and then the discount offered for one with a broken radio had been impossible to turn down. He regretted having no music. Any melody whatsoever would have acted like a sedative, relegating the storm, making it merely incidental, observable. A thing he'd have had little difficulty poeticising from the padded comfort of the driver's seat. Without it, there was no way of achieving distance, making himself a mere spectator in the scene. He felt part of the chaos, as small and insignificant as the leaves on the road. It would have been insolent and unforgivable, to strike up with a song of his own in the face of that tempest.

If the directions he'd been given at the petrol station were correct, he now had a little over fifteen miles to go. The map was spread out on the passenger seat beside him, but it was nigh impossible to make out the clear lines on it now. He glanced and found only an ever more entangled mess of blue, red, black and yellow veins. He circled his shoulders around and gave the back of his neck a brisk rub. His shirt collar was unbuttoned and the white, neatly ironed lapels framed his face. Collar up, his face lit by the faint reflection of the headlights, he must have resembled an old oil portrait, the kind one finds lying forgotten at the back of an attic or a small antiques shop. His hesitant expression, along with his dark, wavy hair and sombre, evasive eyes added to the impression. He gripped the steering wheel with long, thin fingers, like a raptor refusing to let go its prey. He then bit his lip, revealing the brightest white teeth, shining ghostly out of the dark...

This is how I imagine the journey Max took on the night I first saw him. And it was much as I imagined it, as he confirmed some time later, along with many other details I can still recall with startling clarity. Now, after all this time, it is these memories alone that keep me going. They are all I have of him. I felt sure I could use them to understand my existence to date, but I begin to suspect that a person's life is as ephemeral as the thoughts that possess it, as elusive as the obsessions that drive it and as ineffable as the dreams that torment it. We try to understand ourselves, but something escapes us. Always, lacunae and shadowy hollows which, for all that we inhabit our own skin, remain lifelong enigmas. These same shadows were what finally convinced me of the great heterogeneity of human nature, and how difficult it is to grasp its contradictory manifestations, the ways it expresses itself, without simply notching them up as madness when displayed by a single personality.

My name is Simon – let's say. I know it is a name accursed among Orthodox Christians, but I share nothing in common with that obscure gnostic that a whiter power succeeded in vanquishing. It is my hope – for all that my days unfold now with unbearable, near infinite slowness – to turn seventy-eight next month.

In any case, it is not only myself I wish to speak of, but Max as well: of his life seen through my ancient eyes. I here record all that has occurred since my conscience began to awaken. Believe me when I say there is no more painful thing than the awakening of conscience. And yet, life being what it is, I am surely set to end my days not knowing who I am. But we all must find a truth to grasp onto, and this is mine. Never would I seek to convince anyone that it is the truth. No longer.

Men such as I will never be history's chroniclers.

The truth of certain matters, as I say, may never be known – and yet... Perhaps the time has come to put that term itself in doubt, with its power to condemn so many. I have too much time, and I don't use it wisely – I know. Hence, I allow myself to digress. Or perhaps distancing myself from events is a way of making things easier and safer for myself, and by raising other ideas at the same time, judging others' conduct, I reduce the absolute dominance of those events in my life. Certainly, what is fated creates fear, terror even: to trivialize it or pretend, as I do, that it is just another everyday incident, is, in the final reckoning, only human.

Max has become the obsession about which my very life turns. The mystery that gives it meaning. Every night I go to sleep with the memory of his accursed face, and that same image is all that compels me to open my eyes come morning. I cannot tell my story without telling his. So intertwined are our destinies, so monstrously connected, that to make sense of my own life I cannot do without his.

All that I know of Max is the reason I can talk of him without fear of erring. Our contact was brief, yet I came to know him intimately. Nobody ask how – it was a once-in-a-lifetime business. Sixty years pass and not a single soul have you known, not even your own, and suddenly someone appears whose thoughts you can all but read. I know that my ability to penetrate that closed world of his was down to the strange circumstances of our encounter – circumstances that conspired to connect us. Had we met in any but that impromptu, unlikely context, I know he would never have opened himself up to me. To understand him took more than simply observing all the documents to which I later had access. To understand him took a large dose of empathy and insight and I would go so far as to say that even the obsessive need I felt to truly know him was indispensable in filling those invisible spaces in his personality. All the material that came into my hands concerning Max, the videos, the written reports, his diaries and drawings – whether fortuitously or through predestination, I cannot be sure – I have sought to weave together in such a way that the reader may penetrate the complexities of his world just as I did: without intercession of any kind. So clear is his voice, and so strange my obsession, at times it is as though his thoughts were mine. I have included, in chronological order, the video material and the dozens of documents that came into my possession in the days after our time together. Though only now have I managed to fit the pieces together, you may be certain that I have missed nothing out, not even the smallest detail, should I have judged it relevant.

4

But who – you will ask yourselves – could be driven to record the most intimate moments in a life? And what unhealthy fascinations drive them – and why? Obsessions are at times the single motor for all our achievements. Without them life would not make sense.

It is now, as my life disintegrates before me, and my identity once more begins to give up the contours that define it, that I must hold fast to my reality. Although I begin to understand for the first time that the line separating reality and fiction, truth and appearance, is not only vanishingly thin but invisible.

I could have forgotten everything and in truth that would have been advisable. At my age, choosing to forget is one of the best things a person can do, and one of the least reproachable. And yet at times our memories become our sole truth, the only thing keeping us alive; at times, to forget means death. For even knowing what it means not to renounce the past – as I do – I choose to stick with my own truth, to remember and recreate a reality that will soon die with me. I have decided to start at the beginning. Not the beginning of my life, but the moment in which I became aware of my life. This is my reality, this my life. Not the one the doctors wish to impose on me, but the one that I remember. Events take their course – the single possible course – and it is thus that I wish to set them down…

It all began with my sister's death. A chance discovery led me into a world hitherto entirely unknown to me. Several months after her death I was distraught – not due to the loss but the circumstances surrounding it. I was working in a law firm in central Paris and when I look back to that time it all seems like a drawn-out dream, or a period of hibernation from which I woke not only too late but with a great jolt. Depression, combined with my age, prompted the company to place me on indefinite leave, which finally segued into retirement. I used what was supposed to be a time of ease and tranquillity to embark on a manic, frenzied search.

A long time has passed since I first laid eyes on Max, but the past is my abode now. It is there that I install myself, given how little interest the present holds. Nothing happens anymore, at least not in the external world. All my certainties, no longer mine.

To speak of Max, to be in any way certain about his life, one would need to ask his mother, but nobody can do that because she is dead. Either that, or to have been close enough to him to be persuaded that his character was, ultimately, that of a child who was never given the opportunity to mature and live a normal life. If I am a mystery, Max is the confirmation of the mind as the most enigmatic, impenetrable territory we may ever hope to glimpse.

Though he never knew it, he may have inherited from his mother an interest in the magical. An interest bordering on folly. As she herself said: "It is every bit the domain of intelligent people to interest themselves in the unknown, the invisible, all that the rest of the world dares not so much as to name." She taught him to love losing himself in imaginary worlds, worlds he alone could navigate, and that were discernible to the imagination alone. Those silent ghosts accompanying his every footstep. To anyone unaccustomed or in too much of a hurry ever to stop and think, or to delve into the world of the imagination for the simple enjoyment of it, the persuasion of a person like Max will seem childish or perhaps futile. I would counter that by saying it is dangerous. Futility and childishness cannot, I think, be judged from outside. We are each of us masters of our own time.

In reality, for Max the whole thing began in the manner of a child's game, and carried on so until the two of us met. It is well known that the habits and traits that most define us, whose origin seems so obscure, spring from our early years. And from a young age Max's mother got him to draw pictures of his dreams, sitting at the kitchen table in the morning. She invited him, in almost ritual fashion, to recall a past with which, in the everlasting present of his childhood, he was unfamiliar, but that pulsed within him, nonetheless, awaiting the watchword. Initially, the thoughts were obscure, impossible to make out, but after a time the illegible scribbles were joined by allies that aided their comprehension: the bubbles of letters. These diminutive allies began to mesh, if awkwardly and soon all he needed in order to bring an idea forth, or make visible one of these insistent thoughts, was to move his pen here and there, and out would flow a dozen little symbols, strung together like paper chains at Christmas, an imperishable record of the reflection in question, whether wise or nonsensical. Black, red, blue… Were these the colours in his thoughts? Were his felt tip pens instruments of magic? Max looked after them like his most precious treasure. But did these slender automata really contain so much? No, they did not, because a day came when they ceased to act as his messengers, ceased altogether: they no longer brought forth his dreams. From one day to the next. It was then, after a certain amount of upset followed by an explanation he took time to assimilate, that he first realised how nothing – and no individual either – could last forever. Whatever they had inside, ultimately they would falter and come to an end. After that, one was left with nothing but memories, accompanied by an intense, indelible pain. Beyond that lay the unknown.

He never forgot those early marker pens, his first allies, the first bridge between his most hidden self and the outside world. He never threw them away, keeping the husks in a drawer bled dry like martyrs who had given their ink for the one in whose thoughts and ideas they believed. Rummaging in the drawer, he would find them mixed in with an assortment of objects, no longer capable, with their desiccated round heads, of delineating a single jot; and forevermore they reminded him of this, his first brush with death.

It is no surprise that eventually, as these early doodles improved and once he was old enough to decide, he should have landed the perfect job. It came to him one day that his thoughts would no longer be his alone, but that to share them in exchange for money was no terrible thing. He still kept certain things back, to consider in his free time or odd solitary moment. Everything else, including the most ridiculous and extravagant notions, he sold to magazines. It turned out that people everywhere were willing to hand over their money for stories of the kind their minds lacked the intensity to create. Out of fear, perhaps, or out of squeamishness, or repugnance, or simply inability. Whereas he had this facility for conceiving the most exciting, disturbing worlds, places where chaos reigned, the only true counterparts of which were his soul, itself unfamiliar territory to him. It was just as easy to generate other worlds of splendour and comfort, benign and bathed in light. Some of these stories were the fruit of dreams, others came of introspection. He did not know whence exactly they came, but all were his.

His first job on leaving school was for a magazine that ran futuristic comics in its end pages. It fell to him to produce stories to fit these dystopias, with their cast of monstrous and cadaverous beings populating cities at once gothic and decadent. But the magazine folded after a year, and Max was suddenly in a hurry to find another outlet for his warped universe and all its attendant torments. He had to bring it into this world, to get it out. He had little trouble, as it turned out. Publishers abounded who were in awe of the stories he wrote, with their beautiful but blasted beings, constantly depressed by a sense of their ephemeral existences, plagued by perverse doubles bent on ruining all notion of sanity. In a matter of weeks he joined the staff of Gothic Dreams, the best-selling magazine that had good distribution throughout France.

It was a grey afternoon, three weeks before I first met him, when the letter arrived addressed to his dead mother. Taking it out of the post box, his pupils dilated as though he had seen a ghost. He could not bring himself to open it. He propped it against a plant on the mantelpiece in the lounge. But its presence between the flowers and candlesticks gave him the sensation he was watching over a shroud. He picked it up, uneasily, and placed it on the table by the front door, among the usual bills and letters, before realising the pointlessness of trying to disguise it with the triviality of commercial missives. A solemn air hung about the letter and there was no way to avoid it.

When he finally brought himself to open it, he felt discouraged. Doubt and worry overcame him. He had never heard his mother speak that man's name and was unaware that she had dealings with anyone he did not know. He struggled to accept she'd kept such a thing – anything – from him. He had the idea, fully formed by now, that there were no secrets between them, and far less any unknown persons, strangers who might know more about the two of them than he could possibly understand. The person who signed this letter was extremely familiar with them, knew as much about his mother and indeed about him as he did, if not more. He was repulsed by the idea that she had kept a lover and immediately discounted the notion – yet it was also this that compelled him to try to uncover what lay behind those opaque words.

Max wished to learn about himself. With his mother gone, his point of reference had disappeared. An indecipherable abyss opened up around him. He wanted, needed to know what she had left behind, what other people possessed of her now she was gone. Above all he needed to meet this stranger, this intruder who dared direct such words of insolence and reproach at a person no longer there to defend herself. For his mother had died two weeks before the letter arrived, one leaden evening. Max found her lying dead on the floor of the lounge on his return from submitting a couple of particularly grisly commissions.

Max had grown up clutching onto his mother's skirts, lost among them. The memory of his father was the faintest of blurs. She was his only reference as to what a family might be; for reasons unknown to him, they were personae non gratae for her wider family. Ignorant in the ways of the world, Max believed his mother's lack of a partner to be entirely forgivable, obviously undeserving of banishment and the ostracism exercised by his aunts and grandparents. For her part, she never mentioned the family, still less his father, of whom he knew nothing. It was as though none of them truly existed, as though 'relative' was an invention that applied only to other children, the rest of the world. He guessed there were probably cousins of his age somewhere out there, but never dared ask his mother about them. They had moved around so much, no lasting ties had ever been made, or friendships with children his age, or with anyone in fact. His had been a solitary childhood – he always played alone, and a birthday was an occasion to celebrate with his mother and no one else. She put up no resistance should he ever have a friend to stay, but never allowed him to sleep over elsewhere. They lived alone, like a couple of castaways on a desert island who, over time, come to believe that everyone else has wound up in the wrong place. Max never found the perennial isolation strange – on the contrary, being with his mother was a rare source of happiness. She was the only person in whose company he could really enjoy himself. His life was as happy as that of any person sharing their days with someone they love. Of course he didn't miss his father. That strange masculine figure was oppressive to contemplate, and it was beyond him to understand how other kids could wish to walk home holding the hand of such a person, one who must surely have dripped poison into their maternal relationships. No such intruder had ever darkened their days, thank God. He knew how lucky he was to enjoy his mother's undivided attention.

The discovery of her body left him in a state of suffering as painful as the prospect of a life without her. The record player stylus scratched nothing but silence that day.

"I'm home!" he had called out, to no reply.

He dropped his keys on the table by the door and went into the kitchen to make himself tea. They had been living in Lyon for some time by this point. Over a year and a half and, almost unprecedentedly, it seemed there was scope to prolong the stay indefinitely. They had been skipping from one city to the next: Amsterdam, Lisbon, Brussels, Genoa, Madrid, Munich, Salzburg, Milan… An endless parade of places, of which all that remained were albums populated with photos of the two of them standing in picturesque spots, in front of monuments; an array of buildings and imposing landscapes, but never any other people.

He had alighted the bus that day before his stop and had to walk almost two hundred metres in the downpour. The traffic had been stationary for almost a quarter of an hour and the driver opened the doors for anyone who wanted to get off. The stuffy air inside the bus had combined with the cacophony of car horns to make the journey intolerable.

A diffuse light filtered in through the kitchen window. A light that washed everything in the same grey, as if covered in a thin layer of dust. Removing his coat, he once more called out that he was home, but still no answer came. And once more strained to hear in which room she might be speaking on the telephone. He had picked up on the sound of some exclamation, as though someone had relayed something disagreeable – the kind of thing she was bound to keep to herself should he ask.

He went through to the lounge, where the lights were off. The stylus joggled back and forth at the centre of the record, as though trying to hop back over itself. Lifting it off the record, and with the room now in silence, he heard a faint groan and turned around. He spotted something at ground level, something bundled up in front of the fire. He went over and turned on the light. The vermilion of the blood leapt up at him, and he let out a gasp. There was his mother, lying in a pool of deep, warm blood. Her skin shone white like that of a marble statue. He threw himself to the floor beside her, his knees hitting the sticky blood – he felt its warmth – and looked disbelievingly into his mother's terrified eyes. He went on staring – he couldn't understand. And for a moment, those dried-out felt tips of his childhood returned to him. The blood, an inky, meaningless smudge. The spreading pool, a picture still taking shape, and impossible to comprehend. Max whispered to her, a question he perhaps expected an answer to, but all he received was her final breath as he brought her body closer. The slashed wrists, the squalid red, life still bubbling out. Eyes rolled back in her head, spinning in pain. He stayed on his knees, cradling the body, until the female concierge rudely knocked on the door, calling out for the day's rubbish.

"These stairs will end up stinking if it's any later!" she cried.

Max took the rubbish bag to the door, handing it over as usual. He moved like an automaton, completely expressionless, and it was only when the woman screamed that he came round. His shirt was covered in blood – looking down, feeling the red sticky layer beginning to stiffen, he started to hyperventilate. A gush of heat rose from the pit of his stomach and he was immediately sick.

This had taken place a month and a half before, but his mother remained entirely present for him. It was difficult to convince himself it hadn't all been a dream. Often in the middle of the night, in the fleeting moment before waking, a deceptive touch of happiness had come to him, the liberating sensation of knowing our nightmares are nothing but fabrication. But upon fully waking, he found himself inside the very reality that seemed so strange, and the only course now open was to embark on a kind of fetishism, to usurp the space she had left empty. He still caught the occasional waft of her perfume, which hung in unexpected pockets throughout the apartment. Her bedroom, full of a sweet, warm aroma, haunted him with hundreds of memories past. Her dresses still gave off the aroma of the living but he could only bring himself to erode it gradually, to breathe in the wardrobe smell any time his desire became too much. He knew that in time this perfume, her essence, would also die, and it was an added pain to contemplate this second passing.

He loved to be in his mother's bedroom. It felt warm and safe, a place in which the sun never seemed to go down. The sunlight slanted in, flooding every corner with a white, velvety light. Next to the window, which was at the height of the treetops, stood her dressing table with its well-ordered rows of coloured pots. A silver-plated hairbrush, an oval, beautifully inlaid powder compact, a carved wooden jewellery box and the little clay vase he made for her in primary school and in which she always kept flowers. Following her death, he replaced them regularly. He went to the Sunday market and enjoyed picking out the kind of bunch she would have liked, something delicate and cheerful. He placed the vase on the right hand corner of the dressing table, which got the sun until late in the afternoon and on warm days he threw open the balcony doors and let the fragrance of the room mix with the flowers and fresh aroma of the gardens, which in some way were also part of her essence.

For Max, to set out on a journey on his own, leaving behind the maternal hearth, the still-warm uterus of his dead mother, was to immerse himself in the unthinkable, in the chaos of the world; quotidian for everyone else but insurmountable and out-of-joint for someone whose existence and experiences had always been restricted, and carefully managed by her. The outside world was a place he only ever visited, like a tourist among those human avatars. Like those mythological beings, half gods, half men, that never found their way or their true place, spending a life caught between the unattainable wisdom of Olympus they will never attain and the cruel brutality of the world they will never eliminate.

It was all too unreal, too seemingly fictional, that this world, a world he knew so well and that centred on his mother, should have been dismembered so grotesquely, with such flagrant disregard for the rules by which they lived. If death was a mystery, suicide was to renounce the very basis of rationality. Illness, accidents – these now struck him as so entirely natural, enviable, as easy to understand as the motion of the sun and the changing of the seasons. But to die like this, in silence and desperation, neither of which he would ever have associated with her, triggered a constant burning in the chest, the kind of smarting sting that can never be soothed.

So, when the letter came, all he didn't know was compounded by doubt. Summoning all his courage, he went in search of an answer, some logical explanation to douse that inner fire. Laying himself bare, he struck out into the world alone.

# II

## SATURDAY

For he's reported as having one appearance
when he comes into the village
and another on leaving it.
The Castle
Franz Kafka

The petrol gauge hovered close to empty, and still he was driving down that funnel of a road. A flash of lightning illuminated a small road sign to the right: he had to be approaching someplace or other. He slowed down and strained to make out what it said. The sign indicated a steep, winding track to the right: Shimts. 3 miles.

Pulling over, he looked at the map for the mark made by the man at the petrol station. He thought it was another ten miles, and his sense of direction wasn't usually this bad. Checking the map once more, he decided this had to be the turning – hardly likely there would be two towns with the same name. Doubtless it was small and remote. Half the places he had passed did not feature on the Michelin map. He rotated the two maps, doing all he could to establish his current location. These maps were impossible to handle, bulky and stiff as starched sheets.

He took the turning. The track was as muddy and narrow as the previous one, and just as strewn with rocks. And steep. Though the rain had slackened, all he could make out through the fog was a short stretch of track. It wound between a gorge with rocky walls much like those he had just left behind. He peered out in hope of some light or sign of life, but the visibility was dire and he tried to imagine how anyone could wish to live in such a barren and inaccessible place.

Several miles farther on, and more than three for sure, the track flattened out and ceased to wind left and right. He saw a wooden construction up ahead, from which various horizontal trunks stuck out. It was a crude, makeshift-looking bridge, stretching some ten metres across a gully. It looked far from sturdy and having to cross it was not the happiest prospect. The river running beneath the mouldering timbers had swollen and was close to breaking its banks. On the side of the rock face, the bridge was some ten metres high. A drop from such a height wouldn't do the car a great deal of good. He started across, half expecting to find himself tumbling into the river. He flinched at every creak, and tensed his whole body as if thereby to strengthen the loose, half-rotted joinery. Once across, he breathed a deep sigh of relief. There was a wind-battered sign a little way ahead, once more announcing Shimts. But all remained in darkness, still no trace of any town. The track turned steep and winding again. Potholes threw him from side to side, as the wheels stuck and skidded on the boggy, rain-soaked track. He was beginning to lose patience. If the sign had been correct, he should have arrived by now, and yet still the track went on, still he found himself rolling around in this swamp.

"Three miles!" he muttered incredulously, cold to the bone by now. Winding down the windows had been the only way to clear the windscreen.

Just then, half an idea came to him, but it felt far from the right moment to indulge his inopportune gift for invention, to stoke the situation with such thoughts – as he always feared might happen if he gave them a single second more. It was an absurd idea. The road sign, whipped by wind and rain, seemed a remnant of a long-distant past, and for a brief moment he felt perhaps it only stood there because nobody had bothered to take it down. Perhaps he was squandering his little remaining petrol only to bring himself out at some derelict ruins.

The track swung abruptly to the right, and finally, there in the distance, a cluster of lights appeared. Entering the town, he pledged to make the most of whatever else the night should hold. But one look at the place told him it was a promise he would not be able to keep. Dense fog shrouded everything. A scattering of streetlamps lit a wide, straight street, leaving huge areas in darkness. Old stone buildings lined the street. There were no lights in the windows and nobody walked the pavements. The name of the town was written on a wooden sign away to one side, and beneath it a legend Max neither understood nor particularly registered: Do What thou Wilt.

Leaning forward in his seat, he examined the place, quite unsettled. He was apparently driving along the high street, exceedingly drab through the streaming rain and the steamed up windscreen. No smoke rose from any of the chimneys, and no neon signs or boards suggested the presence of a public house in which to warm his bones.

He continued along the road until he finally saw a sign:

*Cravensworth Castle.*
*200m*
*Second left.*
*Bed and board. Guided tours.*

Without stopping to think, he went on a little further and turned down a steep, narrow street, on either side of which stood gloomy houses with small, unkempt front gardens, and soon came to a mossy stone bearing the inscription:

*Cravensworth Castle. 50m*

He stopped the car. There, at the end of a dirt track, on the far side of a tree-lined path, rose an enormous, ill-shaped edifice. It lay in near darkness, but a number of oil lamps prevented him from missing it completely. His headlights swung across a broken-down metal gate, which stood wide open. A sturdy wall enclosed the entrance, and to one side he saw a metal sign with an inscription:

*Welcome.*
*Opening hours: 8 AM to 2 PM.*
*Closed on Saturdays.*

The winding dirt track, bordered by well-kept hedges, led to a gravel courtyard. He brought the car around a fountain and parked as close as he could to the front door. He turned the key and the engine fell silent. Stretching back in his seat, he breathed in the clean, damp night air, which speared icily into his back. Nine hours at the wheel, back tensed and eyes trained on the road the whole way, had left him exhausted. It was no easy thing keeping to the wrong side of the road, having to remind himself where he was supposed to be at all times. A strange sensation had come over him several times glancing at where he and the steering wheel should have been. The back-to-front roundabouts, the taxing rules of the road, had sapped him completely. The same went for overtaking: any time he found himself on the other side of the road he always forgot to move back over to the left. Even on the airport bus to the car hire place, he had felt something strange, as though he'd passed through a looking glass almost too large for his mind to take in.

He looked out through the window. The mansion was a solid stone construction whose every cornice, chimney and window betrayed the ravages of time. He pressed on the car horn a couple of times and peered through the misted-up windows at a small lantern swinging to and fro over the doorway. And stayed sitting for a few minutes longer, until it became clear no umbrella-carrying bellboy was about to show up to carry his luggage.

"Knowing my luck, they'll all be deaf!" he grumbled, and got out of the car.

He had forgotten his umbrella, and perched his trench coat over his head; his other hand held his overnight bag and a small, worn suitcase bearing his beloved notebooks. He looked around despondently, before a smile spread on his face as Roger Corman came to mind: the gloomy scenario would surely have delighted him. He was soaked within seconds. Rivulets of water ran down his face, and he had to blow to either side of his mouth where it was tickling his cheeks. An involuntary shudder ran through him. He rang the doorbell a couple of times, but after several minutes' wait, he became sure that nobody had heard. And yet, he grumbled to himself, he could hardly get back in the car and drive away. The petrol tank was all but empty and he didn't know if he'd find anywhere else to spend the night. Bone-weary, he leant against the door, and felt utterly stupid and absurd. The trip was surely further proof of his inability to overcome adversity, his lack of maturity. There he was, completely soaked and exhausted after a day on the road. And all of it down to his obsession with the identity of the man who had written a letter that in any case made no sense whatsoever.

It was then that I saw him for the first time: looking down from a first-floor window, peeking through the curtain. I observed that young man, blowing water away from his mouth like a Renaissance fountain, and already had a sense of looking at a castaway, a lone soul finally reaching terra firma after a terrible crossing, when he'd floundered and floundered grasping hold of a splintered old barrel. Then someone turned the key in the lock and the door inched slowly open.

# III

In the secret kingdom of the unconscious, nothing
is quite what it seems to be. The dead talk and the living
are dumb. The phallus is a cannibal god gorged with
blood. The moist womb solicits the rapist. The rapist
violates for a love he cannot experience. Janus, the
two-faced guardian at the gate, sees the past and the
future, but is blind to the present and unconscious of the
eternity which includes them all.

The World is Made of Glass

Morris West

**"**So sorry!" said the woman in English, her accent thick and the words
spluttering out like little coughs. "I expect you've been standing here
a good while. Nobody can hear a thing, what with the storm blowing."

Max was taken aback.

"Come in then, won't you? You'll freeze to death," she said. "Here,
I'll take your suitcase."

Max looked at the woman as though she were a ghost. She wasn't
one, but he was disturbed by her attire. She smiled affably and stood
back to let him past. Her body was shapely and firm. She wore no
make-up, and her face, with its symmetrical, delicate features, shone
under the moisturiser that softened her impending wrinkles. Her
cream-coloured, semi-transparent nightie, fell as far as her bare feet.
The sheer dressing gown she had hastily put on top – without time to
do the buttons – was embroidered along the sleeves and hem.

Max had no need to call on his powers of imagination to appreciate
the woman's body, and it was this that must have taken his breath
away. She seemed not to mind in the least. His suitcase in hand, she led
the way without another word, and Max barely noticed the mediaeval
decorations and interior, as he stared at his hostess's rear, jiggling side
to side under chiffon and lace knickers.

For my part, I was not in the best of humour, looking on from the door of my room. When the bell had rung, I was in the process of acquiring some highly valuable knowledge as to the sexual customs of the Highlands, delighting in that same hotel manager's insatiable zeal as an educator. We'd had to interrupt a most interesting lesson, full of concepts so new and fascinating that I remember cursing aloud upon seeing Bezel (that being her name) jump up to attend to the running of her business, which entailed picking up the phone and uttering a brief, "He's here." When it became clear she wasn't coming straight back, I shut myself in my room, diving into one of the books I had brought with me. Calmer by now, I thought that some rest and a little work would do me no harm. I had been at the hotel for four days by this point, and my reasons for being there weren't really so different from Max's. Though this would not become clear until several days later.

An old record player struck up somewhere in the castle, distant strains Max could not entirely make out. He felt uncomfortable, sensing he had interrupted something, but not wishing to mention it, for fear that the woman would tell him exactly what it was – she seemed capable. Though it wasn't a disagreeable sensation, his stomach felt tight and he found it impossible to speak. He supposed she must think him quite stupid, but as hard as he tried to find something to say, nothing apt occurred. She turned to address him and, watching her breasts swing around with her, he felt a touch of nausea.

"It's this way."

They came into the large kitchen, lit by the glow of a fire. The woman, putting down the suitcase, coaxed him to go and warm up.

"How dreadful!" she said. "You're soaked through! I'll bring you a dressing gown. Get out of those wet clothes, you'll catch pneumonia."

She went out, and Max stood feeling quite disoriented. He went over to the fire, reaching out his hands, and his mind was fired up too. Shaking out his hair, he took in his surroundings. It was a very old kitchen, with high ceilings and stone walls. The wooden furniture was old but clean and well looked-after. A large walnut table stood in the centre, the six chairs around it bearing blue-chequered cushions. Small pictures of fruit hung on the walls, and copper pans from hooks. The same blue-chequered fabric had been used for the curtains. Two lamps resembling small lanterns gave the room extra light. The whole place had a simple, homely and feminine feel.

Hearing the woman's footsteps, he hurried to remove his clothes.

"Still got all that on? Come on, put them down by the fire and get this on. Cat got your tongue? You haven't said a word since you set foot inside."

She took a seat facing him, and though she closed her legs Max could make out a mass of pubic hair through her knickers.

"Sorry," said Max. Then, before he could think of anything more sensible – unable to do anything but stare at her body: "I thought this must be a house of the deaf"

"Sorry?" said the woman, looking bemused.

"Apologies. My name is Max Sinclair," he said, eyes still lingering somewhere around her thighs. His English was impeccable. Peeling off his wet garments, he continued: "I've taken a few days off to come and visit an old friend, and I've been driving since dawn. Very nearly got stuck in that canyon before the diversion. The storm started just as I was coming across."

He wasn't altogether comfortable undressing in front of a stranger, but given that he had little choice tried to act naturally. In any case, she didn't appear to mind.

"Lucky's what you were," she said bluntly. "If your car had got stuck, you'd have had to shelter inside it till they came for you."

Max didn't understand.

"Wolves," she said.

"Wolves?"

"You heard correctly."

"I didn't know there were wolves here."

'Well, now you do," said the woman, getting up from her chair. She came forward, her considerable cleavage on full show. "Hungry?"

"I am, as it happens. But please don't bother yourself…"

"Eggs and bacon okay?"

"Wonderful."

"Fine," she said. "I can do that, you just get out of those clothes, or it'll be pneumonia for you."

When she turned away, Max quickly shimmied out of his trousers and wrapped the dressing gown around him. The woman, aware of his haste, smiled to herself as she took out a plate and cutlery. The music continued to drift down from somewhere high in the castle, slow, haunting, and barely perceptible. When Bezel turned away again, he took a closer look. Her skin was taut and supple. She had broad, rounded shoulders and generous, fleshy hips that nonetheless looked not to have an ounce of fat on them. A lyrical part of Max saw her skin shining beneath that diaphanous film, like thin, highly polished glass, but the thought was fleeting and he made no attempt to convert it into poetry. Her long, toned legs were strong and firm, and her bare feet rested blithely on kitchen flagstones, apparently impervious to the cold. She suddenly turned around and caught Max leering. Bezel chose to say nothing about his inevitable inspections, but merely smiled. He sat down and when she put the plate in front of him, it was his turn to pretend he hadn't noticed the obvious suggestiveness with which she did so. He began to choke down a knot in his throat, and it was she who broke the silence with her warm voice.

"How long will you be with us?" she said, picking a mouthful from the piece of bread she had put next to the plate.

"I can't actually be sure," he said. "I had a letter from a friend…"

There was no reason to tell this stranger the truth about his trip. He was a long way from home, and from all his day-to-day affairs too – the perfect situation for dissembling, he thought. Here in this remote place, sitting with someone he had never met before: he could be whomever he liked. And yet, when he tried to put his powers of imagination into action, so easy in the stories he wrote for his comics, it struck him that one also needed courage in order to pretend in real life, and could only bring himself to say:

"He invited me to spend a few days together, and I thought I'd take the opportunity now I have a couple of weeks off."

"What's your friend called?" she said, crossing her arms. "Maybe I know him."

"Vladimir Drake Emilianov," he said, as naturally as he could. He'd have liked to keep the reason for his visit secret, but he hadn't envisaged it being such a small town. Everyone probably knew everyone, and it would have been ridiculous to make up a name, especially since he didn't know exactly where the man lived or what kind of person he was, plus the fact he would need some help.

"Drake's a friend of yours?" she said, incredulous.

"Well, not exactly," he said, correcting himself, surprised that she knew him. "He was a friend of my mother's."

"I see."

"I guess it won't be difficult to find where he lives, but you wouldn't happen to know… The truth is, all I know is that he lives in the town. I don't have an address."

"You've absolutely come to the right place," she smiled. "Your journey's almost at an end: he lives right above us, in the top part of the hotel."

"Here?"

"On the top floor. He was the one who restored the castle, over twenty years ago now."

"Twenty years? How old is he then?"

"Well! That's something of a mystery," she said quietly.

"I thought this was a hotel."

"It is. But when Mr Drake decided to have it restored, he did so on the condition that the top floor would be his alone. And nobody objected – pretty much the whole town is his, so I'm not sure who would have."

"What do you mean, the town is his?" asked Max. "What does he do?"

"I mean, the town is his. He owns the corner store, the bank, the bar, pretty much all the land for forty miles around and all the livestock... Then there are his business interests on the east coast of the United States. Aren't you impressed?"

"No, I mean, of course," said Max.

He never remembered his mother talking about having anyone in her life. She had never brought a man back to the house. The young guys who used to carry the shopping in were the only ones ever to cross the threshold. Try as he might to imagine the relationship, he could not. When would they have seen one another? Perhaps when he was at school? Sitting up straight in his chair, he put the fork down on his plate, his appetite gone. Bezel noticed his unease but went on as though she hadn't:

"Strange he never said anything to you."

"About what?"

"Well, he isn't around at the moment. He is away on a trip and won't be back until Wednesday. Seems strange to me he wouldn't have mentioned it, what with you coming such a long way to visit."

"Actually, I didn't tell him I was coming. I wanted it to be a surprise."

"In any case, he'll be back in a few days. And meanwhile, you can see the sights."

An uncomfortable silence descended, not helped by the discovery of that setback. Bezel spoke first.

"You are French, right? Yes?"

"From Lyon," he lied.

"Ah! I adore France," she said, her gaze drifting up to the ceiling as she recalled a pleasant memory.

"So I imagine you must know Paris well," she said, her tone honeyed.

"Everyone knows Paris well," said Max, swallowing some bread. "Actually I've only been there a couple of times."

"Yes, but you're French," she declared, as though nothing more were needed to meet her full and wholehearted approval.

She tied the hair at the back of her neck, giving him full sight of her smooth, white armpits. As Max used the bread to mop up the remains on his plate, he saw just how absurd his story was. If a friend had invited him, why would he have come to a hotel rather than to the friend's house, why wouldn't he have known where the friend lived, or indeed failed to telephone ahead… But he had already told the lie, and now the worst thing would be to admit it. How could he have known that the man lived on the top floor of this very establishment? Or that the one hotel in town belonged to him? That he was somebody everybody knew – how was Max supposed to have known any of this? He felt nervous in the woman's presence. He didn't know where to look. Look at her, and it was impossible to avoid drinking in the sight of her shapely body; look away, and she would surely know how flustered he was. He didn't want to come across like a schoolboy. Then again, he had little choice in the matter, given that apart from his mother he had never seen any woman naked.

They chatted a while, about Paris, and the crazy nights Bezel had enjoyed in that city she adored. The rhythm of her speech slowed, and as silences began to punctuate her utterances Max wondered if she were drawing the conversation out, waiting for him to take the hint and step out of his dressing gown – and with the violence acceptable in one his age, tear off that gossamer sheathe around her body. But then she stood up all of a sudden. She gathered his plate and cutlery, put them in the sink and said she would show him his room now. She'd grown tired of waiting, Max thought, feeling ridiculous. Should he have acted sooner, done as she had clearly been suggesting? Then again, he wasn't sure what she might have been suggesting, or indeed expecting from a stranger possibly twenty years her junior…

And indeed, Bezel had grown tired of waiting. The young man had given her no signal to pounce on him like a hungry lioness, and, remembering that, though old and far from lithe, I was upstairs awaiting her return, she felt some consolation and dispatched Max without another thought. For her it was a relief to have a man at hand, ready to go.

"This way," she said, no longer seductively. "You bring your suitcase, I'll bring the bag."

"My car's parked right by the door. Maybe I should move it."

"Oh, don't worry about that. There's only one other person staying, and he never leaves his room."

They went along the hallway and took the stairs. Max was still unable to wrench his gaze from the firm rump swaying a few inches in front of him. Not that he wanted to touch it – the slightest contact with those smooth curves, and he would surely have fainted.

The stairway, a lengthy succession of gleaming wooden steps, brought them to the first floor, where an ornate banister stood to one side of an expansive corridor covered in rugs. Bezel walked slowly ahead, coming to a stop at the third door on the left.

"This is it," she said, pushing on a heavy door, which opened onto a large room done in a true Scottish style of five centuries past.

Through the high, discoloured windows, Max saw that the rain continued to come down outside.

"Does it ever stop?" he said, placing his suitcase down by the bed and glancing around the room. It looked far more luxurious than he could afford.

"It might do in about three months, but then the snow'll start, and that will be much worse, believe you me."

"Well I won't be here in three months," he smiled.

"Are you sure?" the woman said, smiling sardonically, before turning and shutting the door after her. There was no time for Max to respond, but in any case, he thought, they were the words of a woman spurned. He had no idea what she meant, but quickly put it aside. His body felt stiff, and exhausted, his knees and neck in particular, and he could barely stand up. The memory of Bezel's smooth neck returned to him, and an erection immediately ensued. All that time in her presence he had managed to control himself, or perhaps his concern for guarding against her advances had suppressed all desire. Anxious, as if someone might be reading his thoughts – he tried to switch off, clumsily rummaging for his pyjamas. He never usually wore pyjamas, occasionally just a comfy old shirt. But for the trip he had brought along a set his mother had given him, and now placed it by the fire.

The room was cold. Though the fire blazed, and the hearth was large enough for a person to climb into it, it was anything but cosy. He stood with his back to the fire for a good while, pleased to warm it up. He heard some noises beyond the door and as he began doing his buttons, he went over, vaguely curious. Several people were creeping slowly down the stairs, clearly making an attempt not to be heard. Max didn't dare to open the door and look out. If that woman had nocturnal assignations with other guests, or with some townsperson, he hardly thought it his business. Coming back past the window, he was about to get into bed when something outside caught his eye. In the distance, on one of the town's streets, he saw a collection of lights, dozens of shimmering lamps or lanterns. They were moving in a single direction, and upon reaching the high street joined a larger group of lights; together the entourage then moved off, heading out of the town. Max tracked the procession, intrigued. The cluster of lights stretched vertically in the rain streaked windowpane, resembling will o' the wisps on fire. They grew smaller in the distance, eventually being lost from sight altogether. He climbed into the bed, wondering what such a gathering could be doing abroad at that hour, and in such tempestuous conditions. Tiredness soon overcame the curiosity. Asleep within minutes, he drifted into dreams, to thoughts of the comely Bezel as she stood making bacon and eggs.

# IV

## SUNDAY

He was a young man, and a life
So full of golden dreams,
Is already gone, before childhood tears
Could dry.
He remembers childhood,
And his mother who weeps for him,
Dying now, thus,
When so lovingly she weaned him!
On Death Row
José de Espronceda

He woke late in the morning to a rap-rap of Bezel's knuckles on the door.

"Mr Sinclair, it's me, Bezel," she said softly. "I've brought your breakfast."

"One moment," he said, pulling the sheets up to his chin to cover himself. Then, somewhat doubtfully: "Come in!"

Bezel appeared with a tray of delicious-looking food, not nearly so eye-catching though as her latest outfit. It was a tight silk shirt, pearly grey and semi-see-through: Max had a clear view of her nipples. They brought to mind the rubbers at the ends of pencils. The skirt, long and figure-hugging, was the same colour.

"Good morning, Miss Bezel," he sniffed as he sat up in the bed. "You needn't have troubled yourself."

"Good morning, Mr Sinclair. Good night's sleep?"

"Very good, thank you," he said, remaining courteous.

His dreams, he now remembered, had been full of her – dreams in which she had awoken more than just his curiosity. But dreams were one thing, and reality quite another.

She smiled and slowly sashayed over to the bed. She fancied the idea of doing what she'd done the previous night to unnerve the young man.

"God knows how much rain fell last night!" she said, sitting impishly down on the bed "Sorry to be the bearer of bad tidings, but last night, not long after you came in, the river flooded again and washed away the lower part of the bridge. It isn't that surprising, the thing was completely rotted." She glanced at Max. "It means we're completely cut off."

"Seriously?" Max felt annoyed, but in fact more concerned with the liberties the woman was taking.

"From what I've been told, the bridge has been destroyed. The road to Shimts is cut off. Nobody's going to be coming in or leaving till the river drops." While she said this, she sat carelessly dandling her finger between her legs.

Max scrutinised the woman, unsure of how to respond. Complicated involvements were the last thing he wanted; his only desire was to meet the person who'd sent the letter, get to the bottom of whatever linked them, and with any luck be on his way furnished with a clear and simple explanation. He was astonished by Bezel's provocative ploys. He was having the kind of thoughts he usually suppressed. It wasn't only that she was so much older than him – there was the unthinkable prospect of a dalliance with a presumably sex-crazed stranger. He felt vexed in the same way his mother had always been vexed by any overfamiliarity toward him from other women. Sex featured in Max's life as nothing more than a few back-and-forths of the wrist, and that infrequently. To him the impulse was a little like having a headache: bothersome, but easy to get rid of. Yes, a part of him desired her, but the other part simply loathed such frivolity, and such brazenness, it made him want to…

"It also means, I'm afraid, that your friend Mr Drake will have no way of getting back into town, nor you of getting out of it." She smiled. "Now isn't that a shame?"

"Tell me, Bezel," said Max. "Is Mr Drake married?"

"Heavens, no, Mr Drake is the wealthiest, most eligible bachelor in all of northern Scotland. He owns hospitals and various businesses on the east coast of the US, in New York and Boston. He is one of the most famous psychiatrists in the world. A man of renown. Did your mother tell you none of this?"

Max shook his head. He wasn't in that much of a hurry to get home – nobody awaited his return – but neither did he plan to stick around any longer than absolutely necessary, least of all in a hotel as expensive as this one. The more information he could extract at this point, the better.

"And what will they do now?" he asked. "I mean, how long will it take to repair the bridge?"

"Oh, I don't know, but there's nothing to worry about. We have everything here a person could need: doctors, shops, restaurants, a pharmacy, the dancehall."

"Even so…" insisted Max.

"It isn't so bad," she said. "Personally, I can think of nothing worse than life in the city. Everyone running around, never any time to get to know people, it's lunacy. We live well here: it's quiet, people are happy. We've got everything we could possibly want. Though I suppose for a young man like you, with your city ways…"

Bezel had begun to lean in close, and Max gave her a cold stare. She stiffened, ignoring the look, as well as his apparent disinterest.

"Well," she said, feigning indifference as she got up and went towards the door, "do enjoy your breakfast. I'd hang around but, you know, things to do. Afterwards you could go for a walk in town, you're sure to like it."

She went out and Max heard her going up the stairs. Seconds later, the old record player started up, and melancholy strains of music, a languid voice singing over the top, flooded Max's room. The music seemed to soften the walls, to make the old, cold building altogether less alien and uninviting. The melody, a tad familiar to Max, though he couldn't place it, caused something in Max to give. Something within him shook, came to life like a drowsy lizard feeling blood coursing through its veins again. He stared at the ground for several minutes, trying to pinpoint the tune. Then, as though awaking from a dream, he found himself standing before the fireplace, hands by his side and fists clenched. He touched his face and found a tear rolling down his cheek. Dabbing it, he looked down at his finger in disbelief, hypnotized, not knowing how the tear had got there. He was crying and yet could pinpoint no feeling that might have provoked tears. He dried his face with both hands, rubbing vigorously, as though trying to clear a footprint frozen in the snow. Then he began moving aimlessly around the room, still finding no explanation. There was no sadness he could identify, no happiness or pain to provoke such a reaction. Nothing.

He tidied his clothes away and got in the shower, resigned to remaining curious. He ate his breakfast sitting by the window, and it became clear that from his position in the castle, by that window, the entire town was his to observe. It wasn't a large place – he could see all the houses and buildings from where he was. He finished dressing and went downstairs.

A sweet fragrance emanated from the kitchen. It was warm and homely. Max thought that maintaining an establishment of this quality in a town so small and remote must cost a fortune, one surely not recompensed by guided tours and still less the rooms. But in any case, he thought, there would be nowhere else to stay, and if it came to it he could talk to Bezel or Drake himself and come to some arrangement.

Firelight played on the faces of Bezel and the woman she was chatting with at the table over coffee. Max came in and greeted them politely.

"This is Mrs Hoffman," said Bezel in that wry tone of hers.

"Mrs Hoffman," said Max, nodding.

"Are you the foreigner who arrived yesterday?" asked the fair-haired, light-skinned woman in her early sixties.

"Yes," said Max. "I'm in town to visit a friend. I had heard Scotland was a green country, but I didn't know it had to pay for it with days like this," he said, doing his best to appear sociable. "I haven't seen rain like this in years."

"Have you already decided where to be?" asked the older woman.

"Be?"

"Yes. Where are you going to live? There are properties available on Neung Street." Then, with a mischievous smile: "Perfect for a young bachelor – which is what you are, isn't it?"

"I am single," said Max, "but I won't be staying on more than a few days. Once the bridge is repaired and I have a chance to see my friend, I'll be leaving."

"Leaving?" said Mrs Hoffman in surprise, looking quizzically at Bezel.

Max looked at her too. Her response was simply to beam knowingly which seemed to satisfy Mrs Hoffman, though Max could make neither head nor tail of it. It felt to him as though Mrs Hoffman had a screw loose, and he bid her goodbye, saying he felt like a walk around the town.

The rain drummed on. Max decided to leave the car where it was: it would be absurd to try manoeuvring it down the small streets. The thought of the wait to meet the stranger filled him with impatience – the stranger who, for some reason, had seen fit to write to his mother as though he were a close friend, to the point, as Max saw it, of insolence. He turned up his jacket collar and began picking his way down the steep track. It was not long before he lost his elevated view and found himself within the town proper. The streets were paved with old cobbles and lined with even older buildings. Coming to the high street, he passed small two-storey homes, all of which had a dismal, run-down aspect. Narrow, winding streets and tracks broke off left and right, the majority precipitous and threading sinuously up towards the main hill. There were long, low buildings surrounded by leafy vegetation, and old mansions hidden behind their respective tangles of bush and tree. Breathing in the cold air he sensed, beneath the smell of wet earth and the hills around, a gentle aroma that caused his heartbeat to quicken. Taking a deep lungful, he noticed something shift inside him. Suddenly he found himself lost in a memory of summer – of one day in particular, eighteen years before: on a holiday he and his mother had taken together in Biarritz.

It was hot that day, the air stuffy and still. It was the first day of the holidays and by nine thirty in the morning they were on the beach. They weren't the only ones out early. Numerous families were spread across the sands with their parasols and hammocks. In a couple of days, few would still be coming down so early, but it was the first day of the holidays and most wanted to make the most of it.

There were rows of dark clouds in the sky, that also seemed to have settled in for the day. They slipped by slowly overhead, almost imperceptibly. The sea was an expanse of soft golden sparkles, its surface smooth as a gigantic silver plate. When Max came down to the shore (he had learned to swim some time before and his mother now let him go in on his own), he looked down at that mirror in wonder. He had come away that summer with a new idea in his head: he felt sure he would be able to walk on the water without sinking. He gazed out across the immensity of the water, which gave off an intense smell of summer, of afternoon strolls and strawberry ice cream. The early morning stillness had yet to evaporate and towards the horizon a thin, gauzy veil seemed to cover the sea. Max put one foot in the water, and it sank – which did not surprise him at all because, so close to the beach, there was still movement to the water, it was a polished mirror no more. But he was sure that, once he went a little further out, he would have no trouble walking on that shining surface.

He looked towards the beach. The sand stretched away from him, soft and cool. His mother was lying in the hammock writing in her diary. He looked her way, and then turned back to the sea. With the warm, golden ice rink of the sea before him, he walked slowly forward, staring at the horizon. He was convinced that when he got to that point, there'd be no difficulty doing as he imagined. He couldn't remember the story exactly but had heard that someone had done precisely this: that it was possible to walk on water.

He went on through the warm shallows, still feeling hopeful, until he was in up to his chest. At his next step, he felt the water eddying in cold spirals around his ankles. Now he was on tiptoes, and when the water reached his chin, he turned to see his mother was still there. And she was, reclining quite placidly, but a long way off now.

He took another step forward, and the sandy depths vanished from under his feet: no more views of the ice rink, the sun, or the summer heat. Everything went black and the cold water went up his nose. His stomach churned and he felt it in his gullet. He was sinking into a cold, dark place, down, down, untouched by the summer sun, and all he could see was a line of silvery bubbles. He felt something tugging on his foot – he had vaguely sensed it before, but not taken it on board. There it was though, no question: something pulling him down. At first the shock had stopped his flow of thought. The next thing he knew, he was unable to breathe. He looked up, and saw the water moving quietly above his head, still burnished a soft golden hue. Looking down, he saw a large hand with a big shining ring on the index finger, and bubbles – coming not from his own mouth – rising toward the surface... Then, everything went black.

The next thing he remembered was his mother's lips on his own, her soft hands at his chest and the pain in or around his heart that stopped him from breathing. He finally vomited a jet of water and coughed violently. His eyes stung painfully. There were people all around him, kneeling and on foot, all staring down at him, and when he got unsteadily to his feet his mother drew him close, taking him in her arms. Warmed by the sun, her skin smelled of suntan lotion and she was crying, though he had no idea why.

He soon felt right as rain once more. He was at the first-aid station on the beach, but there was nothing wrong with him. His mother bought him a strawberry ice cream and made him comfortable on the lounger. It was then that she introduced him to the man:

"This is the gentleman who saved your life," she said. Max remembered her tanned face, the wheat coloured hair hanging down from under her sun hat.

Max switched the ice cream cone to his other hand and wiped his sticky fingers on his bathing robe. He held out his hand to shake, as he had seen men doing. It was then that the real fright came. The man wore a ring identical to the one Max remembered seeing under the water. Dropping his ice cream, Max threw his arms fearfully around his mother's neck. She scolded him, told him not to be so rude. The man said there was no harm done, but the smile he gave Max sent a shudder through the boy. He began to cry, he couldn't help himself...

The memory ended as abruptly as it had begun. Not a trace remained – except, on the far side of the smell of damp Scottish earth, a hint of his mother's skin that day. He had somehow forgotten that incident eighteen years in the past. Until now it had been buried in the recesses of his mind, only for an unexpected association to revive it now; it was beyond him how he could have forgotten such a thing. The truly incredible thing wasn't that he had nearly drowned that day, or perhaps nearly been murdered – this didn't interest him in the slightest. Most significant was the manner in which the day had been evoked in his mind. The level of detail. The smell of the sea shells on the beach had come to him with utter clarity, the diffuse, moist air that summer morning, the smell of his mother's skin when she drew him close and, of course, the distinctive ring of the man who had saved his life – after first trying to kill him.

A melancholic smile spread on his face. There was no way for him to know what was real and what details he had added, nor why, until this moment, he had relegated it to that dark corner of his mind. Perhaps the incident in the water had affected him more than he believed.

Rain was soaking his face, but he'd barely noticed. Back in the present, he found he was standing in front of a house with grey walls and a mansard roof. He carried on towards the centre of town as if sleepwalking, still swathed in the memory, the evocative smells floating a little way above his head. He came to the high street. Here the buildings were cheek by jowl, and none more than three storeys high. Rows of balconies and windows capped with charming sloped roofs and tall chimney stacks. Some of the front doors were flanked by crumbling, ornate pillars made of dark stone.

The dampness gave rise to airy exclamations around the heads of passers-by, as in one of his comics. Though it was a little warmer now, the morning remained wet and blustery. Max wandered along with no particular destination in mind, simply observing what the place had to offer, and not fully registering his surroundings, still half-immersed in that vivid memory. And yet gradually he became aware the memories were beginning to fade. He could still see the images with complete clarity, but something evaporated with each step he took, with each new thought that came into his head. And then he had a familiar feeling. The kind of fear he had experienced after the death of his mother. It was to do with the very essence of things, with that which keeps them alive. It was within his power to avoid an important loss. He had to record the memory, prevent it from vanishing entirely; had to commit it to paper, in as much detail as he could, while still fresh in his mind. He decided to look for a quiet place to have a cup of tea and transfer the whole thing to his inseparable notebook.

Max took his notebooks everywhere he went. To his mind they were irrefutable evidence of his existence. Being able to reread the vignettes that were a representation of his own life mitigated his loneliness. Representations of himself, of his mother, of the houses as they'd lived in them, their travels... He kept a copious record: words, gestures, expressions and moods. Thoughts, even, all that went unsaid, were visible in the little bubble-clouds floating over his characters' heads. This obsession with conserving the passing moments, with transforming them into something to look upon later, had been inculcated by his mother – a wise move. One of the ways she controlled him and was able to know what her beloved Max was thinking at all times.

Max quickened his pace, glancing furtively at the buildings, taking little interest in the faces of passers-by. These people meant nothing to him, they were mere objects, like the mansions or the trees. The truly important thing was that memory because what he desired above all else was to find answers, and what he had just seen might possibly mean something. He came to a sudden halt. The street he was walking along had petered out, and with it the town. To either side, a pair of identical, solemn buildings marked the dividing line. Beyond them lay the track he had entered along the night before. Looking at the dense forest up ahead, he gave a shudder at the stark border separating the town from the rest of the landscape. Disquieted, he turned around and, for the first time since his arrival, left behind his inner monologue to evaluate the picturesque spot where everything appeared to him once unremarkable and quite abnormal. It was a small isolated backwater where everything unfolded sedately. People walked down the centre of the street, no kind of hurry to their movements, and no more noise around than the murmur of their voices, their footsteps, and the rain and wind. It all seemed quite normal, like anywhere else. He stood still for a short time on its perimeter, feeling neither the cold nor the rain that soaked his trench coat and face. Lifting his gaze, he saw the hotel on the promontory away to the left. It was a jagged, ungainly black lump of a building, out of proportion with the rest of the town in its enormity, and spiked with thin, narrow towers and overhanging balconies. It stood dark – nearly black – against the leaden grey sky. From where he now was, the building seemed strikingly out of keeping with its surroundings. As though imported from some other scenario and plonked down clumsily, simply because it had been surplus to requirements. Suddenly the cold air began to bite, and he set off walking once more, eyes still on the castle until it was concealed behind buildings once more, at which point he concentrated on finding a café, and quickly. He hurried along the street until he met a pair of older gentlemen in animated conversation. They stopped talking and looked him over with some interest.

"French, I presume?" said one, seemingly the older of the pair.

The man wore a voluminous dark green scarf that hid his face almost entirely. Grey hair fell on either side of his face like a couple of skeins of wool.

"From Lyon," Max said, repeating the lie.

"If you're looking for something to warm you," said the younger of the two, "go up that narrow street, and you'll find a café. Third building along."

"He's better off going to Hausen's," said the first man. "That place is so dark inside, you can barely see two foot in front of your face."

"Yes, but Hausen's hardly the earliest of risers, he might not be open for business yet. Not the most reliable sort, as you know."

"Yes, but Hausen's is closer, and always has been. If it isn't open, there's always Freyser's."

Max stood saying nothing, waiting for the two men to decide.

"Well, try this one then," said the first man, pointing to a nearby building with a large entranceway. Then, pointing at the narrow street once more: "If they aren't open, you can always try the first one I said."

Max crossed the street and went in through a gloomy doorway thick with the smell of perpetual damp. Coming inside, to his right stood a double door, the lower half of which bore a worm-eaten etching in the wood, and the upper two glass panes with cream-coloured curtains. It was heavy, and an effort to push open. Inside was spacious and musty, and worn flooring concealed somewhat by several tables with blue flowery tablecloths. The counter stood at the back, and beyond it wooden shelves crammed with drinks and cups and glasses of every size and colour.

"Hausen's out of bed then," Max murmured to himself.

Inside it was warm, almost what one might call homely. It had high ceilings with thick wooden beams. Approaching the bar, he rubbed his cold hands together and waited. A white-haired man in his fifties with dark eyebrows stepped out from behind a lace curtain.

"Good morning, Mr Hausen," said Max affably.

The man smiled but did not ask how he knew his name.

"What can I get you this morning?" his tone was friendly, though he spoke with a lisp.

"A nice, hot cup of tea, please."

"Take a seat by the fire. I'll bring it right over."

Though the man did his best to enunciate, it still sounded as if he had a sweet stuck to the roof of his mouth.

Max sat near to the fire. A few minutes later Hausen came over with a tray. He ceremoniously set down teapot and cup, the sugar bowl and a saucer with two slices of lemon, a small jug of milk and a selection of pastries in a basket. The man moved with some difficulty, as though each step he took were an impossible challenge that he nonetheless found a way to overcome. One of his legs was twisted and the foot on that side did not work: skewed inwards, it looked long dead and apparently only still clung to his body out of compassion. The man went off and began cleaning behind the counter, while Max sipped his tea in silence, leaving the pastries untouched. He took his notebook out of the right pocket of his jacket and began jotting down all that he could remember of the summer's day. As the heat from the fire begin to enter his bones, he immersed himself in his memories and set down the sequence of events, delineating his characters and their attendant speech bubbles with precision.

Once it was done, he took a deep breath. He was unaware how much time had passed, but he didn't mind that. He had nothing to do until the bridge was repaired, until Mr Drake returned and Max was able to find out about his relationship with his mother. He tried not to think about it but there were moments when his mind went blank and his stomach would turn as if stirred by an enormous worm awoken only by the awful memory of a bright red pool of blood. And it was the memories, those that bring back sensations we thought were gone, or that begin to populate our daily life with ghosts, that had awoken Max from the lethargy that had marked his existence for nearly twenty years.

"How much is that?" he said, reaching into his pocket.

"Seventy pence. You here on holiday?"

"I am. Beautiful country you've got yourselves here, terrible weather though." He looked out the window. Still the rain teemed down. Hausen gave an embarrassed smile, as though the incessant rain were his doing.

"Rain is good," he said. "It makes the grass grow, and the cows eat the grass."

Max nodded as if he were talking to a small child who had struggled to reach a simple, if correct, conclusion.

"You're right," said Max with a smile, "but I don't happen to be a cow."

He glanced around nonchalantly, the look of a person entirely at leisure, and leaned on the counter:

"Where's the petrol station?"

"No petrol station here," said Hausen, struggling to get his words out. "Did someone tell you there was?"

"No, I just imagined..."

"Ah ha!" said the man, cutting him off. "You imagined."

"Where's the nearest one?"

"Next town along. It's twelve miles away."

"Next along?" Max said, smiling. "Strange sense of 'next along' you've got here."

The man gave Max a look he couldn't decipher, before adding nervously:

"I would like to help you, but I can't. I'm sorry."

Max had no idea what this was supposed to mean, or why the man's delivery was so deadly serious. For a moment he wondered if they were speaking at cross-purposes.

"And you wouldn't happen to know if anyone could sell me some petrol? I think I'm too low to make it to the petrol station. Is there anyone?"

"Yes," said Hausen, looking Max in the eye.

Max waited for him to go on.

"Well," said Hausen doubtfully, "if you're lost, perhaps you won't know your way back."

"I'm not lost," Max said. "I'm on holiday, like I said. I know where I am, and I know what way to go when it comes time to leave. All I need is some petrol."

"Ah! In that case... No, I can't help you."

"But you just said you could."

"That was because I thought you were lost, but if you know where you are, that's... different."

At this, Hausen moved off, dragging his bad foot painfully along.

"What's different?" Max asked, following him.

Hausen said nothing. Max was having second thoughts about talking to this man. But he still needed to find out who could sell him petrol, and, taking a deep breath, insisted:

"Okay, Mr Hausen, let's see. Who in this town can sell me a few litres of petrol?"

"I'm really not sure what to say..." Hausen was now cleaning a glass with a dry cloth.

"But you were about to give me a name. What was it?"

Hausen hesitated for a moment before answering:

"Head over to Vahlenkamp's. Mrs Vahlenkamp sells just about everything."

"Thank you, Mr Hausen," Max said, and, feeling a little calmer, went to leave.

"You are too young to get lost."

This threw Max once more and though he felt like asking Hausen to explain himself, he thought better of it, raising a hand in farewell and went out.

Coming outside, he took a deep breath of the cold air and looked up at the grey sky. The shop was on the other side of the street. An old sign hung above a half-open wooden door:

*Vahlenkamp's Emporium*

It was spacious and quiet inside. The dark wooden walls were finished with a gleaming varnish. The floorboards, in contrast, were worn with footfall. Max cast his eye over the assortment of wares. It seemed a great jumble of things, and yet not entirely without order somehow. All kinds of items were for sale: from dresses to trousers, chairs to rolling pins, scarves, pots and pans, plants, porcelain figurines, gloves, lamps, candles, table-cloths, curtains, cushions, plates, shoes, tables, toothbrushes, towels, rocking chairs, bottles, paintings, books, rugs, mirrors – and an endless assortment of knickknacks besides, all of it somewhat tawdry and homemade. A woman was standing behind a counter at the back, a kerchief over her head, wearing a plain, dark brown dress. She looked to be about fifty years old, and watched Max with interest.

"Good morning," he said, coming up to the counter. "I've been told you might be able to help me."

The woman said nothing but continued to consider her new customer with some interest.

"You wouldn't happen to have some petrol you could sell me?" he continued.

"What's your name?" she said quietly.

"Max Sinclair," he sighed. It seemed he was going to have need of his patience once more.

"Max. Okay, Max, how much petrol do you need?"

"I don't know… A five-litre can would be enough."

"Enough for what?"

"To get me to the petrol station," he said.

"Surely you aren't leaving so soon? Don't you like our little town? Have you seen the castle, Max?"

"Yes," he said.

"Where are you headed?"

"Why all the questions?"

"Want my help?" she said gravely. "Well then, help me by answering my questions."

"I just don't see why you want to know where I'm going or who I am," he said, beginning to lose his temper. "I just want some petrol."

"And I just want to know who you are. Or do you think I go around selling petrol to just anyone?"

Max nearly burst out laughing, but there was nothing funny about the situation. He imagined going into a petrol station in London or Marseilles and formally introducing himself to the man working there, getting out his family photos, his C.V, and then having to wait nervously for the man to consent to selling him a few litres of petrol.

"I'm no one, is what I'm trying to say. Passing through. Is that so hard to understand?"

"No, I suppose not. And tell me, what do you intend to use the petrol for?"

"To put in my car! What else?"

"There is no way I could stop you from going out and burning down somebody's house. And if you were to, the whole town would know I had sold you the petrol. My licence would be revoked, and the consequences of that – unthinkable."

"Good God!" Max exploded. "I haven't the slightest intention of burning anything. What gave you that idea?"

"Those are the rules." Then, coming out from behind the counter, she continued: "Please, take yourself off for a walk now. I'll bring the petrol to the hotel later on. I'm guessing that's where you're staying."

"Why can't you sell it to me now?" he asked, bewildered.

"Because there's none on the premises."

"But later on there will be?"

"Yes, later on there will be. Listen to me, Max. I can't promise anything, but I will keep you updated." Her tone had turned conciliatory. "In any case, you can't leave. As you surely know, the river has burst its banks and there's no other way out of town. One of the downsides to living in the countryside, but let's see what we can do to get you your petrol before the day is out."

"I suppose it isn't anyone's fault that the river overflowed..."

"Please, go for a nice stroll. I'll make some enquiries and look you up later on." This last part she said as though the matter were a delicate one.

"How long could the bridge repairs take?"

"Oh, difficult to say. But if I were you, I wouldn't be in such a hurry…"

That comment, along with its curt delivery, piqued Max, but he chose not to get wound up again. He had already seen there was no point. He knew nothing about this place, but it was clear that the people here had their ways. Perhaps there was something in the water, or sheer isolation – they really were an incomprehensible bunch. Each of the three people he had spoken to had succeeded in getting on his nerves, no easy thing: he was never a person to become agitated. He was someone who kept his thoughts to himself, yes, but not to the point of rudeness. And in the course of a single morning, he had lost his patience no fewer than three times – and, something told him, it could well happen again if he were to enter into conversation with any more of the townsfolk. He came away from the shop both enervated and confounded, and started back in the direction of the castle.

On returning and going upstairs, he found the door to his room open. Bezel was inside. She had her back to him when he entered, and was rummaging around in his suitcase. He went straight up to her.

"What are you up to, Miss Bezel?"

But rather than turn to face him, she went on going through his things as though she hadn't heard. He came around and stood in front of her, at which she slowly got to her feet, smiling at him.

"I was looking to see if you had any dirty clothes," she said blithely. "I'm doing a wash."

"I don't need you to wash my clothes," said Max, taking a pair of socks from her hands and placing them back in the suitcase.

"No need to be angry," she said.

Bezel took a few forward steps, until her body were all but touching his. Max was dumbstruck, once more caught between desire, repulsion and an inexplicable touch of fear.

"I should be off, Miss Bezel," he said solemnly. "I only came to get a jumper."

"Go ahead," she said, smiling maliciously. "What's stopping you?"

"You have no right," he said, raising his voice, "no right at all to go looking around in my things. You shouldn't –"

"I know I shouldn't," Bezel said, stroking one of her breasts with the palm of her hand, "but I'm naturally inquisitive. We all need to be aware of our flaws, and I am of mine."

"You're a real…" He wanted to say something quite vulgar – wanted to call her a whore – but he stopped short. Instead, he composed himself and went on: "If you don't mind, I'd like to know how much I owe you for the room. I'm leaving."

She moved away from him, laughing loudly

"Nothing yet," she said.

"Enough of your nonsense," Max said, trying desperately not to lash out. "I am leaving. You need to tell me how much it is, right now, you won't get a chance later on."

"Fine, go then," she said casually. "But you won't find anywhere else to stay."

"Fine. If you don't want your money, thanks for everything."

Gathering up the few things he'd brought with him, he left the room and went down the stairs.

"See you soon, Mr Sinclair," Bezel said tauntingly from the landing.

Max didn't answer. He left the building, his blood boiling. Throwing his things in the back seat, he set off. Once on the high street, he had to slow down. People sauntered along in the middle of the road, seemingly oblivious to the vehicle behind them. He honked on the horn, to looks of surprise. People moved reluctantly aside, muttering to one another, words he failed to make out – though he couldn't have cared less.

He was soon out of the town, making his way along the track that led back to the main road. After a few minutes, he began to calm down. Glancing in the rear-view mirror, he saw the entire town collected in that small rectangle, the crooked castle included. He drew breath. He wanted to get away as quickly as he could. The place, the exasperating people: there was nothing to like. With a little luck, he might make it to the main road, or near to it at least, and then wait for somebody to give him a lift to the petrol station. Once he had solved the petrol problem, he'd come back and have his talk with Mr Drake; better to drive the twelve miles every day than spend another night in the company of that flirt. The dark-mud track had grown less passable still in the rain, the car felt as though it might slide from under him at any moment.

Coming to the top of the track, he saw how pointless his efforts had been. The final incline leading to the bridge had been completely washed away. He stopped the car and took in the scene. The bridge was in tatters. All that remained were two uprights on one of the banks and a section of railing jutting out of the water. Before him was a ten-metre high rock face from which dangled a battered length of wood. He got out of the car and walked down as close as he could. The river had burst its banks and a considerable amount of the track now lay underwater. The river ran fast, roiling and tumbling by in a torrent. He looked around and weighed up the options. All about him was jagged, rocky terrain. The river wound down through the valley. The town lay at the lowest point, hemmed in by clearly impassable mountains. His only means of accessing the outside world was gone. The river was twice as wide now and the dark water pounded against either bank. Max doubled back, searching for some way out, but it was soon clear that the sheer wall of rock was quite insurmountable.

When Bezel told him they were cut off, his reaction had been one of indifference (more concerned as he was with shaking her off), but the implications now dawned on him. If there was no way for him to leave the town, it meant going back and having to put up with her sarcastic remarks and insinuations. He could think of nothing worse. When she said they were "cut off" she hadn't exaggerated, but Max had thought that perhaps it would be possible to find some other means of reaching the main road. He had not imagined the land to be so precipitous. He had been unable to see further than a couple of metres in front of his headlights the night before.

His shoes squelched through the mud. Wrapping his trench coat around him, he went a little way along the river bank, sweeping the area for a way across, but the further he went from the broken bridge, the clearer it became that this was the narrowest point of the river; doubtless the reason why it had been chosen for the building of the bridge. The rain continued to fall, and he gritted his teeth against the biting wind. There was no way out. He gave a deep sigh, and was about to head back to the car, when something caught his eye. With little mind for where he was putting his feet, he came up to the water's edge. The upright on his side, half-collapsed, stuck out over the river at an angle. Squinting, he took a few steps forward. The wood had a cut in it. A neat, straight cut: there was no way the river could have produced such a clean break.

Dumbstruck and at a complete loss (he found all the explanations that came to mind unconvincing), he got back in the car. Absurd as it was to think that someone would have made such an incision on purpose, he had seen it with his own two eyes: it could only have been made with a sharpened object, an axe or a saw, never the force of the water. Perhaps the cut had occurred after the bridge broke. It was possible that a section of the bridge had become caught up and was stopping the current, and they had decided to remove it before further damage was done. That seemed the only possible explanation. Or at least the only one that settled his mind. There was nothing to suggest anything else had happened. It was obvious that no one would want to be stuck in a place like this. And yet, none of the people he had spoken to seemed worried or bothered in the slightest at being cut off like this. They were most likely used to it. Perhaps he was the one making a mountain out of a mole hill but… He suddenly felt claustrophobic, a choking sensation at his neck. Now, he thought, he had to go back to the town, the hotel. Put up with more of Bezel's smart comments and call on his already thin reserves of patience while waiting for the waters to subside. It was bad luck, but there was nobody to blame. Who could you blame for the stormy weather? Or for the river bursting its banks? Maybe he should go back to town and give Miss Bezel a slap? Or shake the woman in the emporium by the shoulders and shout in her face for her to stop the rain, stop it or she'd be sorry?

He rested against the steering wheel, feeling drained. There was nowhere for him to go. Half-heartedly he began counting the raindrops on the windscreen, laying little bets with himself as to whether the trickle on the right hand side would end up joining the fat rivulet snaking down the left. In the end all became a single stream. Then, as earlier on, when he had sensed that smell beneath the wet air, his mind was once more transported – just as rapidly – to a rainy day that same summer, several days after the incident at the beach.

It was raining that day as well and he remembered the feeling of disappointment at not being able to go down to the beach. He was kneeling on the sofa in the living room, leaning against the sofa back and looking up at the window, imagining the raindrops racing one another. He was bored and had a cold. The beach incident had become the single subject of their conversations and his mother forbad him from going off on his own. And though he had learned to swim at the age of five, now when he wanted to go in the water, he had to put an unwieldy flotation device around his waist. How he had managed to catch a cold in summer was beyond him. He associated colds with wintertime, when temperatures dropped and you were at school. But for some reason he had a high temperature, and every now and then gave a tremendous sneeze. There were friends of his around but he wasn't allowed to play with them until he was better, for fear of them catching his cold. And that was only fun, his mother said, when you are in school and it meant a few days away from classes, sitting in bed reading comics. Nobody would thank him for it in the summertime.

The day was dull and grey. Nobody was out on the street with towels over their shoulders or lilos under their arms. There was a glimpse of the sea from the living room, in between the other houses, and it gave a less than happy impression: murky and lacklustre, not so dissimilar in colour to dishwater. He caught sight of the occasional greenish ripples of foam, bubbling up, then vanishing almost immediately, before re-surfacing when he thought they were done. He soon tired of watching the sea and, leaning his chin on his arms, turned his gaze on the garden. He saw how the pond in front of the house had grown darker as well and the still water been covered in a layer of rotting leaves which trembled under the bombardment of the intermittent drops of rain. Then he heard a creaking noise. It was the garden gate. Someone was coming into the garden. Maybe a friend had taken pity on him and come to play. He dragged himself on his knees over to the left, straining to see who it was. He could tell that it was a man, though the large umbrella in his hand hid everything but his legs from sight. His shoes were polished to a high gleam and his beige trousers had turn ups. He shut the gate carefully behind him, as if wanting not to make a noise, and took a few steps in the direction of the house. But then he stopped. He stood there, as though straining to hear an infinitely quiet noise of some kind, trying to establish where it was coming from. Then, closing the umbrella, he turned, slowly and deliberately, and looked straight at the window where Max was. Then he recognised him. It was the man who had dragged him out the water. The man, a smile playing about his lips – as though he had read Max's thoughts – took his hand out of his pocket and raised it, before swapping the umbrella into that hand, and raising the other. None of his fingers sported rings. Max, however, was far from convinced by the show, and continued looking warily out. Eventually the man started forward again, covering the short distance to the front door. The doorbell rang, shattering the silence of that rainy morning.

"Don't go, Mummy," he said, grabbing onto her skirts in desperation. "Don't open it." Amused, she turned and picked him up with a smile. Max clung to her neck, nuzzling her smooth cheek. Together they opened the door, and the man stepped forward, a smile on his face and a bunch of flowers in one hand. Max was quite taken aback. Where had the flowers been before, he wondered? And where had the umbrella gone? His mother was pleased to see the man and, letting go of Max, took the flowers and invited him in for a cup of tea. Max looked up, clinging to his mother's dress, tugging on it for her to carry him.

"You are awfully big now for me to pick you up, sweetie," she said, stroking his cheek. "Why don't you show Mr Drake the living room while I boil the kettle?" Max thought about it for a moment, before grabbing her once more:

"No, I'm coming with you."

"Oh, don't worry," said Mr Drake, "let's all go into the kitchen." And he too grasped at Max's mother's dress. This made her laugh – she put a hand over her mouth. And though Mr Drake had immediately let go of the dress, Max didn't like it one bit that someone else should have the right to do that. Something other than fear woke inside him at the intrusion. Jealousy was what he was feeling, though he didn't yet know the word.

Mr Drake had an unusual way of dressing, bordering on the extravagant. He wore silk shirts and cravats, and bright, garish jackets, much like his manner. His voice was hoarse, unnervingly so, and he was forever touching him. Max didn't like being touched, and when Mr Drake pinched his cheek, he flinched and drew back, glaring at the man in a fury. But that didn't seem to bother him, his seemingly immovable smile remained in position, and before long he reached out to pinch his cheek again. Max also didn't like the way he talked. Almost every utterance began with a "My dear" that sounded seductive on his lips.

They took their tea in the living room, under the watchful gaze of Max, who kept staring at Mr Drake's mouth: he wanted to work out whence precisely that low sound came from. His mother didn't seem to mind the man's voice and smiled from time to time at the things Mr Drake said. Max found none of it the slightest bit funny. Drake spoke slowly and deliberately, as though each word, each syllable, were premeditated. Everything he said landed in such a way that it was impossible to ignore. Max didn't understand a lot of it, but he supposed, given the manner of the delivery, it must all be terribly important. Drake drank his tea very gingerly, as though there was a large insect inside his cup, which he did not want to swallow. Several times Max peered into the cup, but all he ever saw was tea.

At one point, as an aside from the conversation, Mr Drake invited them to a party he was due to give that coming Saturday at his home.

"You simply must come," he announced. "We'll have a fine time."

"I'm sorry," Max's mother said. "I don't think we can. I can't leave Max."

"That's not an issue, Irene," he said. "Naturally, you can just bring him with you. If it goes on late, you can put him to bed in one of the rooms."

Max's blood froze at the idea. It was beyond him to even imagine entering that man's house, which would doubtless be as unpleasant as he was. Where hideous voices like his would resound down long, dark corridors. No chance he was going to sleep in some room full of shadows, while everyone else was having fun downstairs. Mr Drake kissed his mother on the hand, and then, in that deep voice of his, turned to Max: "So, see you on Saturday, little chap." Max hid behind his mother's skirt, and they laughed After Drake was gone, Max took his mother's hand and kissed it as he had done: he was the man of the house, and there was no way he was letting anyone else push him aside. She ruffled his hair affectionately. She wore a blue dress that day, and her loose hair cascaded over her shoulders. Standing in the front door, hands propped against the small of her back, she smiled as Mr Drake went away.

How beautiful she was.

Max emerged from the memory, feeling quite astonished. He was leaning forward over the steering wheel, eyes wide with surprise, staring out at the drops of rain. "Drake!" he whispered. He looked deep within himself, as far as his sight would allow, trying to break down the memory. It was useless. Never until now, as far as he knew, had he had any contact with this man. He straightened his back, as though by making his posture symmetrical and upright, he might discover the source of the bells he'd heard jarring within him. He must be delusional, surely it was some kind of dream: there was no way those memories were real. Those simply were not scenes from his life, not part of it, like a father was not, like going to friends' houses on Sundays was not. It was beyond him how his mind could generate such memories, as it was to know why it had chosen this particular moment to do so.

Straightening his shirt collar, he ran his hands slowly over his eyebrows. Maybe it was this place, he thought, looking around. He couldn't be sure that it was a coincidence. If it had happened on different days or in different places, the thought wouldn't have occurred, but today was the first day anything like this had happened to him. Like anyone, random days sometimes came back to him, happy days from childhood – but always somewhat consciously, always with a sense that a memory was rising up. Here it was as though his mind had spontaneously set itself in motion, and with no prompting whatsoever was making an inventory of all the memories stored in an enormous, cluttered attic. He needed to find some rational or at least comprehensible explanation for why these memories had remained dormant inside him for such a long time and why now, with no apparent stimulus, they had risen to the surface, like cork freed from the rock where it had been embedded. The functioning of the brain was not something he understood, not even his own, but he did know that its mechanisms were as mysterious to man as the turning of the spheres.

For all that, he could see that he'd always found it easier to invent new worlds than to cast his mind back over his own. Until the death of his mother, he'd had no need of memories: his days were always happy enough. Nor was there anything about the past that he missed. The present moment, and sharing it with his mother, kept him fully satisfied. Perhaps his memory, atrophied from lack of use, had allowed for boundless imagination to rush in, and that long-standing dearth of evocation was now being nourished in some way with memories deep and unexcavated, events cast out from the kingdom of his mind. Wasn't it true that the mind shut out wounds and difficult emotions, just as files are closed once they are filled? But he surely wasn't so old as to have forgotten so much, or for his own short life to throw up this kind of surprises. Why was he afraid? Perhaps out of a suspicion that forgotten memories were not always pleasant. Perhaps he sensed that certain experiences were better forgotten... This last thought, which had surfaced randomly, left him petrified. Did such experiences exist? Events in his life that were hidden from him? He sat up tall again, sharpening his inner vision. What on earth could have prompted him to ask such a question? He'd forgotten a couple of scenes from his childhood, and now that made him a total stranger to himself? The question had presented itself so abruptly, as though thrust upon him by that innermost being we all possess and which Max loathed, though he didn't know why.

He took out his notebook and began writing and drawing pictures – all of which I would later see: committing to paper the memory of that rainy day, everything about Mr Drake and his deep voice and the reflections that flowed from the discovery. A new set of sketches, those wispy figures of Max's with the speech bubbles emerging from their mouths, filling the pages of the notebook that would later come into my hands. He worked in a hurry, driven on by the fear that those memories would be lost once more.

*It all began in the car, as the raindrops on the windscreen turned to fat rivulets...*

He concluded with a paragraph which, like many of his stories and pictures, seemed to emerge from some secret compartment, some unfathomable place inside him, a place emanating a sadness that bordered on desperation. Having filled an entire page, and waking from his 'trance', he was stupefied by what he saw before him. The last thing he had written was the following:

*Nature abhors a vacuum, however there are no vacuums, therefore nature hates in vain. One misstep and the debt with the stronger spirit is settled. So sad to live a hidden life, stifled by a fearful nature, stuck in the abyss, ever disconsolate. I call out, but nobody hears my cry. There is nobody there. The chains begin to chafe on my bones. I see through to the muscles, pinkish beneath my skin. The way out, the way back, lies somewhere hidden behind me – not damnation. We should all be able to live, even if only ultimately to die.*

He could only put down what had happened on the day of Mr Drake's visit – nothing before or after. He noted down with great precision all the feelings, the quality of the light through the windows, the smell of the tea, the blue of his mother's dress, the words that had been exchanged... He relished it all, as though his senses had opened up a spiral in time, taking him back with an awareness so sublime of every single detail that he could even feel the mucus that had run from his dripping nose. When eventually he looked up his neck was stiff and his hand swollen. Dark had fallen without him noticing. Peering out into the blackness, he wondered how much time had elapsed with him immersed in this delicate dreamscape, a place where he handled himself like an expert juggler. He knew that it began getting dark there at four in the afternoon, and by five was completely dark, but he couldn't believe he had been there more than two or three hours at most. The clock on the dashboard wasn't working. He had turned on the interior light some time before, but couldn't even remember doing so. He decided to park the car to one side of the track, and got out, taking his notebook and bags with him. It seemed best to leave the car there. It would be in nobody's way, and when everything was sorted out at least he would still have a little petrol to get him to the main road.

He peered around, eyes twinkling in the dark. His life to date had been a warm soup whose flavour he knew only too well, and the recently added ingredients had left a bitter aftertaste to which he still was not accustomed. When his mother was alive there had been nothing to worry about. He was a prince living in a glass tower, safe from both the world and himself. His entire life had been regulated by his mother's love, by that chain – no less cruel for being invisible – with which mothers seek to shackle their offspring, reminding them that should the umbilical cord break that will be the death of them. He, like so many others, had believed the tale and had never dared break that which joined them, or even to pull on it very much. He was ingenuous as only those are who have lived too long clutching their mother's skirts – mothers whose possessiveness wears the mask of protectiveness - weak as a lion born in captivity. But now, in this short space of time, he had gone from spoilt child to solitary man. A bloodless sacrifice had taken place without his knowing, and there was nothing he could do but wait. He suspected that this sudden realisation (Drake was no stranger after all) had not come to him by chance. His curiosity, so piqued since his mother's sudden, baffling departure and the arrival of that letter, had been given added fuel by this new discovery.

He started back towards town, bags in hand. He could hear the roar of the river behind him in the distance – only hear it, as it was now too dark to see. On and on it flowed, its endless burble like low voices at his back. He walked quickly. In the dark it was difficult not to stumble and slip on the muddy track he had to follow. The pelting rain clouded his eyes and the cold once more settled in his bones. For a short while, Max's inner monologue went uneasily silent. What to think? This trip was turning into a nightmare. He would end up catching pneumonia if he stayed on in a place where the rain was an everlasting lament. Or, what was worse, being driven mad by so much mystery.

# V

I see the future. It is there, poised over the street,
hardly dimmer than the present.
What advantage will accrue from its realisation?
Nausea
Jean Paul Sartre

When he reached the town he was out of breath and shivering. His feet were covered in a sludgy layer of compact mud. The bags seemed full of stones. The handles kept slipping and his trench coat had ceased repelling the rain; it was merely one more burden it was so soaked. He was alone on the high street. He walked past the corner with the sign: Do What Thou Wilt that sounded far from unfamiliar. Stopping at the sign, and without knowing why, he read it aloud a couple of times over: "Do What Thou Wilt, Do What Thou Wilt." His voice was shaky, hesitant. The wan light from a streetlamp picked Max out, a faint figure in the dark, deserted high street. Nobody's lights were on, in homes or shops. He was struck by the terrible air of solitude in the town, how entirely lifeless it was. It was as though everyone had fled an impending nuclear disaster. There was nobody to be seen through the lace curtains at Hausen's. He immediately headed to the emporium; he needed to talk to that woman. She had promised to have an answer before the day was out.

Hurrying along the darkened streets, something dawned on him that he had missed the night before: the town truly was deserted. The old, ramshackle buildings had a different aspect than in daylight. They seemed abandoned. As he walked, he saw that some of the windows were even smashed and the interiors looked forlorn. He didn't stop to look inside. Coming to the shop, he pushed hard on the door to open it, but it was locked. He put his eye up to the window and peered inside. Closed. He rapped his knuckles on the window, but nobody came. Going back out into the middle of the street, shielding his eyes from the incessant rain, he looked around for a light, any sign of life. He found none. Turning to look up at the castle, he saw its flickering lanterns. Then a thought struck him and, arms straining under the weight of his bags, and water pouring down him like a fountain in a park, he started walking again, looking out for the sign that had pointed the way to the hotel the previous night. It had disappeared. Someone had taken it down.

He carried on all the way to the end of the high street, but there was no trace of the sign. He didn't understand. Or perhaps it wasn't this alone that disturbed him. Perhaps it was the general air of unreality. What was he doing out in this never-ending storm after dark, standing in a town no map will ever show you, looking for a sign to tell him the way to a hotel which he already knew how to find? What worried him most was the feeling that something ill was afoot. If he recalled how he'd got there, why and where he'd come from with his suitcases, it didn't seem at all strange. Isolating the moment, separating it from his awareness of time, from that unbroken flow made it seem unbelievable. Even the most basic, normal events would stop making sense if you started abstracting them in such a way, he told himself. Any life, captured in a jumbled series of slides, and taken completely out of context, would become nothing more than an indecipherable hieroglyph. It was the warning light that had turned on inside him – alerting him to danger like a lighthouse – that was his true concern. A danger he could discern only faintly, unaccustomed as he was to its odour.

He set off walking once more, still scanning the shadows. Where was everybody? All the people who had been out on the streets in the morning, all walking around so calmly? The fruit seller's stalls, the clothes shops, the pharmacy, the jeweller's, the bank… He walked slowly on until he was halfway along the street. A chilling vision. Hidden behind the clouds, even the moon seemed irremediably to be withdrawing to a remote point. For some reason he had the sensation that hundreds of silent eyes were watching him from the darkness. He wasn't wrong.

He smiled nervously at the absurdity of his own thought – how ridiculous! He felt embarrassed at being so afraid. There was nobody there. And if nobody were about in the street, he thought, it's because it is raining, and late, and cold. And possibly these buildings have fallen into misuse – the offices or storehouses of the shops, no longer inhabited. It was like the bridge: there was nothing to suggest anybody had destroyed it on purpose. With his bags weighing in his hands, he strode unwaveringly in the direction of the castle, like someone returning home after a hard day's work. The rain ran from his hair into his eyes, he had to blink constantly to see where he was going. Starting up the steep path to the castle, he could barely hold the bags. He was no longer bothering to dodge puddles.

Suddenly he felt safe as he reached the door – though he couldn't attribute that to the monstrous building itself, still less the prospect of Miss Bezel and her extravagant ways. "Get on with it," he said, pressing the doorbell, girding his loins for her remarks and infuriating insinuations. He knew she was going to laugh at him, with all the reproachful sarcasm that came so naturally to her, but then again she was right: he had been forced to return. And even so, he rang the doorbell in the hope that it would be Bezel who opened it, that she at least was still herself. And he wanted her to be wearing some new provocative outfit. The key turned in the lock, and he wasn't disappointed. The door opened and there was Bezel, barely covered by the skimpy nightie she wore, the sight of which prompted a relieved smile in Max – at least nothing had changed on that front. Her sinuous, tangible curves instantly chased away the furrows gouging out his brain. The warmth of her body, and her apparently constant willingness to be taken, soothed his senses, and he relaxed:

"Told you you'd be back," she said condescendingly. But Max had expected that and didn't react. "Pretty determined to catch pneumonia, aren't you? People have been round asking for you," she said, swapping a nail file into her other hand and standing back for him to enter. "Good heavens! What a sight!"

Coming in, he heard music soft and enchanting as a snake-charmer's flute, similar to what he had heard the night before. It drifted down from somewhere in the castle, gently echoing off the cold walls.

"I went for a walk," was his dignified answer. He removed his trench coat, little more than a sodden rag by now, and his shoes, two great muddy clumps. Bezel gave him a quizzical look, but said nothing.

"You must be frozen. Come into the kitchen and get yourself in front of the fire. What madness, going out all day in the rain. You're sure to have caught quite the cold. What a strange boy you are."

Max could hardly understand. He was the strange one? He, who had so struggled to adapt to the version of "normality" that reigned in the town and among its inhabitants? They went into the kitchen and again, at her offer of a dry dressing-gown he undressed. Taking his clothes off in front of Bezel was becoming a habit.

"Eaten since you left?" she said, making it clear she was happy to cook.

"No," he said, smiling. All that had passed his lips, he realised, was the breakfast she had left in the bedroom and the tea he had drunk at mid-morning in Hausen's café. "If it isn't too much trouble."

"No trouble at all," she said, cutting him off. "Do you like chicken soup?"

"Yes."

"I'll heat you some up," she said kindly. "Then you can have some chicken."

"Thank you," said Max, feeling genuinely thankful.

He glanced apprehensively at Bezel, like a fearful child not entirely sure what it is afraid of. He didn't know if he could trust her. There were times when she seemed so normal, like now, asking if he liked chicken soup. As normal as any woman. But he sensed that the other Bezel could emerge at any moment from behind such behaviour and renew her strange and vicious sniping. Nonetheless, he decided to try; he was feeling uneasy, he needed someone to talk to, and right now she was his only option.

"Miss Bezel," he said, clearing his throat as she went on making the food. "You know the river's burst its banks and there's no way to get out of town?"

"I do," she said, going on with the cooking. "I told you so, but you didn't want to listen."

"And… did you know the town's deserted?" He did his best to sound unconcerned. "There's absolutely nobody around on the streets and everything's closed. Abandoned."

Max examined the woman as she prepared his meal. And, for some reason – truly there was no basis to it – the chilling sensation came to him that everything she did was an act, and all her apparent poise nothing but a front. He rested his elbows on the table and crossed his arms. He went on watching her, inspecting her every move – trying to uncover something that might confirm his suspicions. There was no way he could simply come out with a question like, Miss Bezel, is it true the bridge was destroyed on purpose? Or, why on earth have I been having visions of episodes in my life hitherto completely unknown to me? Or even, why do I feel you're putting this all on, just like that woman in the shop, just like Hausen too? Is it my imagination, which I rely on in my work, or is there something to it? Or, guess what, it turns out I do know Mr Drake?

No, he was sure she wouldn't answer his questions, because he wasn't sure about anything either. All the same, he decided to try:

"By the way… Where is everybody?"

"Everybody who?" said Bezel, feigning disinterest.

"You know what I mean. The people from the town."

"Erm, how should I know? In their homes? I don't spend my time spying on people, as I'm sure you can understand. What a question!" she said, shaking her head.

"I know you don't do that, but… where do they live?"

"Where does who live?"

"No one in particular," he said impatiently, "people."

"You want me to make a list of where everyone lives?" she laughed. "So what if you don't know anyone?"

"No," said Max, getting slowly to his feet and going over to her. "Why does the town seem like it's been abandoned? Why is there nobody in the streets?"

"Perhaps because it's two o'clock in the morning? People go to bed early here. This isn't Paris," she said, though her tone was gentle.

"Two o'clock in the morning?" He went and sat down again.

"Yes, and if there's no sign of life, possibly it's because people turn out their lights when they go to bed. Or maybe where you come from people sleep with the lights on? Don't tell me it's we who are the weird ones. Are you trying to say that anyone in their right mind would go out walking on a day like we've just had, and stay out until two in the morning?"

"I didn't know it was so late," Max said, guessing what Bezel was thinking. "The day went by just like that."

In truth, he was also confused by how completely he had lost track of time.

"Sure," said Bezel with a half-smile.

"What about the sign for the castle?" Max insisted, unable to shake the feeling he'd had on the street. "Why's it been taken down?"

"Really though, what's going on with you?" Bezel smiled. "Everybody here knows their way around. When the wind gets up like this, the signs are taken down so they don't go flying into people's windows. There was one time when a sign came loose and smashed two shop windows, then it flew right into Mr Doran, broke the poor man's collarbone. Since then, the signs get put in storage over winter, or any time the weather turns nasty. The only one that occasionally gets left up is the one for the hotel, but it's been so windy that probably it just got put away too. What do I know? Plus, nobody can get in, the town's cut off. Remember?"

Bezel gave Max a satisfied look, pleased at having so roundly dispatched his queries. Once more he had the feeling that she was making it up as she went along, either that or she was hiding something. On the other hand, everything she said seemed quite reasonable, indeed credible enough that perhaps it was his tortured mind making everything seem unreal and nightmarish. He decided to take her word for it. The truth was, it wasn't so strange for a sign to have been taken down, given that nobody could access the town. The truly strange thing – she was right – was for him to have been out for upwards of twelve hours and for it to have felt like... Three? Four, perhaps? He thought back through the day, trying to recall everything he had done.

"Did I say you had a visitor?" Bezel said, breaking the silence.

"You did, but not who it was," Max replied, without a great deal of interest, still staring into the flames.

"Vahlenkamp."

"Who?"

"The woman who runs the emporium"

"And what did she say?"

"That she wanted to talk to you, and that the petrol would have to wait a couple of days, till the bridge is mended."

"What else did she want to talk about?"

"How should I know?" Bezel said. "She just asked me to pass that on."

"Do you know Mrs Vahlenkamp?"

"Everyone knows Mrs Vahlenkamp."

"I mean do you know her well?"

"What do you mean by 'well'?" Bezel said suggestively.

"Come on, Miss Bezel! You know what I mean. Who is she?"

"She's the woman who runs the emporium. Trying to tell me you didn't go by there this morning?"

"I did," Max retorted, refusing to lose his patience. "But why's she so... odd? When I went in the shop, she started asking me all these questions. All totally irrelevant. It was like being interrogated."

"She must have liked you," Bezel said, with no suggestion she would clarify what she meant.

"It's impossible to have a serious conversation with you," rasped Max. He clearly wasn't going to find anything out.

"Problem is, you talk too much. You ought to think less, relax a little." At this, she parted her nightgown, giving Max a clear view of her ample cleavage and firm breasts with their aura of warmth and softness that Max could barely contemplate.

"Another time, Miss Bezel," Max said, looking away. "I could relax, but please understand, I have to see Mr Drake. I wasn't planning on getting stuck in this town, or spending all my money staying in a hotel of this quality. I don't even know if I can afford two nights here..."

"Oh, I forgot. Mr Drake called from New York this afternoon, and I mentioned you were here. He said he was sorry not to be here to welcome you, that you shouldn't worry about the bill, and if there was anything you needed, it was on him."

'What?"

"He'll cover your costs," Bezel said. "At the end of the day, it's our fault you aren't able to leave. Were it not for the bridge, and Mr Drake's absence, you'd be gone by now. Right? And if you're a friend of Mr Drake, that's more than enough."

"Mr Drake said that?"

"He did. I already told you he's the boss around here. I guess he was pleased you'd come all this way to see him. He says it's the least we can do for you. It means you can relax. Stick around till the Polster guys have mended the bridge, which'll be a few days. First the river has to go down."

"And did Mr Drake remember me?"

"Yes, of course. He sounded extremely pleased to know you were here."

Max rubbed his face with both hands. It seemed the memories were not an invention of his after all. They really had met.

"Well... I'm very grateful. But why doesn't someone call for the emergency services to come from another town? Don't people mind being cut off?"

"We're used to it by now, and well prepared. It isn't that unusual..." She gave an amused smile. "You just happen to have been caught out this time."

"I'm afraid I don't see the funny side," Max said. "But in any case, thank you. I was worried about how I was going to pay." Then he regretted saying that.

"We've already found a way for you to do that," she said suggestively.

Max finished his supper, but felt jittery. He knew there was nothing to worry about, that his common sense would out. But the sensation of constantly being stalked was bothering him. "Doubtless she's had her fill of the men in the town," he thought, "now here I am for her to prey on. Probably the only one she hasn't tried yet." And, a stock image in cartoons and comics, he later went on to draw himself as a succulent chicken, turning golden in the oven, while a buxom she-wolf in a nightie stood by licking her lips.

Feeling inquisitive, he eventually broke the awkward silence:

"Is it only you running the hotel?"

"Oh, no! I just do the organising. I'm free to do as I see fit running the place, that much is true."

"Don't seem to be that many tourists in this town," he said, doing his best to be friendly. "There isn't that much to do, I mean, and it isn't even marked on any maps..."

He was not going to sleep with her, but, after the truly surprising courtesy she had shown, it would be rude not to chat a little.

"And," he said, "to be honest, I was pretty surprised to find a hotel like this in such a small town."

"Scottish castles are like mushrooms. You can find noble heritage in any place you care to look. And it's thanks to people like Mr Drake that such places are still standing. It's true, not many people come through, and particularly when the weather's like this. In summer, the odd tourist who's taken a wrong turning. I know it's far too nice a place for this town, but if it weren't a hotel it would be in ruins by now. So, though it doesn't make much money, it gets looked after all the same. It's more a museum than a hotel, to be honest. It's my job to keep it shipshape, and," she added with laugh, "to look after any lost souls who don't have a clue where they've wound up."

"If I'd have got a flat tyre, I could be being devoured by wolves in a ditch right now," he said, remembering the comment she made on his arrival.

"You don't believe there are wolves, do you?"

Max looked at her uncertainly.

"The hills are crawling with them. Plenty of day-trippers have been ripped apart by the wolves hereabouts. I've seen them with my own eyes: they're like dogs, only bigger and much more ferocious."

"Miss Bezel, you are going to give me nightmares."

"Are you laughing at me?"

"Oh, not at all." Now it was his turn to be sarcastic. "I believe you. I do."

"Wouldn't you like a drink?" she asked, seeing he was more talkative than usual.

Max hesitated, but telling himself that nothing would happen if he did not want it to, he said he wouldn't mind a cognac, much to her astonishment.

"I'll be right back," she said.

She left the kitchen, and he heard her footsteps going away down the stone hallway.

Max sat staring into the fire. That was the downside of someone else paying for you, it meant you had to be sociable. It made him uncomfortable to suddenly be in Bezel's debt. She might mistake it for something else, and that was the last thing he wanted. He knew she would need no second invitation… He broke out in a sweat. It wasn't as though she was paying for him to be there, so in fact why be nice to her? In truth, he didn't feel like talking to Bezel at all. Why had he been so quick to agree to a drink then? A contradictory feeling came over him and he realised it wasn't a good idea. He didn't feel comfortable in her company, and if they started drinking, his unease could well intensify. He wasn't much of a drinker. Getting up, he went out to the reception to tell her he'd had second thoughts and that –

"We can't tell him," he heard a man's voice say. "How do you think he'll react? He isn't ready."

"He has to find out sooner or later," said a woman in reply. "What if we just left him to adapt? The important thing is that he recall his past."

Max tilted his head slowly to the left. In a room to one side of the stairwell, an argument was going on. The part of Max that was suspicious of everything and of everyone, and that at times whispered to him with such clarity, told him they were discussing him. His face flushed, certain as he now was that the bridge had been destroyed intentionally. He went quickly through the reception area and threw the door wide open. This kicked up a dark cloud of dust, and he stood blinded for several seconds. There was nobody in the room. He stood there in bewilderment, rooted to the spot. Through the greyish dust that hung over the sheeted furniture, he glimpsed a room of considerable proportions, with high ceilings and windows. A strong musty smell. It must be some joke, thought Max. He moved forward between the furniture. All the windows were closed, and there were no other doors. He backed unsteadily away, and on reaching the double door once more, took hold of the two handles and pulled them softly shut. He stood for a moment with his forehead against the door, eyes shut, straining to hear if the voices came back. Bezel's footsteps behind him interrupted his train of thought.

"What are you up to now?" she said, her tone forbearing, as if speaking to a mad person whose extravagant behaviour has begun to get on people's nerves.

She was carrying a silver tray with a cut glass bottle and two small, wide glasses. Max gave no answer but, still holding the door handles, turned around with a smile, showing his perfect set of teeth. She gave him a conspiratorial smile back, as though she knew what had just happened but was trying to make it seem like she didn't.

"Why do you go around in a nightie at all hours, Miss Bezel?"

"Oh, so you noticed," she said, as though it were a compliment. "I didn't think you'd even realised."

"Aren't you cold?"

"No, quite the opposite," she purred. "Pretty hot, actually. And you?"

"No. I'm frozen, Miss Bezel. I'm… frozen." Then, in a tired voice: "I'm going to bed. Excuse me."

He went slowly up the stairs while Bezel watched smilingly on. Entering his room, he collapsed on the bed still fully dressed. He shut his eyes and tried not to think, but that proved impossible. The part of him that only came out, ghost-like, when the rest of him slept was now on full alert. The part whose single function it was to extract whatever was going on inside him proved unable to resist, and like an automaton Max took out his notebook and began to describe in a kind of desperation what he'd just experienced. The last paragraph was dramatic:

*Did it really happen? Or is it just a dream, my mind playing tricks? My solitary soul alone knows how fragile my sanity is, and what a feat it is to keep on two feet. Might I perhaps ask for what I already have? Those voices. Those voices that continue to resound in my mind like echoes from the past, bitter memories. Does my body now seek the chaos which my soul seeks to flee? Whose game is this? Who watches on? Who laughs last? Dispel the time-devouring ghosts hovering by landscapes drenched in scarlet. Powerless I stand before their onslaughts – beaten and defeated before stepping into the arena.*

*Fight, for the love of God! Do not surrender now!*

His hand went limp and his thoughts dissolved into dream. He shut his eyes, and his hair splayed out across the pillow, ominously. He slept for a while – how long he did not know: time loosened its grip on him. But then a sudden noise woke him. He blinked a few times and, realising where he was, lay back in the bed, asleep or awake, or whatever this state in fact was. He was soon fully asleep, but his dreams were far from restful.

# VI

"It's almost impossible to believe that other people
are conscious beings, aware of their own inward
feelings, as we ourselves are aware of our own," said
Françoise. "To me, it's terrifying when we grasp that.
We get the impression of no longer being anything but
a figment of someone else's mind. But that hardly ever
happens, and never completely."

She Came to Stay
Simone de Beauvoir

Bezel drained her glass of cognac by herself. A shiver ran up her spine. He was right: it was cold, and she felt it too. Of course, she would be happier in cotton underwear and a pair of trousers! But she had to parade before him half-naked and, despite the cold, it was not the worst she'd been made to do. Wrapping the gauze-thin dressing gown about her body, she gathered the plates, disconsolately humming a tune. She turned out the lights and left the kitchen. She did not go upstairs straight away, but went to the room in which Max had heard the voices. Pushing on the door, without turning on the light she peered inside. All was quiet. She didn't know what Max had heard precisely, only that she had found him looking ashen and afraid. She had pretended not to know what was happening, and, as was required of her, had acted concerned. Acting concerned – acting in general – was her metier. Going up to the first floor, she stopped in the hallway to see if she might hear anything. Not a sound.

She carried on up the stairs to the top of the building – the third floor. At the end of a long corridor of closed doors, hung a painting by some romantic landscape painter. Bezel advanced quietly along the hallway and stopped by the door adjacent to the painting for a few seconds. She then knocked lightly. Taking a key from her pocket, she moved the painting a little to one side to reveal a keyhole. She opened the door gently. It was – as always – dark inside the room. Without fully opening the door, she reached her head around it, unable to make anything out in the darkness. A deep voice came from the far end of the room:

"Alright, Bezel. Go to bed."

"Thank you. Good night."

She received no reply. Closing and locking the door, she put the picture back in place. She went along the hallway and down the stairs without making a noise. Her room was on the second floor, directly above Max's. The first thing she did on entering was to remove the insubstantial nightie, throwing it to the floor and donning a cotton one instead as well as a more comfortable pair of knickers. She lit a cigarette, her first chance to relax all day, and moved around the room taking deep breaths. She looked at the clock. It was almost three, but she wasn't tired. She got into bed and turned out the light. There was nothing for her to do now and she had to be up and about again at half past six. The next day was bound to be hard. Max might try to escape or take fright at the next set of memories – which she thought were sure to be unpleasant – and it would be up to her to calm him. Yes, she'd have to behave around him, soothe his worried mind, make him believe he could trust her like his own mother. As if she were his mother.

# VII

## MONDAY

"Ah, but it is necessary to corrode.
And to confound. Above all else, to confound.
Dream with waking, fiction with reality,
the true with the false; to confound them all
in one homogenous mist.
Mist
Miguel de Unamuno

She was there with his breakfast at half past eight. Slipping noiselessly into his room, she found him fast asleep. She went over to his bed and picked the notebook up off the floor.

"Poor Max!" she murmured, smiling to herself glancing at the last thing he'd written before falling asleep.

She opened a button in her shirt and arranged her hair.

"Max! Wake up. I've brought you breakfast."

Max lifted his head, not knowing whose voice it might be, and, turning over several times in the bed, eventually opened his eyes. The sight of her seemed to bring back the previous night's events. He fumbled around for his notebook, finding it on the floor, where Bezel had just deposited it.

"Wake up, sleepy head," she said with a smile.

Max responded with a courteous smile and, still half asleep, thrust the notebook into the pocket of the jacket he was still wearing.

"Good morning, Miss Bezel. Is it still raining?"

"I'm afraid it is, Mr Sinclair."

"Mr Sinclair?" he said, stretching.

"Max," said Bezel, correcting herself.

"What's the time?"

"Half past eight, breakfast time."

"Nothing time," he said wearily. "I have no idea what I'm supposed to do in this place for a whole extra day. I expect the bridge is still totally impassable, right?"

Bezel nodded.

"Great," he smiled, a strange twinkle in his eye. "Another day in mystery town, the place where anything is possible."

"Don't be so melodramatic. It isn't that bad. There are all kinds of things to do. I'm sure you'll find some way to amuse yourself."

Max didn't mind Bezel coming into the room this morning. He seemed to accept that, as guest of honour, he had no choice but to be her primary focus. Personal attention, he thought, and it was free. What more could he ask for?

"I'll let you have your breakfast," she said, seeing he'd slept in his clothes. "And sort yourself out."

"Have you had your breakfast?" asked Max, feeling he didn't want her to go.

"Not yet. I'll have it downstairs," she said, though in fact she'd had her coffee some two hours before.

"Well," he said. "Maybe we could eat down there together."

In truth he was frightened at the prospect of being alone and hearing the voices again. The previous night's events had been proof enough that all in this place was not as it should be. Insubstantial and confused proof it might have been, barely tangible, given he understood nothing, but there was something going on. Whether in him, or in the building, or the town generally, he couldn't say, but the feeling he had was of teetering at the edge of a precipice. The memories, the feeling of losing control, and above all those voices… He didn't want to experience anything like that again. He was fearful. Bezel's company, however fraught, was still preferable.

"Must be boring for you being stuck in a place like this," said Bezel, sitting across from him once they were both in the kitchen. "Especially coming from a big city."

She was not going to try her feminine wiles on Max this morning. Not try to make him nervous, nor sting him with irony or insolence. This morning was for playing the nice girl, extricating all the information she could about his life and his parentage, anything she could do to get the memories whirring. Yes, she was going to be a nice girl today…

"Well," said Max, cup of tea in one hand, "I'm not actually in that much of a hurry. I can't say I'm over the moon about my present situation, but neither am I going to despair at the prospect of a few

days here. And I feel easier knowing I don't have to pay for the room."
Every word of this was a lie.

"Why should you worry about the money?" said Bezel forthrightly.
"If Mr Drake hadn't said he was going to pay for you, you could have
wired me the money further down the line, or just brought it when
you came to see us again."

Max hesitated.

"But you don't know me at all. Who's to say I would send you the
money, or show my face again?"

"How wrong you are! You're a good person, I can tell from your
face."

It was she who was wrong, Max thought. As soon as he'd had
a chance to talk to Mr Drake, he'd be gone, never to return. There
was nothing that could induce him to return, still less after what had
happened the previous night.

"So, you aren't married then," said Bezel, sticking to the script.

"No," he said indifferently. "I like to live alone."

"Oh! You live on your own?"

"Yes, completely."

"And what about family?"

Max scrutinised the expression on Bezel's face. She looked back
with a curiously open smile, waiting for him to reply as though her
question had merely aimed to keep the conversation going. But she
knew such directness was a high stakes strategy. If he decided none of
this would be of interest to her, the next stage of her plan would be
in jeopardy. Perhaps she should have been more roundabout in her
approach, but... she had started now. Max, watching her as he chewed
on a piece of pastry, decided there was little point, now, in this context,
in being his usual tight-lipped self. He'd be gone within a matter of
days, never to see this woman again. What did it matter, shooting the
breeze for a little while? He could always make something up again.
Lies, lies and more lies.

"My mother died quite recently, and my father..."

His father. Where was his father?

"Yes?" said Bezel encouragingly. She noted a change on his face.

"I don't actually know where he is," Max said. He got to his feet,
abruptly ending the conversation. "I never met him."

"Are you leaving?"

"Yes, I'm going for a walk, being that I'm a tourist and all."

"As you wish," she smiled. "Nice chatting to you."

Max said nothing, but shot her a cold look as he shouldered his
jacket. His trousers were badly creased and his shirt was bunched up

beneath his jumper. He had slept fully clothed, but it didn't seem the day to worry about how he looked. He hadn't even showered. He smoothed out his clothes a little and left the hotel intending to go back to the shop.

He had found it impossible to lie. It should have been easy, yet he'd been unable to make up a story about his father. It was something he didn't want to talk about, falsely or otherwise. Period. Particularly with a hussy like Bezel. What was it to her where his father was? Why should she care, when even he didn't? Max walked quickly down the steep track and walked through the castle gate. He went along, eyes downcast, at a furious rate, unable to see any further than his own thoughts. He stumbled and fell to his knees. He felt a searing pain in his kneecaps.

He couldn't get up again because there, before his eyes, was his Biarritz house, exactly as it had been in the summer of 1978. The vine-covered stone façade, the stone garden wall and metal railing, the windows with their emerald green frames.

Max was nine years old. It was that same summer. He was wearing a pair of blue trousers and a yellow shirt. The laces on one of his plimsolls were untied and his socks (covered in bits of straw) bespoke the hours spent playing in the fields and his newly recovered freedom after shaking off a cold. He approached the house slowly, and then caught sight of a figure inside. It was Drake, that sinister man, he thought fearfully. Why was he so afraid of him? Stealthily he opened and closed the garden gate, as if in a game of cops and robbers. He came up the steps to the window on the other side of which Drake and his mother were deep in conversation. Crouching down so as not to be seen, he tried to make out what they were saying.

"How did you find that out?" said his mother, her voice close to breaking.

"Who do you think you are talking to?" Drake said condescendingly. "I know everything about the two of you."

"You tricked me," she said, pacing the living room. "I trusted you. You're still one of them after all."

"I'm not. I can assure you, Irene. I am prepared not to tell anyone anything, if you work with me. But understand this: Max means a great deal to me."

"I need some time to think, let it sink in. I'm still getting nightmares. I wake with them. I'm still afraid of him – Aldo is unhinged. I thought I was free of him, of all of it, and now…"

"But you're right, you don't have to worry about him anymore. Take all the time you need," Drake said affably. "Max is very important.

Don't you find it incredible that our paths have crossed again: and not by coincidence, if you ask me. I need Max, and you ought to be aware that you won't be able to hide him for long."

"Forget all that. The whole thing was a front. I did it for money."

"You know that isn't true. You did it because you believed. My dear, Max is not like other children. It isn't a burden you can shoulder alone."

"That burden happens to be my son," she said, beating her chest. "And I will do whatever it takes for him to have a normal childhood."

"An endeavour that will be entirely pointless, and you know it. Put the past behind you, think about us – you, me, Max. Aldo can't hurt you anymore, you have my word."

"We'll see."

"You know how fond I've grown of you, my dear, and of Max. I can give you everything you both need."

"No," she said firmly. "Max would hate it. I don't even want to think about what would happen."

"See? You're afraid as well."

"But... He's just a child..."

"You know that couldn't be further from the truth. You can't go on like this. The two of you, constantly moving around: you don't have to spend your life like that. Aldo's deteriorating by the day, he doesn't even recognise me now. You don't need to worry. If you will just let me do some tests on Max, just for a few days... He won't suffer, I guarantee it. He'll be fine."

"I'm all he's got. He's all I've got."

"I need both of you. And you need me. Ask him. You can make Max do whatever you want. You and only you. He adores you. He'll do anything you say. Really. I wouldn't lie to you."

"I don't know. Seems pretty awful, tricking your own child..."

"It isn't a trick. Who said anything about tricking anyone? He's just too young to understand."

"I have to think about it. We'll see."

"Of course, of course, you have a think. I want you to know that I'm at your disposal." He took her hand and kissed it. "I should go, Max will be back any minute."

He didn't know precisely what the issue was, but had heard enough to tell something significant was going on. What could be so important? Why did his mother seem worried, and where did that note of distress and doubt come from? Drake moved away from the window, and Max hurried down the steps and hid himself in the garage. He very nearly clattered into the metal watering can, before kneeling behind the car. Drake came out of the front door and made his way slowly, almost meditatively, towards the gate. Upon reaching it he stopped and stood there for a moment, without turning around. It was as though he were tuning into some subtle vibration. Watching him from inside the garage, Max didn't move a muscle, didn't dare breathe either. Eventually, lifting the rusty metal latch, Drake spoke in that booming, grandiloquent voice of his:

"Good day then, Max."

And away he went down the street, leaving Max crouched behind the car like a frightened rabbit, with a sensation of ridicule that in seconds would turn to rage. He was fed up with Drake. Always with his self-important utterances and cheap magic tricks. That man made him nervous, he thought as he brushed the dirt from his hands. But above all, Max was intrigued by him. "That Drake," Max had once heard a man say at one of the parties in their house, "he's like a fly that no one dares to swat." The gravel floor in the garage had dug into his knees, leaving white indentations in the skin, along with a pleasant stinging. He strode up the steps to the front door, advancing resolutely, pretending he had only just returned.

"Mummy!" he called out airily. "I'm home."

His mother didn't get up. She was sitting in a chair by the fireplace. She limited herself to looking anxiously at Max. Salty summer air wafted in through the open door.

"What's going on?" he asked.

"Max," she said holding out a hand. "Come here, come and sit with me for a moment."

He went over, and she hugged him tight. Then, putting her hands on his shoulders, she gazed into his eyes. Irene's eyes had a sheen to them, seemed about to shed tears. Max felt tense. He'd never seen his mother look like this, not even half as bad as this.

"Max," she said, unsure of where to begin. "You… You know that I love you, don't you, son?"

"Yes, Mummy," he replied, a lump in his throat.

It was beyond him to imagine what she might be about to say, but he was prepared for the worst. He and his friends had been playing in the white meadow, a place where the grass grew higher than your head and where, sometimes, if you didn't tread carefully, you could find yourself in a deep, slimy bog they all called quicksands. He wasn't afraid of his mother. She'd never given him reason to be. The fact that she was afraid though – that was frightening. He could feel it. It was like a cloud surrounding her and spelling out in smoky letters: Fear.

"You…" she said. "You love your Mummy, don't you?"

Max nodded.

"… And Mummy has never done anything… anything bad to you."

Max shook his head.

"You know that anything I ask of you is always for your own good," she said cautiously, to another nod from Max. He had no idea what his mother was referring to. She had been acting so strangely of late. For several days, speaking so quietly he'd been unable to hear her and sometimes coming and talking to him when he was asleep. At one point he had woken up and found her there, sitting by his bed, gazing down at him and uttering meaningless words.

"If Mummy asked you to do something," she said, "you'd do it?"

"Of course, I would!" he said, offended at the question. He'd do anything for her, anything.

"Mr Drake… "she began tentatively.

She knew Max was frightened of him. Max was just a boy, and Drake a daunting man, with that deep voice of his and a bearing capable of intimidating even an adult. The look on Max's face changed, and she drew him closer.

"Mr Drake," she went on, "is a very important, and a very clever man. You do know that?"

Max simply shook his head. He had already decided his answer, no matter what the question might be.

"Listen, Max. You know I'd never do anything to hurt you. There's something I want you to understand, and that's that you are a very clever boy, and Mr Drake thinks there are lots of interesting things you could learn."

Max went on shaking his head, as it sank down into his neck. His shoulders were almost up about his ears, his body completely rigid, and he was on the verge of tears.

"It's okay, don't worry. We'll talk about it some other day, but Mummy would be really happy if you went and spent a little time with Mr Drake."

At that, Max began to cry.

"There, there," she whispered, holding him close. "Mr Drake is also very rich, I'm sure he'd be able to buy you a new bike, maybe even that one you've been pestering me to get you."

Max wept in her arms. He was inconsolable. But she seemed not to realise how greatly he was suffering, the absolute horror he was feeling. Still she persisted:

"Please, Mum, please! Don't make me, please, I love you, I love you so much…"

When she saw her son trembling in her arms, she could hardly believe this was happening. She looked down at him, as his small hands gripped her dress. His nose was running, and there was a pleading look in his eyes. She pulled him close once more, squeezing him tight.

"Shh, don't cry. It's okay. We aren't going anywhere. Forget about it. See, all forgotten, okay?"

She cradled him in her arms, rocking back and forth. He was sweating, his shirt covered in tears and snot. Irene gave a distraught sigh. How could she be so insensitive, thought Max? She knew he was afraid of Mr Drake and yet, all the same, had pushed and pushed on the question. What on earth did they want from him?

Max was still down on his knees back on the Shimts path. Head in hands and weeping, the fears of that distant day utterly real to him once more. His chest felt tight and he tasted salty tears in his mouth. He had to take two or three deep lungfuls of air for his breathing to settle. Rubbing his face, he looked suspiciously around.

It had happened again. Once more those memories had hypnotised and transported him back, when least he had expected it. He wasn't upset, but such a lapse of consciousness, to lose control like that... The memories had been even clearer this time, even more real, and yet... The incident he'd just remembered had taken place over eighteen years ago, if it had happened at all. How was he to know? He had no trouble recalling the beach house, 'Queen' – his bicycle – and the recently forged summer friendships with André, Louis and Claire: those long afternoons spent looking for treasure in derelict houses, an endless number of childhood episodes beside. All of that had happened, no doubt. All of that was part of his past, his life. Though, where had those other memories been hidden all this time?

Rubbing his face once more, he got to his feet. His trousers were covered in mud, his shirt was untucked, his hair a mess. His eyes were bloodshot and his nose puffy. He took a couple of unsteady steps, trying to remember where he'd been going. Staggering a short distance, it then came back to him, and he changed course. He glanced bashfully around, checking to make sure no one had seen him fall. He made a vague attempt to tidy his hair. His hands were dirty. On he went, still somewhat falteringly, clumps of mud in his hair as well. He came to the high street. He saw Vahlenkamp's emporium on the opposite side of the street and, a few doors along to the right, Hausen's Café. He finally opted for the café, reaching into his pocket for his notebook.

He needed to go in and start writing, and needed to do so now.

He pushed on the door, but it didn't open. It looked dark inside. He hammered on the door and someone came out from behind the curtain next to the counter. The shadowy figure dragged itself over, a key turned in the lock.

"You sleep too much, Hausen," said Max, shoving open the door as the disabled man looked on in surprise.

"I'm not… I'm not open yet," said Hausen.

"I don't need long," said Max, going straight over to the table he'd occupied the previous day. "I won't be any trouble."

"Well, something to drink?"

"Yes please," Max said.

Hausen looked him up and down. Max's shoes were covered in mud. The cuffs of what had been a very white shirt were filthy, and poked out untidily from the jumper sleeves. Max had already forgotten the man's presence, already immersed in his writing.

"I'm guessing you'd like tea?" said Hausen, but received no reply.

He went over to the counter, keeping one eye on Max, prepared the tea and brought it back over. Looking up, Max thanked him.

"Had a fall?"

"No, I mean, only onto my knees," Max said, reaching down to touch them. He realised now how much they were stinging.

"Those trousers need a good wash," said Hausen, pointing at them.

Max smiled at the man, almost ignoring him.

"Not got any more clothes?"

"What's that?" said Max, annoyed.

"Your clothes," said Hausen, struggling to pronounce his words correctly. "You're wearing the same clothes as yesterday."

"Yes. They are the same as yesterday, but I need to do some writing now. Why don't you go back there with Beth while I finish off?"

"Beth!" said Hausen.

"Yes, your wife is called Beth, isn't she?"

"Yes, she is," said Hausen, going gloomily back over to the counter.

It suddenly struck Max that he didn't know who this Beth woman was. In truth, he didn't even know if Hausen was married or not. He didn't know why he had said what he had, but it seemed he hadn't got it wrong. Lifting the cup of tea, he observed Hausen as the man stacked Coca-Cola bottles on the wooden shelf behind the bar. Feeling flustered, Max ran his fingers through his hair, causing bits of dry mud to drop onto the page. He looked down at them as though he'd seen a ghost. Brushing them away, he took up the pen and went on sketching his memories in the notebook, try to chase the thought of Beth from his mind, whoever she might be.

# VIII

We can also see that the perceptions of our senses,
even when they are vivid, must necessarily contain some
confused feeling. For since all the bodies in the universe are
in sympathy, our body receives the impressions of all the
others, and although our senses are related – to everything,
our soul cannot possibly attend to each particular thing.
Thus, our confused feelings result from a downright
infinite jumble of perceptions.

Discourse on Metaphysics

Gottfried Wilhelm Leibnitz

*The mirrors are buckling, they only reflect monstrosities now, deformed, self-hating beings who take shelter in reality in order to look pure. Behind them, down in the depths, the beast awaits to devour the remaining shards of glass. Death may come even without crossing the threshold, the one keeping us far from the masquerade, the one terrifying us with its motley lights, with dreams of what once was or what will simply be. If you have no dreams, you must kill to have them...*

He stopped writing and took a sip of the tea, stone cold by now. He pushed the cup away bitterly. Bottles rattled at the back of the café. Going over to the counter, he called Hausen.

"Just doing a bit of sorting," Hausen said. "You all done?"

"Yes," Max said, his tone apologetic. "Sorry for coming in like that, but I had to write something down before I forgot."

"That's fine. I was about to open up anyway."

"Tell me," Max said, uncomfortable at what he was about to ask, or, more precisely, what the answer might be: "Tell me, is your wife really called Beth?"

A dejected look came over Hausen's face:

"Yes. Her name was Beth. She died thirty-two years ago."

Suddenly, Max felt a stream of searing heat rise from the back of his neck to his ears. He braced himself against the counter, unable to speak.

"Are you okay?" Hausen asked, concerned.

"Yes," said Max. "Yes, I think so."

"Maybe you ought to sit down," Hausen said, seeing the blood drain from Max's face. He came out from behind the counter and took him by the arm. "You don't look so well, sir. And look, your clothes are all wet, you'll catch a cold."

Max ran a hand over his jumper. It was true. The garment was soaked, and not only now; it had been like that for nearly two days. He had slept in these clothes, and they'd got drenched again that morning. He smiled limply, quite embarrassed to think of the impression he must be giving.

"You probably think I'm a hobo."

"I do think you should go back to the hotel and change. A nice, hot shower would do you good."

"You're right, Hausen," Max murmured, getting to his feet. "I think you're right. I'm a sight. Aren't I?"

He fished in his pocket for some change, but Hausen motioned for him not to bother.

"No need for that," he said.

"Thank you. I'll take your advice and go back for a shower."

He couldn't bring himself to apologise for his tactless comment. He couldn't have known that she was dead. How could he have, if he didn't even know he was married? And yet, he had known her name, even down to the fact Hausen called her Beth – not Elizabeth, not Mrs Hausen! He rubbed his face vigorously. He had started to grow a beard, he realised; it prickled. He smiled anxiously.

He walked quickly but unsteadily back to the hotel, like a drug addict in need of his daily fix. He didn't want to think about what was going on: because he lacked the answers to calm his troubled mind. How had he known that woman's name? He bit hard on his lip, nearly drawing blood. He'd been feeling out of sorts ever since his mother died. Everything had happened quickly, so horribly quickly... Coming to a sudden halt, he balled his fists up, trying not to cry. He didn't know if this was the way things worked: one's mother just committing suicide for no reason. She had abandoned her only child. Left him all alone, and that child had then lost his mind, so intense was his despair. Maybe such things happened. And was hearing voices, and somehow guessing the names of dead people, part of that madness? The worst part was having no one to share his thoughts with. He was alone in the world and, as if that weren't enough, trapped in some town in the middle of nowhere – where the prospect of confidants was little more than a joke. Who could he turn to? Could he open up to Bezel, to put aside the repulsion he felt for her and talk about everything he was going through? She would laugh, take him for a child – and her only solution would likely be a bit of nooky in the kitchen. Looking around, he felt his energies fading. Everything about the place seemed hostile. Though, why fool himself, so was the world in general. He had never felt at home in it. His own insignificance horrified him. He couldn't handle it.

He came to the castle door feeling haunted by dark thoughts. He had the sensation of being watched, of some stalking presence beyond the trees, beyond the mountains, beyond his brain. Pushing open the door, he came into the entrance hall. Nobody was around. He'd not been the boldest of boys growing up, not even particularly brave, but that was because he'd always had an advance sense of danger: if he felt afraid, that was his signal to avoid a coming situation. It was as though one of his senses preceded him, telling him if a grazed knee or cut hand were in the offing. He felt afraid now. He sensed a huge predator was lurking. And worst of all, he didn't even know what shape it might take. If it were something one might fight off, or rather if, as it seemed, it were within him.

Soft music echoed down off the high, sturdy walls in the lobby. Max went slowly forward, heart in mouth. He thought he was about to hear those same chilling voices again. The music was coming from somewhere far away – where precisely, he couldn't tell. Its gentle yet piercing tone suffused the atmosphere. It filtered between the stones in the walls. Almost breathing them. The sun came out – for the first time since his arrival – and he looked on hopefully as the light entering through the arched stained-glass windows left a multi-coloured tracery on the stone floor. Dust motes hung in diagonal shafts of light. His cheeks felt pleasantly warm for a moment or two. The entrance had assumed a golden, homely hue, transforming even the decor, usually so dour and gloomy. But then a noise shattered that feeling. Looking up to the top of the banister, he caught sight of something on the first-floor landing, though too fleetingly to be sure what. He gave a couple of incredulous blinks, but whatever it was hadn't gone away.

Eyes wide and a hand over his mouth, he went towards the stairs, and began making his way up... The sun went in again, taking with it the cheerful brightness; all was grey and dull once more. Coming to the first floor, he advanced to the start of the passageway, peered around. His heart was pounding. Very slowly he inched his head around the corner, only to find the passageway deserted. Arranged along it like tarot cards, rugs foretold a future that, blind to his own fate, Max failed to decipher. A faint light came through a window at the far end of the passageway. "Me against the light," he thought, not knowing what that implied. The door to his bedroom was open. He slid along, keeping close to the wall like a salamander. His temples pounded as he went forward. He had to find out what it was he'd seen. He truly had no idea what it was that had shot down the corridor. He needed to know whether he was hallucinating or beginning to lose his mind. It was beyond unintelligible, even if he was going crazy. There had to be a rational explanation for everything, or at least half rational. Maybe he was being poisoned. It couldn't be his mind. He wasn't capable of inventing such preposterousness – in fact, that wasn't right: he'd spent his entire working life writing the darkest of comic strips. He was famed for it. Weird, demoniacal beings were his stock in trade, creatures from beyond the grave, slavering extra-terrestrials, schizophrenic housewives, unstoppable mass murderers wreaking their gory havoc. He had been the author of hundreds of scenes like the one he had just experienced – and yet, he could not find the words, not even an image, to express his current state. It was as though some formless, faceless, voiceless being had gone along the passageway calling out to him, its words at once mute and penetrating. A weary sigh came from inside the room.

Max took a few steps back, and then a deep breath, before going to look inside. If he wasn't crazy and this was real... If this, whatever it was, wasn't some kind of insanity, he might be in peril. A touch of depression could be cured, he thought as he edged forward, but the ineffable presence he'd sensed before would be worse than any depression, any nightmare. The cheery music had grown louder.

Breathing deep, he readied himself to look in the room – there was no more putting it off. Leaning back against the wall, he peered inside and choked down a second cry. He stood rooted to the spot, rigid as a plank of wood.

"Max, sweetie," came the silky voice from within. "Are you okay?"

His pretty young mother was standing before him. She wore her favourite blue dress, and her hair was up in a yellow ribbon.

"Mummy!" Max whispered. Was this terror or amazement he was feeling? "Mummy!"

"You don't look so good, sweetie. What's wrong?"

Above all else, Max wanted to tell her everything. He needed someone to talk to, and who better? But perhaps the person before him wasn't his mother? She was dead. Perhaps it was another hallucination, or perhaps...

"Come on, tell Mummy what's wrong." She smiled, arms

outstretched. "That's it, come to Mummy."

"Mummy?" he said incredulously.

He stepped forward hesitantly, but suddenly stopped.

"Who are you?" he said, his mouth dry.

"What do you mean? It's me, honey. Don't you recognise me?"

Max then had a strong feeling of déjà vu. Looking around, he saw that bedroom wasn't the one in the Shimts hotel, but his mother's in the house in Biarritz. And he was not an adult, but a nine-year-old boy once more, face flushed, breathing shallow. Before him was his mother, looking rather lifeless. So luminous and beautiful only moments before, her face looked drawn, and her eyes, always so alive, were glazed a sickly yellow.

"Mummy! Are you all right?"

"No, sweetie. Actually, I'm not." Then, gesturing to the buttons of her dress: "Help me take this off, will you?"

"Of course," Max said, ever ready to help.

She sat down on the bed while he undid the three buttons at the neck. Then the zip beneath, which was snagged on one side, before pulling the dress upwards. She subsided onto the bed, and Max tucked her in. Her skin was tanned, soft and firm. Her round, gleaming shoulders were bare.

Max watched in silence as she breathed painfully. Her face was so pale it seemed to belong to a different body.

"What can I do, Mummy dear?" Max asked in a low voice.

"You know, sweetie. You know."

He did. He knew what she wanted. But he couldn't accept that this was her desire. It was all too much, it made him so afraid he didn't even want to think about it.

"Why don't you help Mummy, just do what I ask?" She spoke gently, but with a reproachful edge to her voice. He couldn't stand it when she talked like that. In some way it suggested her illness was all his fault. And, though he couldn't say why, he knew it was true. He'd refused to go away with Mr Drake for those few days, and that, he thought, was killing her: and if I don't do as she says, I'll be dead too. If she dies, I'll die too. He couldn't stand to see his mother suffer. Just to think that it might be his fault made him feel like a monster. He couldn't go out and leave her to suffer on her own, even to go and play with his friends. He didn't want to, not if it meant her being all alone in such a state.

"Max, will you do it for me?" she asked. "Mr Drake is a friend. He's very fond of you."

"Yes," Max said, resigned. "I'll do it for you, Mummy."

"What a good boy you are." She gave a satisfied smile. "I love you."

"And I love you," he said, his stomach in knots.

He wanted to say that he'd said yes out of fear, out of the feeling that if he didn't, something terrible would happen to both of them. He wasn't sure if she knew. She had such a good heart; he could hardly believe that she'd have come up with such an awful idea. No, it wasn't her idea, it was Drake's – he was behind it all. Max had known it all along. Ever since the day Drake had held out that ostentatious ring of his, Max had known life was set to change. He knew, too, that the man was controlling his mother, that in some way she was being drawn into his orbit, and that she was the unconscious thread dragging Max along.

Max came to on the floor of the hotel room. Bezel had her hand on the nape of his neck, and I was there with an empty water glass, having just splashed his face. Bezel gave him an affectionate smile. Sitting up slowly, he cleared his throat a couple of times.

"Are you okay?" I asked.

"Yes… What happened?" he said, clearly confused.

"We heard a noise," Bezel said, though she didn't specify where we'd been or what we'd been doing, when we heard it, "and came in to find you lying on the floor. You must have caught a cold. Your clothes are soaked."

Max cast his mind back. He remembered coming back to the hotel, planning to get out of his dirty clothes and take a shower. Hausen had let him in to do some writing, he'd somehow known the name of Hausen's wife… And after that he'd seen and felt that thing crawling into the room. He glanced suspiciously around.

"There was no one else here?"

"Here?" Bezel said. "There's nobody else here, Max. Come on, let me help you out of those clothes. You don't look so good. I'll run you a hot bath."

"Okay," said Max, clinging to our necks.

We laid him down on the bed. Bezel went through into the bathroom and turned on the taps. The sound of running water reached through into the bedroom.   "Come on then, let's get you undressed," I said. "You smell of fish. What have you been up to, my friend?"

Max did nothing to resist. He seemed calmed by my presence. Bezel appeared worried, eager to help him, and he was amenable. We got him into the steamy bathroom and lowered him into the bath.

"Better now?" Bezel asked.

"Yes, I think so."

"I don't want to alarm you, but you should see a doctor. You could have caught pneumonia, your clothes are wet, and then fainting like that… It doesn't bode well."

Max didn't answer.

"I'm going to make you some hot milk," she said, clearly wishing to help.

"Miss Bezel!" he exclaimed, as she went to leave. He didn't want her to, but at the same time, how to explain such childish behaviour? If she asked, what could he say? I'm afraid of being on my own because lately I've been hearing voices and there's some invisible thing wandering the hallways…

All he did say was:

"Could you bring me my notebook, and the pen that's in my trouser pocket?"

"Of course."

Bezel went out, and at that point Max looked at me as though he was noticing my presence for the first time.

"Who are you?" he asked in surprise.

"I'm Simon Bughin," I said, holding my hand out.

Max shook it, and I felt the moist warmth emanating from his palm.

"I'm staying at the hotel too," I explained. "I don't leave my room very often, hence the fact we haven't run into each other. We don't seem to have had the best of luck with the weather, and to be honest I detest the rain."

The steam in the bathroom enveloped our bodies – as though the mystery enveloping that encounter had assumed a physical form. I noticed Max glance nervously around. Then I began to wonder what someone like him, so young, was doing all alone in such an isolated spot, and above all what was wrong. Why was he so afraid?

"When did you get in?" I asked, though I already knew the answer.

"Two days ago, I think."

"You don't remember?" I said, smiling.

"Yes, yes, I do," he said, more certain now. "Two days ago."

"Here visiting family?"

I also already knew he'd come to see Drake. Bezel had told me so in the midst of one of our anatomy lessons, which I had been making the most of to extract all the information I could about that man; I too had come to Shimts to see him.

"No, I've come to see a friend of my mother's"

"Your mother's friends with that man?"

"Was," he said, staring into my eyes. "My mother's dead."

It was then that I saw something terrible was happening to him. His gaze was cloudy, like that of a man possessed, those who think they are visionaries, lunatics too.

"I'm sorry," I said, and I was. "Recently?"

"A month and half," he said. Taking a sponge, he began to wipe his face.

"How awful. I lost my mother as well. Though I was too young to suffer in any conscious way."

Max seemed interested by what I had to say, as though for the first time in a long time he had someone who understood his language. He seemed to relax, and I took that as an invitation to go on asking questions.

"Would it be terribly forward if I asked, how did it happen?"

The fact was, I felt as though I already knew. From the first moment I saw him spitting water in the hotel doorway, I'd had an intuition that his arrival wasn't fortuitous. He hesitated for a few seconds, but finally, clearing his throat, he answered in a cracked voice:

"She committed suicide." Once more he rubbed the sponge over his head.

Now that I know Max, having read his notebooks, followed his steps on the videotapes, observed his point of view and studied the documents, I know that for him to have said this out loud would have been like a weight off his chest. He looked at me pleadingly, as though he'd finally found someone with whom to share his nightmares. The distrust still evident in his face began to ease as his swarthy body relaxed in the warm water. I failed to appreciate the gravity of his answer at first (I was more concerned with observing his reactions), but when I finally did realise what he'd said, my curiosity revealed a reality too obdurate and premeditated to be true.

"Your mother committed suicide, you said?" I asked, rather tactlessly.

"Yes." His reply seemed intrigued rather than indignant. "Why are you so interested?"

"No reason," I said. "Just curious."

I believe that Max, just as had happened with me two days before when I saw him in the rain, suspected that some hidden urge had sparked my curiosity. And since he, like me, had come to this place in search of answers, he pursued the conversation, and now started to harry me with questions:

"What about you? What are you doing in this place?"

"I already said, passing through." Now it was my turn to satisfy his curiosity. "I'm in the middle of some research and needed a few days' rest."

"Are you here on your own?"

I nodded.

"Do you know Drake?" he said, going straight to the point.

"No," I said, trying to appear uninterested. "Who's that?"

"He owns this castle, and most of the town in fact. He's the person I've come to see" he said, as though confessing something. "I met him when I was a boy."

"Ah! So it's a reunion" I said stupidly.

"Exactly," he said gravely. "A reunion with the past."

Then we heard Bezel's footsteps coming closer, and Max hurried to cover his body with foam.

"Feeling any better?" she said.

"Yes, much better," he said.

She placed a tray with milk on a small bench she'd pushed by the side of the bath

He slid down into the water up to his chest, and I couldn't help but laugh at such extreme shyness in someone his age. I thought that if I'd been his age, and in the presence of a woman like Bezel, the reason I'd want to cover myself in foam would be altogether different.

"You gave me quite a fright," she said, leaning against the doorframe. "Such a strange boy. I know we don't know one another, but you seem worried. If there's anything I can do for you..."

Max rejected her "help" in the politest way. I could see his disinterest bothered Bezel. An uncertain look had come over Max's face. He was unsure about everything. Maybe Bezel was telling the truth, and he was the one looking at the world in a distorted way, and the people in the town were just that, sincere, friendly townsfolk. If anyone had been acting strangely, doubtless it was him. Perhaps it was only a coincidence that his mother's suicide had begun to hit him in this place. All the changes were taking place inside him. The town had been like this before he arrived and would go on being just the same after he left. He looked at Bezel again. Perhaps it was only his imagination, but still, better to wait and see, just in case.

"Feel like you're getting a cold at all?" said Bezel, kneeling down next to the bath.

"I've got a headache," Max said, abandoning the flow of his thoughts, "but an aspirin and that glass of milk, and it'll go."

"Max, I think I'd better call the doctor."

"No, no, I'm fine." He smiled. "Just a bit out of it, things on my mind. Honestly, I'm not in pain, let's just wait and see if I get any flu symptoms."

"Bezel," I said, "I think he's old enough to know whether he's ill or not. Don't harass him."

Bezel shot me a reproachful look. It was a warning: if I tried to meddle, there would be consequences for me in private lessons. But I also knew her, and knew she'd be trying to get into my trousers the second we were alone, and I went on undeterred:

"Why don't we leave him to have his bath in peace? I don't think he can be very comfortable with the two of us in here."

I could tell that Max appreciated this, whereas Bezel frowned even harder. No doubt she would have been delighted to give him a nice back rub and get her hands on the rest of that firm, swarthy body. She smiled vindictively.

"Okay, Max. Simon's right, you're quite old enough, but if there's anything I can help you with, you know where I am."

"Thank you very much," he said, mimicking her apparent sincerity.

"By the way, I forgot to tell you that the rain's stopped. The sun has come out, it's a lovely day. If it's nice tomorrow as well, we'll go out on an excursion. We'd love you to come too... If you're feeling better, of course."

"Well, I guess the bridge hasn't been fixed yet..."

"Wonderful. Now, don't get cold in there," she said, bringing the towel over to the bath. "Food will be ready soon..."

"I'll be down shortly in that case," said Max, not wanting to eat alone in his room. Bezel gave a satisfied smile and the two of us went out, leaving him alone.

It was then that Max took out his notebook and began writing down all that had just gone on, from guessing the name of Hausen's wife, to the encounter with his mother and subsequent fainting fit. He drew highly detailed pictures of the 'old' memories that had come to him. That day, his mother had been ill and he thought he knew why. Now he remembered that even at that time he'd known why she was poorly: she was afraid, terrified even, and he was the cause. He also knew that Drake was forcing her to do something. Though he was a child, he suspected that it was all because of him, and that Drake wanted something from him. That strange behaviour, the things she'd been saying, that made no sense, that terrible request, none of it was down to her.

What he didn't understand was why his mother didn't just free herself of Drake. Why she played his game, and suffered in silence. They were both so vulnerable. She was a young, trusting woman, he a boy of nine... And Drake – who was Drake? What linked him to them? Why did his mother not make it clear he was unwelcome, as she had with other men when they made their advances? What united them?

Looking up, Max saw that the steam in the bathroom had begun to thin out. He could remember nothing else. His mind only allowed him to access information in a calculated, measured manner, as though impelled by logic he couldn't fracture. He was sure there was much left to discover, that the memories were leading him to somewhere specific, and that it wasn't by chance they were being parcelled out like this. He'd remembered that Drake had wanted to take him off someplace, and that he had given his consent. He'd succumbed to his mother's pressure. It was impossible not to, and Drake must have known only too well. Drake had engineered that...

# IX

How would you like to live in Looking-glass
House, Kitty? I wonder if they'd give you milk
in there? Perhaps Looking-glass milk isn't good
to drink[...]

Oh, Kitty! how nice it would be if we could only
get through into Looking-glass House! I'm sure it's
got, oh! such beautiful things in it! Let's pretend
there's a way of getting through into it, somehow,
Kitty. Let's pretend the glass has got all soft
like gauze, so that we can get through.
Through the Looking-Glass,
and What Alice Found There
Lewis Carroll

Max felt edgy as he got dressed, looking up suddenly at any creak of the floorboards or a gust of wind that rattled the windows. His head was buzzing with questions, flapping and fluttering like birds gone crazy. He felt tense, bracing himself for another blackout, another moment when he'd be dragged back into those memories. He waited for a response to the decision he had taken. That summer, he'd made a promise to his mother, and was sure he must have kept it. He couldn't recall now, but knew that the images would come to him when least expected, and then he'd discover what had ensued. Straightening his shirt in the mirror, he forced himself to smile, like when someone we don't want to see waves to us in the street, and we smile politely back.

But he was the only one there, and he was no stranger. Yet, he realised, he was avoiding looking himself in the eye. It struck him that when he did so, he'd glimpsed something strange glinting deep down. Clearing his throat a couple of times, he was about to start whistling. But he never whistled, and thought that if he did, the sensation he was trying to conceal, would be brought into relief. What he did was quite odd. He knew himself well, and confronting frightening situations wasn't exactly his favourite occupation. And yet, driven by some irrational impulse, by atypical derring-do, he stepped closer to the mirror. Going right up to his reflection, he scrutinised whatever it was he thought he'd seen moments before in his own eyes. He rolled them around, myopically, swaying his head slowly, seeing if that strange glint that had so shocked him might show itself again. But all he could see were his own large, dark brown eyes and thick black eyelashes. He leaned closer still, resting on the frame, peering at the image of himself like a lunatic. The mirror soon steamed up with the warm air coming out of his nose, so the image disappeared behind the mist, which came and went, eventually obscuring his entire face. He reached up to wipe the condensation away, and fell back with a cry, bumping into the bed. He clapped his hands over his mouth. When he'd wiped the mirror, he'd seen something. Something alien. And he thought he'd seen (because it couldn't be true) a pair of heavy-lidded, bestial eyes, half-swollen by a dark, viscous layer of fat. And inside the eyes he had seen, or felt, a terrifying force that had made him shudder. What he'd seen in the mirror was not himself. It was a deformed, abominable being with a menacing, self-satisfied smile on its face. He'd never seen anything so terrifying. Yes, he'd seen it, he thought with a shiver. He'd just "seen" it a moment ago. It had slouched through this very place, and he had followed it, and yet he still didn't know what it was. It was just a feeling, as insubstantial as a wicked thought. He couldn't bring himself to look in the mirror again. He sat on the bed and slumped down shivering. How could this be happening? Was he feverish? He didn't think so. Despite the visions, despite the voices, he could still distinguish the normal from the abnormal His mind was clear. He screwed his eyes shut and held his breath. Something inside him was about to explode. He didn't know if it was better to let it out, or resist, resist until he had nothing left – and until whatever it was grew to bursting-point. How was it possible for life to change so much? Could all this be part of the same existence? If he cast his mind back to the happy days when his mother was alive, days full of so much hope and laughter, they seemed part of a different and distant life. Drying his eyes, he curled up in bed, trying to remember those happy days as he always had. But it soon became clear that he couldn't conjure them in all their detail. They were a blur, barely perceptible in his innermost thoughts.

In his anxiety, he tried to recall a pleasant memory: the day when he won the drawing prize at school. He tried to take himself back to the unsullied pride which spread on his boyish face, when, before his peers and, most importantly, before his mother, he had received a trophy in the shape of a pen from the headmaster. Everyone had applauded – most passionately of all, his mother. She had helped him, assuring him he was certain to win. He had, and her kisses and radiant face proved the greatest prize. He would never forget it... Or at least so he'd thought until now, because when he tried to remember what he had drawn, he couldn't. And he didn't have the relevant notebook with him. When he tried to recall the party his mother had thrown, the images of the day, the guests' faces, everything floated in a haze, like ghosts at a banquet that had been called off. He was losing his memories, and that was truly terrifying. If he lost the ability to remember his mother, and his early days, what would be left? Nothing but a profusion of lines, spoken phrases contained in bubbles, an infinity of lifeless sketches. He had already lost his mother and his own life was now slipping between his fingers. He was alone in the world, alone with his visions, with his fear. And there was nothing solid to help him stay on his feet. He felt he was floating upwards, flying at such high speed that he could barely breathe.

But what kind of illness was it that made him forget his own memories, and forced him to rekindle forgotten moments? How many memories were due to beset him, how many to cease to belong to him? He curled up into a ball, at a loss, afraid to look at himself in the mirror, afraid of hearing those voices again, seeing such deformed creatures, and returning to a past he didn't recognise. Perhaps it was best to wait, see what surprises were in store. He looked around, afraid to move. He was paralysed. He heard Bezel calling, but couldn't move. Then he heard footsteps coming closer.

"Food's ready," Bezel said, appearing in the doorway. Seeing Max in bed, she went over. "Max! What's wrong? Say something." Then, turning back to the door, she shouted out: "Simon, come up here quick!"

She sat on the side of the bed and took hold of Max by the shoulders. His body was limp.

"Max! Come on, you're frightening me," she said, attempting a smile while slapping his face with the back of her hand.

"Miss Bezel, don't go, please, don't leave me," Max said, becoming aware of her efforts to revive him. "Please, stay here."

"I'm not going anywhere, Max. Don't worry," she said, drawing his head to her bosom. "Easy, easy."

"Please," he whispered, relieved to have somebody close. "Don't leave me."

"No, no. Now relax. Here, get under the covers, and let's get you out of those clothes. You need a lie down. I'll bring you something to eat, maybe you're just exhausted."

"No! Don't go," he pleaded, grabbing her arm.

Bezel gave him a sympathetic look and perhaps even tenderly brushed the hair from his sweaty brow. The boy needed her. Finally, she'd done it. He wanted her to stay. Her victory seemed complete, and yet it didn't feel that way. When he'd grabbed hold of her, it had shaken something inside her. Nothing libidinous, or sensual but rather a maternal, compassionate tenderness. And yet, she knew she had still to play her part. She wasn't going to throw it all away for some silly sentiment, not having got this far. She pulled herself together.

"Come on, Max, take it easy. I'm going to call the doctor, you just try to rest," as she said this, she began slowly to disentangle herself. But, rather than moving away, she leaned over and whispered in his ear: "Hurts, doesn't it, seeing your own soul on the wrack?"

It was as though Max had not heard the words, but rather intuited them. When she did move away, and the twisted look on her face yielded to one of kindness, it was unclear to him whether he had just imagined those words.

"What's going on?" I asked from the door.

"He's all pale and cold," Bezel explained. "You stay with him while I go and call the doctor."

I laid him down. He made no attempt to resist. He wearily peeled off his clothes and got into the bed, eyes closed. He felt too afraid to open them.

"I'll be right back," Bezel said. "Just try to take it easy."

Sitting on the side of the bed, I looked down at him pityingly.

"I won't be a minute," Bezel said from the door.

Max was lying with his back to the door, curled up with his arms crossed at his stomach. He tried to think, but his thoughts remained entangled, ensuring that any attempt at order was thwarted. The build-up of tension, sadness, hate, incomprehension and fear those past weeks had been too much. Max wondered if all that was being released, and once he had assimilated his new reality, he'd be himself again.

I leaned closer and, as he was shivering, tucked him in. He flinched, but turning and seeing that it was me, he seemed to relax.

"It's all right," I smile. "The doctor's being called."

"I don't need a doctor," he said quietly. "I need my mother."

I felt a lump in my throat.

"Max," I said carefully. "There's no logic to life. It's always beyond us. Only if you understand that, will you realise there's no point beating yourself up trying to make sense of things. We will never understand."

Wearily he sat up in the bed, scanning the entire room in an attempt to meet my gaze – as if he might find my eyes on the ceiling, or above the mantelpiece. He needed me, needed my words more than anything. He was alone, and his world, just a few months before so perfect and hermetically sealed, had evaporated. I later learned what a key moment this was. It was then that he allowed me into his peculiar existence, when he truly opened up to what I had to say. I had no experience in such things, had not even had any children. I was a solitary person, always avoiding commitments, feeling no need for any. My sole motivation in life was to solve a murder that had taken place eight years earlier, a case the police had closed, writing it off as suicide.

"Simon," he said, grimacing. "I'm losing my mind."

I moved closer in order to hear better. I believe it had become impossible for him to keep it all to himself any longer.

"I'm having visions. I pass out, and then find myself in places I know from my childhood. It's as though I lose consciousness in the present and then come to in the past. And," he said, moving closer, almost whispering to me now – he seemed tremendously lucid but at the same time full of the terror anyone experiences when madness threatens to take over, "Drake has appeared in each of these memories. The man I talked to you about. I think my mother's death has affected me more than I believed, because until yesterday, I knew nothing about this man. I'm not even sure I'm not just making it all up."

He tried to summarise what was going on, and in doing so compared his life with his mother to his current situation. This he did wishing to demonstrate that there was nothing peculiar in that former life, and to convince himself, and me, that what was currently happening was strange and terrible. However, I could see from the small detail he recounted that in fact he had always lived a strange life, not so different in kind to his recent experiences. He was immersed in his own reality, just as I was in mine. Spending so much time consorting with his own ghosts had made them cease to seem anything out of the ordinary. But if there was anything his life smacked of, it was the extraordinary.

Max had no clue about the person he had come looking for, had no idea what kind of individual he was. I, however, had spent too long investigating Drake, and the things I had discovered about him made it impossible to believe that Max's case was simply one of madness. I knew things that Max didn't, not only because he was young and inexperienced, but because what I knew about Drake was unimaginable to the majority of people; and what we cannot imagine, simply does not exist. It's unnerving to think that the best-kept secrets, the most dangerous, are those that do not form part of the collective unconscious. There are beings with nothing in common with their fellow men apart from physical appearance. Their obsessions become a way of life. To come to believe that individuals such as Drake actually exist, that they live in the same society as the rest of us and supposedly breathe the same air, takes some doing – takes a wholesale alteration of the senses. Oft-times the actions triggered by these dark thoughts are not so different to those activated with far less sinister ends in mind. It is in the depths that, if one truly begins to dig, their true nature becomes apparent, and it is at that point that one must be ready to accept something that I term an aberration of principles.

I had no idea how to explain to Max what I knew, or where to begin doing so. For anyone not versed in such thoughts, they may be beyond the realms of the believable and even deeply unsettling. At least in my case they had been. I went from fascination to bewilderment and then on to repugnance. I needed to tell him that he wasn't going crazy, far from it: Drake was manipulating his mind. I didn't know if he would believe me, but I could back it up with evidence. Eight whole years of evidence to prove to him that I was inventing nothing. And, to stop him worrying for his sanity, he needed to know. For all that, the knowledge meant entering a space that would engender a different kind of pain. One pain for another.

"Max, listen closely," I said, sitting down on the bed. "You aren't going crazy."

He looked at me suspiciously – how I could be so sure?

"Your mind isn't falling part. I believe it's being tampered with."

"By whom?"

"'Drake."

"So, you do know him?" he said, clearly excited.

"Yes, I know him. I didn't mention it because I didn't think there was any way all this could involve you."

"What is 'all this'?"

"I am also here because of a death. But I never thought I'd find someone in the same situation. I don't know where to begin, it all happened so long ago. Well, my sister died eight years ago, and all the evidence suggested it was suicide… But I know that she was murdered."

"Murdered?" he said, thoughts turning to his mother.

"I was first led to the idea by coincidence, when I was clearing out her house a few weeks after she died. I decided to hold onto some of her belongings, among them her books…"

Max gave me an uneasy look. For a moment I regretted having begun my tale. Doubtless he wouldn't believe me or, worse still, he would, and that would lead him to realise that the risk he was running was far worse than the prospect of losing his mind. But it was no good now going half-cocked, giving him some edited, easy-to-swallow version. It wasn't an easy story to tell, and far less to hear. Maybe it was my selfishness that pushed me to continue. I was also in need of help, and he might have some information to fill out my suppositions.

"Among the books were twelve or so that caught my eye. They were old, and well thumbed, with sandpaper covering the jackets, so you couldn't see the titles. I ripped the covers off to find they were all concerned with questions of magic. Lots of them featured passages that had been highlighted and underlined, or there would be notes in the margins. It was the first I'd heard of my sister's interest in such subjects. As I read on, it became clear to me that she'd had this secret world, a double life, that nobody had suspected, not even me. I found a bundle of papers slotted in the back pages of one of these books, the handwriting in which was exceedingly cramped, almost impossible to read, and then another bundle of letters written in an elongated, antiquated hand. No return addresses. I put the letters in order of date and began to read. It seemed that my sister – how and through whom I still do not know – had been in contact for several years with a sect that practised black magic. Initially the letters were polite if a little standoffish, somewhat condescending and secretive. Then the tone changed. It seemed my sister had met with the people in question, and the language became less formal, more direct but at the same time harder to understand – for the uninitiated. The correspondence covered a period of seven years, in which time I assume my sister had gone quite deep into that dark world, a world more powerful than she was. After rereading the cryptic language, the letters and the books, and schooling myself in the terminology, a picture began to form: it seemed that my sister had accepted a large sum of money to conceive – there was no mention of who the father might be – and later hand the baby over to the Rosicrucian society of the old Church of Carmel The doctor who carried out the autopsy revealed she was two months pregnant None of us could believe it. We had no idea who the father might be. I can barely bring myself to think of it now. Though full of ambiguities and obscure phrasing, the last letter revealed the existence of a pact. She was reminded of her duties to the community, and of the impossibility of going back on pledges she had made. It was clear that she had got involved in something where one paid a heavy price for mistakes or weaknesses. The threats, though veiled, were unmistakeable. From her own notes, in that cramped, semi-illegible handwriting, it was clear to see that she was afraid. A fear that she could share with no one, I imagine because of the magnitude of the mistakes she'd made, and the similarly great barbarity of the acts she might have committed (or been forced to commit), all of which was too terrible for her to confess. Those notes made it clear to me that she wanted out. Her final letters had been written in a state of outright terror. The last days of her life must have been very sad indeed. She must have known where her choices were leading her.

"At the end of each letter, she was told to destroy all correspondence after reading them. I don't know why my sister kept those letters, from the first to the very last, but my sense is that she suspected from the start she wouldn't be able to last the course. I believe she was always on the verge of opting out, and decided to keep this evidence of her lapse into the inferno as a kind of future punishment, for when someone like me found out what she got up to in her free time. I never judged her. Quite the opposite. It became obvious that solitude and insecurity compelled her to find acceptance in a group. My sister's behaviour seemed to me to have been induced by third parties. It was clear that somebody, somebody to whom she was attracted – a man, doubtless – had been the one to initiate her in the mysteries, and that, only once the game was underway, had she realised it was all a trap.

"I've spent the years ever since searching, trying in vain to make contact with the society in question, or with anyone who might be able to give me information about it."

"Did they dress up her death to make it seem like suicide?" asked Max, as though weighing up the possibility.

"I am absolutely sure that they did. Look, Max, these secret societies exist in every city in the world. They may be impossible to locate, but they're there alright. And they know all too well to select new members from among the weakest and most disadvantaged, the most stupid, and most gullible. If anyone tries to contact them, it's pointless, whereas if they get some poor beggar in their sights, that's that. I have spent years looking into secret societies and sects. I even spent time trying to make everyone I came into contact with believe that I was prepared to sell my soul to the devil. But I guess they struggled to trust someone who made such a fuss. Nobody ever made contact with me. I never found any kind of trail that might lead to explanations, it was pure chance that led me to refine my searches. I spent a number of years working for a law firm in Paris which took on fairly small-scale cases: divorces, *crimes passionnels*, murders over inheritances, manslaughter. At some point I remembered that a very elegant woman had come into the office some ten years before, the kind of person who, when they want to hide some misdeed, or a family secret, try to find someone from the lower classes to pin it on. This woman's son had disappeared without trace, and she had come to us to appoint a private detective to find him. It seemed that the woman – Sophie was her name, I can still remember – knew that her son had been in contact with people who, according to her, were involved in some kind of shady business, the kind of people you wanted to avoid, unless you wanted to acquire the habit of dipping communion wafers in warm blood before going to bed.

"Sophie maintained that her son had been drawn into a secret society that forced him to live away from home, to take drugs and practice the rite of kundalini, which more or less means letting someone fuck you in the arse on the basis that it's all part of a respectful initiation ritual, in which everything gives the appearance of being very chaste and symbolic (I never could imagine what kind of symbolism they meant, the whole thing seemed pretty explicit to me). When I recalled that incident, I visited my former colleagues who readily supplied Sophie's address. (I had to say I was lusting after her). I went to visit her, and found out that her son, whom our detective never did manage to find, had died two years earlier. The woman, who had rather lost her looks since last we met, received me at her house on Rue ***, and told me everything she could remember about her son's friendships and the final conversations they'd had. With the names I got from her, I was able to find my way into the highest echelons of Paris society, and it was there that I finally understood that I would never find the information I was looking for: not only were all those rich bastards bat-shit crazy, there was an unbreakable pact of silence between them. Nobody would ever dare talk about anybody else, because if the truth of their shared activities were revealed, they knew that they'd all get dragged into the mire."

"I don't get it. How is this place connected to what you're talking about?"

"A great deal. If there's anything good about being poor, it's that you'll always be helped by others who are also poor, in full knowledge that they'll never get anything back apart from simple gratitude and friendship. It was the housemaid of one of the families, whom I won't name, who gave me a couple of surnames she'd overheard being spoken, while doing her chores about the place, and it was those names that, a good while later, led me to this place."

"And what's Drake's connection?" Max asked impatiently.

"One of the names I was given happened to be that of a man who had belonged to the same sect as my sister. Turned out he'd had problems with some of the other members. Seems he had some rather eccentric tastes, and never bothered to hide them. They threw him out. Just imagine what he would have had to do for these people – who wouldn't think twice about gnawing on the skulls of their victims or washing in sperm produced in a magic rite – to think him a risk. Being expelled not only meant having to leave the sect, but the city as well, and moving to New York. It was either that or stay in Paris underground. But this guy was well connected. There must have been someone in the society who liked him, and who helped him stay on. He got a job with an investment company in New York, and this is where it gets interesting, because the main shareholder turned out to be none other than our friend, Drake Emilianov. Unfortunately, the man in question is dead now. Take a guess at how he died?" Absorbed in my tale, Max shook his head. "In a ritual, off his head on mescaline, he cut off his own penis and bled to death. Can you imagine a more ridiculous way to pop your clogs? But I didn't let myself get bogged down in any of that. Drake turned out to be the real goldmine. He ran the sect in New York, and most of his clients and patients were also members. He wielded considerable authority among them and had contacts in the higher reaches of secret societies throughout the world. He knew who was who in every religious movement, every cult and every secret society. Anyway, all of this has been going on for years... I'm not sure how to explain it all," I said, faltering, "there's so much."

"What do you mean?"

"Just that what seems at first sight some silly kind of entertainment for eccentric rich folk with too much time on their hands, has a far darker, far more sinister history..."

While we talked, Bezel made her way quickly to the top of the stairs. She began to descend, but after a couple of steps stopped and, taking off her shoes, turned around and came back up, as quietly as she could.

Once on the top floor, she hurried on tiptoes to the end of the unlit hallway. She knocked gently, opened the door and slipped into the dark room. Regaining her breath, she squinted and peered around. It was very cold in there. Once her eyes adjusted, she was able to see her breath before her, and the faint purplish light from several television monitors in one corner, on which my conversation with Max was being recorded in all its detail. She crossed her arms and stood waiting uneasily. A number of minutes passed with only their breathing to break the silence: hers shallow and uneven, Drake's deep and slow. Then it struck her that he was perhaps asleep.

"Sir?" she said gently.

"Yes, yes," came his deep voice, from an indeterminate point in the room. "I'm not asleep."

"Sir…" she went on. "He's in bad shape. I don't think he can take it."

"Nonsense!" Drake said, in a half-groan, half-shout. "Perhaps it's actually you who's struggling?"

Bezel knew it was impossible to hide anything from him – even speaking out loud was in a sense absurd. He knew her inside out. He was too intelligent, always several steps ahead of anything she might be about to say, as though capable of reading her mind. It was no easy matter to lie, he had a view of everything from this room. But at times she thought that wasn't the worst of it. Worst of all was being in his hands. And yet, for all that, she was still an individual in her own right, her powers of judgement or feelings had hardly deserted her, and there was no way to go on like this without becoming truly anguished. He had to understand.

"We're not making any headway, Bezel." Drake spoke in a flat monotone. "You're never going to get better, never. I do everything I can for you, but time and again you disappoint me. You're clever, but there's no denying that you're also ill."

Another shiver ran through Bezel. It was very cold in the room, the kind of cold that gets into the bones, that seeps in through the pores. She felt it in her aching eye sockets – blinking brought the heat of her blood to her corneas. She was all too aware of her reliance on Drake, that she had given her word – more than that – and that there was no turning back now.

"I really think he's suffering, sir. I'm concerned he might fall ill before we get to where you want to get to. He's very sensitive. I don't think he's ready for all of this."

"You don't?" Drake said scornfully. "Since when did you know anything about psychiatry?"

"Well, he's had a rough time, he's trying hard to resist but… he thinks he is crazy."

"And he is crazy," he said, his tone softening. "Bezel, my dear, you haven't the first idea who this boy is, so please, spare me your sentimental warbling."

Bezel heard movement at the far end of the room, the sound of shifting clothes. She strained to see, but all she could make out were shadows.

"Downstairs with you now, and call the doctor," came his voice, no longer his previous monotone "And don't forget I'm watching you. I'm watching all of you."

"Doctor? Which doctor?"

"Which doctor? Dr Graham, of course!"

"But the man stinks, he's a –"

"He's a doctor. At least he was until a few years ago, and very efficient about his work, I can assure you."

"But now... He's been struck off, and Max needs –"

"Are you trying to tell me what to do?"

"No."

"Do as I say. Call the doctor or get ready to start living like the rest of the town."

"Certainly," she said, backing slowly away. "I only wanted you to know –"

"Bezel!" he cried, making her jump. "I don't want you to do what you've been doing: no more whispering in his ear, no more trying to put the frights on him. No more!" he growled. "Don't become a problem for me, you know I could dispose of you without so much as a second thought. If it weren't for me you'd be lying in some stinking alleyway, or in some tin-pot NHS psychiatric unit, or dead. Don't forget it. Don't forget that you still need me. And I'm the only one who can help you, but..." and now his voice took on a paternal edge, "I need him to believe in you. It isn't so difficult. I can assure you. Now, off you go."

Bezel went out, shivering. She shut the door behind her. Breathing in the warmer, fresher air in the hallway, she immediately felt better. She slipped silently down the stairs. Coming into the lobby she headed to the left and opened the door into the lounge. She went in without turning on the lights. The windows were closed and only a few shreds of light entered through the old, uneven catches. She quickly made her way to the far end. Ancient paintings and fraying tapestries hung on the walls. There was a seven-metre long table across the centre of the room with straight-backed chairs along either side. Going over to a cabinet at the end of the room, she took out a personal organiser and a telephone. Flicking through, she dialled the number with trembling fingers. The doctor gave her the creeps. He was a disgusting man, with an even more despicable history.

"Doctor? It's Bezel here. You need to come right away." There was a silence. "Yes, he asked for you. I'd never have called you myself." Another silence. "Well, you know what that will mean... I can't force you to, but… Sure."

Putting the telephone and the organiser back into the cabinet, she left the living room. The doctor would be there in under ten minutes. He lived close to the edge of the castle property and never had any patients. The occasional person with a cut finger, or a broken arm or wound from some fight, but that was all. People in Shimts didn't fall ill in the normal way, at least as far as he knew. They hardly ever got colds, or stomach ulcers, or had heart attacks, or suffered from cancers or any other illness. In Shimts, accidents rather than illnesses tended to be the cause of death. A slit throat while shaving, a gash to the wrist while chopping vegetables, a most unfortunate fall from a top floor…

The doctor's eyes were a dull blue, like the sky on a cloudy day, and his nose was covered in reddish warts. He smelled of cat urine and whiskey sweated through the pores of his crumpled body. He arrived at the castle short of breath, and Bezel let him in.

"He's upstairs," she said, feeling on edge.

"And what's wrong with him?" he said, not so much looking at the woman as he made for the stairs.

"He's cracking up," she said, following the doctor. "He's beside himself."

As he entered the room the doctor sneered. Max was still lying in the bed. As if a thought transfusion was in progress, the most hare-brained ideas whirled chaotically around his mind. Talking with me had produced a shift in him, he was calmer now, but the image in the mirror had so terrified him that he said he never wanted to look at another in his whole life. The doctor shuffled in and we had to put off our conversation. His shoes had bits of cat excrement on them and his clothes gave off the sour stink of a drunkard's sweat. He approached the bed, placing his medical bag down on the bedside table.

"Right, young man, let's have a look then."

The man spoke as if he had a mouth full of sweets, or his tongue couldn't touch the roof of his mouth. Max sat up and shot Bezel an interrogative look. The man smelled awful.

"It's the doctor," she said to calm him.

"Right then. Something hurting?" he said, readying to put his claws on him. Max couldn't hide his disgust and seemed to forget the vision in the mirror for a few seconds.

"No, don't worry. I'm fine. I just need a little rest."

"Well, that isn't what I was told," the doctor said, looking over at Bezel.

It dawned on her that Max would rather go mad than have those greasy hands all over him. She saw the disgust on his face, and the way he flinched as the doctor came close. Wanting to help him out, she clarified:

"He' all right. Perhaps a little edgy. A sedative would probably do it."

The doctor was about to say something, before deciding that it was none of his business. If it was sedatives he wanted, that wasn't a problem – he had the lot. He opened his bag and took out a box of Valium.

"If this is all it was, you could have saved me the trip," he grumbled. "This will give you a nice long rest. Don't go necking too many, or you'll be going into hibernation. Ever taken one before?"

Max shook his head.

"In that case, one will do the trick. If you're feeling really worked up, you can take two."

"Thanks," said Max, wishing the man would just go away.

He looked over at Bezel, who gave him a nod. The doctor closed his bag and went out, leaving his awful odour in his wake. Bezel showed him out and went straight back up. She looked at Max apologetically.

"He's very efficient sometimes," she said, half smiling.

"No doubt," I said. "That smell would wake the dead."

"There's very little work for him here. He drinks to pass the time."

She brought Max a glass of water and a pill.

"I think you should take it. It will do you good."

Grudgingly, Max took the pill from her, swallowed it, only for his face to darken once more when he remembered what had been going on.

"What is it?" Bezel asked.

"I wouldn't know where to begin," he admitted, clearly still feeling troubled.

"Maybe it's a build-up of tension."

"Yes, maybe," Max said in a low voice. "Tension... I've had problems recently."

"You mean since your mother died?" Bezel hastened to ask.

"Yes. I've been very tense. Sorry."

"Don't torture yourself" she said encouragingly. "Problems come, but they also go away again." Max looked unconvinced, and she quickly reframed her comment: "I mean, with a little bit of rest, in a few days you'll be right as rain. As it turns out I think you've come to just the right place. If there's anything you can do here, it's rest. Make the most of the bridge being down, after that it's unlikely you'll have lots of time to be lying around."

"Right. Maybe I've been lucky after all."

"And your girlfriend too," said the tireless Bezel.

I gave her a disapproving look. Though our encounters were nothing if not fulsome, and though I was always willing to satisfy her indefatigable appetites, for her it wasn't enough. Neither the laws of physics nor statistics seemed to apply in that department. I knew she was using me, but never have I taken so much pleasure in being used, and I submitted all too willingly. It didn't bother me that she should find Max attractive. He was a good-looking, fit young man, and his stamina might be more suited to the task. But even at that point I had a sense that Max's misanthropy and dislike of society extended to a strict, unswerving brand of celibacy. I couldn't help but smile at the futility of Bezel's innuendos.

"No," Max said wearily. "I don't have a girlfriend."

"I find that difficult to believe," she said, playing up her surprise. "A guy like you must have them queuing up..."

"How about we let him have a rest?" I said, coming to his aid.

This won me a sharp look from Bezel, tinged with desire. I think she thought I was jealous, and that turned her on, briefly putting Max out of mind. She gave me a suggestive look as if to say we should go out together, but Max intervened, just as I had thought he might.

"Simon," he said. "Would you mind staying with me for a bit?"

"No, of course not," I said, rejecting Bezel's invitation with a sardonic smile.

Her face flushed red. Doubtless she wanted to strangle me there and then, but I somehow failed to take the hint, and sat down on the bed once more.

"Well, I'll be off then," said Bezel. "Have fun, you two."

She just managed to prevent herself from slamming the door, and we heard her footsteps going away down the stairs.

"She'll be putting poison in our food," I said with a laugh.

"I don't like her."

"If you manage to get out of this hotel in one piece, someone's bound to give you a medal. You must be the only man who's resisted her advances in decades."

"It isn't that I don't like women," he said apologetically, "but I couldn't... I guess I'm old-fashioned. My mother was too strict in the way she brought me up, there's no getting away from it."

"You might be right, but at my age there are certain dishes one simply can't send back. You never know when you might get another taste. But matters of the bedroom are one thing, trust is another. I try to prise information out of her, but all she ever does is put me off. I'm convinced she knows more than she lets on."

"She might just be a lowly employee."

"Don't be naïve, Max. I wouldn't be surprised if she turned out to be one of Drake's concubines."

"Concubines?"

"Drake goes along with the ideas of the esoteric society founded by Crowley."

"Aleister Crowley?"

"Know of him?"

"Vaguely. I've read a bit about him."

"That's more or less where we were before we were interrupted. When Drake felt he'd established enough contacts, he definitively removed himself from the societies he was a member of, and poured his energy into running one he himself had set up some time before. It was based on the same precepts as Crowley's Astrum Argentum. I don't know a great deal about the society Drake currently runs, but I have tried to get to the bottom of that previous order, and from what I have been able to make out, Drake was into all kinds of sexual rituals, including Tantric Magick sex."

"Including what?" he said, baring his teeth.

"The idea is that it's a way of reaching one's full psychic power. They believe that orgasm is a way of reaching a higher state of consciousness, one that allows them to see God. To them it's a mystical act."

"I don't believe it."

"Well, it's true. And it wouldn't surprise me if Bezel turned out to be one of his acolytes, or that he used her in his rituals. She's told me that she used to be a patient of his, that she first met him while on a detox treatment."

"She was a drug addict?"

"More than that. But let's stay on topic. Crucially, what did Drake have to do with your mother. There might be something there to help me get to the bottom of what happened to my sister. We have both buried a loved one and here we both are – directly or indirectly, because of Drake. Maybe he isn't the author of your mother's death, but the coincidence seems pretty enormous. Wouldn't you say?"

"If he did have anything to do with it," Max said, suddenly furious, "I'll kill him."

"Take it easy. I don't think it will be as simple as that. He's a very powerful man, and I fear he might have surprises in store for you. Come on, think it through, Max. Do you believe it's a coincidence that these memories come to you just now, in the place he resides? I don't even think the letter he sent your mother was a mistake. He must have known she was dead, and simply wanted to entice you here."

"But why would he be interested in me?"

"Well," I said "I am certain that your presence here, and the death of your mother, have more behind them than a simple kundalini rite. You could begin by telling me everything you remember about Drake and, above all, what linked you and your mother to him. Maybe if we start piecing things together, we'll form a picture of what the two deaths have in common."

"I've been making notes of all my memories in this notebook," he said. "I know it might sound strange but –"

"That's where you're wrong," I said, cutting him off. "I'm at a stage where nothing seems strange anymore."

"I'm not sure that everything I've remembered is true, but it's so real. A lot of it I don't understand, it's all very confused."

"May I?" I said, looking at the notebook.

Reluctantly, Max handed it over. He wasn't used to opening up to others but something must have told him that allying himself with me was going to be his only route to answers. His notebook, as I've already said, featured a mix of comic vignettes and text. A mishmash of a heartfelt magazine, drawing the reader in with the sheer chiaroscuro beauty of the lines. Such was Max's world, an unreal, desolate world in which words emerged in bubbles over people's heads and their impenetrability was offset by the characters' expressive gestures and looks.

"Beautiful," I said, and I meant it.

He nodded.

"Tell me, Max: where's your father?"

"I never met him."

"And you've no idea who he might be?"

He shook his head, saying nothing.

"When you've met Drake, did you have the feeling that your mother already knew him?"

"I think so," he said, annoyed. "But what are you trying to say?"

"It's far from likely, but perhaps Drake had something to do with –"

Max sat up in bed. His eyes glowered indignantly.

"You think he's my father?"

"No, no, but…" I said slowly. "There's always the possibility… Perhaps…"

"What?"

"Well, I know nothing about the kind of company your mother kept, but…" I stopped there, waiting for an answer.

"She didn't have lovers, if that's what you mean. I was her –"

"Her what?"

"Nothing," he said defiantly. "She just didn't have any lovers."

I couldn't bring myself to ask about his relationship with his mother. It struck me as both too obvious and too cruel to go rooting around in such personal terrain, and I decided to change tack.

"What I mean is, perhaps your mother, like my sister, had some debt outstanding, one she was unable to pay."

"My mother?" he said, clearly amused. "No, that's not possible. You didn't know her. She was a good woman."

"I'm not trying to say she wasn't. My sister wasn't a bad person either, but they both were, or were soon to be, single mothers. Perhaps your mother had relationships that were just as secret as my sister's."

"I would have known," he spat.

"The same way you knew that she knew Drake?"

Max said nothing, pondering the fact my hypotheses might not be so wide of the mark.

"You think she was killed because she failed to keep up her side of the deal"

"You told me you never had visitors, that the two of you lived alone, and that you were constantly on the move. I'm sorry, Max, but it's pretty clear that your mother was trying to get away from something, or someone. Maybe she was trying to hide, or trying to hide you."

"But why do you think it has to be like that? Just because something happened to your sister, doesn't mean my mother was involved in that kind of –"

"Trust me, if your mother was involved in any way with Drake, you should discount nothing. They aren't the kind who let you off if you owe them something. Look, I had no idea about any of this before, but in eight years I've seen so many things, all I can do now is be suspicious of everything. It can't be a coincidence that I'm here in this place. I've put so much time and effort into finally joining the dots that show Drake was involved in my sister's death. I risked my life repeatedly poking my nose where I shouldn't and asking prying questions. I know that he indirectly ordered her murder, though at this precise moment it would be virtually impossible for me to prove it. And that's what's so terrible. These people, they're like moles, they go around the world covered in a layer of impunity, they are untouchable. Or like worms, they chew their way through society, from the inside slowly, never losing their patience. They might seem normal but," I said, recalling my sister, "behind them is an invisible world that even those close to them have no idea about. What I'm trying to say is," I went on, searching for a way to put it that wouldn't cause him more pain, "perhaps your mother had some kind of interaction with Drake and his people, and later thought better of it."

I couldn't just come out with what I thought, at least not without hurting Max. Perhaps his mother had agreed to conceive him in one of those satanic rituals, in exchange for an elevated position within that secret society, and a considerable sum of money. All the people involved in that society turned out to belong to the very richest echelon of society; all of them were powerful, immensely wealthy and immensely unhinged.

It was true that in all my years of researching, I had failed to learn very much about the Rosicrucian society of the old Church of Carmel (which my sister was involved in), but I had begun penetrating other groups which, though more accessible and less off-the-wall, allowed access to all kinds of people and helped me form an understanding of just how far man will go to achieve a kind of power which, to my mind, is not within his gift. The elite of which I speak is untouchable, but one can find out a good deal in eight years, and slowly but surely, I had begun to gather sufficient information to paint a very embarrassing picture indeed for more than one internationally prestigious family. Everybody knows that a great many families in French and European high society, and high-ups in the Church, have in the past been linked to these societies. What perhaps fewer people know is the kind of rituals carried out in the previous century under the auspices of a subsequently excommunicated priest by the name of Boullan (a name that is also no longer secret now). This society, to which Drake had belonged for over forty years, was a replacement, a hair-raising version, of the old Rosicrucian society of the Church of Carmel, which had its origins in the Works of Mercy, an organisation founded in 1840 by a seer by the name of Vintras. He was a hysterical, perverted homosexual who dedicated himself, among other things, to teaching his disciples mysterious forms of prayer, many of which involved group masturbation. Drake had joined a latter-day version of this society as a young man, but quit it some years later with the aim of putting on his own show: a society based on the teachings of the Satanist magician, Aleister Crowley. It is likely that Drake encountered these ideas in his youth, and was charmed by the magnetic aura of the magician. There was no surprise in that. Crowley had been a rich, eccentric child, with a magnetic personality and a way with people, and no compunction about going where others who also called themselves magicians feared to tread. When he left the Golden Dawn he founded

Astrum Argentum. The main motto was Do What Thou Wilt, and the primary aim was to revive ritual magic – the one abolished by the advent of Christianity – the kind that built altars to Priapus and Isis.

Drake was one of a number of remaining Crowley followers, a fanatic who believed in magic and in the power of orgasms to enable people to achieve full psychic potency. But he was a world-renowned psychiatrist too, and publicly renounced conventional psychiatry, sharing Laing's ideas on mental illness – though he was even more radical. In Drake's eyes, mental illness was a social phenomenon – a view similar to Foucault's, who compared it to leprosy. Drake believed that a madman did not live in the same reality as the rest of the world, but did not deserve to be locked up as a result. He had become an expert in lost causes, visionaries and mystics. Like Freud, he viewed the unconscious as being governed by different laws to the conscious mind and his principal studies and research focused on showing that behind every Charles Manson there dwelt an unknown, perhaps diabolical force, impelling the subject to act according to codes of their own. And it was those codes he sought to decipher.

He took on the most radical cases. His clinics, which I had visited some years before, hosted an endless parade of characters who believed they had the secret to the philosopher's stone and the meaning of the universe, who swore they conversed with angels and demons, and even had a direct line to God. Drake and his team studied each of them closely. He believed that the truth was hidden somewhere there. The truth that philosophers and mystics had been trying to uncover over the course of centuries. He thought that the field of perceptions of those known as madmen – and whom he, after Foucault, referred to as lepers – was more extensive than those of people in their right mind, and that only by investigating and coming to understand the core of them could the deepest, darkest secrets of humanity be known. He proclaimed the power of the mind, of willpower and the usefulness of hypnosis in influencing people's actions. He sought to convince the world that magic, as a controlled inner power, was dormant at the deepest level of human nature and that if we were to awaken to this other reality then the logical laws of physics, which he compared with the conscious self, would eventually cede to those of the unconscious, in which true power resided.

Quite aside from the truth or otherwise of my theories, it was clear that since Max's arrival in Shimts, he had been experiencing visions that were beyond his control. I suspected that Drake, using his knowledge and the mental powers he claimed to possess, was manipulating him. It was only my opinion, but the whole thing had an undeniably dark side to it, too sinister to think that he had come there of his own volition. Max did not know that Drake's theories were about the mind and the power of an unknown force in the unconscious; about the existence of certain "controlled influences" already discussed in the key doctrines of modern magic; or that he employed all of the above in his sessions with patients. To date I had never seen with my own eyes how these theories would work in practice. They had always struck me as too abstract, too farfetched, to have any empirical impact. But from the look of things our friend Drake was using Max to try out a theory previously formulated by Eliphas Levi, an occultist from the early nineteenth century. Levi claimed that the human will was capable of achieving anything whatsoever as long as it was correctly developed and channelled, and compared it with steam power or the galvanic current in an attempt to convince the world of its natural and not at all obscurantist origins. In a mesmeric story by Edgar Allan Poe, "The Facts in the Case of M. Valdemar", which also talked about that from the perspective of Mesmer, a pioneer of hypnosis, there was a masterful account of subjugation. Whether or not you agreed with Drake Max's current experience had all the signs of subjugation, of a post-hypnotic suggestion. It was quite clear from those losses of consciousness, from those visions and memories that, if not Drake, then someone possessed of a strong will was manipulating his mind.

I didn't know how to break this to Max without tipping him directly into terror-induced madness. He struck me as too sensitive and vulnerable, and going through a difficult time to boot, so I decided against rehearsing all my thoughts about his mother and his current state of affairs. Max was going to be revisited by these visions of his past, and I was certain that they would help us uncover – before it was too late – who was behind the death of my sister and perhaps of his mother.

While we talked, Max gradually gave way to sleep. The Valium had hit him hard, and he was now resting peacefully. Safe from all his fears. I stayed with him until I was sure he was asleep, and then headed downstairs to make up with Bezel. After all, we all get hungry at some point, and the dishes she cooked up – why deny it – were entirely to my liking.

# X

I never experienced any of this previously.
I came home peacefully. I walked around my home
and nothing disturbed my serenity of mind.
If anyone had told me what sickly, silly fear
was going to attack me one day, I
would have split my sides laughing.
He?

Guy de Maupassant

Someone went into Max's bedroom while he was asleep, taking up position at the foot of the bed and regarding him in silence. It was Bezel. She was wearing a loose-fitting dress, quite unlike her usual attire. It was white and made of thick, rough cloth. Only her face was uncovered, and it was pallid and grimly set. She gazed unblinkingly down at him, and Max felt he was being watched, hounded relentlessly by a stern, domineering gaze: it made him shudder. The room quietly began to fill with people. They all wore the same spartan attire. They came silently and stood around the bed, watching Max: some with looks of disdain, others with a mocking sort of compassion, others with more loving, respectful expressions. Cut off from the warmth of the fire, he shivered. Those people's icy looks pierced his skin and penetrated his bones. Those glassy, frozen looks chilled all feeling and thought – all that was warm inside him. His limbs felt stiff, liable to shatter into a thousand pieces should he so much as move. He lay still, unable to speak out or flinch. He could feel nothing sufficiently strongly to react. He realised he lacked air to breathe, a point came when his eyes were unable to bear the pressure any longer: and he woke bathed in a cold sweat.

It was nighttime and the room lay empty in the dark, but the feeling of a lack of oxygen still weighed heavy. He took a deep breath and lay staring at the embers in the hearth. He hadn't had the kind of nightmares one wakes from with a start for a long time, and this one had left him with a profound sensation of loss. It meant that his mind was trapped within an obsession, a deep fear. Years ago, he'd worried about losing his mind when those petrifying visions came to him in his dreams, and, on waking, a small voice told him those nightmares were part of some future reality. He wasn't wrong. If she were still alive, Max thought, perhaps his nights would not be so dark nor his dreams so dire. Life wouldn't seem like a succession of incomprehensible moments and he would finally find it within himself to make that effort to understand.

Feeling afraid, he curled up beneath the sheets. Closing his eyes, he tried to get back to sleep. He felt that a colossal hole was ripping open his chest, a dark and massive rift dragging him irremediably down to some awful nadir. He was alone, completely alone. There was nothing so terrible as that sensation of not belonging of having no one, of not being part of anything. He could die that very moment and nobody would care. Nobody would come to claim his body. He tried to understand how this could have come to pass, how family and friends alike had become so distant, and people in general of no importance to him. They were simply objects going by in the street, things at the periphery of one's existence. They were there, but who were they? He no longer knew. He and his mother had been cast aside and forgotten, and he couldn't fathom why.

After leaving Max's company, I spent a couple of hours with Bezel, before returning to my room completely spent. I knew that it wasn't my sex appeal she went wild for: she was simply a woman who went wild. I tried to avoid thinking about the games she would have submitted to in Drake's sessions with his disciples. The kind of thing she liked was too recherché for a simple country woman. It was as though her freakishly deviant suggestions were intended to show how utterly uninhibited she was, how totally lacking in restraint. As though someone, claiming it as flattery, had told her that acting like a tart was her forte, that she ought to feel proud of it and use it as her greatest weapon. Maybe that was why she took it so hard when Max failed to respond to her advances. When he made it clear that in his eyes she was a nobody, a shapeless shadow.

By the time I made it back to my room it was quite late. I'd left Bezel sleeping, but I wasn't tired. Going down the stairs on the way back to my room, a strange sensation came over me. There was the usual quiet stillness of the small hours, but for a moment the hotel's apparent calm and isolation struck me as fake. I felt a shift, something unseen, a sense that on the other side of the walls, and all around, someone was watching. Only Bezel, Max and I were there, and each one of us was engrossed in his or her own life, our peculiar obsessions and desires. And yet I felt that something was breathing at our backs. I had the somewhat delightful thought that, perhaps it was true, all Scottish castles came with their attendant ghosts – but even that seemed overly simple and romantic, too reductive for a mind like mine, having by this point begun to move in the world of thought of Drake and his coterie. At the time it didn't cross my mind that someone might actually be watching and listening to all that we did.

Back in my room, I began to undress, my mind full of the images and text in Max's notebook. Of his mother. I could well picture the two of them living under the same roof. He, submissive and devoted; she, sweet and possessive, using love and kindness to control Max, even down to his most fleeting thought. The two of them supporting one another in the solitude of their lives. I pictured trains and aeroplanes, cars and low-class hotels; suitcases and hand luggage; memories that would ultimately be lost because nothing mattered in their lives and this closed circle of theirs. I wondered whom they might be running from, the reasons for that endless moving about and unrootedness.

As I buttoned up my pyjamas, I thought I caught sight of something outside the window. Going over and looking out, I saw a group of twenty or so lanterns being carried along the high street. They were heading towards the forest. My curiosity overcame any need to go to bed, and even my intense dislike of the rain. I threw on my jacket and silently left the room.

Exiting the castle, I made a dash in the direction of town. I hadn't been out for several days and the cold night air pricked my skin, penetrating the lethargy brought about by the warm fire in my room. There was the smell of open fields, of the wet earth, of smoke and the expanse of hills. I came to the high street, where one could just about pick out the buildings in the wan light from the streetlamps. The procession was almost out of sight by now – I could still glimpse the last of them disappear among the trees where the town segued into woodland. I ran as fast as I could to the end of the street, keeping my eye on the lantern at the back of the procession. As the trees began growing thick around me, I had to slow down. I could hardly see my own feet, but knew that if I stopped I'd lose the procession; I stumbled on, making sure I kept an eye on that last glimmering light. I couldn't think what all those people might be doing out in such weather, and at that hour. It had to be something abnormal. For a moment I hesitated, one of the lanterns seemed to hang back from the group, and I was worried about being seen. The general glow around the group was very faint by now. I walked past a boulder and noticed a small shadow behind it. Then there was the sound of something cracking behind me, and my heart jumped. There was someone behind the boulder. The faint glow of a lantern gave that individual away. I backed off in fear. My foot caught on a root and I fell onto my back. Several seconds of confusion ensued, I tried to pull myself up by a low hanging branch, and saw the shadow come out from behind the boulder. A cold sweat sprung up on my forehead and I tried to get up, while at the same time backing away. The shadowy figure turned up the lantern, came slowly over and held out a hand. I grabbed the thick white fabric of the sleeve. It was a man, and he calmly turned to look in the direction of the receding lanterns: then I knew he meant me no harm. I let go of his sleeve. Putting a finger to his lips, he whispered:

"They mustn't see us together, but let's meet tomorrow evening at the library. Get yourself to the library. There's something important I need to tell you."

"What's important? Who are you?"

"Don't you remember me?"

Then one of the lanterns up ahead seemed to be coming closer, and the man turned to leave.

"Not now... Believe me. I know everything about you people, everything."

"What do you mean, you people? What are you referring to?"

"Do as I say: tomorrow evening, the library. Now, get out of here."

The man looked fortyish, fragile and unhealthy. His voice was cracked and his gaze dull and lifeless. There were black rings under his eyes. As he moved off, I didn't dare follow. My heart was still pounding after the fright. Regaining my composure, I hesitated for a moment, before deciding it was pointless to go on with my pursuit – I'd only end up falling in some hole or getting my head bashed in. Wrapping my coat around me, I retraced my steps. Coming to a clearing, I caught sight of the dim streetlamps in the town. A faint glow glimmered above the craggy mountains. It was like finding oneself at the bottom of a funnel, trapped at the foot of a gigantic well. I simply couldn't think what it might be that the man needed to tell me, nor why he would have lain in wait for me in the forest. I didn't feel like going to bed. It was close to three in the morning and a large group of people were out in the forest getting up to goodness knew what. I felt as though I was missing something, something important. Unbidden, a shiver ran through me and I was reminded of the last time I saw my sister. Her body was white, nearly blue. Each of her wrists had thick, coagulated black scabs on them, and her lips and eyelids sparkled as though they had been made up for a carnival. She was cold and stiff. But above all I felt she was very much alone.

# XI

So we remain necessarily strangers to ourselves, we do
not understand ourselves, we have to keep ourselves
confused. For us this law holds for all eternity: "Each man
is furthest from himself." Where we ourselves are
concerned, we are not "knowledgeable people."
The Genealogy of Morals
Friedrich Nietzsche

The Valium had sent Max into a deep sleep. But a moment came
when, still inside his dream, he was unsure whether he was asleep
or awake. Everything was too real.

He lay still under the sheets, staring up at the ceiling, until he
noticed somebody whispering, murmuring away over in one corner of
the room. He sat up slowly. The fireplace was no longer there; in its
place stood a large, heavy wardrobe. It had been pulled back from the
wall to expose a hole some three or four feet wide and high, leading to
a flight of mouldy stone steps. A strong, musty smell came from the
opening, mixed with the smell of the sea. Rubbing his eyes, Max felt
how his hands were small and chubby. He was a boy once more, lying
in a strange room, in the dark and alone, completely alone. Just as he
was in Shimts. He had been deeply asleep, and his body felt numb.
He looked about warily. To one side of the room he could see a black
shape rocking back and forth... And words issuing from it, but none
that he could make sense of, a seeming stream of gibberish, spoken in a
flat monotone, like an old lady telling her rosary. On the opposite side
of the room was another dark bundle of a figure, intoning the same
solemn sequence of sounds. Sitting up, Max felt a chill run through
him. The tip of his nose felt icy and his toes were uncomfortably stiff.
He did not recognise the bedroom.

The shadows began to take shape before his eyes. The huddled
figures on either side of the room each wore thick black tunics. Only
the darker openings in front of what were presumably their faces gave

a sense of the provenance of that unintelligible rosary, that incoherent litany. Straightening up, Max peered into the dark, trying to see what or who it was. Light came from a couple of candles positioned above the heads of those dark shadows. The murmuring was making it hard for him to think.

The steps beyond the wall descended in a spiral. From the depths of that passageway came a briny smell, mixed with a sharp aroma of seaweed and desiccated crustaceans. His toes searched around instinctively for his slippers, which his mother always left on the floor by his bed, but they weren't there. Whatever he was wearing was rough against his skin – a white ankle-length habit, he now saw. The sleeves were wide, difficult to wear, and he struggled to get his hands out of them. A faint bluish glow came from somewhere far down in the passageway. Max wanted to cry out, call for his mother. If only he could speak her name. He was shivering with fear, but above all he was very cold. The air felt damp and heavy. The only thing for it was to try to get away without those two dark figures seeing. And then he remembered: he had made his mother a promise, and now he was in Drake's house. He could not remember arriving in this room, or having been given these clothes, but there was no doubt: this was what he had been afraid of all that time. On went the two figures with their low, bewildering chant: "Munnnmammm Saunnnommmm Daunnnmummm".

On a dresser to his left, he could make out an object, but he did not know what it was: a kind of urn with a metallic lid.

He wanted to go home but had no idea how to get out. The door was a distance away, and too close to one of the figures; the other way out, the steps down into the passageway looked like the entrance to hell. For a moment he was so afraid that he thought about getting back into bed and curling up into a ball under the sheets. His nose was running. He wasn't going to cry, but he had known – he absolutely had – that if he went along with his mother's request, with Drake's really, something like this would be on the cards. He waited for a moment but the two figures went on intoning exactly as before. He thought perhaps they wouldn't notice if he went very slowly. He crawled over to the gap in the wall and peered down. Music was floating up from inside, some cheery tune, and there was a subdued light, as on a cloudy day. A faint breeze carried the smells of the sea: some mild and perfumed, others with a stinging salty tang. Either side of him, the shrouded figures went on rocking back and forth, undeviating, blind to his presence. He sat on the floor, one foot resting on the other on the top step, hands nestled between his legs, watching the two faceless guardians out of the corner of his eyes, puzzling over what could possibly lie beneath those mantles. He imagined deformed, diabolical faces, eyes perhaps red and flashing. Suddenly the fear became physical, throbbed and it was an effort not to wet the rough garment that was making his whole body itch. Gathering the tunic about him, he began walking down the steps. Nobody followed. On he went, not looking back, his mind still full of what might have been behind those dark shapes. The sound of the sea gradually grew louder. The music too, cheerful and distorted, seemingly coming from an old record player.

*I found a million dollar baby...*

The ground felt damp underfoot. It was beach sand, virgin and compact. He advanced holding the habit up.

*The rain continues for an hour...*

The rotund moon hung heavy in a cloudless sky. A damp breeze whipped his face and hair. The sea was a little way off, drowsy and interminable. It was a clear, calm summer night. There was somebody lying on a lounger, looking up, as though sunbathing at the wrong time. And next to the lounger was an ancient gramophone, scratching out the same song over and over. On one side stood a high, thick wall, and on the other, the sea stretched away into infinite silvery glimmers.

*Love comes alone, like a popular song, any time or...*

Distant clouds slipped quickly by, as if going somewhere. The music stopped and a hand reached out and put the needle back on the first groove of the record. A wintry cold emanated from the door into the house, but there it was the height of summer.

His fear had given way to curiosity, and he went on, confused by all the contradictions. Who could be so stupid to go out moonbathing? Could you get a tan that way? He crept forward, feet sinking into the increasingly soft, wet sand.

"Come and sit next to me, Max," said a voice up ahead. "Look how lovely it is."

Going nearer, Max saw Drake lying in a hammock, enjoying the balmy night. His face had a serene, welcoming look.

"It's cold in the house," Max managed to say. "And you can't get a tan from the moon."

Drake turned towards him with a smile. Max smiled back.

"It can't be cold in summer," insisted Max, "and in the house it's super cold."

Sitting up, Drake took another puff on the cigar he was smoking.

"Well," he said, "it is."

Max said nothing. He went over and sat on a towel spread on the ground next to the man, and looked out to sea.

"Where's my mother?" he said, feeling no fear, gazing at the horizon.

"She's okay, she's alright now."

"Good."

"What about you?" Drake asked.

"My feet are cold," Max said, bringing the towel up to cover them.

"But it's summer, they can't be."

Max smiled, as though he'd just been caught lying.

"It's from before," he admitted.

*It was a lucky April shower…*

"Same song again?" Max protested.

"You don't like Bing Crosby?" Drake asked, without looking at him.

"Mm, don't know really."

"I like him," Drake said blandly. "A lot."

He began humming along, swaying his head.

"Sounds old."

"It is old. That's why I like it."

"I know a better song," Max said.

"Maybe you ought to forget it," Drake responded, smiling.

"Yes…"

"This one's better." He turned up the volume. "Listen, really give it a good listen."

The song rose up into the night and Max felt as though the stars were listening too. The music expanded, flooding the waves, drenching the sand, filtering down through the holes between the rocks and into his ears too, wriggling like a worm.

He said something but it couldn't be heard over the music – he could smell, feel the music every time he took a breath. Drake swept his hand from side to side in time with the music. It was just the two of them, sheltering together on a tiny inlet. Swivelling around, he could see the door and the foot of the steps that led back up to the bedroom. A little way above, at the top of the stone wall, there was a railing and beyond that, immense and upright against the sky, Drake's mansion.

Max recognised it immediately. That old building had always terrified him. A knot would form in his stomach whenever he had to go past it. He always chose to cycle on the other side of the street, keeping it as far from him as possible. Now he sat absorbed in the sight, feeling no fear as he contemplated it, and it felt wonderful. It was a clear night and the moonlight fell on the uneven roof tiles and slipped over its cold façade like the finest of gauzes. He felt no fear now: he kept on looking and felt no fear.

A sudden rush of happiness broke over him, and the music seemed very lovely – like a forgotten melody that suddenly comes back to us, bringing with it delightful, comforting memories.

"This house…" Max said, still looking at it, still not understanding why he was no longer afraid. "I want this house for myself."

Drake burst out laughing, slapped his thigh and replaced the needle at the start of the song.

"And you will have it, dear boy," he said, still laughing.

"But those shadowy shapes… I want them gone," he ordered.

"They won't hurt you."

"Okay, it's just that…" but Max didn't know how to make his case.

"Tomorrow is your last day. When you get home, I want you to give your mother a big kiss. She's missed you."

"Why?"

"Because she hasn't seen you in a whole week, and she loves you very much."

"And I love her. Beautiful, isn't she?"

"Very."

"I didn't want to come here," Max admitted shyly. "Before, I mean."

"I know. But now, see? You came to no harm."

"No, but I can't remember anything."

"You don't need to remember anything. You will be able to, if the moment comes when you need to."

"I will come whenever you like. I'm not afraid of you anymore."

"Want to sing with me?"

"I don't know the words."

"Sure you do, sing."

They broke into a hearty duet, accompanying Bing Crosby's crooning with their own out-of-tune but heartfelt effort. And Max was surprised to find that he did indeed know the lyrics. The song came to an end and an austere silence settled. The needle hissed repetitively on the still-turning record.

"Do you know that very often the most insignificant things are what decide our entire future?" Drake asked.

"What?"

"When I was a boy, similar age to you, something very surprising happened to me. It was a winter's day, and my mother left the house very early. The place where I lived was very cold in winter, very, very cold."

"Where did you live?" Max interrupted.

"In Yaroslavl, a city to the north of Moscow. There was never any lack of kindling where I lived, but there had been some big event and none of the fires had been lit. There were a lot of people around, a lot of commotion, which wasn't usual. Nobody seemed to notice me. At some point all the commotion died down, and the house fell silent. I lay in my bed waiting for the maid to come and light the fire in my room, but the wait was in vain. For some reason things were happening differently that morning. I forced myself to get up. There was no one in the house. The windows in the living room hadn't been opened properly, and it was dark, just a few cracks of daylight coming in. At first, I didn't realise, but then, looking over at the dining room table, I saw my grandfather sitting at the head. Elbows up on the table, chin resting on his hands. There was a clarity to his face, it almost looked lit up. I walked slowly over to him and asked where everybody was. 'Making the preparations for my funeral', he smiled.

I didn't know what that meant. I went and sat next to him, hoping for one of the fantastic stories he always used to tell me. My grandfather was a really great guy. The person I had the most fun with, without a shadow of a doubt. He always had some new tale to tell, or activity for us to do. He had boundless energy.

It was very cold in the house, but being close to him I became aware that he was even colder than I was.

'Listen', he said. 'I think I've hit on something really important, and I decided you ought to know about it.'

Lifting me onto his knee, he came out with a single phrase: 'Do what you want,' he said. 'Don't forget it. And if anybody asks, don't tell them I was here. They'll think you've gone crazy like your grandfather.'

'You're not crazy, grandpa,' I said.

'Oh, yes I am. But,' he said, whispering in my ear, 'it's so very wonderful.'

He kissed me on my forehead, and left. It was the last I ever saw of him. A few hours later, the house filled up with people again. It seemed that my grandfather had died that morning. He'd gone out in the snow with hardly any clothes on, and frozen to death. Everyone was crying, and though I wanted to tell them that he wasn't actually dead, I remembered my promise. He didn't want them to lock me up, to put me in a cell like they had him. So I kept it to myself. It's a very dangerous thing, knowing more than other people do. And those who are mad know more than everyone in the world put together."

"Your grandfather was mad?"

"Yes and no. In the eyes of the doctors and my family, he was. But to me, he was this really entertaining person, and completely different to anyone else – someone who did things no one else would dare to do. It wasn't until many years later that I understood the meaning of that phrase, but it's thanks to him that I am who I am now, and that's why you're here. You're just a boy, and you don't understand, but when you grow up, you'll grasp many hidden secrets. You'll come to see that there is more than coloured ink inside people, dear Max."

Max frowned. He felt as though Drake had discovered something about him that he had thought secret.

"But when?" Max said impatiently. "I want to know everything."

"We never know everything, and still less about ourselves. But perhaps, perhaps, when the time comes – when you've forgotten all about me, and about yourself as well. When everything becomes definitive."

"What?" he asked, totally at a loss.

Drake smiled and tousled his hair.

"Are you rich?" Max asked.

"Very."

"Can you buy everything?"

"No, not everything."

"What can't you buy?"

"The moon," Drake said, looking up at it as though it were a photo of a beloved woman.

"And the sun?"

"Not the sun, either."

"A thousand lollipops?"

"Mm," Drake smiled. "Yes, I think so."

"And will I be able to buy whatever I want?"

"More than that."

"Like what?"

"You will be completely free from all the pressures, all the deceptions that simply suffocate the rest of humankind. You will achieve the things you failed to achieve when you were someone else. This time you will achieve it. I know who you are, and I will help you to find yourself."

"I don't know," Max said, losing interest. It all sounded a bit beyond him.

"You won't remember it now, but you yourself told us that you would return," Drake said, becoming intensely excited. "You won't remember, but it's true. And we helped you to come back. Now you can make a fresh start, and if you really are there, I'll find you. You'll be first among men," he said triumphantly.

"What men?"

"All men."

"To what end?"

Falling silent, Drake reached over and put the record on to play again.

"To reach the plenitude you deserve," he said. "From this point on, you will be Perdurabo. You mustn't forget it, little man."

"Perdu-what?"

"He who endures beyond the end of time."

"What's that?"

"Magic, Max. Magic."

"And the lollipops?" Max insisted.

"Yes, the lollipops too."

"And…" Max tried to think of other delicious things. "Cakes and pastries, and bikes and marbles?"

Drake made a face as though weighing the request and nodded. Max rubbed his hands together in excitement.

"And what about my friend Claire?" he blurted. Then, sadly: "I think she likes Louis."

"She'll be yours too. They all will."

"When, when?"

"I already told you: when the time comes. No sooner and no later."

"Do you have everything?"

"Yes, everything…" Drake said pensively.

"Like what?"

"A whole town."

"With real people in it?"

Drake nodded.

"They are the world's lepers. My very own lepers. The unwanted. But they are the true magicians, the true sages. Not even they know it, but it has fallen to me to help them to understand their lives and their dreams. Marvels, each and every one."

"They have dreams?"

"Of course they do, and I help them to understand themselves. They have little affection for the world as they find it, they hate it and the world hates them for being unique, and for being infinite. They hold the answers, they ask the questions nobody else dares ask, and they dream the boldest dreams. They can fly, Max, they are comets, leaving their fiery trails wherever they go."

"I know what you're talking about," Max said, turning serious. Suddenly he looked far, far older.

Noting the change, Drake observed him closely.

"They are crazy people, it's a town of crazy people."

"But what is it to be crazy, Max? Who decides that a person is crazy?"

"Doctors, doctors who work in lunatic asylums."

"I'm a doctor, and I work in one of those asylums. And I can assure you, I am thousand times happier in the company of my patients than that of any sane individual."

"They're more boring.

"They are more, that's all. Do you believe that the majority is in the right? Answers, Max, answers are all important. What does it matter if we don't understand them? We aren't ready, that's all. Did we understand Jesus Christ? No! We crucified him. Now there was a true lunatic, right? The best that ever lived."

"Mummy says Jesus was God."

"He was. And you will be too."

"I don't know who I am.

"You will, little man. All you need is to let yourself go. You must get used to remembering."

"Sometimes I forget things, that's why I put them in my notebooks. But I know that Mummy knows them."

"I know. It's better that way. Sometimes a legacy is the greatest burden."

"We're always on the move, I don't like it. I lose my friends."

"Don't worry, you'll have friends."

"Sometimes I think that if you make people need you, they'll love you more," Max said seriously, staring out to sea. "And if they don't love you... you kill them."

Drake pursed his lips. The smile faded, and he gazed warily at Max:

"What do you know about that?"

"Why?"

"You don't know?" Drake said. "Killing is a sin. Everybody knows that."

"I don't," Max laughed.

"You do, because I just told you."

"I don't remember," Max said slyly.

"Now that's a sleight of hand."

"Maybe, but nobody's going to punish me for it. Right?"

"Sometimes you remind me so much of your father."

"You knew my father?"

"Yes."

"What was he like?"

"He died."

"Yes, but what was he like?"

"Off to bed with you now," Drake said gravely. "Tomorrow I'll take you home."

# XII

## TUESDAY

> As for the liberation of the insane at Bicêtre, the
> story is famous: the decision to remove the chains from
> the prisoners in the dungeons. [...] He asked to
> interrogate all the patients. From most, he received
> only insults and obscene apostrophes. It was useless to
> prolong the interview. Turning to Pinel: "Now, citizen,
> are you mad yourself to seek to unchain such beasts?"
> Pinel replied calmly: "Citizen, I am convinced that
> these madmen are so intractable only because they have
> been deprived of air and liberty".
>
> A Treatise on Insanity
> Philippe Pinel

A jubilant beam of sunlight pierced the window of Max's room, breaking through a gap in the ranked clouds moving sluggishly across the sky. Max blinked, wrinkled his nose and turned over in bed. He was reluctant to wake. Screwing his eyes shut and lying still proved futile, the light was too intense. He sat up in bed. He felt lethargic. He was sweating, hair plastered against his temples. He heard voices on the floor below. People talking in loud, animated voices. The only one he recognised was Bezel's. Rubbing his face, he sighed deeply. The sunlight gave everything a more cheerful air. The mirror to his left caught his eye. It glowed bright and colourful, but its fretful sparkles sent a shiver through him. The recent memory, whether dreamed or revived, suddenly came back to him. He clamped his hand over his mouth and immediately took it away, unsure that the limb was actually his. Still looking at his hands, he took out his notebook and began putting down – as throughout the two days of his stay – the last memory he had of Drake, just as unreal as all the others, just as impossible to forget as previously it had been to recall by any act of will.

At that time in his childhood, there were seven completely blank days and nights behind him – no trace of them remained. They had been lost, suspended in time and he hadn't a clue what he'd done for their duration. Seven nights on which something had been introduced beneath his skin. Even on the inside the most essential aspects of his physiognomy had been under observation. Max hesitated. The anguish and fear he had experienced when leaning close to the mirror came back to him like one more dream to add to the notebook, one more anecdote. Everything seemed connected and yet he was powerless to establish a link between the horror of the memories and those visions. All they now induced was confusion. The terror he'd experienced but a few hours earlier began to fade. He remembered everything: all journeys into the past, the voices in the lounge, the reflection in the mirror... But they seemed somehow far away, as though they'd all taken place a long, long time ago, as though the violence of the feelings had diminished, leaving only a bitter taste in the mouth. He was certain that behind the memories lay an invisible thread, some shared point of departure from which the uncertainty arose. But it was a point Max simply could not access: they had closed down that path long ago. The entrance was sealed and camouflaged in such a way he couldn't even remember if it existed.

He closed the notebook, his latest memories now inscribed within it, including his cryptic conversation with Drake. In those moments the man had seemed like a friend, an ally of the kind with whom we happily share our most incriminating secrets, knowing they will never be disclosed or ridiculed. He had seemed fun and powerful, with a serene, enviable kind of energy. A halo of distinction surrounded him, separating him from the rest of the world, from all that Max knew. A feeling of confusion returned, as though the memories had revealed to him a facet of himself that he'd only been able to behold for a few moments. His own words seemed awful and impossible to fathom. He had spoken in such an offhand way about terrible things; he'd been so carefree and childish. He couldn't believe he'd have said those things.

Drake had mentioned a town in which all the people, or almost all of them, were under his command; quite clearly, that place was Shimts. This was Drake's redoubt, the place where every soul belonged to him because none believed in the world at large or in themselves. Now Max understood that not only did Drake own the businesses, even the people's lives belonged to him. They were the lepers of whom he had spoken. They were the insane! And Bezel, and Hausen, and

Vahlenkamp: were they insane too? And what of his father? Max had included in his notes Drake's mention of his father. That hazy, ghostly figure. Drake would have lots to tell him when they finally met. Max dressed and went down to the kitchen, where an unusual number of people were milling around.

"Ah, Max!" Bezel said, clearly pleased. "You're up. And looking so much better."

She was wrapping up some food in tinfoil. Over to one side there was a wicker basket containing bottles of wine, fruit and food containers.

"Simon," Max said, taking me by the arm.

"How are you feeling?"

"Good, but…"

"Are you going to come along?" I said, cutting him off.

He clearly wanted to tell me something, but it wasn't the right moment. Ever since I'd been at the hotel, I'd been trying to win Bezel's trust. I had insinuated that, given the fact I had neither family nor professional obligations, I might consider staying on in Shimts. She had seemed extremely pleased at the prospect, and, as though trying to sell a cruise ship, told me what a lovely, quiet place it was to live in, how everybody got on, and how happy I would be if I did decide to stay. She had promised to introduce me to Drake whenever he showed up, and given me every indication that not all the people in Shimts were as dull as they might seem. A little patience, and I could find out for myself, seemed to be the suggestion. I'd decided that their reserved nature was a family secret they couldn't yet reveal to me. She had made it clear that, should I stick around, she'd use all her influence to help me be accepted as a member of its most select community. Hence my wish to avoid the impression that Max and I were hiding something, and seem fully behind the plans for the spread they were preparing.

"Yes, I'll come," Max said, though with little enthusiasm. "I've got nothing else to do."

"Wonderful," Bezel said. "Max, you grab this basket, and you," she said, giving me a complicit look, "that one."

In the kitchen three women had just introduced themselves to me, and their Teutonic build left Max speechless; they'd just finished preparing the picnic. They wore tightfitting cotton blouses that left little to the imagination in terms of what fine fettle they were in: each was blessed with generous, matron-like bosoms, and the soft, tight fabric of their trousers showed off fine, toned legs. They smiled at Max, who knew neither where to place his feet nor how to respond to such courtesies.

"Everyone ready?" Bezel said, linking arms with me.

"Ready," I said.

"Let's get going, then. Sunshine and the countryside, what more could we want?"

We left the hotel, carrying our bundles like a happy family off on a day-trip. Max fell in behind, walking in silence like a soul condemned to an endless, mind numbing pursuit of the living. I knew he wanted my ear and that his youth and inexperience made it hard for him to contain himself. He lacked the necessary composure. He was lost and I was his only purchase on the world. I could feel his eyes on me as he walked. I hoped that his latest discoveries would help in my investigations, and doubtless they would, but for now I was more concerned about what I believed to be the charm I was bewitching Bezel with – ignorant of the fact Drake was pulling the strings, and that like Max I was another pawn in the game, for all that I might be having a nicer time of it.

We went down the high street, leaving town along the same path I'd taken the previous night when tracking the lantern-bearing procession. Max stopped in front of the sign that read Do What Thou Wilt, staring at the words as though trying to decipher a code, as though those words alone could provide an answer to the questions weighing down on him.

"Max!" I shouted.

Starting out of his trance, he fell silently in behind us. We came through the lightly wooded outskirts of the forest, baskets and blankets in our arms, and the thickening canopy of trees made it seem as though clouds had covered the sun once more. The Teutonic ladies went in front, arm in arm, joking and laughing as they picked their way between boulders and low hanging branches; their derrières, round as a collection of sponge cakes, drawing us on like the Pied Piper of Hamlin. Bezel kept her arm in mine, like a bride on the way to the altar, maids of honour ahead and followed by Max, who could cling to the invisible train she dragged through the dewy woods. And yet Max remained engrossed in his own thoughts, with no discernible nuptial enthusiasm. On he trudged, holding tight to the notebook in his pocket, wanting nothing more than to open it and share his latest round of memories with me, like intangible trophies from an imaginary hunting trip. On we went, the forest growing thicker still. On and off the trees grew so close together that the Teutonic ladies had to unlink arms, as did Bezel and I, in order to make it through the gaps. There was an intense aroma of damp, virgin earth in the air, and it seemed to shudder at our intrusion, at the songs of the Teutonic dames up ahead, who like prepubescent schoolgirls lifted their tittering voices to the sky.

"A fine time we are going to have," Bezel said, glancing back at Max who remained a couple of paces behind.

"Come on, Max," I said. "Cheer up. You can't tell me this isn't all exceedingly lovely."

Max nodded apathetically, trying to get my attention with his show of silence, not realising I'd already picked up the signal. The vegetation thinned once more and we came to a small clearing. Some metres ahead there stood a doorway that seemed to have grown of its own accord between the trees, an apparently spontaneous, self-generating feature, as much part of the place as the plants in the forest. There were no kind of railings or fences to be seen. There the door stood, anchored to the forest floor between the trees. We walked under the wrought iron frame, with its Gothic twirls and filigrees, and as we came through, I noticed a rusty metal sign that read: No Trespassing. Private Property.

Beyond the door, on a bench bowed by the woodland damp, an old man was sitting eating grapes. He made no sign that he had seen us.

"You'll catch cold," Bezel almost bellowed at him.

I assumed he must be deaf. Looking up, he reached out and gave Bezel's bottom a generous pinch, and grinned to show a set of teeth as rotten as the bench slats.

"Wouldn't mind a bit of you!" he growled.

Bezel and the other women, with smiles and blushes, quickened the pace to elude the old man's clutches, as he reached out for a handful of more youthful flesh.

"Check out, granddad!" I said.

"He's older than the town," Bezel said, "but believe me, he's got more petrol in the tank than any number of guys who could be his grandsons." Here, though she didn't look his way, she was doubtless referring to young Max.

I noted Max's growing alarm. As well as the fact that all the females present seemed to have been on the receiving end of the old man's amorous attentions in the past.

Letting go of Bezel's arm, I went back and joined Max.

"Come on," I said, giving him a push. "You need to learn to enjoy yourself. You're too serious," I added, winking as a way of telling him I'd noticed his nerves. Clapping him on the back, I went and joined Bezel again.

"What was that door doing there?" Max said, finally speaking up.

"It's an entrance way," Bezel said, without breaking stride.

"An entrance way to where?" I said.

"You'll see, nosy."

Nobody spoke again until we came to another clearing, the scene inside which could have been straight out of a Ruisdael painting. It was a circular glade with a small fountain on one side and a gazebo on the other. Groups of people were lying on blankets on the grass, enjoying meat pies and smoked and marinated salmon pies, salads, fruit and home-made desserts – the smell of the food was mouth-watering. I glanced over at Max encouragingly, and he smiled, a little more animated now given the magnificent sight.

The wine was flowing, the food being shared around. Bezel and the Teutonic dames picked a spot near the centre, next to a plinth which supported a large circular stone.

"This will do us just fine," said one of the girls, spreading a blanket out on the short grass.

Out came the food containers, the fruit, bread and dairy desserts, the smoked meat and the wine, and they motioned for us to sit down. Bezel went to swap a piece of meat pie for a slice of game pie.

"Mrs Van Geyn makes the best game pie in the world," she said, offering us a slice.

One of the Teutonic ladies with a blonde ponytail, came and sat next to me, handed me a glass and proceeded to pour some wine.

"Come on, Max," I said, tugging on his arm. "Take a seat."

He sat down next to me, looking around wide-eyed but at the same time apprehensively. The Teutonic lady held out a glass, and Max took it without looking at her. These women, with their firm cheeks slightly flushed from the walk, must each have been fortyish, but they gave off a fresh, carefree air as if still in the throes of puberty. They had robust, sinewy necks, and the golden hued skin I guessed, signified long hours spent working in the fields. They spread another blanket out and sat down alongside us, handing out paper plates overflowing with delicious flavours. Even Max began to unwind, savouring the cool, refreshing wine and the food. People seemed serene and free of worries. It was like a photo in a travel agency window, everyone enjoying an unending, joyous occasion, devoid of stress or shadows. They sang songs that everybody knew, until someone else started on another, louder tune, to lots of laughter and gesticulating. Bezel came and sat next to me, smiling triumphantly:

"Someone's having a good time, I see," I said.

In truth, I had not expected anything like this. I thought we were on our way to take part in some macabre ritual, like the ones I'd read about in all those books on magic, and this simple countryside gathering had wrong-footed me altogether.

"I told you we know how to enjoy ourselves," she whispered in my ear, brushing her breasts against my shoulder.

"I never doubted it for a second," I said.

"Yes, you did. But soon you'll have the chance to find out that we know how to enjoy all that we are, completely naturally and pleasurably."

"Come again?"

"Pleasure, Simon. The endless wellspring of pleasure each of us has inside. Our bodies are perfect machines, entirely self-sufficient."

"Self-sufficient?"

"Eat your food and relax," she said, smiling as though she had some wonderful gift hidden behind her back.

We drank and we ate, letting all our senses feast on honeyed, invigorating smells, on flavours that conjured more explicit, carnal pleasures, simply sweeping aside any lack of appetite. The food itself was easily digested and only fuelled the high spirits. Until, gradually, the clearing became a closed space in which the only sounds were laughter and song, with many a toast proposed to the cooks of the day. By now lots of people were off their blankets and dancing merrily around. Cavorting in the centre of the circle, they waved empty bottles, while others sang in unison and clapped along. Two of the Teutonic ladies had come and sat on my lap, and I had begun caressing their ample breasts at my leisure, keeping my lust on a leash. Max timidly turned away from the attentions of the third woman, who had sat next to him on the blanket. Somewhere a bagpipe struck up, adding to the din of the singing and jubilation. The air suddenly became pure and crystalline, making the mountains glow.

It was a sound that entered into the bones, passing through us as though we were ghosts, insubstantial beings upon which the notes could nonetheless come to rest. One of the pair on my lap began kissing me, and I took in the warm, acid smell of the wine on her lips. Her shirt was unbuttoned, and her overflowing breasts hung on the air before me. I ran my hand along the edge of one, feeling its warmth. As I went to lift it to my mouth, I felt Max yank hard on my sleeve, rousing me from my reverie. I looked at him reproachfully.

"Simon!" he said, losing all semblance of cool. "I know what Drake meant with that line of his, Do what thou wilt. And why he called me Perdurabo."

I let go of the breast and turned to Max.

"When did he tell you that?"

"Last night. I dreamt or remembered it, I'm not sure now. It's all in my notebook."

"He called you Perdurabo?"

Nodding, Max held out his notebook to me. Reaching for it, I clumsily knocked its side and it fell onto the blanket. The wine was clearly glazing my mind and I smiled apologetically. Then, looking around to see if anyone had noticed my drunkenness, I was presented with a jaw dropping spectacle. The scene had changed. The whole aspect, the festive air, had all been corrupted. Even the smell had turned sour, and what I now saw before me was a scene of unbridled degeneracy. The air had thickened, as though the sky had pressed down upon us, condensing the now-restricted space in the clearing, or as though the cavities, which suppurated juices and oozed secretions, had muddied it somehow... The people around us, those light-hearted, affable souls who just a few minutes before, or so it seemed, had been singing without a care in the world, had now given themselves over to a degenerate display of licentiousness that made the eyes smart. In groups or in pairs, their games had crossed the line into orgiastic territory, and between their tittering and moaning, under the aegis of, or perhaps spurred on by the sound of the bagpipe, they masturbated one another under the blankets or in plain sight, making unintelligible, head-spinning sounds.

I sat up with a jolt, knocking the two Teutonic ladies from my lap. Barely noticing, they tumbled onto the grass, content to pleasure one another.

"What on earth?" I said, gazing on the scene.

Grabbing Max's arm, I pulled myself to my feet.

The wine, or whatever they had spiked it with, turned my thoughts into a dense, floating mush. I could hardly believe my eyes, or that I wasn't in fact delirious. I was sickened by the sight of all that flaccid, jouncing flesh, the toothless mouths gasping and groaning, the dull, vapid eyes with crows' feet rolling around in ecstasy, white thighs pulsating in the breeze, potbellies too old to ever conceive... Observing that spectacle produced a sensation of unspeakable shame, not for myself, but on behalf of Max, for whom I in some way felt responsible.

"Come on, let's get out of here. This is too much, even for me. We're better off out of it."

I took a blanket and wrapped it around his shoulders. My jacket was beneath one of the Teutonic dames, who was writhing around like a fish out of water as she moaned softly, as though the agony of choking to death were a pleasure.

"Come on," I said, putting an arm around Max's shoulders.

I turned to see what had become of Bezel, only to find her down on the grass being mounted by the old man we had passed eating grapes in the wrought-iron doorway. Numerous other men, equally old, had gathered around. From the look on her face, Bezel looked completely gone, as if in some kind of trance. Her breasts beat like bells hysterically tolling for a wedding or warning the townsfolk of a fire. Max and I hurried away. We made our way through the forest without a backward glance, ducking and swerving branches and roots. Max's teeth were chattering, I don't know whether from cold or fear, and he kept repeating: Perdurabo, Perdurabo.

Once we were out of earshot of the orgy, I halted and turned to face him:

"Take it easy, Max. It's just us now. Tell me, what did he say?"

"Drake called me Perdurabo, I didn't know why. But on our way out of town earlier on, seeing that sign, I was reminded of you telling me that he's a long-time follower of Crowley's."

"Let me see the notebook."

"He thinks I'm Crowley," Max said, giving a pained smile.

I quickly read Max's latest jottings and, from the looks of the cryptic conversation with Drake, it seemed he wasn't wrong. For some reason, Drake associated Max with Crowley. Perdurabo became the magician's name when he joined the Golden Dawn as a novice. He addressed Max like an adult, as if speaking to Crowley himself. He was trying to prompt him to remember a past that did not exist, for Max was just a boy and Crowley nothing but a ghost.

"My God!" I said with a gasp. "Drake is crazier than the whole lot of them."

In the notebook it described Drake talking about the people in the town, and calling them lepers. If Max's memories were correct, that made Shimts his own personal sanatorium. The entire town was an asylum, a laboratory in which Drake placed his beloved lunatics beneath the microscope and tried tapping into their fantasies. I began to see why the town was so cut off, and the reason for its inhabitants' behaviour, and for the prompts posted about the place on signs and notices. I had always believed Drake to be a gross eccentric, but it was now clear to me that he was as unwell as the farthest gone of all his patients. His obsession with discovering the divine spark in man – a spark lost or perhaps stolen – was his single motivation in life.

I had to face it: I was trapped in Drake's talons. He had drawn me to this place, allowing me to believe that I had discovered his game, his secrets, when in reality I was nothing but his prisoner. I knew about his rituals, his manipulations, his practices and the murders he had tried to pass off as suicides, but it made no difference. In the place I now found myself, knowing all of this was tantamount to knowing nothing at all.

Max glanced at me fearfully. I felt for him. Not only had he suffered at his mother's hands – a woman whose sanity I was also starting to doubt – he'd also had to put up with Drake's intrusions, heaven knows how many absurd analyses and tests the results of which were intended to prove that Max was Crowley, back from the dead.

"I think," I said, "Drake wants to turn you into an object of worship. He's trying to fabricate a life history for you to make you end up believing you're someone else."

"How can a past be invented?"

"If he's known you since you were a boy, it could be that quite unawares you've been under his control all your life."

"But that's ridiculous. I can't be anybody but myself. We can't be turned into other people."

"Of course not, but Drake is a madman who thinks you can."

"Madman! But what does madness mean to you? He's a maniac, I don't question that, but you're telling me that he's reinventing my past, my personality, as though I were but a doll. I'm a living, breathing person. People can't be moulded like that."

"No, but they can be manipulated. They can be made to believe things that haven't actually happened."

"Impossible."

"In that case, how do you explain this recent spate of memories, events in your own life you knew nothing about? Did you remember all of this?" I said, shaking the notebook at him. "And how are you to know that this place is anything other than a run-of-the-mill town? It's all in here," I held the notebook out again, "in your very own hand: this place is a lunatic asylum and all the inhabitants are Drake's patients. Do you think that normal people go around having orgies in broad daylight? That it's normal to follow up your slice of meat pie by masturbating the person next to you under a blanket in a forest clearing?"

"That's no proof that the things I've been remembering are real," he insisted.

"But it does show that Drake knows you better than you know yourself, because he doubtless remembered all that, and many other things you still don't know about. That's the reason you're here."

"What are you trying to say?" he said, looking me in the eye.

I didn't answer.

"Are you saying I'm crazy as well?"

"No."

"Yes, you are. These things that have been happening to me are... caused by the stress of my mother dying!" he was furious now, shouting. "I know. That's all it is."

"Easy, easy. That wasn't what I meant."

"Yes, it was. I don't care what you think, trust me. I know why I'm here, and that's the only thing that matters. I don't need you to understand, I don't even know why I let you."

"Why you let me what?"

"Start coming up with all these ideas about me."

"I haven't come up with any ideas. I've just been trying to find an explanation for all... this."

"All this is me."

"No, Max. All this is this," I said, gesturing at the things around us, the place. "Neither you nor I belong in this place, we're just visitors here."

"I'm always just a visitor. What about you?"

"What do you mean?"

"What are you doing here?"

"I told you. I'm trying," I said calmly, "to find evidence to link Drake to the death of my sister."

"Are you sure?"

"What do you mean, am I sure? Of course I am. Max, you need to calm down. You're all strung out, and that's to be expected, but we won't get anywhere fighting one another. We need to get a handle on what's going on. There are lots of way-out things around here. I'm going to help you, don't worry."

He gave me a wary look, running his fingers back through his hair: "I have no idea what's happening to me, Simon. Absolutely none."

"It's Drake," I said. "He's behind it all."

"But where? Where is he?"

"He'll be here soon, and then we can take it up with him. Don't worry."

Max looked at me, unable to voice his fears, but I could tell what he was thinking. I too felt a tingle, a shiver down my spine. I guessed what he wanted to ask:

"How is he going to get here, right? Good question," I said, sitting down on the grass. "The bridge is still broken and nobody's bothering to fix it."

"Maybe they're waiting for the river to subside," Max said, unable to admit to his fears.

"The river? This is the twentieth century, Max, for goodness sake. It's hardly the mightiest river in the world. If they had wanted to, they could have built a bridge that wouldn't fall to pieces after a few drops of rain, a bridge that would always actually be there... "

"Do you think...?"

"Just enough for us to be able to cross it, for us to have got in. This town is completely cut off. There's no other way in or out. It's a mental asylum, and mental asylums aren't the kinds of places you can just check out of when you feel like it."

Until I heard myself utter these words, the full horror of our situation hadn't struck me, the fact that we were cut off and shut in. That was our reality and we had to deal with it. I felt distressed, a touch of claustrophobia that I tried to brush aside in order to think clearly. Everything seemed normal but the fresh air, houses, shops and open spaces and hills around were all part of the deception. It was an enclosed version of normal life, with strict boundaries. Appearances suggested that we were free to do as we chose, free to leave whenever we liked, but that couldn't have been further from the truth.

"Now more than ever I'm sure that Drake was involved in my sister's death," I told Max, my spirits sinking "If not, I wouldn't be in this situation."

"They can't keep us here against our will. "

"Really think so?" I smiled. "How many people know you're here?"

"No one."

"See? Nobody knows I am either. They can do with us as they wish. By the time anybody realises we're gone, we could be six feet under by one of these trees."

"All the same, I'm not going anywhere. I have to talk to Drake."

"Feel like sticking around, do you?"

"What I want is to find out who I am. There's a lot he knows about me."

"If you stay here, you'll end up forgetting who you are. You'll become one of Drake's patients, and the same thing will happen to you as has happened to that lot... Going down to the woods to rub off a friend."

"He's all I've got. He knows more about me than I do. I know it sounds terrible, but it's true. I'm not going anywhere," he said, as though that were his final word on the matter.

"I don't think you understand. They are going to swallow us up, turn us into one of his specimens. It won't be long before you're going around in a straitjacket, fucking Bezel on the ground in front of people out for a picnic, and at the same time believing this is the best place in all the world…"

"Hey! What are you up to?"

We turned to find a man marching towards us. Well-built and dark-haired, he looked to be somewhere in his forties. He was dressed in country attire, in corduroy trousers and a checked wool jacket.

"Not taking part in the picnic?" he asked in a strongly accented English.

"No."

"You guys are new, right? I haven't seen you around before."

"New?"

"Guests, visitors," he said. "We don't get all that many people coming through."

"I can well imagine. What about you, who are you?"

"Me? Nobody."

"Uh-huh."

"And you?" he asked Max.

"I'm nobody as well," said Max, visibly annoyed.

"Right, you must be Max," the man said with a mischievous smile. Max blanched.

"How do you know? "

"I've heard about you."

"From who?"

"Mr Drake, of course. He told us you'd be coming this week. Of course, not all of us know. I'm one of the select few –"

"You're lying!" Max cried.

"Why would I do that?"

"Because nobody knew I was coming. Not even I was sure that I would."

"Seems Mr Drake knew."

"All right," I said. "You might be nobody, but you've still got a name. Or not?"

"Yes. I'm Ávila. José Ávila, I'm from Spain."

"And what is it that do you do here, Mr Ávila?"

With another mischievous smile, he answered confidentially:

"I work here."

"Doing what?"

"I'm a watchman"

"A watchman? What kind of job is that?"

"Just a job."

"What do you watch?" I asked.

"The town."

"What is there to watch?" I went on.

"To ensure everything is as it should be," he said, shrugging.

"Hey, do you know when they'll fix the bridge?' I asked.

"What bridge?"

"What bridge?" Max said in irritation. "The bridge I crossed three days ago. It's still broken and I might feel like leaving quite soon."

José Ávila folded his arms and smiled cynically.

"Sorry, I don't know anything about any bridge."

"Nobody knows anything about the bridge," I said. "I'm starting to think it doesn't exist."

"Really?" Ávila asked. "In that case, how did you get into town?"

Max looked at me, Ávila looked at me, and I cast my mind back. I had come in a week before, arriving late in the day and...

"How did you get here, Simon? I didn't see your car at the hotel."

I realised I couldn't remember how I had got there. There was simply a blank in my memory. I knew why I had come, and when, but not how. Max, a startled look on his face, started backing away.

"What is it?" I said.

"Who are you? Max said.

"What do you mean, who am I?" I laughed. "I'm Simon!"

Standing with arms crossed and a smile on his face, Ávila watched the two of us. He seemed to be enjoying himself.

"I just can't remember right now," I said, feeling flustered. "God, this is ridiculous! It must be Drake. You know he's doing this to you."

"I don't know anything," he said, continuing to back away. "I don't know who you are. I let you read my notebooks and I don't know who you are," he said, pointing at me.

"Max, listen to me. And you," I said turning to Ávila, "stop smiling!"

The man held up his hands apologetically, then placed one over his mouth.

"Max, you can't seriously think that I'm one of them. You have to realise that, for some reason, they're playing with us, with both of us."

"I don't know."

"Where is Drake?" I spat at Ávila.

"Don't get excited, mister," he said calmly.

"Don't talk to me like that. Don't be stupid. I must see Drake."

"Why don't the pair of you go back into the woods," said Ávila, "and have a little fun?"

"Because, back in the woods there, there's a ghastly orgy in full swing. If you're the guy who's supposed to be keeping an eye on things, perhaps you should start by imposing a little order."

"I can't stop them from enjoying themselves. They're all raving mad, you know," he said, coming closer and lowering his voice as if to avoid being overheard. "They have to let off steam somehow, it'll only end up coming out in some other way. Mister," he said, looking me in the eye, slowly nodding and smiling, "bear in mind that nobody winds up in Shimts by accident."

"I know what I came here to do, and Drake knows too. That's why he wants me here, because I know all his dirty secrets, and those of his friends. I know far more than he would like. Max is being made to think he isn't himself, and now I'm being told to believe I'm crazy – but it won't work."

"Let's not start getting uppity," Ávila said sternly.

"I'm not getting uppity," I said calmly. "It's Drake who should be uppity. Max, let's go!"

He didn't seem completely sure, but the certainty in my voice must have convinced him that he was better off with me, and finally he came over and stood next to me.

"You can't get out," said Ávila, modulating his voice. "Don't waste your energies. You are in a place that's completely isolated, there's no way to get over the mountains. You'll get used to it. You just see."

"Shut up!" I shouted.

"I'm not even going to stop you from going and having a nosy around. Go on, off you go, you'll see for yourselves, no way out. There must be some reason you're here, something you don't understand now, but I can assure you that you need Mr Drake's help. Everybody here does."

"Ávila!" said another male voice from somewhere behind us. "What are you doing here? You should be in the waiting-room; they're looking for you. It's your check-up today."

Max and I looked at Ávila in surprise, and he gave an embarrassed smile. A grey-haired man of about fifty, with a big belly on him, came wearily out of the forest.

"Damn you, Ávila," he said. "I've been looking for you for the past half-an-hour. You know it's your check-up today. They're going to be angry with you."

"I was on my watch," he said apologetically.

"You can do all the watching you like, but you can't miss appointments. You know that only too well."

"Don't get angry, Howard. Look. I found a couple of deserters. They were trying to escape."

"No, no," he said walking up to us. "There will be no escaping, you know that. Go back to the clearing."

"I demand to see Mr Drake," I said.

"I'm afraid that isn't going to be possible. Mr Drake will see you when it's your turn. In the meanwhile, you are free to enjoy the countryside, the fresh air, the picnic…"

"Who are you?" I asked.

"Howard Harris, I'm one of the nurses in Shimts."

"My God!" Max grasped, backing away in horror, seeing that we really were in a lunatic asylum, that the things he'd been writing down in his notebook weren't ravings after all. He stumbled backwards in amazement, and nearly tripped over a stone.

"Don't be afraid, Mr Sinclair," said the nurse solicitously. At the same time, Ávila mimicked his movements, drawing a disapproving glare from the nurse. "There's nothing to worry yourself about. You'll feel very welcome here, you'll have everything you need."

"No! No!" Max cried, clearly frightened. "I want to get away from here. No! I must talk to Drake. None of this can be happening, none of this is real. Right?"

"Please calm down," Howard asked him. "Take some deep breaths. Everything is going to be fine."

"No! Nothing is fine. I demand to see Drake as well. Now!"

"That's not going to be possible. Mr Drake can't see you yet. It's too soon."

"Too soon for what?" I asked, grabbing onto his shirt.

"Don't get excited, Mr Bughin. Both of you need to calm down."

"How do you know my name?" I said, "Who told you my name?"

Ávila put his hands over his mouth, stifling a laugh.

"I told you. I work here. I know who everybody is." He took a walkie-talkie from his belt, and moved a little way off, speaking a few concise words in a low voice.

Ávila had sat down on the grass and was imitating everything Howard did as he spoke into his device. At the end, he slipped an invisible walkie-talkie into his belt, and turned to look at us.

"If you'd like to go back to the hotel, you're free to," Howard said. "You can do what you like."

"Except getting the hell out of here," I pointed out.

"That's not up to me. Mr Drake will fill you in when he sees you."

"Mr Drake plans to keep us here indefinitely," I said.

"Then that means you need to be here indefinitely."

A voice came through the walkie-talkie, and Howard lifted it to his ear, as Ávila continued to mimic his movements.

"Received," he said. "Ávila, you come with me! They're waiting for you. I've wasted enough time over you already this morning."

Jumping to his feet, Ávila brushed down his trousers.

"I've warned you already," Ávila said, copying Howard's voice, then letting out a laugh.

"And what exactly are we supposed to do?" I asked Howard. "Go back to that clearing and join in with that pack of nutcases?"

"No," Ávila said. "They aren't nutcases. You can't call them nutcases. We won't tell them we heard you say that, but don't do it again."

"Enough, Ávila!" Howard said. Then, to us: "There are no other activities today, I'm sorry. Everything else is on hold, because of the picnic."

"Orgy day, orgy day," tittered Ávila. "Orgy's the only thing on the menu today… Either you go with them, or come with us. Orgy or check-up. Check-up or orgy."

"Ávila!" cried Howard. "Want to carry on being a watchman Then shut your mouth. As for you two, there's nothing to worry about. Everything's fine, try to enjoy yourselves. "Come on," he said, taking Ávila by the arm, "let's go."

"Try to enjoy ourselves?" I said, barring their way. "Look, Howard. Neither Mr Sinclair nor I ought to be here. We've come for different reasons, but not on account of any madness. We both need to talk to Drake. It's of the utmost importance. You have to help us."

"You don't remember a thing, do you?" Howard said, shaking his head in commiseration.

"What are we supposed to remember?" I asked.

"When the time comes, they'll give you their undivided attention. Until then, I'm afraid you'll have to get on with it, like the rest of the guests."

"Guests?"

"You happen to be in the best sanatorium in the world," said Howard. "This place is just what both of you need. Anything you do here has no consequence in the outside world. You're freer now than you have ever been. Can't you see that?"

Max and I stood there in silence. The two men turned and went off, arm in arm as though out for a Sunday stroll.

"We're going to be stuck here forever," said Max numbly.

"Nobody forced us to come. We're here for a very clear reason. I for my sister, and you because of that letter."

"So?"

"So, our will is not subordinate to Drake's."

"Simon, until six days ago I didn't know I was going to come, yet he knew that I would. And you heard Howard. He's able to control what I do. He knows what I'll do before I do."

"Nonsense. We won't allow it."

"So, what's your plan?"

"For now," I said, slipping my arm into his, "I plan to see just where Howard and Ávila are off to. Maybe they'll lead us to him."

Going the same way as the two men, we picked our way through the trees until we reached a narrow path that stretched off into the forest. To begin with, the plants and leaves were only flattened a little by cumulative footfall, but after a while it became a wider, well demarcated footpath, where someone obviously came to clear away the sticks and leaves.

We walked on in silence, each of us deep in thoughts we were unwilling to share lest we should discover that someone else had thought them before. Until then, I thought it was only Max who needed to watch out for Drake's manipulations, that his control didn't extend as far as me. But after what Howard had said, it seemed evident that I too needed to be on my guard. It was far from inconceivable that he'd lined up a place for me in his asylum, that all my research had bothered him to the point that he had decided to shut me up for life in this hole. He had let me do as I wished for eight years, allowing me to come to my own conclusions, and gradually draw nearer to him. He could have finished me off in any other way, but I had the impression that this gave him most satisfaction. Of course, there was no way I could swear to forget all that I knew if he only let me leave, that I'd put more than eight years of enquiries behind me in exchange for my freedom. It was too late to take a backward step. All I could feel confident of was that there would be some way out, that some person would take pity on me and help me to escape. Such a person did not exist, I knew that, but I'd be ready to use force if the opportunity arose. Looking behind me, I saw Max walking quickly, hands in jacket pockets and a look of supreme resignation on his face. I knew he wouldn't leave without the answers he'd come in search of. Plus the fact the questions he'd come up with had by this point increased tenfold. There were more and more reasons to stay, fewer for leaving. Drake had infiltrated his mind, acting on him like a drug on which Max was increasingly dependent. He was destroying Max's willpower, and yet Max had no idea. Max thought Drake would be the one to resolve his doubts, to rid him of all the pain, and banish the uncertainty. It struck me that Max had stopped seeing Drake as an enemy, and rather as his salvation, someone to help him piece his life back together. Which was precisely the view of everyone else in Shimts: the great saviour, the great listener, the one who valued them... Max had forgotten that his current situation, all his doubts and fears, were a direct consequence of Drake's input into his life. I was the only one who seemed to see all that.

The path gave way to a levelled area. Ahead of us, a long hedge of bushes spread left to right, obscuring whatever lay beyond. And in the middle, by way of an entrance, the path led straight through an opening. The bushes curved out of sight. I put my finger to my lips, and Max and I crept slowly forward. We could hear the murmuring of water on the far side of the hedge, and a voice in the distance, perhaps Howard's. We reached the opening from one side and peered out. What we saw drew a gasp from Max, and from me stunned silence.

# XIII

We took a few forward steps, emerged from between the bushes to see the start of a vast, levelled area crisscrossed by stone paths and extensive lawns. Just inside the entrance stood a three-tiered fountain with an angel balancing on one foot and holding a cornucopia that spurted out water. At the far end of one of the paths, away to our left, there was a square, four-storey building with a mirrored façade reflecting the surrounding woodland. It was an enormous glass cube. A gigantic, four-sided mirror both blending in with and giving back an image of the landscape. For all that it sought to be a part of nature, it was really just a trick because the building's cold rigidity, its perfect, studied symmetry, was all too obvious.

Its surface reflected the trees, the green of the lawns and the fountain as though it were all an optical illusion. A shudder ran through me at the sight. It was something so subtle that I was barely able to take it in. The building, and what it presented to us, were using nature, always lovely and wholesome, in order to hide its own horribly angular edges, of which it was nonetheless completely aware and indeed proud. The only sounds were the water in the fountain and the birds singing indifferently in the trees. Beyond this first building were several smaller buildings, reflecting back diminutive versions of ourselves. They were cubes of various sizes, each reflecting a delightful natural scene which, in being so reflected, became less beautiful, and more mechanical and studied. Multiple paths with lawns, trees and bushes stretched into the distance, gradually becoming lost among their doubles. Looking farther ahead, one couldn't tell where reflections ended and nature began. Dozens of reflected, non-existent trees and curved paths going nowhere.

To the right, beyond the trees, we glimpsed another large clearing, entirely devoid of vegetation. We approached slowly. Picking our way through the undergrowth, we entered a clearing of sinister proportions with a cement platform in the centre. Two small helicopters were on the far side and by one of them a metallic hangar whose interior lay in darkness.

"What is all this?" Max whispered in astonishment.

"There it is," I said. "Your one and only way out."

"I don't want to get out."

Max turned and carried on, and I followed silently after. We took the path that led to the nearest building, the largest of all. We advanced feeling we were penetrating a non-existent world, a place in which reality and mere reflection were more prone to confusion than anywhere else. Max came to a halt. His pupils were dilated. Our reflections in the building were terrifying. We were but a pair of minuscule, insignificant figures. On that surface, our reflections seemed possessed of a life of their own. I didn't want to look.

"Come on, Max," I said, grabbing his arm.

We went on walking with no idea whether someone was watching us from inside. Coming to the door, it took all I had not to turn around and bolt. There Max and I were. I sensed that to cross through that mirror meant penetrating the deepest parts of ourselves.

"We must go in," I said, addressing Max's reflection. He nodded in reply. I saw a profound terror flicker in his eyes. I didn't feel brave enough to mention it, but I suppose that, just as I had, he had seen something in his reflection, or perhaps in mine, that had made him shiver I pushed open the door, which opened smoothly.

The interior was as aseptic as the outside. White and cold, the walls rose up around a deserted vestibule. We turned around. Through the glass, the world outside appeared wrapped in a greenish mist. The birdsong and rustling of branches had been put on mute. Nature was presented to us as in a painting, as though the unreal now lay in this mute, perpetual image offered by the garden, with its green accoutrements and repetitive movements. I took Max by the arm and we pushed on a second door that led into a lobby.

We entered a gallery of white, lifeless walls. All around were doors, dozens of metal doors. All of them closed. Nearby, on our right, there was a stairwell going down four flights underground. Peering down, we saw at the bottom people coming and going with an air of utter normality, documents or folders under their arms. To the left, the stairwell went up another four floors. The physiognomy of each floor was unchanging: metal doors and flat, unbroken expanses of wall. The ceiling was a glass vault, with four panels rising up in pyramid fashion, flooding the interior with light. Voices from the basement floor rose up, echoing off the sterile walls. I tried a door on my right, but it was locked.

"Down," I said.

I descended all four flights with Max in tow. As we reached the bottom, the natural light waned and was supplemented by fluorescent strips. The white marble floor sparkled icily. Wide corridors stretched away in all directions. Looking up, we saw eight floors with metallic handrails, surrounded by countless identical doors. Up above, the sky had cleared of clouds and the sun cast slanting rays on one side of the gallery. A man holding a clipboard came up behind us. He wore an immaculate white coat. His black shoes contrasted with the whiteness of the floor. He wore thin-framed glasses and had a pleasant, well-kept aspect.

"Are you lost?" he said in a friendly tone.

"Yes," said Max nervously.

"Are you here for a check-up?"

"No."

"You don't have an appointment?"

"No," I said.

"You've recently arrived," he said, as though everything now made sense.

We nodded.

"Nothing to worry about. You shouldn't really be here. Not yet. But no cause for concern."

"We want to see Mr Drake," I said, taking the chance.

"I imagine you do. Everyone does. But he has only one body and the same number of hours at his disposal as the rest of us."

"I'm Max," he said as though that might help.

"I know who you both are," he said politely. "But even so, you shouldn't be here."

We both felt a tinge of disappointment. Everybody seemed to know who we were and what we were doing, as though nothing we did could surprise anyone.

"We saw Howard," said Max apologetically, "and we followed him."

"And do you know why you're here?" said the man, seemingly unflappable.

Neither Max nor I said anything. I was about to say yes, I did, that

136

I'd come to accuse Drake of a murder, but the moment didn't seem right.

"I understand," said the man. "Now, time for you both to leave."

"Why?" I asked.

"You're supposed to be at the picnic, if I'm not mistaken."

"But we aren't the same as those people. All we need is to talk to Drake Nothing else."

"Mr Drake is just as interested in talking with the two of you, but you must understand, there's a time for everything."

"What's he waiting for" I said, raising my voice. "For us to actually go mad?"

The man smiled elegantly and gestured for us to follow him. Which is what we did, following him down a wide passageway. Through a number of open doors, we glimpsed large meeting rooms with long, polished tables surrounded by chairs with symmetrical backs. They looked like university lecture theatres, with a sophisticated, aseptic air, and gleaming, well-swept side rooms containing semi-circular black leather sofas.

"Here we are," he said.

He pressed a button and a lift door opened. He went in and waved a small black fob in front of a panel. Pressing another button, he came back out of the lift, gesturing for us to enter.

"It's best if you both go up. Believe me. Hard as you might try, things won't go any quicker than they ought to. Be patient. I know you have hundreds of questions. If you're able to live with the uncertainty and keep calm, your efforts will all be repaid in the future. Go on, take the lift."

We got in. The man stepped away from the door and it slid noiselessly shut. We felt a slight jerk and the lift began to ascend. Neither of us said anything. It was as though the man's friendliness, his sincere words, had obliterated our wills, or perhaps it was just fear. We felt another jerk and the lift door open. We were at ground level again. Smoked glass walls surrounded us. On the other side was the fountain and the path alongside the hedge by which we had entered. The door remained open but neither of us took the step to go out.

"What shall we do?" Max said eventually.

"Know how to fly a helicopter?"

"No."

"In that case," I said, not giving it much thought, "we must go back in again."

"Why did we let him kick us out like that?"

"I don't know."

We pressed the button for the lift to go down again, but it didn't move. We stepped out and found ourselves back in the garden, and turned onto the path we had walked along a few minutes before. Once more our reflected images began to tremble the closer we got to the entrance and then I had the impression that this new attempt to cross through the door, to try to find answers, was a mistake, that we had been lucky to get out in one piece. I felt we were defying our own luck That the gods had smiled on us, one of those invisible gifts they make us for no apparent reason, like when we miss a plane that ends up crashing or avoid a falling section of roof by inches. When this happens, we are quite unaware because everything happens in accordance with that fate to which we are blind. We made our way back, now almost ready to bend destiny to our will, creating what we believed we deserved, or perhaps another outcome altogether, one we didn't even dare imagine.

# XIV

That is, this person has come to have attributed to
him behaviour and experience that are not simply
human, but are the product of some pathological
process or processes, mental and/ or physical,
nature and origin unknown.
Sanity, Madness and the Family
R.D. Laing, Aaron Esterson

We were less taken aback by our reflections this time, as though
the repetition of the repetition reduced the feeling of danger
and at the same time ramped up our sense of unreality. I believe we
had both concluded that the worst outcome would be to get trapped in
that place: it was vital to leave, to be free of the pressure it exerted on
us, not to mention the uncertainty. It was beyond us to suspect that at
times our doubts are the very thing that keep us moving forward – that
definitive truth may paralyse, ossify or atomise our awareness. Very
often, the truth we seek so hard to find isn't necessary, or even advisable
We also believed that our tenacity would be rewarded, that somebody
would step forward and offer us assistance, as soon as they realised
how badly we needed it. But as always, the importance or otherwise of
things turned out to be relative; our concerns were wholly at odds with
what seemed relevant in that place, as was our idea of "help". In any
case, I think both of us were unlucky men and we knew it. Not even
we were hopeful of success, of getting what we wanted, and returning
to the world victorious, with truth arrayed at our side. And yet, we
went on with a measure of confidence, knowing that sooner or later
our questions would be answered.

Max was no longer worried about being there; he needed somebody
to show him the way forward. Now his mother was dead, he was a lost
little boy, unable to discern what was prudent, or right. She had taken
his voice, his self-awareness, with her. I sensed he was nothing more
than a zombie now, a being that moved and was apparently alive, but

has lost his inner, defining identity. Though Drake still hadn't put in an appearance, his presence in our lives was becoming more and more palpable. He had become the motor driving us on, the reason for our present situation and the mystery of our past.

We came through the door and entered the reception area. Dense black clouds had moved in front of the sun, presaging another downpour. We went down to the bottom floor not saying a word, and waited for several minutes not sure where to go. The passageways stretched into the distance in opposite directions, as though our possible fates lay in wait at the end of those silent corridors. We couldn't decide to strike out in any particular direction. There was no knowing which was the right way. All we could do was choose one, and hope. I took Max by the arm, and we began down a passageway lined with doors bearing signs. The place seemed deserted, and it wasn't until we reached a circular vestibule that we saw another soul; a man emerged from a room we'd just passed holding a test tube of liquid containing something amorphous and pink; he was deep in thought. Not noticing our presence, he turned and made his way down a winding corridor at an even pace. We walked to a fork formed by two much narrower passageways that ended abruptly. To our left, a series of glass doors gave us a clear view of the rooms inside. Crouching down next to the first one, the door to which was ajar, we looked in and saw a neatly dressed, affable-looking man taking notes while another lay back on a divan and spoke and gesticulated as though shooing flies. A glass screen separated the pair, but we could hear the voice of the man on the chaise longue quite clearly; it sounded tinny and amplified. Max and I remained down on our haunches, trying to glean what we could from this conversation. We only caught the occasional, unconnected phrase, none of which seemed to make sense:

"... I was starting to fade, when it struck me that the scab surrounding me was getting harder, and I was going to be completely isolated... My father hit me, but it didn't hurt because my armour plating was too thick... I don't know if you remember, but it was the "other" who had to kill her... I only managed to gather a little of the sperm, but enough to bury it under the earth... No, I don't think my wife has a clue. He buried June in the garden, just above my sperm... He'll be a wonderful boy..."

Max shuddered. He looked deathly pale. I could see that he needed air. I helped him over to a sofa we had passed. He took a deep breath and gave his face a vigorous rub, as though to banish an unwanted thought.

"I feel frightened," he said, not looking at me.

"What of?"

"Of becoming one of them."

"Don't be. People don't go mad for no reason. Schizophrenia only comes about through a quite specific process, lots of different things have to happen, whereas psychosis only happens through some significant or repeated event." I said, sitting down beside him. "That guy in there is genuinely insane, a lost case He killed that woman, but doesn't know it. He's created another self, a false self to convince himself that it wasn't him. Excision isn't as simple as…"

"What isn't?" Max said.

"Excision," I said hesitantly.

"How come you know so much about that guy, when we could hardly hear what was being said?"

I didn't respond.

"Come on, what's excision? How come you know what's happening to him?"

"Maybe I've read about it somewhere. But it was pretty clear: he was showing signs of a personality disorder created by a divided self. My god," I said, jumping to my feet, "what am I saying!"

"What's wrong?"

"I don't know," I said in anguish. "I think I need to lie down. I've suddenly got a splitting headache."

"Wasn't the idea to find Drake?"

"Yes," I said uncertainly. "You're right."

"Are you waiting for somebody?" said a woman from behind us.

We spun around in surprise.

"Yes," I said. "Drake."

"Mr Drake isn't here…" She came closer. "Oh, it's you two! Did somebody call you already? I didn't think it was…"

"What?"

"What are you doing here?"

"We told you, we want to see Drake."

"But he's not here?"

"You're lying," I said. "He's here, he's expecting us."

"You, maybe, but Max shouldn't speak to him yet."

"Yes, I should!" Max said, jumping up. "I need to –"

I grabbed his arm, interrupting him:

"Fine, take me to Drake." Then, to Max, with a wink: "You ought to get out of here."

Max didn't understand my signal, because not even I had a proper sense of what I was planning to do, but I felt this was my chance to see him: finally I'd found someone who could actually take me to him.

"Follow me," said the woman.

She led us back to the same lift.

"Go on, Max," I said firmly. "You get in."

"But…" he protested faintly.

"Max!" I cried. "Get in the fucking lift and go for a walk in the town."

"You said you were going to help me," he said, astonishment on his face. "You said we'd see Drake together."

I grabbed his collar and shoved him inside.

"You," I said to the woman: "Push the button."

She did so, and as the doors slid shut, Max screamed:

"Simon…!"

"Go to hell, Max," I said.

The door shut and I caught a glimpse of his confused stare.

Not thinking what I was doing, I strode back into the building. I heard the woman's high heels on the floor as she followed me without saying a word. I made my way along two wide hallways, took a passageway on the left, then one on the right, which brought me into a small room with blue walls. There was a desk with a female receptionist sitting at it, and she looked up, surprised at my entrance:

"Sir!" She said.

The woman gestured for her to let me go in. I opened the door and found myself in Drake's office.

"All by yourself," he said from his desk. "Well done, Gerald!"

This stopped me in my tracks: the name seemed somehow familiar, and Drake's tanned, smug face reminded me of some terribly far-off moment. I'd found his office by myself, I realised, that was what he meant. How was that possible if I'd never been there before? Drake looked back at me from his maroon chair, a malevolent smile on his face. His indescribably blue eyes held my gaze. He struck me as more detestable than ever and for a moment I forgot why I was there, and a feeling of confusion was unleashed inside my chest.

Two men in white coats came in and positioned themselves either side of him. Drake always was fond of a theatrical touch, of giving the impression that everything was under his control, that he'd missed nothing.

I glanced nervously around. A brightly coloured painting hung behind him. A smiling blue sun hovered in a yellow sky, and a green dragon with hooked teeth flew over the surface of a white lake. On an island in the shape of a hand – with only four long, gaunt fingers – there stood a man with a halo holding a red-burning torch. Beyond this figure stood another saintly man, who'd caught an orange fish he didn't seem interested in taking out of the water. To the right, a man with Asian features was rowing in a small boat. On one edge of the picture, a face I immediately recognised looked on in satisfaction.

"I'll kill you," I said quietly.

I charged towards the desk, only for Drake's men to leap forward and grab me. I ordered them to let me go but to no avail, of course.

"Gerard, you can't go on hating me," said Drake, his voice steady and relaxed. "Come on, give it up. You've got no chance against me. I'm the one who's in charge now."

"You're a dead man," I whispered, as though that were my one reason for living.

Hate surged violently from the centre of my chest. I was frightened. I had no idea why he was calling me Gerald, but at the same time didn't care. All I knew was that I had to put an end to him, that I had to kill him with my own hands.

"You didn't think it would be that easy?" He smiled. "I'm your doctor. Remember? I know all there is to know about you."

"You aren't going to convince me that I'm crazy. I know who I am. You're not going to mess with my mind. I'm here to make you pay for the murder of my sister, and I'm not going anywhere until I have."

"Come now, Gerald! You know very well that your sister is alive, just as alive as you or I. When are you going to stop pretending?"

"I knew this was going to happen. I just knew it. You trying to convince everyone that I'm crazy, when in fact you are the madman. Hey," I said, looking at the two nurses, "he is the one who should be in a lunatic asylum. He's a murderer. He's tortured children and women and uses them in his rituals."

"Gerald, that's you," he said quietly from his couch. "You're the one who did all that. Don't you remember the last time we spoke? I said you'd never escape the punishment you deserve because, though you're unwell, you are at the same time far too self-aware. And that, you more than anyone should know, is a big problem."

"You and I have never spoken before."

"Nonsense. The last time we spoke was in Boston. We went out sailing on your yacht. You'd been allowed out under surveillance, only to make a hash of it by killing those two tourists."

"None of that is true. I don't even own a yacht. I couldn't afford one."

"That's the way you'd like things to be, right? To be poor and so terribly honourable. Have your conscience as clean as those little babies you liked torturing. You know you aren't well. You know as well as I do, given you're also a doctor. One of the best psychiatrists around."

"It isn't going to work. What do you want? Do you think you'll get your own way as usual? That I won't tell the world everything I know?"

"What do you know?"

"That you've been buying children for years to use in your stupid black magic rituals. That you've used virgins to conceive children and make them demented so they'd respond to your extraordinary questions. I'm sure there are a lot of perfectly sane people out there you've got locked up purely in order to study their behaviour, to watch the way their minds degenerate, like Max and me."

Leaning forward, Drake bellowed with laughter, but in a constrained way, as if to suggest via his tempered response that my accusations were nothing but the ravings of a lunatic.

"Poor Gerald," he muttered, feigning sympathy. "You so persist in believing your own lies. Why not cast your mind back to everything you learned at university about schizophrenia? Don't you remember the time we spent studying together? Even then, even when we were just youngsters, you were ill, Gerald. Yet you were always my best friend. I admired you, know that? I admired your madness, your energy. When you put your mind to something, nothing could stop you. I'm the only one who knows you, Gerald, and that's why you want to kill me. Just as you wanted to kill your sister when she found out what you were really like."

"You killed her!" I cried hoarsely.

I knew he'd had this whole story ready for a long time, and how much he was enjoying finally having me there, unable to defend myself. This was one big display of power, to impress upon me that he could do whatever he liked with me if the feeling took him. He could lock me up for the rest of my life if he was minded. One word, and I would never see the outside world again. I decided to calm down, not allow my nervous state to lend weight to his claims.

"Fine," I said, taking a deep breath. "I should have known it wouldn't be easy."

"What wouldn't?"

"Proving that you killed my sister."

"And how were you planning to prove it?"

"I had a plan," I said, hesitating. "When I sent Max up in the lift just now, I thought I did, but…"

"Max?"

"You know exactly who I mean. It's awful the state that young man is in."

"Funny you should say that," Drake said, half closing his eyes. "I was sure you'd end up succumbing to his charm, his innocence. I knew leaving the two of you together for a few days was the best idea ever. Have you forgotten his mother? Have you forgotten that you were in love with her? You and I both were. She was so beautiful, so sweet…"

"I don't know what you are talking about."

"Yes, you do. Tell me something: do you like the painting?" He said, pointing up above his head. "I saw you studying it with some interest."

"No. It's hideous."

"You bought it. More than thirty years ago. It's a Crowley: Isle of the Magi. We were together when we first saw it: I remember how enthralled we both were. You more than me. Cost us both a pretty penny. You said that one day you would have your own isle of magi, a place away from the world where everybody would be saints, visionaries or… madmen. I always admired your ideas, your madness. You can't imagine the number of times I loathed my own sanity, the way you were able to have fun in those extravagant parties, seeing you enjoy your unhinged exploits, with those delusions of grandeur that occasionally overwhelmed. It's thanks to them, to you, that I am the person I am today. Forgive yourself, Aldo, there's nothing you should feel sorry for. You've found your way to that dream island, and if you wish, you can share it with me. I'm your friend."

"Don't call me that."

As Drake spoke, I looked at the painting. It was a nightmare landscape, an absurd collection of faces, of clashing colours, like a kind of bad dream prompted by the worst indigestion. And yet I felt it was vaguely familiar. Perhaps I've seen it reproduced in a book I'd read about Crowley.

"It leaves me completely dead," I said. "I think I might have seen it before in a book."

"No. You had it in your home in Boston, next to the fireplace. Don't you remember? Then, when you were admitted to the hospital, I took it away. I thought you'd be pleased to see it. Crowley might be living, Gerald, you know that as well as I do. You and I assumed the task of making it happen."

"Are you listening?" I said in satisfaction to the two men and the woman who were with us. "There is all the proof you need. He thinks the boy is Crowley, and he's messing with his mind the same as he is with mine. All of you know that's impossible. Listen to what I'm telling you, I beg you: this man is a murderer, he's truly, truly unhinged. I assure you; I've known him for a very long…"

Then I fell silent. A blurry image came to my mind. Drake and I were in New York, entering a glass building, a skyscraper on Fifth Avenue. We were both wearing black suits and had big smiles on our faces. But no, it couldn't be. I knew the whole thing was some illusion, some trick of fabricated reflections he was projecting on my mind. Nothing was real. The whole thing was pure manipulation, my thoughts were no longer my own. The images in my mind were invented memories. I had never experienced any of this personally. Somehow, he had gained access to my mind, perhaps via drugs. Perhaps Bezel had been doctoring my meals without my realising, dropping in a little something to make me vulnerable, to stun me as I was now stunned.

"It's not so easy to persuade someone they are crazy," I said firmly.

"What have you dreamt up now? Do you think I have the power to do something like that? How fond you are of these tricks! I'd certainly like to be able to do that, I won't deny it, it would save me a lot of time and money, but unfortunately, I have to disappoint. I thought that by presenting you with the truth, I'd get a reaction. What a shame! Sooner or later you will have to stop pretending, and then the shock will shatter you. The violence will turn you into what you truly are. I'm sorry for whoever happens to be close to you at the time," he said, with a satisfied laugh. "How long were you about to say we'd known each other for?" he asked, "I haven't brought you here to argue. I got you out of jail, Gerald. If it weren't for me, you'd be serving a life sentence. I am your friend. I accept you for what you are. Everybody here accepts you. You can even go back to practising if you want. Nobody will find out. We are all on your side, please understand that. An isle of magi, Gerald, for the two of us: a place where one can live free of any laws, a place where the truth is available to find, and Max here with us, Gerald. He's our creation. I thought you would remember when you saw him and read his notebooks, but I now realise you're in an even worse state than I thought. Even so, I know you will remember, I know you will finally accept yourself. You are who you are, and that's fine. But until you accept your past you won't ever be yourself again. I love you, Gerald," he said, getting up and coming around the desk. There was a sincere, distraught expression on his face. "You know I'd never let anything happen to you. You don't need to worry any more, you're safe. Believe me."

"Safe? I'll never be safe. You killed my sister. Nothing can change that."

"Your sister is alive, Gerald. For all that you would wish it otherwise. You killed her in your mind when she found out the truth about you, what you're really like. That whole melodrama you came up with about the sect, about the awful things she'd done, only then to repent and supposedly kill herself – pure fantasy, the lot of it. She was never involved in any of that. It's all an invention of yours and it was she who discovered the things you had been up to, and that was why you attempted to kill her, because you couldn't stand her knowing your true identity. And you want me dead because I'm the only one who knows. It's all one big farce, Gerald. You're trapped inside your own fantasies, you're a prisoner of your own delusions. But all this will pass once you forgive yourself, once you accept yourself. You made the whole thing up more than twenty-one years ago to convince yourself that you were a good man. You aren't poor, Gerald, you don't live in a Parisian hovel. You're wealthy, immensely wealthy. All of this has been built thanks to your money and mine. It's ours. And if you join me, we can keep it going."

"The story you told Max about yourself is pure fantasy. Your personality is so split you no longer distinguish truth from lies. Your life is a patchwork made of bits of other people's lives, some real and some made up, things you wish had happened. I've been watching both of you since you arrived. The story of the man you followed, who led you to me, the one you said worked for me and then died from loss of blood after cutting off his penis. Remember? Well, that's just a combination of different memories. The man you were talking about was an absolute nobody, an underling in a law firm in Paris. Nobody expelled him from any sect, it was you who was expelled, and you who cut off his penis, who killed him. Then you took on his name: Simon Bughin, that was his name. You couldn't face the crimes you committed. What you believe to be your life is nothing more than a montage you have created in your mind to shield yourself from your terrible deeds. It was you who drank blood, you who killed Sophie's child. It was you who conceived Max. You are his father, Aldo."

"How do you know what Max and I spoke about?"

"I've got cameras all around the town, Gerald. It's dressed up to appear otherwise, but this is a hospital, as you know. I've been watching you ever since you got here. Why do you think you can't remember how you arrived? Because I brought you here under sedation from New York. And I did that because I knew Max was on his way, and I wanted you to be here to receive him. So, you see, I prepared everything so the two of you could meet, as is right and proper, and so you could build a more gradual picture of who he was. He is our creation. Our boy. Don't you remember? Why are you trying to act as if you hadn't listened to me? Did you hear what I said about Max? You are his father."

"No," I said feeling faint. "That's impossible."

For a brief moment, my mind severed the thread that translates the outside world, and I was unable to distinguish what was real and what wasn't. Something inside me was falling apart, and the damage was considerable. My headache returned and it was impossible to escape from that place, from his words, I wanted to cry out, cursing his name, but every ounce of energy was gone. I knew I would end up being the person he'd decided I should be, that he could turn me into whatever he wanted, madman, killer, or whatever. I didn't have it in me to fight back, to show who I really was.

"If you don't believe me," Drake said, "I can get your sister to come and see you. She could be here tomorrow morning."

"No!" I cried. "You won't do that. She's dead."

"So now you remember?"

"No – there is nothing to remember. The fact that a place like this exists helps me to know that I am not crazy. There are things that will never happen however much we try."

"Perhaps. But what is bound to happen cannot be avoided. Listen, many years ago, a few months after you were committed for the first time, I found Max and his mother in Biarritz... But you know about this, don't you? You read about it in Max's notebooks. I never said anything to you because she was so frightened of you, she always knew you were unhinged. I know I should have told you but..." He gave a weary sigh. "I loved her. I always did. Now I don't know if I did the right thing. If I'd have brought her with us, she'd still be alive."

"I don't know what's happening to me," I said, feeling sick. "I need to think, and I can't. I don't know what's wrong with me. My head's aching."

"Don't worry. Margaret will give you something to calm you. All will be well, you'll see," he said, clearly happy with the way things had gone. He settled back in his chair and gestured to one of the nurses.

# XV

… sanity or psychosis are tested by the degree of
conjunction or disjunction  between two persons
where one is sane by common consent.

The Divided Self

R. D. Laing

I came away with my head spinning, unable to string a sentence together. My thoughts were a jumble. I have only the vaguest memory of whatever took place after Margaret gave me a couple of green pills. I know they laid me on a sofa along from Drake's office, and I must have fallen asleep there. When I woke up, in a small, windowless room, the headache had gone, and a swarm of dark details and blurry memories had taken up residence in my brain. I'd never felt anything like it. It was difficult to create any link between the information I now confronted and what I recognised as my life, my real life. In the tangled mire of my mind only one thing stood out with any clarity: I had to get free of Drake's clutches. He posed a great danger to both Max and me. That man would be the end of me, I was now in no doubt. Glancing up at the ceiling I saw the tiny insect eye of a CCTV camera scrutinising me.

I couldn't allow myself to get into another exchange with Drake: that way disaster lay. It was imperative that I end his life, little as I knew how I would approach such a task. The mere fact of his existence meant large numbers of people had to renounce a normal life and all ties with their real past. It wouldn't be easy getting to him, but nothing was easy. The next time we were face-to-face, I would break his neck, or perhaps plunge something into his throat, a pen for example. I realised I didn't feel impatient or furious. I knew this was the one thing left for me to do in life, and that I would have no regrets. All my nervousness had disappeared following our conversation, or following the pills, perhaps. I felt angry at being so naive. What had I thought? That I would come, point the finger – "You, sir, are a murderer, please

accompany me to the police station." "Of course, I'd be delighted." –
and head back to Paris with my conscience clear? I couldn't remember
what my plan had been on arrival. It was as though it had been erased
from my mind. What had I been planning? Ever since I'd arrived
in town, I'd been hoping to meet him, and the second I had, all I
could think to do was to murder him. I was in a rage and could barely
breathe, so desperate was I to have him before me again. I never
thought I would hate him this much. I felt so repelled by the thought
of his smug face, those blue, vainglorious eyes, that endless Olympian
attitude of his. I shuddered to think of the life he'd planned for me.
He'd created a whole biography for me in his twisted imagination. The
most frightening thing was that I might come to believe the story too.
For now, I merely vacillated, but within a few days I could be foaming
at the mouth in a padded cell, while Drake observed me from his
maroon couch.

The door opened and Margaret appeared. Blue-eyed and blonde,
she wore her hair in a careful bun and had it not been for her air of
cold superiority, I suppose she'd have struck me as attractive.

"How are you feeling?" she asked, though she obviously could not
have cared less.

"Having a whale of a time."

"I mean how is your head."

"Still on my shoulders, but if you really want it…"

"You're free to leave."

"Leave?"

"Mr Drake told me to tell you. Time for you to go back to the
town."

"Where's Drake?"

"You needn't worry about that. When you've decided what to do,
he'll send for you."

"What to do? About what?"

"About yourself. You know what. Whether you are going to be a
doctor or a patient. It's up to you to decide. Nobody but you has the
right to choose your future, but you must understand that decision
may lead you down very distinct paths."

"Choose to be someone I am not? Do you think it's as simple as
that? Today I am me, and tomorrow whoever Drake decides…"

"Better that than being nobody, don't you think?"

"And did you also have to choose?"

The woman didn't answer. She opened the door and stood to one
side, inviting me to go out.

"And what precisely am I supposed to get up to in the town?"

"You can do whatever you want."

"All the while, you lot will be watching, right?"

"Nobody wants to do anything that isn't for your best. When you are feeling steadier, you'll see things differently. Mr Drake only wants to help you, don't you see? You would be rotting in a jail cell if it weren't for him."

"No, no, no," I interrupted. "I'm not going to listen to that spiel again. I know you've been practising it over and over, and you want to get me to believe it too, but please, not now."

I tottered out of the room. A shiver ran through me when I realised I'd been in one of the rooms off the gallery. Looking over the handrail, I looked at the eight floors with the identical metal doors and the large spiral staircase leading to places all exactly the same. We were on the fourth floor, and looking up, out through the glass pyramid roof, I saw dark clouds jostling in the sky. It was still light. Two nurses waited patiently by the stairwell. I followed Margaret and we descended to the vestibule. On reaching the lift, she nodded, and I got in without complaint.

"See you soon, Gerald," she said with a smile.

"Goodbye," I said.

The lift door slid shut behind me and I stood feeling paralysed. I sensed I'd been caught up in a great lie. I tried to stop the door from shutting but it was too late. Why had I answered to that name? Who was Gerald? I was being infected, something like a virus was growing within me, silent but implacable. Madness? How had I succumbed so easily to Drake's manipulations? Who was I? Couldn't I even defend my memories to a stranger? If all of this could happen, if a man could control the will of another, put an end to his thoughts, and turn him into another person, what would be left of our own self? What would we be reduced to? Just like Max, I was having memories unconnected to my own past that I didn't believe were my own. Was it really so easy to fabricate a life story? How many people with made-up pasts might there be in the town? How many were going around with memories that were not their own, living lives designed for them by a group of madcap psychiatrists? I knew about Drake's unhealthy obsession with uncovering the secrets locked inside shattered minds. I knew that his boundless interest in deciphering and discovering the functioning of the brain had led him to make his very own group of mad people using cruel and inhumane methods, to turn normal, everyday people into psychopaths, merely to study their behaviour. Now, I was another one of those test cases. The hunter had been hunted. I had thought I was pursuing him, that I was the sleuth, but unbeknownst to me, this reality had become one more lie. All I had been doing was approaching his lair – his laboratory. I had fallen into the trap without needing a push from anyone, just as he'd said when I entered his office: "All by yourself."

# XVI

[Freedom] has to be its own past, and this past is
irremediable. It even seems at first glance that freedom
cannot modify its past in any way; the past is that which is
out of reach and which haunts us at a distance without
our even being able to turn back to face it in order to
consider it... I cannot conceive of myself without a past;
better yet, I can no longer think anything about myself
since I think about what I am and since I am in the past;
but on the other hand I am the being through whom the
past comes to myself and to the world.

Being and Nothingness
Jean Paul Sartre

I got out of the lift and made my way slowly through the garden. My migraine had come back without me noticing. Now, I felt something in the back of my brain, a small lump I never remembered being there before. It was hard and ridged to the touch, as though a crumpled piece of paper had been inserted behind my left ear. I felt it pulsing. I brought my hand away, suddenly terrified at the idea that they might have inserted something. I knew that couldn't be. I was letting my fears go too far. It must be a knock I'd sustained when I was being carried out of Drake's office, nothing more.

I made my way back through the forest, expecting to cross paths with someone, but there was nobody around. The clearing where the picnic had been held was a scene of devastation, with the grass flattened, and empty cans, bottles and shreds of tinfoil strewn around. I started back along the path towards the town, but felt far from sure, as though afraid I might find something worse there than what I'd left behind. Plucking up my courage, I told myself that nothing was going to happen to me, that the fear I was experiencing was the result of the conversation with Drake. The sensible thing was to keep my cool, while readying myself for a new round of accusations, and a fresh

153

onslaught of confusing misinformation. They could say anything they wanted, and it wouldn't shake me: I knew who I was. I wouldn't let them rock me again. I would be on my guard, now that I knew what to expect...

And yet, there was a thought I could not shift. Drake's accusations, the incredible stories he'd invented about me, or the idea of being stuck inside this inconceivable farce weren't stressing me out. Worse than all of that was my inability to remember how I'd arrived in the town. There was a gap in my mind, a dark, murky lapse in time, I couldn't fill with any image or memory. I briefly thought how terrifying it would be to be unable to rely on oneself, trust one's own thoughts or discern whether what we know, and what we recognise as our own, is the truth. Not just a truth, but our truth. Without that certainty, the confidence that drives us to choose ourselves and choose between different options vanishes and we are simply robots, with only the slightest memory of what used to be our consciousness. Perhaps this was all that Howard, the watchman, had meant when he suggested we enjoy our time in Shimts; that it was better to be in a place where one's acts are neither measured nor judged, but merely observed. The inhabitants of this place were like a colony of wild monkeys, existing under the illusion that they were a part of the world at large, while their lives unfolded inside a perfectly simulated scenario, playing roles that held significance only for people like Drake. He and his doctors were the spectators, the ones who gave meaning to the show, and it was they who marked out the parts and named the streets. They ruled that there would be no rules. And in the midst of this madness I found myself, half man, half automaton, afraid of being devoured by hundreds of eyes, eyes avid for information.

Looking up at the trees, I noticed a small camera turning between some branches, swivelling around like the head of an owl. Looking for prey. A camera that registered conversations, orgies, flights of madness, moments of anguish, hundreds of moments that ought by rights to be lost in time, becoming vague memories or being forgotten about altogether. But they captured it all, analysing it to the nth degree. They would turn the past into the present, into a curse, like Prometheus's liver. An act that would regenerate at the push of a button. They would never allow us to forget the worst of ourselves.

# XVII

I believe I am in Hell, therefore I am.
Night in Hell
Arthur Rimbaud

I had reached the town and was making my way towards the high street. I was almost all the way out of the forest before I realised. Those final steps were lost to my memory, but I knew that they would never go away entirely. I glanced instinctively back and saw myself covering that same route a thousand times over. An inanimate contraption had been given the task of proving I had been there.

I was given a rather chilly welcome by the sign bearing the name of the town and the quote from Crowley. The invitation now made sense. Not the magician's, but Drake's. He had manipulated it, as he did with everything. The original phrase invited a superior self, a kind of wise and diligent super conscience, to act in the same way that this "thou", a sacred, elevated kind of "you", would. But Drake knew only too well that not everyone would grasp the message's hidden meaning. For some it would be taken as a chance to give free rein to their darkest desires; to others, justification for every sort of madness. How could those people be asked to act of their own will, if nobody there was sufficiently self-aware? Was the idea that by invoking the truth, answers would come? Idiotic madman! It was he who deserved to walk the dusty streets, to breathe the claustrophobic air of this sham town, to live under the microscope like some insect.

The nodule behind my ear kept pulsing slowly, as though it were feeding on my thoughts, thoughts that were perhaps no longer my own. But what did it matter! I didn't know how to show my hand, or how to get away. All I could do was wait, keep my eyes peeled for an opportune moment to deal with Drake. That would be my one satisfaction, my one victory. Meanwhile, I would allow myself to be observed like an ant in his glass ants' nest.

Coming past Hausen's bar, I heard a flat voice call my name. I turned around and found Max before me.

"Simon!" he said, his voice dull. "I thought you'd be in a test tube by now."

"Perhaps you'll live to see it for yourself."

He turned around and went into the bar. Surprised, I followed him inside, taking the seat next to him at the bar.

"I thought you didn't drink," I said.

"I didn't before this morning," he said.

Looking in his eyes, I saw an unwonted sheen there. He was completely drunk.

"Hey," I said, my tone apologetic. "What happened in the lift was only to save you from something nasty."

"Leaving me on my own and telling me to go to hell is saving me from something nasty?" he said, smiling bitterly. "Next time, don't be so considerate."

"There won't be a next time. Don't worry."

"What would you like?" said Hausen, emerging from behind the curtain.

"Whiskey, of course."

"Of course," said Hausen.

"Well then?" said Max, still staring into his glass.

"Nothing to report. Drake, precisely as I thought, wants us to stay on here, whether we like it or not."

"Yes, we knew that. But what did he say to you?"

"He tried to convince me that I'm crazy, that he and I know one another, and..." I scrutinised Max for a moment. "And a lot of nonsense besides."

I couldn't tell him that Drake had also tried to convince me that Max was my son. He was in a very vulnerable place and any big revelations could throw him into greater turmoil.

"Nothing interesting, it seems," Max said.

"No, nothing. What about you?"

"Me?" he said, laughing hysterically. "I'm still dreaming away. One step forward, five steps back... Something my mother used to say when she got angry," he turned his seat around towards mine, "You're going backwards, like crabs do. Well, that's where I am at the moment."

"Have you had any new memories?"

"Think I'm drinking this crap because it tastes nice? Whiskey is the most disgusting drink on earth" he groaned, banging his glass down on the bar top.

The noise made me jump. Max laughed dejectedly.

"Okay, so?" I said.

"Everything's starting to make sense, Simon. A couple more swigs of this, and even sense won't matter anymore."

"Come on, Max," I said. "What have you remembered? You can tell me."

He drained the glass with a grimace and placed it on the bar top. He didn't look at me. He ran his fingers back through his hair and took a deep breath, before covering his eyes and shaking his head, as though refusing to accept something that had already happened.

"Max," I said, gently touching his shoulder.

Hausen gave me a look and disappeared behind the curtain.

"It's all one big lie, Simon," he gasped. "Everything."

"What do you mean?"

He didn't answer. I heard him struggling to breathe beneath his hands. He was hiding his face.

"You got what you wanted," he muttered.

"Who?"

"My mother!" he cried.

He spun abruptly round to face me, and I saw his alcohol-reddened eyes and the tears.

"My mother and Drake, and you, you bloody liar!"

"What?"

"What do you mean, what? You know exactly what."

"No, I don't."

"All those years I spent thinking there was nobody else, it was just me and her. You and your stupid conclusions."

"Max, I don't know what you're trying to say."

"And you never will, because you're completely off your rocker," he said jabbing a finger at me, his face swollen by alcohol. "I trusted you, and it turns out you're nothing but a sadistic screwball. The kind of father figure everyone would like to give a beating to."

"But who told you that?"

"I don't think that's important.

"Of course it is. Whoever it is has sold you a lie."

"Think I'm not clever enough to tell?"

"I think that somebody is having a lot of fun at our expense."

"You're wrong. Nobody here would dare mess with you. I know that now. Although," he spat, "what should a madman's opinion matter!"

"Okay, that's enough!"

I grabbed him by the neck and was on the verge of hitting him, but something held me back.

"Though of course..." said Max, stumbling back towards the tables. He knocked into a chair and nearly fell over. "... Of course, I am too."

"What do you mean?"

"You know: a chip off the old block..." he said, sitting down hard in a chair.

"Max, what did they tell you? Please, you must tell me."

"Same as they told you, I guess."

"And you believed it?"

"To be honest, I did. Why wouldn't I?"

"Because all they want is to drive us mad. Don't you see?"

"I don't, actually."

"You can't believe a word these people say, Max. Everyone here is crazy."

"No, Simon. There are people here who aren't crazy," he said, his words spilling out as he concentrated on enunciating his thoughts. "I now know who I am. Though I can also see that the price I paid is too high."

"Aren't you going to tell me what happened to you?"

"It isn't so bad. I shouldn't be so upset" he said wearily. He was on the verge of collapsing. "It isn't so terrible here. In the end, it's the place we deserve, don't you think?"

"No, I don't think that. They are succeeding, Max, they're muddying your mind. Don't you see? When you arrived, you weren't like this. They're doing something terrible to you."

"So what?" he cried. "Hausen! Bring me another."

The man came out and poured another whiskey.

"Look at this poor guy," he said with a laugh. "There he goes. Whole day stacking bottles in the back of his bar. OCD, I guess... Know what that is? Of course you do. You're a psychiatrist, and a good one at that. He repeats things a hundred times over, checking and checking again, because he's off his rocker as well. Haven't you noticed the way he's constantly stacking bottles back there? But he didn't used to be like this. He used to have a beautiful wife, then she died in an accident. He nearly died too, but here you have him, stacking bottles, stacking and stacking them till kingdom come..."

"Don't drink anymore."

"Why?"

"It isn't good for you."

"How do you know what's good for me?" he spat.

I knew then that something horrible had happened, that his most recent memories were hiding something terrible enough to truly make him insane. I could hardly believe this was the same young man looking back at me. Until now, he'd been withdrawn, polite, steady. This person before me was not Max.

"I want to help you, Max," I said, and I meant it. "Talking to Drake has brought home the fact that I can't do anything for my sister now, she's dead and nothing is going to change that. But she's only one of many wrapped up in all this madness and… You, you are alive. There's still a chance for you."

"And who's going to give me that chance, you?"

"I can help."

"Do what?"

"Discover whether all these memories you've been having are real. And to get past all of this."

"All of this, all of this – don't you realise that all of this is me? Are you going to help me get past myself? Are you going to make me change? Can you change the past? Who do you think you are, God?"

"What happened to you? Tell me. Talk to me, Max."

"It's impossible," he went on, thinking out loud, ignoring my presence. "There's no way to change the past. Sometimes we would like to, sometimes we'd give our very lives for it but… What life? Who would want a life like mine?"

He took another sip and gave a forlorn smile.

"The only way we'll get out of this is if we work together. If we let their lies divide us, we'll both end our days in a straitjacket."

He had collapsed forward over the bar and seemed quite changed, as though the few hours we'd spent apart had been years in his life. He seemed really old and subdued.

"Hand over the notebook," I said firmly.

"Dream on. I made that mistake already. I don't intend to repeat it."

"Max, give me the notebook," I said, holding out my hand impatiently.

He lifted his head and looked me in the eye. Something there struck me as tremendously familiar and at the same time awful. I averted my gaze, hoping he wouldn't see how frightened I was.

"Max," I said, "there's something I need to know. I want to do something for you or for me, for whoever. I don't know any more. I feel useless, impotent at the idea of spending the rest of my life in this hole, at the sense there's nothing I can do to avoid it."

"You're wrong, you can do whatever you want."

I looked at him uncomprehendingly. There was something he was trying to tell me, and at the same time to hide from me.

"We are both crazy," he said, trying to stand. "And those of us who are crazy can do what we like because the rules governing our chaotic world are different and we won't be judged by any of our actions. Think about it. In the world out there, people are judged every day because of what they do, they are prey to the things other people say, they must constantly repress their urges and not overstep the rules, and everything seems normal, right? But what would happen if people were studied individually, every single man and woman? It would become clear that what is known as schizophrenia exists as an unavoidable facet of modernity. And what would happen then?" He was babbling now. "The world would show itself to be one gigantic lunatic asylum! Not so different to what it already is. And yet," he said, pausing, "those of us here don't have to pretend. This is a chance to act, to experience this environment exactly as we want to. Drake is benevolent in this way, you ought to know that, you know him better than I do. He doesn't discriminate, he doesn't reduce his "guests" to mere test cases, he lets them live their lives, lets them be… Can you think of a better way to grow old? Here I've got a chance to settle down, to feel as though I'm a part of something. I've spent my entire life running in no particular direction – completely lost. Now I've got a place I can call home, somebody who understands me. Everything's marvellous. Now all that's left for me is to understand myself," he said dejectedly, burying his face in his drink.

"Who's been putting all these ideas in your head? What is there to understand?"

"Universes, all these many unknown universes hidden one within other. We aren't what we seem," he said, suddenly frightened. "Nobody is. My mother wasn't, Drake isn't, not even you, Simon. A day will come, and you'll wake up and, bang, you're somebody else."

"It isn't as simple as that."

"That was what I thought. I thought I was me, at least until my mother died. Now I know they were having me on, she and Drake were having me on."

"Why?"

"Don't you know? Drake and my mother were lovers for many years. Nobody knew, not even me. What a liar that woman was… That's right, my whole life has been spent believing lies… Mummy's little boy," he bellowed, "mummy's little monster!"

"Let me see the notebook."

"Not only have you lot stolen my past from me, now there's no way for me to even get back," he said accusingly. "And do you know why? Because I've got nowhere to go. There is no identity I can live in peace with. I'm a bastard, the product of degenerate minds. But..." he added, trying to make a show of satisfaction, to convince himself, "I came here looking for answers, and now I've got them. Although, it's strange, I thought that knowing who I was would make me feel better. The fact is, the more I remember, the more I wish I was crazy."

I'd had just about enough, and I grabbed him by his shirt collar. He tried to fend me off, but was far too drunk, and only managed a couple of clumsy swipes at the air. I put my hand into his jacket pocket and took out the notebook. There was no need for me to hit him, he fell back into a chair before collapsing onto the floor. Hausen peered out from behind the curtain.

"He'll sleep now," I said sharply. "It'll do him good."

Drying his hands on a cloth, Hausen weighed up the situation, finally deciding to stick to his side of the bar. With a shrug, he went back to his bottle stacking.

I sat down by the hearth, and opened Max's notebook. He and his mother were leaving Biarritz on a rainy summer's day. Once more leaving something behind that it would be necessary to forget, a memory only she would retain.

"I remember yours was a clean birth," said his mother, looking back at him from the driver's seat. "What a bonny boy you were, with those big, dark brown eyes of yours."

Max was lying in the back seat, covered by a towel, pretending to sleep. Irene spoke as though sleepwalking, in a halting monotone. Max saw himself resting there, curled up beneath the towel. Now Irene began to weep, drying her tears on the edge of her blouse, while keeping her eyes on the road ahead. Max stayed lying down, a bruise on one cheek. Three days earlier something irreparable had taken place.

Max had gone out to play with his friends, after his week away with Drake. They had cycled out to the white meadow, a place they loved though it was banned by all the parents. It was dangerous to go walking there; the earth was hidden beneath a blanket of white grass which, in certain places, grew higher than their heads. There were potholes everywhere, once filled with earth and stones. Water erosion had made the potholes bigger still and compacted the earth artificially mounded there, creating a patchwork of small, muddy swamps, into which a child could easily sink. Though they knew they weren't supposed to, Max and his friends spent entire afternoons playing hide and seek in the dust, earth and mud, while insects made nests in their hair and their shoes and socks became covered in golden burrs.

Max felt wonderful that day, as though he'd been given a new toy. On his return from the stay with Drake he felt full of a new kind of strength. Drake was right and he couldn't remember the reason for his happiness, for this expansive, exalted feeling. They left their bicycles at the entrance to the meadow, hidden behind some shrubs so other kids wouldn't steal them, before diving into the grassy jungle.

"Over here!" cried André. "A big one!"

They all ran over to join him by the ants' nest. The ants bustled around under the midday sun: entering and exiting the mound bearing morsels and building materials, preparing against a future of which, for all its regimented insignificance, they were only too aware.

"Look at that little fatty," said Louis. Then, with a laugh: "Like your sister, Claire."

Claire gave him a push, but smiled, while still looking down at the ants' nest, shifting her feet so the insects wouldn't swarm up her legs.

"The queen is in there somewhere," said Max. "She's the biggest of all. She's about this big," he said, holding up forefinger and thumb.

"That's impossible," said Andre. "You don't get ants that big."

"Yes, you do. And in Africa, there are even bigger ones. They eat people."

They tittered nervously.

"They're like some of the tribes you still get in certain places," said Max. "They don't have individual awareness, or a sense of themselves as separate from the colony. They're gregarious."

The others frowned. They had no idea what he was talking about.

"What?" said Max, confused that no one was saying anything. "What is it?"

"You sound like somebody's dad," said Claire with a laugh.

"Shall we, then?" said Louis, lifting a foot. "Should we destroy it?"

"No!" cried Max. "Leave them."

"Why?" said Louis. "Isn't this what we came for?"

"Yes, but what's the point in destroying the place where they live?" said Max, fascinated by the activity in the nest. "They'll never know what caused their misfortune."

"What?" said Louis.

"What's the point of destroying it?" said Max sombrely. "They've been working on it all summer, in this heat. They go out looking for food, they create this great big store for all their food, and then we come along and, bang, we take their house away."

Now the others looked at the nest with new eyes, and with not a little remorse. Louis brought his foot back to the ground and leaned in to take a closer look at the tiny tireless creatures.

"You can't hurt somebody, without that person knowing it's you causing the pain. It makes no sense," said Max, barely blinking, allowing the words to flow. "If you want to do someone harm, you've got to make sure that person knows you did it to them," he said, glaring angrily at Louis.

"Are you crazy?" said Louis, unable to fathom his twisted thinking.

"No, you're the crazy one," said Max, his blood suddenly up. "You're crazy if you think you're going to take Claire from me. She's mine," he said, grabbing her by the arm.

The girl was still engrossed by the nest and hadn't noticed what was being said. She jumped when she felt Max's hand on her.

"Hey?" she said.

"Claire likes me, kiddo," bragged Louis.

"No!" shouted Max. "I can do whatever I like, and she's mine."

"You're my girlfriend, aren't you, Claire?"

The girl nodded.

"Not anymore,' declared Max, pulling her towards him. "She's mine now."

"Ow!" screeched Claire.

"Let go of her," growled Louis.

"Any closer and I'll kill you," retorted Max.

Louis took a step closer, but saw something in Max's eye, a glimmer he couldn't comprehend, one that left him speechless, pinned to the spot.

"Let me go!" asked Claire.

"No, I won't," said Max, gripping her arm more tightly still.

"Hey, Max," said André. "You're hurting her."

"This is so you know who's boss," he said, and punched Louis on the nose.

The boy fell to the floor, blood pouring from his nose. Claire gave a yelp and went over to help him.

"You're crazy, Max," she said sobbing. "I'll never be your girlfriend."

Max saw Louis crying on the ground, his shirt bright red with blood. Dozens of ants were crawling up his trousers and filling his shoes. André looked at him in pure terror; Claire with undisguised hate. Suddenly he felt nauseous, with a painful prickly heat around his ears. He grabbed his own shirt at chest height and yanked it furiously up to his neck. He began gasping for breath, and, wide-eyed for a moment, fainted, hitting his face on the top of the ants' nest. When he came round, he was in bed. His mother, sitting on the edge of the bed, gave him a worried look.

"What happened to you, Max?" she asked, her voice tremulous.

"Nothing. Why?"

He worried that she knew what he was thinking. There was a good deal of telepathy between them, one always able to feel what the other was thinking; it was something they had fun with. But this time, he didn't like the idea.

"You hit Louis," she reminded him, "and he's your friend."

"He had ants going up his leg," Max said, eyes rolling back. "Lots of them."

"What got into you, Max?" she asked, a lump in her throat. "You've never been a boy for fighting, you've never hit anyone."

"Haven't I?"

"Of course not, dear. You're a good boy. You always have been."

"I don't know what happened. He had blood on him, it was all down his face."

"Because you hit him. Don't you remember?"

"I don't think I do," said Max, rubbing his face and running his hands through his hair.

"Why did you do it?"

"I don't know."

"Try, my love. It only happened about an hour ago. Please," she said, wanted to appear calm, "try to remember."

Max couldn't see why it was so important to her, but if she wanted him to do something – anything – he would.

"I think... I wanted to be with Claire," he said, embarrassed. "And he said... That she was his girlfriend."

"Is that why you hit him?"

"Yes," he said. "Claire has to go out with me."

"Claire will choose her own boyfriends. People can't be forced to love."

"She's going to be my girlfriend," he said obstinately.

"No, Max," said Irene, visibly unsettled. "You can't force people. Max, look at me. You're a good boy. You're going to go to Louis' house and ask him to forgive you, he's your friend. We have to be good to our friends, respect them. He really looked up to you, and now he's feeling rotten. Please, listen to me, always try to –"

"– to be my best self," said Max unenthusiastically. "I know, I know."

"Max," she said, mastering herself. "I don't want anything like this to happen again, ever. When you feel like you want to hit someone, you have to count to ten, try to think of another solution. Agreed?"

"Someone hit me once as well. I'm not the only bad one."

"That was a long time ago," she said nervously.

164

"Yes, but I can remember."

"Well, you ought to forget. Bad things are best forgotten," she said, staring him in the eye. Max felt suddenly curious.

"Why?"

"Because… It isn't good."

"But that boy hurt me. I got blamed, and I was only defending myself."

"I want you to forget that. It was a long time ago."

"But…"

"Max!" she cried, her voice breaking. "I said you should forget that!"

"Okay, but sometimes I remember without wanting to. I can't stop myself. I don't know how to make myself forget."

Relenting, she gathered him in her arms.

"You're right, sweetie. It isn't easy to forget. But sometimes we have to, because if not, it stops us from living. That was… Well, you weren't a good boy that day, either. But the best thing is to put it aside, move on. You were just defending yourself."

"Like today with Louis," he hurried to say.

"Yes, like today."

"He made me do it."

His mother gave him an imploring look.

"No, Max, nobody makes us do that. If you find yourself feeling those things again, you must promise me that you'll try to think, take yourself off somewhere quiet, and think about what's going on. You can't just go around threatening people. They'll start to hate you."

"Yes."

"Promise me you'll go and say sorry to Louis this afternoon"

"I promise."

The doorbell rang, and his mother tucked him in, saying:

"Good boy. Now, you stay here and rest a little while."

She blew him a kiss from the door and shut it softly behind her. Max got up, went over to the door and tried to listen. It was a day when he felt he wanted to know everything.

"I thought you weren't coming by anymore," he heard his mother say wearily.

"I had to see to some things," said Drake. "How is he?"

"I don't know. First, he says he doesn't remember, then that they made him do it. He still remembers the incident from four years ago. Not clearly, but still…"

"What did he say?"

"That someone hit him too. He doesn't remember at all clearly."

"He doesn't remember how… How he hit the other boy?"

"No, I don't know," said Irene, becoming desperate. "He should forget it."

"I already told you about my sessions with him. He's very unwell. Sooner or later, all that's inside him will come out. It isn't as simple as it seems, Irene. You can't hide him," Drake said gently. "You should let him come with me."

"No!" she cried. "Don't even think about taking my boy away."

"Irene, he needs help. He could get worse, he's just a boy now but he'll grow up… We don't know what might happen. He isn't right."

"I don't believe any of all that. He's a normal boy."

"No, he isn't. He's the same as his father and you know it."

"His father is a murderer," she snarled. "God! I can't believe this is happening."

"Calm down, my dear. It's going to be okay."

"How could we have been so irresponsible?"

"We weren't, we were just trying to -"

"To what?" she cried. "To bring one monster back to life via another monster. All those ghastly ideas, all those absurd beliefs… We were stupid to follow him, to believe him. He's crazy, it shouldn't have taken us so long to see. And now Max will have to shoulder the burden his entire life."

"There's nothing we can do now, except wait and see if we've been successful. Think that maybe it wasn't simply the madness of three boisterous teenagers…"

Irene shot him a hard look.

"There are only two possibilities," said Drake, brightening up, "and both are quite fascinating…"

Irene shook her head as though to banish a ghost.

"If the ritual was successful… And he is Crowley."

"Says somebody who claims to want to heal people? Your head's so full of nonsense. I can't believe you think that's all real."

"We know nothing about the mind, or about the soul, or whatever it is that remains after death, if indeed anything does."

"You're right about that. We know nothing."

"And what if we believe it was an adolescent game but in fact it did actually happen?"

"If so, may God forgive us for bringing a demon like that back to life."

"You used to think differently."

"I used to be a little girl, spellbound by a couple of eccentric young men, by fantastical ideas about magic, superhuman powers and immortality. I would have done anything you asked of me. In fact," she said dejectedly, "I did. I can't believe you still think there's any truth in those ideas."

"I know that I will find something in that the end. I don't know where, or how, but I will."

"And how many lives will you destroy in the process?"

"I don't know," said Drake pensively.

"You're so like Aldo sometimes. You'll stop at nothing. You believe you're the only ones who have the right to life. I didn't think you were on his side."

"I'm not. I'm working alone now. Aldo is too unwell – not a description I like but… I must say, he's getting worse all the time, not that anybody knows."

"You'll end up behind bars as well for covering up his insane doings."

"Forget about him," said Drake. "Max needs help. I have my own sanatoria where he could stay, he'd want for nothing."

"You already know my thoughts on that subject."

"You can't hide him forever. Something terrible will happen one day."

"Shush, he'll hear you!" she said suddenly. "Look, you ought to go. I don't feel very well."

"As you wish, my dear. But don't say I didn't warn you."

There was a silence, and then the sound of the door opening.

"Call me if you need anything, anything at all."

"You know I will," she said, calmer now.

Max jumped back into the bed when he heard his mother's footsteps coming down the hall. She pushed open the door softly, in case he was asleep. She smiled, and he smiled back.

"Hungry?"

They ate an early lunch before lying down together on a lounger in the porch for their siesta. It was a warm, sticky afternoon. When they woke up, their hair was plastered across their foreheads and both were sweating copiously.

"You look like a little chick," she said, pushing his hair to one side.

She kissed him on the crown, where he had a cowlick, while he rubbed his eyes, bleary from the heat.

"Go take a shower," she said. "Then you need to go to Louis' house."

Max nodded mechanically.

It was ten past five when Max cycled off in the direction of Louis' house. The road brought him to the dirt track that led there, but he stopped for a moment. In the distance, he could see Villa Belza shining in the sun. He half closed his eyes. The sea shone and glittered intermittently, as if to send him an encrypted message he had to unlock. He suddenly felt wonderful, with a great rush of energy that was beyond his childish understanding. He turned the handlebars and cycled decisively in the direction of Louis' house. He stopped in the road outside, getting down from the bicycle and walking it slowly toward the garden wall. Standing on tiptoes, he glimpsed Louis lying beneath a tree reading a comic. He had a piece of blood-stained cotton wool poking out of one nostril.

"Psst... Louis," whispered Max.

The boy looked up and saw Max between the bushes.

"Hey, Louis, come on. Come over here."

Louis put a hand to the cotton wool. He pushed it further inside his nose as a reminder that he was injured and got grudgingly to his feet.

"What do you want?" he said from the other side of the wall.

"To say sorry for this morning."

"Right," said Louis dryly.

"I'm really sorry, Louis," said Max, hanging his head. "I didn't mean it. You're my best friend."

"Well, it doesn't really hurt now," said Louis, without rancour.

Max stood saying nothing, as though mute with remorse.

"Seen the new Bygone Heroes?" said Louis, holding up the comic, unable to make Max feel guilty any longer. "Mum and Dad got it for me this morning. That's the good thing when bad things happen, they always buy me a present."

Max looked up and gave the cover an interested look.

"Why don't we go out for a ride?" said Max. "We can find some place to read it."

"I'll go get my bike."

Louis disappeared for moment, before emerging with his bicycle and crossing the garden.

"My parents are having their siesta," he said in a low voice. "I need to be back before they wake up."

They mounted their bicycles and took the track that led to the white meadow. The heat was unbearable. The only noise was the low drone of the cicadas, along with the occasional bark of a dog in the distance. The blinds on the houses they passed were all lowered, to keep the heat at bay. The entire town seem to be under a self-imposed curfew, everybody hunkering down inside the cool, stone houses waiting patiently for the heat to pass. The boys left the bicycles against a small oak tree and made their way into the golden meadow. Max went first with Louis behind, the comic rolled up under his arm.

"Where are we going?" asked Louis, who was bathed in sweat.

"There's something I want to show you," said Max, not turning around.

They stopped in front of a foul-smelling pothole. It was some nine metres deep, and perhaps a metre and a half across. It was the only one around where a metal fence with spikes, now useless and broken down, had been erected to prevent accidents.

"I saw something down there the other day," said Max.

"What?" asked Louis, curiosity piqued.

"I don't know. Something golden. I think it was a gold coin."

"No way."

Stepping over the fence, they both peered in. Unlike the other potholes, the interiors of which were marshy at best, this still had a little water at the bottom. No more than a few centimetres of muddy liquid, a rank, rotten-smelling soup moistening the stones.

"I can't see anything," said Louis, screwing up his eyes.

Max had stopped looking inside the pothole. He was looking intently at Louis instead, disparagingly. He knew what he wanted to do. He'd known ever since he saw the sea glimmering in the distance. But why would he? Louis was his friend. He was genuinely fond of him. But, he thought, that was irrelevant; he'd also been fond of Philippe when the two of them had fought four years earlier. Then, too, he had sensed a terrible urge to react to the love he felt. He could no longer recall why he'd thrust the pen into the roof of the boy's mouth, but he couldn't forget the blood that had come gushing out of his mouth, splashing down on the tiles in the school toilets. He looked at Louis again: truly, he liked him. He was fun and friendly. Max could even understand why Claire preferred him. Louis always made them laugh, always shared his sweets, while everyone else always kept their favourites for themselves. Going up behind him, he put one hand on his head and one on his waist.

"What?" Louis stammered.

"Nothing," said Max, giving him a push.

Louis' head made a sickening crack upon contact with the wet stones at the bottom. This was followed by a brief splashing, as though the boy were trying to swim in that dirty puddle. After a few seconds, his legs stopped kicking, and everything went silent. Max glanced indifferently down and caught a glimpse of Louis' crumpled form. He'd fallen headfirst, and his arms were stretched out behind his body like a pair of broken oars. One of his shoes had come off, and one leg was twisted upwards against the pothole wall, as though he were trying to do a handstand.

"Louis," whispered Max. "Louis, can you hear me?"

There was no answer.

"I have to go. I promised my Mum I'd come and say sorry, and then be straight back."

Turning, he picked the comic up off the ground, straightened it out and rolled it up again. He left the meadow and got on his bike. Before cycling off, he wondered for a moment if he shouldn't leave the comic in the basket of Louis' bike, but Louis wouldn't be needing it. Nobody would accuse him of stealing it. He pedalled slowly away. It was too hot to go any faster. He took a small detour, up and over some mounds of sand that recreated a motocross circuit; cresting them, he stood up on the pedals as he'd seen people doing in rallies. He went back towards Louis' house. Propping the bike outside, he went to the front door, and tried to make as much noise as he could. The whole world lay in silence, as though everything had stopped and everyone, except him, had been thawed by the heat. Though the door was open, he rang the doorbell and waited. Louis' mother soon appeared, looking somewhat sleepy, her hair dishevelled.

"Hello, Max," she said quietly.

"Who is it, Barbara?" came a voice from inside the house.

"It's Max, my love," she called back. Then, turning to Max with fingers interlaced: "Well then, Max: what was all that about?"

"Nothing, Mrs Jacob," said Max, chagrined. "It was all my fault."

"I don't like you boys fighting. You're great friends."

"What do you want, young man?" asked the father, making no attempt to hide his displeasure.

"Pierre, please," said the wife. "They're just kids, it's normal for kids to fight."

"Well, let it be the last time," said the father, wagging a finger.

"Pierre! Be quiet. Please, come in, Max," she said, giving his hair a stroke. "Louis is probably in his room. Go on, go and make up with him. I'll make some lemonade."

Max went in, glancing around as though actually expecting to find Louis sitting playing with his toy cars. Up in his room, he saw his toys, his tennis pumps, a couple of pairs of socks rolled up into balls, Louis' insect collection. The window was open and a light breeze was blowing – Finally, though Max. He closed the door and went to the kitchen.

"Mrs Jacob."

"What is it?"

"Louis isn't in his room."

"Oh, I'm sorry. He must have gone out to play with David. I think they'd been planning to meet up. But don't worry, when he gets back, I'll tell him you came by to say sorry."

Max nodded, smiling.

"Here," she said, holding out a glass of freshly squeezed lemonade. "It's so hot!"

Max drank while Louis' mother made coffee for herself and his father. When he'd finished, he thanked her and said a polite goodbye. Louis' father looked up from his book as Max passed him on the porch.

"Bye, Mr Jacob," Max smiled.

He gave no answer, going back to his book without moving a muscle. When Max reached the gate, he heard Louis' mother reprimanding her husband: "You're more of a child than any of them..." When he reached his bike, he saw the comic in the basket. Instinctively, he picked it up and flicked through. There was absolutely no doubt in his mind: Bygone Heroes was the best comic out there. The stories were amazing, its heroes were the bravest and the female characters the best-looking in any comic anywhere. He spent a short while reading, before dropping it back into the basket. He liked to draw as well. And, according to his mother, he wasn't bad either. He thought he'd spend the rest of the day at home, see if he could copy the pictures. Maybe one day I'll get good enough to do them exactly as they are, he thought.

His mother was at the sink doing the washing up when he got back.

"Talk to Louis?" she said, pushing the hair back off her brow with her forearm.

"No. He wasn't in."

"Oh, that's a pity."

"Going to my room for a bit," he said casually.

She said nothing, but simply watched the small figure of her son walk away, soon to become a gangly teenager, soon to lose that childish roundness and become full of incomprehensible edges and corners. When Max went into his room, she sat down next to the window and began writing in her diary. The same diary that Max read in secret when she wasn't around, and thanks to which he was privy to her thoughts in crucial moments. Irene saw Max as a sweet boy, but one with character, something she liked. He acted strangely from time to time, agreed, but so did all children. Max was intelligent, far more intelligent than other children his age. Drake's comments meant nothing to her. Max was a normal boy. Well no, he was special. But being different was no sin. She would see to it that all went well for him, and Drake would be forced to eat his words – all those expert diagnoses. She would show him, and the rest of the world, that Max was a normal boy, a good boy. The mistakes she had made in her youth wouldn't come back to haunt him. Unlike Drake, she had grown up; and, unlike Aldo, she was sane. She knew what she had to do. Max was her son. Nobody knew him like she did. She would make an upstanding man of him.

Though it pained her to do so, she wrote down her memories of her younger days, a time when she'd been so taken by Aldo and Drake and had allowed herself to be drawn into dubious but fascinating territory with the promise of incredible new abilities and powers. She scorned all that now, and despised herself for having allowed an outside party – an innocent, defenceless one at that – to get caught up in such madness. Max had been conceived on the basis of a macabre proposition. And only afterwards, when it was all too late, had she realised the magnitude of her mistake. Her fascination with the pair passed, and the reality of her situation imposed itself. Then she realised that what she had seen as originality was, in fact, madness; what she had thought audacity, was but immaturity. Aldo had used her to carry out his murky plans, and Drake, just as enthralled as she was then, had succumbed to Aldo's incipient madness, with no thought for the consequences. Though she knew that Drake loved her, Aldo represented the culmination of his most profound preoccupations. She realised that Drake had an almost irrational fascination with anyone not in their right mind, and Aldo's eccentricities, far from disappointing him, strengthened their bond.

Aldo had become a megalomaniac determined to put in to practice all the perverse ideas that came to him and Drake, who initially acted as the voice of his conscience, abandoned his Jiminy Cricket role and simply observed him passively, convinced he'd found the oracle he'd always dreamt of. But he wasn't the only one to succumb to his crazy ideas. When Irene realised her son would come into the world surrounded by seers, schizophrenics and desperados who would turn him into a circus freak, an embodiment of their vile minds, she decided to escape, to forsake them and have her son by herself. She didn't know whether it was chance or fate that had brought Drake back into her life, and though she knew he'd never say anything, because he still loved her, she still feared any traces Aldo might have left in him. That phantom would always be there. However, much Drake swore he'd got over Aldo, she knew he found a secret delight in observing her child, that Drake wanted to discover whether Max was a copy of Aldo more than anything else in the world. If his genes marked out by madness had been passed on to his son or if, on the contrary, his infantile desire to resurrect the last great magician in the West had been successful and they were in the presence of a mystery beyond understanding.

She'd had to cede to Drake's wishes, and she would have to go on doing so. She hadn't been able to deny him those days with Max. If Drake were to get angry, she and Max had a great deal to lose. Drake was the only one who could shield her from Aldo, and perhaps help her with Max. If she put her mind to it, she could ensure Drake did what she wanted. Not only because he loved her, but because they represented something important for him. Drake was a man deeply marked by obsessions and fetishes, and she knew that men like that were easier to control. He'd never tell anyone their secrets, and would be sure to protect them just as long as she allowed him to stay in their lives – allowed him to carry on observing Max, if only at a distance. He'd keep the truth to himself merely to continue having her, Max's mother, his most pressing obsession and the wife of the man he'd always admired profoundly. In a way that she found difficult to acknowledge, she too felt something for Drake. But it was a mixture of necessity and familiarity that bound her to him, rather than any sincere or heartfelt kind of love. It was very difficult to live in fear, half expecting Aldo to show up on the doorstep, to force her to share their son. Now though, Drake had him "under control" in one of his sanatoria, and that meant they could perhaps settle somewhere, and begin a new life. She'd allow Drake to study Max at a distance, and that way everybody would be happy. Everybody except her. But she'd accepted some time ago that she must pay for her mistakes, and all that mattered now was that Max should grow up like a normal boy, should have the chance to settle somewhere and make positive, lasting friendships. Perhaps, just perhaps, not everything would go badly from now on.

She took off her apron, left the diary on the coffee table and went to see if Max wanted to go out for ice cream. There was a light breeze now and she opened the living room windows on the way through.

"Max!" she said, bursting into his room. "How about an ice cream?"

Max was sitting at his desk, and gave a start when she came in, hurrying to slide something beneath his drawing pad. It was less the movement than the gleam in his eye that caught her attention. The look was as though he had more to hide than adult magazines.

"What have you got to hide?" she asked, smiling.

"Nothing."

"Nothing? Is that why you jumped ten feet in the air when I came in?"

Max tried to smile, but it seemed more like a grimace.

"Come on! What is it? Not one of those magazines, is it?"

"No."

"Well then, what is it?"

"Nothing. Leave me alone."

His tone made her feel even more worried.

"Max, come on. It's me. I'm not going to tell you off, but if it's a magazine, give it to me. You know I don't like you looking at that filth. You're still a boy. There are far more interesting things for children your age... though you might not think so."

Max sat stock-still, waiting for her to go. But she had no intention of leaving before finding out what he was hiding.

"Max, don't make me angry," she said eventually, making it clear that the joke was over now.

Max pulled out Bygone Heroes, Issue 37, and showed it to his mother.

"Why didn't you want me to see that?" she laughed. "Silly boy. You know I don't mind you reading this. I wouldn't want to spend money on something like this, but if somebody lent it to you, I'm not going to take it away."

Max said nothing. He knew it was only a question of time before she guessed what had really happened, but there was also a chance nobody would work it out. Perhaps they'd think Louis had run away to another country. Sometimes people ran off, like his own father. And you never saw them again. Irene flicked through the comic momentarily, before looking at Max again. Then she knew that something else was going on. He was avoiding her gaze, and she could see something fearful in his posture, a kind of fear she'd never inspired in him.

"Max, what's going on? Think I'm going to tell you off? When have I ever given you reason to be afraid?"

Max said nothing.

"Max, look at me." She went over and knelt down: "You don't need to be afraid, unless... You didn't steal it, did you?"

"No!" he replied, feeling insulted.

"Are you sure? If not, why are you so jumpy?"

"I'm not jumpy."

"Max, tell me the truth. You stole it. If not, you wouldn't be acting like this."

"No, I swear I didn't steal it. I just borrowed it."

"Borrowed it? Who from?"

"Louis," he said quickly.

"You said you hadn't seen him."

Max turned his chair around and leaned his elbows on the desk with his back to his mother.

"Max, look at me. You said you hadn't been able to speak to him."

"I've got a headache, Mummy," he said glumly.

Standing up, Irene sighed deeply. She felt sure he'd stolen the comic, but it was turning out to be a day full of difficulties. Max seemed changed, absent. Perhaps it was better not to force the issue, leave him to himself and talk it over when things were calmer. In the end, it was only a comic. She went through to the lounge, picked up a book and sat down on the porch to read it. The rest of the day passed in silence, with her looking up from time to time, and the occasional contradictory thoughts interrupting her reading – things she noted down in her diary, her one escape from her endless solitude and desperation. Her one confidant. Something was bothering Max. Perhaps Drake's presence was the problem. He shouldn't worry about that: he only need say, and she would put a stop to Drake's visits. She'd do anything to make Max happy. But then, thinking it over, it struck her: why should she worry so much what a nine-year-old child thought? Wouldn't it be more natural for her to impose her will on him, and for him to make the effort to please her? Was she perhaps afraid of making him angry? Putting the book down on the wicker table, knowing it would be impossible to get back into it, she tried to clear her mind. The sun was very low now, almost touching the water. Max hadn't left his room all evening, he hadn't even turned on the light, though by now it would be difficult to see inside. Irene jumped to her feet, as though ejected by a spring. She went through the lounge and into Max's room, breathless with worry.

Max was there, sitting at his desk. Just as he had been when she went out three hours earlier. This time, he didn't jump. Putting down the ultramarine pencil he was holding, he looked up at her in surprise.

"What... what are you doing?" she stammered.

"Drawing," he said simply.

"Okay, well..." she said trying to contain herself.

A horrible, horrifying thought had come into her head. She'd seen him lying on the bed, dead... It had just been her imagination, a vision of death. If he had stolen the comic, it was her fault; if he had hit Louis, it was her fault. Max was utterly blameless. It was all down to her. She went over to him, arms outstretched.

"Here," she said, a lump in her throat.

Max stood up from his chair and hugged her half-heartedly.

"Don't worry about anything, sweetie," she said, raining kisses down on his eyes, mouth and cheeks. "Is there something on your mind?"

"No," he said bluntly.

"Does it bother you that Drake comes to see us?"

He said nothing.

"You don't need to worry. He won't come back again, if you don't want him to. Let's go for a walk along the seafront this evening, have an ice cream. Would you like that?"

Max nodded.

"Will you show me what you've been drawing?"

He went over to the desk and gathered up the scattered sheets of drawing paper. He proceeded to present them to her, like a low-ranking soldier putting his best foot forward on parade.

"They're lovely," she said in surprise. "Max, they're…"

Just then, the telephone rang, and she answered it while still looking at the pictures. Max knew who it was before she picked it up. It was Louis' mother.

"Hello? Ah, Mrs Jacob. How are you?" There was a pause. "Oh, I see!"

A change entered Irene's voice, from affable and chatty to doleful. She turned towards Max's room and saw him feet bare, hair dishevelled, leaning against the doorframe. His toes gripped the carpet. She dropped the pictures, which fell noiselessly to the ground, as one hand went to her mouth.

"Oh!" she said weakly, gasping. "No, I'm afraid not. He's been here all afternoon and evening," she said, trying to hide her breathlessness. "Yes, yes of course, don't worry… Fine, goodbye, Mrs Jacob."

Hanging up, she sat down with her back turned to Max. She couldn't turn around. He watched her from the door, biting his lip. He heard her sobbing. She leaned back against the table; her legs started to shake; her body broke out in a sweat. She couldn't turn around. A sharp pain gripped her chest, making it hard for her to breathe. She knows, thought Max, she always knows everything, just like me.

"Mummy?" he whispered.

"Max," she said.

Her tears were salty, she wiped them with her forearm and rubbed her face. She gave half-turn and looked over at him. How small he looked: it was as though she was seeing him several years younger. Before he had begun to grow, before he had lost that soft roundness she so adored.

"What have you done, Max?"

"Nothing."

"Where's Louis?"

"I don't know."

"When did he give you the comic?"

"Earlier."

"Where?"

Max said nothing.

"Where?" she cried, banging her fist down on the table.

"At his house."

"Why did you lie? Why did you say you hadn't seen him?"

Max said nothing.

"You know where Louis is, don't you?" she said, still crying.

"Yes."

Her hand flew to her mouth. She'd always known that something like this would happen: she saw it now. She'd always foreseen that. It was the fear that had secretly stalked her, day and night. There existed between her and Max a kind of communication that went beyond words. And that silent voice had been trying to tell her something was amiss, that she needed to watch out. Her son's faint voice had been crying out to her for years from the most confused part of his self, he needed help, that there, in the depths of his young soul, great darkness existed. There'd been a suggestion of it, however imperceptible, four years earlier, and she had refused to accept it. She knew that he sensed her thoughts, just as she did his, and yet she had ignored them. She had ignored the signals, tried telling him he was a normal child – a line she herself had bought. But what could she do? Let them lock him up in a sanatorium for the rest of his days? Abandon him to a cold, tiled cell in some remote location, cut off from all human warmth? It was her he needed, more than any treatment, more than any therapy.

"What have you done?" she said.

"If I tell you, you won't love me anymore. You'll send me off some place, I know it."

"What place?"

Once more the feeling of guilt grew in her chest. He could hear her thoughts clearly, as clearly as she had heard his entreaties.

"Nothing you've done will stop me from loving you. Nothing."

"I don't want to go away. I want to stay with you, Mummy."

"You will, but you have to tell me where Louis is."

"In a pothole," he said quietly.

She covered her hand with her mouth. Her head felt like it was about to explode. This couldn't be happening. It was too awful.

"You…?" she said, sobbing.

Max felt the palms of his hands begin to sweat, sweat beading down the back of his neck too. He was afraid. He didn't know what he was more frightened of, Louis's contorted body at the bottom of the pothole, his mother's anguish, or the constant threat of being sent away to a sanatorium.

"Why are you always thinking about the place with the white tiles?"

"What?" she said, still sobbing. "What place?"

She was having difficulty breathing. She felt she was being strangled. Her eyes stung, her eyelids felt as though they were on fire, and she could barely see him next to the door. The image of him was blurry, indistinct.

"Nobody's taking you anywhere," she cried, as if arguing with someone. "You're staying with me. You have to forget about everything, sweetie. I won't let anyone take my little boy away." She went over, knelt down and threw her arms around him. "You don't need to worry. Mummy won't tell anyone."

"I love you, Mummy."

"I know. They won't separate us, don't worry. It's all my fault, sweetie, you're a good boy."

"And what's going to happen to Louis? I'm worried about him. It was very dark in the pothole, and it will soon be night-time."

"Nothing. Nothing's going to happen to him," she said, sliding a hair clip into her hair. "Try to stop thinking about it."

Irene looked around, frightened for a moment that somebody had heard them. She rushed to shut the windows. Night had nearly fallen, and away in the distance the horizon was lit by lightning, though the sound of the storm had yet to reach the shore.

"Nobody must know that you saw Louis," she said, sitting Max down in a chair. "We'll say you were here all afternoon."

"I spoke to Mrs Jacob."

"What do you mean, you spoke to her? When?"

"Afterwards…"

"You went to the house afterwards?" she said, falling back onto a sofa. "My God!"

Her stomach felt like it was cramping up. She couldn't stop crying. She could see no end to it. Everything had changed, and so suddenly. It wasn't her fears any longer, or Drake's suggestions. Something real had happened. If anybody found out, they would be done for. Both of them would be locked up, and they'd never see one another again. Their lives would be spent surrounded by crazy people, murderers, precisely what she'd always feared. All her efforts to lead a normal life had slipped through her fingers… And yet, if they were able to stay together, wherever it might be, they'd be alright. Mrs Jacob came into her thoughts suddenly, and she retched. She tried to run to the kitchen or the bathroom but couldn't stop herself: she vomited across the living room floor.

"Mummy!" cried Max in fright. "Mummy, what's wrong?"

"Nothing, it's nothing. I'm fine. No. Stand back, I'll clean it up."

Max began silently crying. She knew he wasn't crying for Louis or at the prospect of being punished. It was for her, seeing her in this state, and she thought that if she didn't get a grip, the whole thing would become a traumatic memory for Max, and he'd find it even more difficult to forget the incident.

"There, I'm fine," she said with a smile. "All that heat today must have affected me."

Max looked at her questioningly, trying to discern some sign of pain on her face.

"Fine?" he said impatiently.

"Yes, sweetie. All okay."

He sat beside her on the sofa and they hugged one another. They sat quietly for a time, each staring into space, until night fell and the house lay in darkness. At some point flashes of lightning and the booming storm, which had come inshore now, woke them. They had fallen asleep, exhausted by a reality that was too fantastic. In the confusion of thunder and lightning, Max didn't know where he was, or what the time was. Irene glanced around, and remembered. Seeing Max clinging to her, she kissed his head.

"We fell asleep," she murmured. "It must be late."

She got up and turned on a light. Max blinked at the brightness, rubbing his eyes. It was raining hard, as though the heat had sucked up all the waters of the sea and they were now being dumped on the land. Glancing out the window, Max shivered.

"It's after one. Are you hungry?"

Max shook his head.

"Me neither. Let's go to bed."

Max climbed into the bed with his mother. The solitude of his own room was overwhelmingly frightening, as was the damp hole in which Louis' body lay. Above all he feared the storm.

That same night, while the two of them slept, the search for Louis was initiated. Extra assistance had been sent from Bayonne, speedboats and rescue workers. They expected to find the body in the sea. In the early evening, the waves had been good for surfing, and youngsters loved it when a swell came in, loved pushing the limits of what was deemed safe. Someone would drown each summer. The sea always returned what it had, with no apparent motive, borrowed. But this time it wasn't the sea. In the early hours they found his bike propped against a tree and, not far off, a boy of ten, body covered in mud and leaves, at the bottom of a pothole.

The doorbell rang early the next morning. Irene got up, full of foreboding. For a few seconds she went nowhere, still half asleep, but the bell rang again, and then again. She pulled the covers up over Max and padded to the front door. It was Drake.

"Irene, open up," he demanded.

She thought about just going back to bed. She didn't want to see him, but she knew he wouldn't go away. He must have already heard about Louis' disappearance. That was why he had come. Max got up and dragged himself over to the bedroom door, his hair a mess and his stomach in knots.

Drake had the day's newspaper under his arm. Stepping nervously inside, he shut door behind him and searched Irene's face.

"It was Max, wasn't it?"

"What are you talking about?"

"The child they found dead at the bottom of a pothole. That's what I'm talking about."

She gestured for him to keep his voice down and went into the kitchen to make coffee.

"I told you something would happen sooner or later, and you didn't believe me. Think I don't understand these things? That I don't know when somebody is in need of help?"

"Okay," she said wearily. "You were right, what of it?"

"What of it? Need I remind you that a child of ten is dead, and his mother is currently up to her eyeballs in tranquillisers because last night, when the body was found, she just about lost her mind..."

"No!" cried Irene. "Please!" She let go of the cup and fell to the ground. "I can't stop thinking about Mrs Jacob... God! There's nothing worse, nothing in all the world."

Drake crouched down and offered her a handkerchief.

"What do you plan to do?"

"In terms of?" she said, disconcerted.

"Does anyone know... anything?"

"No. Nobody saw them. Mrs Jacob called last night. Max..." she had to take a breath. "Max went round there to ask after Louis, after the..."

"But what did he tell you?"

"I didn't want to ask. If I make him think about it, he won't forget it."

"This isn't the way," said Drake. "You can't just act as though nothing's happened: it could all just happen again. Now we know."

"It won't happen again," she said.

"And how do you plan to go about stopping him? Are you going to shut him up for life?"

"I don't know," she said nervously. "But I won't let anybody take him away."

"He needs help. He's dangerous. You've seen now. How many Mrs Jacobs before you accept that?"

"You have to help me. He's just a boy."

"Your self-deception is endless. Even if you were to see it with your own eyes."

"He's my son!" she said, beating her breast. "He's all I have."

"He's Aldo's son too," Drake reminded her.

"Damn you, Drake! You aren't taking him away, I won't let anybody. Half his genes might be Aldo's, but the other half are mine. I'll do anything to give him a normal life."

"Normal? Like who? Like you? Look at you. You're trying to cover up for a nine-year-old murderer, one whose soul is branded with madness."

"My son is not a murderer!" she cried. "He just needs someone to explain clearly the difference between right and wrong. He's too young to understand."

"Just as Louis was."

She gave him a despairing look, and curled up on the floor once more. She knew her loss was far from the greatest; Mrs Jacob would be in her home, blinds down, breathing a deafening silence, filled by an immense emptiness that nothing would ever fill.

"If you take Max away from me, he'll have died along with Louis, as good as. I need you to help me. I need you to make him forget."

"Madness is not a thing that can be hidden. Sooner or later he will remember who he is."

"You can do it. I know you can. I'll let you study him, let you observe him at a distance," she begged. "That's what you've always wanted, isn't it?"

"And if they discover that it wasn't an accident? Haven't you considered that?"

"The rain will have washed away all the footprints. That meadow's dangerous. It's only surprising that it hasn't happened sooner."

Pensive, Drake ran his hand through his hair.

"Going to tell me you've got objections?" spat Irene. "Did you have any when you were covering up Aldo's 'interests'?"

"Aldo is in a sanatorium."

"He is now, but for a long time you hid the heinous things he did."

"Until I realised that was the only thing that could save him from prison."

"Please, Drake," she said. "I implore you."

"The first thing is to make sure nobody saw them. To make sure there isn't any evidence linking Max to what happened."

"There isn't."

"We'll have to ask Max and then wait to see what happens."

"No. I don't want him thinking about the subject anymore."

"The subject?"

"The more he thinks about it, the harder it'll be for him to forget. You said as much yourself."

"If you want me to help, we have to do it my way. The first thing is for you to find out what the police know. Go and see Mrs Jacob. Offer your condolences, then ask."

"You'll help us?"

"Of course I will. Anyway, I'm too much a part of your... family."

"We aren't a family. Don't even think about bringing Aldo into our lives"

"Yes, my dear. Much as it pains you, you are irremediably linked to him, as is Max. He was your partner. He is Max's father. Nobody can ever change that."

# XVIII

Oh, wash away these scarlet sins.

Lope de Vega

The sun shone in a cloudless sky. It beat down mercilessly on Irene and Max. It pursued them like an implacable finger of blame. They left home at mid-morning. She gave him her final instructions as to how to act at the Jacobs' house. She knew he wouldn't get it wrong: Max was a smart boy, quick on the up-take. She had promised they'd go to the beach after stopping by the Jacobs', and Max had brought his bag with bucket, spade and sand rake. Irene tugged on his hand while muttering niceties under her breath, stock phrases that, when the moment came and Mrs Jacob stood before her, she would have no difficulty repeating. She knew she needed to keep an eye on Max and the things he said, any giveaway looks he might make. Children, even the most intelligent ones, sometimes confuse reality and fiction, and at such a time anything Max said could be picked up on. She was sure they would ask him questions, Louis' father in particular…

"Remember everything I've said?"

"Yes, Mummy."

"Look at me, are you okay?"

"Yes, Mummy."

"If you feel like you can't do it, just pretend you're feeling ill. They'll understand, after all…" She stopped herself. She had been about to say that Louis had been his friend, and that they would understand if Max was sad, but saw that this might not be a good idea.

"Can we go for an ice cream afterwards?" said Max, looking towards the seafront in the distance.

"Yes, afterwards. For now, try to concentrate on what I've told you. If not, you know what's going to happen to us."

"Yes, Mummy."

Coming into the Jacobs' garden, they saw an assortment of cars parked alongside the garden wall. Max looked at the swimming pool and saw that it was covered in leaves and tufts from the lawn. It hadn't been cleaned since the storm. The Jacobs usually kept the water so clean that you could see a hair clip all the way down at the bottom without using goggles. But today the water was muddy, murky, there were even little piles of earth here and there on the bottom. Max thought he'd never get into that dirty water, nothing in the world could make him – it reminded him of the water at the bottom of the pothole…

One of Louis' aunts opened the door. A woman with a pinched, sorrowful look. She resembled Louis' mother somewhat, except for the very grey eyes and the frail, less youthful frame.

"Hello," said Irene. "I'm Irene Sinclair, and this is Max…"

"Come in, come in," said the woman resignedly, as though it didn't in fact matter who they were.

The house looked untidy. The air seemed murky and simulated. That struck Max the moment they set foot inside: the same atmosphere as at home the previous night. Something was missing, as though a hole had opened that nobody could see, but which everybody sensed with every single breath. A couple of men were pacing the living room, each staring at the floor, as though seeking an answer for what had happened from the grain of the floorboards. Three women sat whispering on a sofa and a third man stood, hands in pockets and back to them, looking out into the garden. They looked up and faintly acknowledged the new arrivals, nodding faintly. Then went back to whatever they'd been talking about.

"Barbara's in her room with our mother," said Louis' aunt. "Please, go through."

Irene felt far from comfortable. Squeezing Max's hand, she shot him a look. The light in the Jacobs' bedroom was as she had imagined: blinds down, the sunlight impertinently penetrating through the cracks. So seemingly indifferent in its triumphal brilliance to the awful events, the sun went on shining merrily as ever. Louis' mother had no desire to see the world outside, the way it carried on regardless, and Irene knew it. She didn't want to hear the cries of the children playing on the beach, or the seagulls calling overhead. At this time of day, the beach would be full of people enjoying the summer, going on with their holidays as unaware of her suffering as the sun itself. Next to Barbara was an older woman who looked downcast. She gripped her daughter's hand, which hung limp – gripped it as though fearing Barbara might tumble into an abyss only apparent to the pair of them. Although Irene saw it very clearly: it was right there in front of them.

Louis' mother looked different to Max, more like the woman who had let them in. Puffy-eyed, red-faced. Seeing Max enter, she held out a hand and burst into tears. Max placed his beach bag down on the floor, took her hand and let her hug him. He felt like the hug wasn't for him, that she wanted to feel the touch of a small body, one similar to Louis', whom she would never be able to embrace again. Max let his body go lax. There was a lump in his throat, but he managed to say, very quietly, almost directly in the woman's ear:

"I'm sorry."

She let him go. She straightened his hair and wiped her tears from his face with a handkerchief.

"Thank you for coming," she said.

"This is my mother," he said.

Irene went over to the bed. Her legs were trembling. She felt she might burst out crying herself at any moment, confess that it was all her fault. That her son had only been the instrument that had carried out something for which she was entirely responsible.

"I'm so sorry, Barbara," she managed to say. "I can't tell you how sorry I am."

She meant it. Louis' death was the worst thing that had ever happened to her. Because, after a fashion, it had happened to her too. She would never forget it, as long as she lived – and she would have to live with the memory all her days, just as Barbara would have to without Louis. But she couldn't allow Max to pay for something that was her fault. There would be no point in owning up now, in telling the truth. It wouldn't bring Louis back.

"I'm pleased you came," said Barbara. "Have you met my mother?"

She introduced them casually as if such formalities were absurd to her.

"If there's anything I can do..." said Irene, trying not to appear too affected.

"Thank you, though there isn't really. But I'm pleased to see Max. He and Louis were good friends, isn't that right?" She gave an uncertain smile. "I'm sorry the two of you didn't have the chance to make up."

"We don't want to be any trouble," said Irene, unable to stand it any longer. "We'll leave you in peace."

"Could I just go to Louis' room for a minute?" Max suddenly asked.

"What do you want to do that for?" said Irene, giving him a disapproving look.

"No reason, just to look."

"Of course you can," said Barbara.

Picking up his beach bag, Max hurried through to Louis' room. He opened the door and took a lungful of the air inside. It smelled different. He glanced behind him. Nobody was looking, but he shut the door just in case. Kneeling on the floor next to the bed, he reached into the bag and pulled out Louis' comic. He unfolded it, shook off the sand and flung it under the bed. He closed the bag and gave the room a final once-over. It was too quiet. Something was missing. He didn't like giving back the comic. It was one of the best he had ever read, but he knew he could be accused of having stolen it from Louis, even though he had only borrowed it. He didn't know if Louis was going to need it – wherever he was – but he had it back now just in case. He opened the door and said farewell to the room. He would never go inside it again, he knew. He shut the door and went back through to his mother. Irene was standing in the hallway, talking to Louis' grandmother.

"Do they know how it happened?" she asked.

"He went to play in the meadow and fell into a pothole, they think. Hundreds of times I told him never to go and play there. There are potholes everywhere, nobody bothers to fence them off properly. That means there are bound to be more accidents. I hope something will be done after this but... well. Nothing's going to bring Louis back."

"We ought to do something about it," nodded Irene, watching Max approach. "Demand that they close off the area..."

Max was worrying her. She was barely listening to Louis' grandmother. She'd had already established the key details and was answering mechanically while trying to catch her son's eye. It was clear that nobody suspected foul play. Everybody's ire was directed at the town council – that made her feel better. But at any moment Max could come out with something...

"Max!" she said, grabbing his hand so that he knew she was angry with him. "Let's go and say goodbye to Barbara, right?"

They said their goodbyes, repeating the condolences. Louis' father was at the hospital seeing to things, but they assured them he would appreciate them stopping by.

"Come and see us any time," Barbara said, not once but twice.

Max nodded, though he knew very well they would never set foot in that house again. Once they were out in the garden, Irene yanked on Max's hand, but said nothing. She wanted to put enough distance between them and the house to be able to speak.

"What were you up to? Didn't I tell you not to leave my side?"

"Yes, but…"

"You just had to make me worry, didn't you? Go off and leave me on my own."

"I just -"

"You just what?"

"Nothing."

"Nothing, is it now? What were you doing in his room?"

"I had to give Louis his comic back," he said quietly.

"What?" she said, confounded.

"He only lent it to me."

"But… have you any idea what you've done? How could you do something like that without asking me first? What if they can identify you by it?"

"I didn't think you'd let me…"

"Of course I wouldn't have let you. Nobody's going to be thinking about that comic now, but when they come to clean his room, if there's something in there, something of yours… Dear God!"

"There wasn't, Mummy. There wasn't."

"I told you to do as I said!" she shouted, losing her cool.

"I swear, there wasn't anything," he said. "I gave it a shake, and I looked on all the pages."

"Never again, Max never again. If anything like Louis happens again, I'll let them split us up. I swear it."

Max began sobbing silently. She wasn't joking. Irene quickened her pace, with him following behind at a distance, still tearful, begging her to forgive him. They spent the day on the beach, sitting between groups of normal people enjoying the weather and spending time with their families. Irene was prickly towards Max all day, and the boy spent hours feeling tense, hanging on his mother's every move. He placed his towel directly beside hers and curled up, watching her constantly. He searched her face for any hint of a smile, he collected shells and presented them to her, rubbed sun cream onto her back and was careful not to kick up the slightest bit of sand in her vicinity. But her pique lasted the entire day.

An elderly couple sitting nearby spent the day watching Max. Deeply tanned from head to foot and with lovingly preserved blonde hair, the woman got out of her hammock and winked at Max. He went grudgingly over, making no attempt to hide his low spirits. The woman beamed and offered to buy him a strawberry ice cream, and Max accepted because he'd spent the entire day asking his mother for an ice cream without getting an answer. He ate it under the contented gaze of the elderly couple, and, on finishing it, kissed the woman on the cheek. He knew that old women liked being kissed. Then, going back over to his towel, he heard the woman say she didn't know why some people bothered having children when they clearly didn't want them; God, she said, gave some people bread though they clearly had no teeth.

Max carried on watching his mother in silence. He couldn't bear the situation. He could put up with anything except this. He thought perhaps she was planning to take him to a sanatorium, as Drake had suggested – that she didn't love him anymore and would prefer not to have him around. He felt sickly, with no desire to play: something had changed between them. He had let her down, he thought, and things would never be the same again. But that afternoon, Drake stopped by the house to see them. He and his mother had a discussion: there was talk of money, and Drake offered them a monthly sum on the condition they maintain contact with him. Max knew their travels were not at an end, not because of needing to flee Aldo, but because Drake had discovered Max's inability to love. In the evening, the two adults explained to him, slowly and carefully, that they were all going to play a game together, a really fun game. Max guessed it was a ruse – from the way his mother was so serious, so clearly preoccupied, and from Drake's exaggerated friendliness. They sat him down on the sofa, put on some cheery music by Bing Crosby, and Drake began talking slowly, in a solemn monotone. Max couldn't remember the specifics of the game, but from that day on his mother became loving again.

Two days later they left Biarritz, never to return.

# XIX

The key premise in this argument is the claim that
my actions can be truly mine only if they are caused by
my character or something else about me. Bergson's
account of decision making as we actually experience it
from the inside enables him to refute this premise, for it
shows that there is only one way in which actions can be
truly mine, and that is when they are not caused by my
thoughts, but belong with them in the total flow of my
life history. In that context, they can be understood after
the event, but they cannot be causally explained or
strictly predicted beforehand.
Twentieth-Century French Philosophy
Eric Matthews

Max remained slumped on the floor of the bar. I bent down to take a closer look at him and placed the notebook down next to his hand. His face had relaxed in sleep, but I knew that beneath his deep, regular breathing, every fibre of his being was in conflict, a fight between the person he thought he was and the one he was now becoming. It hardly mattered anymore, I thought sadly. After this latest round of memories, nothing would be the same for him again. His inner cardinal points, those by which he navigated and moved forward in life, had ceased to be immovable constants. At a glance, from the carefree look on his face, one might think his mind was empty of all sinister thoughts, that everything in his life was flowing in a clear direction, driven by his own desires. I couldn't bring myself to wake him, to be the one to bring him back to the hell of consciousness.

It was becoming increasingly difficult for me to believe that these memories were Drake's invention. I myself had been able to verify that many of the things in Max's notebook (such as the fact that Shimts was an asylum, that Drake had an obsession with Crowley and that he'd been born in Yaroslavl) were in fact the case, and the upshot of this was that I felt unable to ignore everything else. Once more Max's degraded powers of recall had shown a surprising capacity for capturing details, for remembering the tiniest thing and ordering it all in an intelligent way. But accepting that his memories were true to life meant doubting certainties of my own. I found unsettling in the extreme the thought that Max had carried these past events with him for over twenty years quite unawares. If this kind of secret compartment existed in him, it could well exist in any person. Anybody might be the victim of a disturbed past. In a life of seeming transparency, one apparently without troubled waters and easy to elucidate might an individual's essence be lurking there, needing only a word or sign to surface? And what if it were true that a parasitic monster was hiding within Max? If his mother and Drake had taken his most elemental instincts and placed them somewhere not even Max could access? Perhaps Max had always secretly known that a being slumbered within him whose sum and substance was utterly at odds with the persona he presented to his mother and the rest of the world.

Max writhed for a moment, a bitter expression on his face. He was waking. I felt sick in the pit of my stomach. What would I say? How could I defend myself against his accusations? He associated me with the dark figure of his father; in his newfound vision of life, I was despicable. I was part of a story which only inspired horror, one in which I'd been the cause of his mother's suffering, of his sickly nature, as well as his rootless, nomadic existence. Without lifting a finger, I'd been transformed in his eyes. As he woke now, I felt he was about to be presented with new codes, a new set of information as to the nature of the world around him. I couldn't help but feel to blame for this new person I'd apparently become. I didn't need to be afraid, but I was. The moment Max opened his eyes, I would no longer be myself, but an image created by Drake's twisted desires. It was then that I was able to feel the full extent of his manipulations. An image of myself loomed over me, one that I didn't recognise but that, like Max, was proving impossible to ignore. This is exactly the way Drake engineers his patients, I thought, inserting in the subjective mind images whose reflections end up supplanting the originals.

How he had managed to prompt these memories in Max, and why at this precise moment, were both things I still couldn't understand. Inside the tangled chronology of a person's memories, is it possible to seize the instant when our present divided, and ceased to belong to us? If Max had reached this threshold it was because Drake wished it so. In the part of the notebook I'd just read, Max's mother had begged Drake to make the boy forget this unsound part of himself. Drake was the only person with the key to this parallel dimension. He was controlling and directing Max's mind like a captain on a ship's bridge. He was carefully parcelling out the information Max received, in a very controlled, very deliberate manner. He had him all to himself now. Finally, here was his chance to study his mind, and learn whether his ridiculous youthful experiments had been a success. Because Drake and the people working with him believed that Crowley could be alive within Max.

Drake had the capacity to keep the necessary inner equilibrium to allow his scientific mind and his mystical-fanatical delusions to coexist, while avoiding any doubt as to the validity of the theories proposed by either. It was that mystical, cruel angle I found most disconcerting. It was capable of destroying a human being's balance, breaking the self to the point of the ultimate, most terrible consequences, treating people like guinea pigs and, at the same time, still believing that inside every person existed a unique, sublime spirit nonetheless as changeable as one's Sunday best. These beliefs peacefully coexisted. One merely needed to look at the man to see how convinced he was of his truth, how he believed in his own theories – no regrets, no doubts. Any sane person would see that he was mad. But there was no inner conflict, and that distinguished him from his patients.

He believed passionately that his studies and discoveries would bring to psychiatry data that would advance knowledge of the human brain. He defended his theories so fiercely that people treated him as a genius rather than a madman. It's true that genius and lunacy have always been close, but it wasn't till then that I realised how fine was the thread separating them. His intellect together with his boundless imagination and huge self-confidence transformed him into someone who was listened to and admired. Drake had something to say. He had turned his personal obsessions into scientific arguments. The mysteries that had fascinated him as a child were now the engine driving his research and it was evident that his forcefulness wasn't simply in his mind, he knew how to communicate it and infect others with his lunacy. It was strange. He was doing all he could to zero in on the madness gene, but it somehow never struck him that madness was a contagious illness.

Max blinked gingerly. He appeared dazzled by the dim light in the café. His eyes were puffy, bloodshot. He glanced around, propping himself up on an elbow, before collapsing forward once more, as though downed by an invisible bullet. He was unconscious, full of drink, but soon he'd be back, and he'd remember murdering Louis. I sat down next to him and took a drink of whiskey. Max was right, whiskey was one of the most horrible drinks around, but it hit you, and had a fire to it and, above all, it helped one to forget. But why was I drinking? I didn't need to forget things, quite the opposite. What I needed was to remember how I had wound up there. Then everything else would fit into place. The image of my hotel room came to mind, my belongings strewn all around, my books and clothes. Would this be just the beginning? Perhaps within a week I would begin to forget the reason for my journey, and in a month I might have forgotten all that I knew about my sister's secret life, and in a matter of a year not even remember I once had a sister. In Drake's office I'd had the sensation that some part of my mind was falling apart. An indescribable terror had come over me, the feeling of something lurching too close – I wanted to flee, get as far away as I could from this loony bin, go back to my home, my life – workaday and monotonous, yes, but mine, when all was said and done. If I did nothing, if I let Drake go on controlling things, I'd end up stuck in this place for the rest of my days.

If it was a game he wanted, I'd give him one. I had no choice. It was that or go slowly crazy in this place. I wondered if it might be possible to make Drake think that I was remembering, that the details of the life he attributed to me were gradually coming back – and thereby make him trust me, and in the process win back my freedom. I knew enough about this Gerald person to play the role. A brilliant psychiatrist with a liking for outlandish things. For now, I didn't need to make an effort to seem to be remembering, I could pretend that something inside me was coming back to life following our conversation, after reading Max's notebook.

But then again, might this not be the very trap he wanted me to fall into? To make me believe that my only option was to convince him that I was the person he had assigned to me – only for me to begin, in time, to get used to being that person? Perhaps Drake had already counted on me attempting to play the role, and whatever I did or said would only serve to tighten the grip of the spider's web into which I had fallen. I again had the sensation that even my thoughts were being observed, directed, that nothing I could do – however spontaneous it might seem – could catch them off-guard. All my options were quite clear to them in their laboratory, and they'd already engineered them so that any movement would be registered in advance of me making it.

Somewhere in the bar a camera was recording everything we said and did. Clearly, there was some place in the town from which this monstrous network of spies was being controlled, and in that place all my conversations with Bezel were being stored, each of our sexual encounters, as well as my conversations with Max and my arrival in Shimts. Yes, all this information had been registered, information that I needed access to more than anything in the world to confirm that I was being manipulated, that in some way I too was being infected.

I was suddenly struck by a thought I had been trying to avoid: what if Drake turned out to be right? And, finding myself in front of that screen, I were to learn that I'd been brought to Shimts under sedation? My car wasn't at the hotel and that was the only way I could have got here. I tried to stay calm. My throat felt tight, tense. This is what they want, I thought, to make you unsure, to force you to submit. The car could have been taken away, and this confusion could be a product of their manipulations. You have no idea if they're drugging you, if they've hypnotised you in your sleep and that was why you knew the way to Drake's office.

I broke out in a sweat. It felt like my hands were trembling. And next? There still wasn't any next. If it were true that they had brought me here under sedation, Drake himself would have shown me the recording. Though there was every chance that his plans were crueller still, and that he wanted me to lose my mind slowly, bit by bit. It was the food, I was sure. And sleeping. I knew that while a person slept ideas could be introduced into their mind that they wouldn't remember until a code word was spoken. The same as happened with hypnosis, it was exactly that.

If they wanted me to act like a madman, I would. If they wanted me to be someone else, I would be. But only until Drake put his trust in me and let me operate of my own free will. If I could avoid forgetting my true identity, nothing would happen to me. I needn't be alarmed by the appearance of unfamiliar images in my mind, because this was only part of the "treatment". They could film my movements and the expressions on my face, but they could not read my thoughts. Those at least were my own. If the feeling I'd had in Drake's office came back, I simply needed to remind myself that all was illusory. Another shiver ran down my spine. I wasn't sure if everything would turn out as I envisaged it, but there was nothing for it but to dive in and take on the choppy waters alone.

In all likelihood, I would end up drowning – but I wouldn't go down without a fight.

I saw myself sitting on a bench in the Jardin du Luxembourg, watching young tourists strolling by, their whole lives ahead of them, and I remembered when that was all I ever did: watch the world go by. A time when I looked ahead to an uneventful, peaceful old age, spending my evenings in the parks and strolling along the banks of the Seine. How far away that all now seemed.

# XX

The relationship between victim and criminal
is more complex than the law is prepared to admit.
The Murdering Mind
David Abrahamsen

I gave Max a few light slaps about the face. He was curled up in a ball on the floor.

"Max," I whispered. "Come on, you need a shower."

"Get off," he groaned.

"Max, you're lying on the floor. Get it together."

He opened his eyes and frowned, clearly wishing I would just go away.

"What do you want?" he muttered.

"For you to get up. You can't spend the rest of your life lying in a heap."

"Are there more important things to do?" he said, scratching his face.

He got laboriously to his feet and took a seat. He looked befuddled, his hair was a mess.

"What's the idea? Planning to spend the rest of your days in a drunken stupor?"

"Not a bad idea. Hausen!" he slurred. "Bring me another one of those disgusting whiskeys."

"No, Hausen, don't bring him anything. We're going." Lifting him up under his armpits, I got him to his feet. "Lean against me. Come on, walk."

We left the bar. Max was having difficulty putting one foot in front of the other. He was still half asleep. His face was contorted, with dark shadows under his eyes that made him look a good deal older. As we went along, he peered at everything smiling idiotically, as though it were the first time he'd seen anything. We went along the high street, which was busy at that hour; passersby looked on with some interest. Max dragged his feet as we reached the small alleyway that led to the castle lane. He was too heavy. He stumbled several times on the way up the incline, could barely stand, and the next time he tripped, took me down with him. When I fell flat on my face in a muddy puddle, Max burst out laughing – unpleasant, hysterical laughter. He too was covered in mud, absolutely soaked. He looked terrible. He was like an instrument gone completely out of tune, playing only dissonant notes.

"Fucking rain!" I cried, getting up. "Come on, on your feet. Now you've got no excuse for not having a shower."

"Neither have you," he said, thrusting his hands into the mud.

We got to the hotel and went inside. As we were on our way through the hall, Bezel emerged from the kitchen.

"What's happened to you two? You look like you've been in the trenches – why are you all camouflaged like that?" she said with a smile.

"Very funny, Bezel. Help me with Max."

"What's wrong with him?"

"He's blotto."

"Our Max, drunk?" she said affectedly.

"He needs a shower. Do you mind helping him with that while I go and get cleaned up myself?"

"Are you joking?" she said, her face lighting up. Of course she didn't mind. She'd been waiting for this since the moment Max had arrived. It didn't take a genius to work it out.

"Don't you worry, I'll get him clean as a baby. You go and take a hot bath."

I left him leaning against the door to his bathroom. He was sufficiently far gone not to protest at Bezel taking over. I waited for her to turn on the taps, helped get him undressed and then went off to my room. I needed to unwind, take a moment to consider my course of action. It could be a few hours until Max's drunkenness wore off and Bezel would be busy with him. That gave me a bit of time for myself, to shut myself in my room and order my thoughts. I turned on the hot tap, shut the bathroom door and took a seat on the edge of the bath. I began removing the grime on my face and hands with a wet cloth.

In Max's room, meanwhile, Bezel took off the last of his clothes. Max made no resistance, letting her strip him and following docilely as she led him to the nearly full bath.

"In you get, then. You're filthy."

Max gave a timid smile and said nothing. He stumbled as he tried to get in, throwing out a hand to grab onto Bezel, or a wall, but he was so drunk all he did was flap his arms, as though trying to take flight. He fell into the water, onto his rear end, splashing Bezel all over. He began to laugh hysterically. Bezel was drenched, her hair plastered down over her face and her clothes dripping. Max suddenly stopped laughing and looked serious. He stared unblinkingly at her; eyes wide in surprise.

"Max?" she said.

Bezel looked down at her blouse. Her breasts were clearly visible under the wet silk. The blouse had gone skin-tight, and Max couldn't tear his eyes away. She gave a mischievous smile, but Max didn't notice.

"One moment," she said, going out of the bathroom.

She went to the bedroom door, took out a bunch of keys, locked the door and put the keys back in her pocket. This was her chance and she wasn't going to let it pass her by. Nobody was going to interrupt. She had him all to herself. When she came back in, Max was still staring at the same point in space, as though she had never gone away and her breasts had remained hanging on the air before him.

"Give me your hand," she said gently.

Reaching over, she took Max's hand. He didn't blink. She brought his hand to her breasts and began gently caressing them. Max's hand was warm, and she shuddered at his touch.

"That's it, touch me. I know you want to. Go on, Max."

Bezel let go of his hand and Max went on touching her. He squeezed one of the breasts between his fingers, firm and smooth, and close to erupting beneath the tight-fitting blouse. Bezel undid one of the buttons, and then another. Max's eyes grew even wider. He brought his other hand up and began to squeeze both breasts, as though trying to milk them.

"Wait, wait," she said, in ecstasy.

She was sure that Drake would be watching; this very likely added to her excitement. Getting to her feet, she undid the zip on her skirt. Dandling the skimpy fabric at the sides of her knickers for a moment, she slid them down her legs, and then stood naked before Max. She ran her fingers over her pubis, stroking the copious covering of hair and reaching out for Max, who in turn reached out – as though across a great distance – and gave that mysterious triangle a tentative stroke. Bezel moaned, and Max drew her violently towards him. She lowered herself onto him in the bath, breasts bobbing against his torso. He gasped and pulled his hand away.

"Oh well, not to worry," said Bezel, with half-smile. "Not so terrible for a first time."

Max, seeming to wake from his trance, blushed. He reached down between his legs and sobbed bitterly.

"Don't be like that," she said affectionately. "It's completely normal. Next time it'll be better, you'll see."

"No," he whimpered. "There won't be any next time."

"Listen to you! Of course there will. Come back as often as you want."

Max looked disgusted, pushing her off him so that their bodies were a little way apart. He glanced at her sternly, and saw her warm, steaming breasts, firm and round. He reached down between his legs again, face turning crimson once more.

"You whore," he said quietly. "You slut, you dirty, perverted trollop..."

"Turn you on, does it, calling me names?" she said impishly. "Do your worst, I don't mind. I'll take it all, sweet boy," she said, puckering her lips.

"Quiet!" shouted Max. He put his hands over his ears and began to sob.

"Don't be such a baby. Nothing's wrong."

"Get off me. Get out of here."

"What's wrong with you, Max?" she said, lifting herself out of the bath.

As she stood before him, her body firm and steaming, Max felt himself retch. He had drunk too much and wasn't used to it. He tried to hold back, but couldn't help himself from vomiting onto his hands. Bezel shrieked and tried to get out of the bath, but, surprisingly quickly, Max grabbed her by the hair and threw her back into the bath.

"Max!" she cried, as the vomit and water covered her body.

"You wanted filth, right?"

He thrust her head into the dirty water. She thrashed around, splashing water everywhere. As he lifted her up, she gasped for air.

"Max!" she said weakly.

"You wanted me to do it," he said, his eyes bulging. The veins on his neck stood out, his muscles straining and stiff. Bezel had gone pale. Perhaps it was now that she realised the danger she was in. Max's face had gone an unpleasant shade of purple. Every ounce of sweetness had evaporated, and he seemed no longer to be seeing her. As though he thought she was somebody else. He gritted and ground his teeth together, producing a bloodcurdling squeak.

"No," Bezel whimpered. "Max, no..."

He grabbed a handful of her hair, winding his hand around it as though gripping onto a rope to save his own life, and proceeded to bash her head repeatedly against the side of the bath. He was up on his knees, and Bezel was unable to regain her balance. He was too strong. He shook her about like a ragdoll.

"Whore!" he said, slamming her head down once more.

Her eyebrow split on the next impact and blood came gushing out. The bathwater reddened and Bezel, dazed, went lax, dropping like a sack into the dirty water. Blood covered her face. Her eyes rolled back in her head and she felt something slipping away.

"Did it not occur to you? Did it not occur, you dirty whore, that maybe I didn't want to touch you? That there was no point?"

Max let go of her. He got out of the bath and walked over to his jacket. Bezel tried to get up, but the blood clouded her eyes. She saw a version of Max in red, through clumps of sticky hair over her eyes. As he went out, she tried to stand, to get over to the door and lock it, but was barely able to move. If she could only get to her feet and reach out a hand, she'd get to the bolt. As she tried to regain her bearings, she saw Max come back in with his notebook and pen. He shut the door and locked it. She looked up at him in horror. Then, turning to the ventilation fan in the ceiling, behind which a camera was positioned, and glancing to her left where another was hidden in the wall, she said:

"Please, please don't let me die like this."

"Who's that you're talking to?" said Max.

But he gave her no time to answer. Mechanically, he took the cap off the pen, threw the notebook to the floor and snatched Bezel up by the hair. He lifted her up and plunged the pen into her neck. With a gurgle, she looked upwards in surprise, as though thinking, this wasn't part of the script, it couldn't be happening. And then, at the very last, I imagine it all became only too clear. She realised that Drake had used her to provoke Max, to bring him to fever pitch, as a way of testing out his theories. She had been nothing but bait, something to fill the gap in a question that Drake hadn't been able to answer. From the very beginning, this had been the way it was all headed. Drake knew it would end like this for her, because he also knew Max and was intent on seeing him in action. Someone, in a white room somewhere, was watching her bleed to death. That person would take some notes, before rewinding the tapes and watching them back, over and over again, just as I was to do later.

Turning to Max, Bezel saw him staring up at the ceiling. Perhaps he was asking himself why she'd been looking in that direction so intently, or perhaps entertaining the idea of stabbing her with the pen again, seeing she still wasn't dead. Bezel propped herself against the wall and saw the bath water red with her blood. Touching her neck, she found that the blood was no longer spurting out so vigorously. She watched as Max went over to the sink and washed the pen, thorough and meticulous as a surgeon. He dried his hands slowly, as though trying to work out how they had got so dirty.

"Max?" she whispered. "I didn't know."

Max turned around and looked at her in surprise.

"Poor Max," she said. "Poor..."

Just then, some cheery music began to ring out from some quarter of the castle. It was a Bing Crosby song. Those crooning, upbeat tones of his, mixed with the poor quality of the recording. It was one of those old records that hiss as the needle goes round. Max's eyes shot open and his body stiffened. As though responding to a signal, he leapt at Bezel and began beating her about the head. Raising the pen up, he plunged it in once more: it pierced her cheek, her left eye and her lower lip, but Bezel felt nothing: she was dead already. In a fury, Max hit her again and again. He wept and cried out in despair.

At the sound of the booming music, I woke with a start. I'd fallen half-sleep in the bath. Going out into the hallway, a towel around my waist, I tried to work out what was going on. Through the music I heard Max's cries and the blows he was dealing Bezel. My heart began to race. Throwing on my bathrobe, I dashed down the hallway. The door to Max's room was locked, and I heard him shouting inside. Cries of pain, despairing howls. I was completely in the dark at that moment and thought that Bezel might be hurting him. I began shouting and banging on the door. I couldn't knock it down – the kinds of doors that give way with a single push only exist in the movies. I was in a fifteenth century castle and would have needed another ten men to burst through. I ran down the stairs. I knew that Bezel kept a set of keys in the kitchen. I emptied various earthenware pots, rummaged through the drawers and cupboards. I finally found them on the mantelpiece, ran back up the stairs and tried each of the keys in the lock. The cries coming from inside set my teeth on edge – Max sounded like he was being skinned alive. He was shouting out random words and phrases, in amongst sobs cut short by his stuttering breaths. Finally I found the right key. Dashing through the bedroom, I again had to try the keys on the bathroom door, but this time I found the right one more quickly. I threw the door, open and found a spectacle I could hardly credit.

Bezel lay naked in the bath, her face a bloody, pulpy mess. The walls were blood-spattered, and the bathwater was scarlet red. Max was sitting on the floor looking vacant. The scant foam remaining was tinged a funereal pink. Gripping the pen tightly in one hand, he stared down at the bloody scrawls and splashes on the floor. The tiles were a slippery mess. Lifting his eyes to meet mine, there was a lost look on his face – a look I hadn't seen before, verging on the inhuman. His hands were shaking and something viscous dripped from the pen.

"It was me," he declared, though it sounded half like a question.

"Max!"

I went over and took the pen from him.

"She never let me be myself," he said, eyes closed.

His face was wet with tears, and his breath once more grew rapid and stuttering. His body began to tremble from head to toe as though he was being shaken. His teeth chattered; his jaw stiffened spasmodically

"'Let's get out of here, Max," I said, taking him by the arm.

"What does it mean?" he said, staring despairingly at the floor. "I don't understand."

"What does what mean?"

I didn't know what he was talking about. I looked at the blood smeared all over the tiles. Some of the splashes were dark and thick, and others, mixed with water, made twisted, meaningless hieroglyphs.

"It's nothing," I said. "They're just smears."

He came with me, though he found walking a challenge. His body was a flimsy mass of flesh and bones.

"Here, lie down."

The music came to a sudden stop, and I was suddenly reminded that we were being watched. Probably they wanted to hear what was going to be said, but I couldn't for the life of me think of anything to say. I felt mute, horrified. They had watched it all. They could have intervened, and yet nobody had lifted a finger to save Bezel. Looking through into the bathroom, I saw her slumped against the tiled wall.

"Is nobody really going to come?" I eventually roared at the ceiling.

Max trembled in fits and starts, still staring at the blood stains on the sheets. I don't know how long I spent standing in silence, hypnotised by the lost look on his face. He was immersed in his own void. From there, he must have been watching from the other side of the looking glass. Night had begun to fall, plunging the bedroom into darkness. Silence and the absence of light seemed to creep across us, as though to devour us. I stayed alert, my body rigid. I strained to keep at bay the hum of silence and single out the echo of footsteps coming down the hallway. But nobody, I realised, was running to our aid.

I looked at the bath, and again I caught the spectacle of Bezel. The blood on her face had gone black by now. Max continued to scrutinise the sheets on which he lay. I was overcome with a feeling of panic. What was I doing there? Why was I watching over a raving murderer, and Bezel's blood-spattered corpse? What was I waiting for?

I got up and went over to Max.

"Max, I'm going out for a minute," I said. "Max, can you hear me?"

He lifted his gaze, and I looked into his eyes again. They were the eyes of a mad man, obliterated by pain. It was the most chilling expression I'd seen in my life. I had to look away. That look contained despair and menace, hate and love…

"Daddy?" he whispered, bemused

I felt a twinge in my chest. Blood rushed to my head, and I felt like running away as fast I could. I knew that it was the first time in his life he would have spoken that word in front of anyone, addressed anyone by it. Like his memories, it had always lain dormant, had never been brought into play. Was he so in need of somebody that he could erase the pain and horror that paternal figure had brought to his life? He was capable of clinging onto anything at all, if it meant not being alone, if it meant giving himself some point of reference, some handle. But I wasn't his father. I couldn't bear such a burden. I felt panic-stricken, and a ghastly fear – of what, I didn't know.

Bewildered, I went out of the room, locking the door behind me. There were no lights on in the hallway and I tripped on the edge of a rug. I was quite out of breath when I came to the top of the stairs. Leaning on the banister, I tried to recover my breath. I exhaled hard, as if to sweep away that word which was still resonating, still flickering inside me. I couldn't leave him in that state. What had they turned him into? What were they turning everyone into? I knew they were watching us, that they had seen everything. How I pitied Bezel. Drake had used her as bait. He had given her precise instructions that would bring Max to boiling point, in full knowledge she'd then be in terrible danger: by playing the seductress, she had in fact been digging her own grave. Such an outcome had been more likely with every passing day, and Drake must have known that. It had only been a question of time. A terrible feeling of guilt came over me. If I hadn't gone and taken that bath, I thought, if I had just stayed with her and Max, she would still be alive. Her death had come down to something as insignificant as a stumble, falling in a muddy puddle. I looked up at the ceiling in terror: what kind of conclusions would they have drawn after Max pounced on her? What notes would they have taken? How many observers would have been standing there in their immaculate white gowns?

I sat down on the stairs. They didn't understand. This was real life, not a play in a theatre, not some drama they could use to hone their practical knowledge of the functioning of the brain. It was my life. It was Bezel's, Max's, and the lives of all the people shut up in this place. A wave of anger gripped my throat. I felt like crying out, but that wouldn't bring Bezel back, and it wouldn't free Max from the future that awaited him, nor solve my predicament – shut up in this place, and on the verge of collapse. What was next for me? Was there nobody in this whole place who acted like a normal human being? The man I had spoken to the previous night in the forest came to mind. I looked at my watch. In the evening, he had said, at the library. Perhaps I might still catch him. He was likely just another lunatic, someone like Ávila who thought he held some special status. But I was hardly blessed with options, however uncertain this lifeline might be. I glanced back at Max's bedroom and quivered in that silence. He would still be lying on his bed, trying to decipher those bloodstains, and Bezel's skin would be growing whiter by the minute, just as my sister's once had.

I got dressed and rushed out of the hotel. My heart was pounding. I felt a crushing sense of guilt for all that had happened. I was the only one who could have prevented Bezel's murder, the only one who could have helped Max with his nightmares. I had read his notebook, and knew that something was looming over him, that he was increasingly confused and afraid. Max was no longer Max. He was a danger now. If the rage that had come over him with Bezel reared up once more, he would be capable of tearing anyone to pieces. And what if he went for me? What would I do? Defend myself? Hit back? I couldn't. I felt a compassion for the young man that was – why not admit it – almost paternal. I felt somehow responsible for him. I was all he had. If I abandoned him to his fate, to whatever awaited him, he would end up becoming a murderer. And nothing else. Nobody was a murderer and nothing more, nobody deserved to have a single aspect of themselves define them, or to become nothing but a guinea pig. Not in my worst imaginings had I ever thought Drake being capable of such extremes, that his cruelty could be so monstrous and inhuman. He thought himself above human affairs and behaved like a god, only bothering to justify his interventions when he deemed it necessary. He would only get involved to bring a situation to the cliff edge, and then, as the tragedy unfolded, step back, put a distance between himself and mere mortals, using the freedom he had given them as his excuse.

What did he have in mind for me? An end like Bezel's? I was not only at Drake's mercy, but also that of the sick individuals peopling the town. What if someone were to be pushed over the edge as Max had been, and came after me? There was nobody to stop them. On the contrary, they'd be gathering around that screen of theirs and taking notes, making bets, amending their predictions. There was no police force to keep order, not even a moral code of conduct. Nothing was taboo. Every single person in Shimts could quite easily go into a murderous rage, begin killing one another, and nobody would care in the slightest. I had to calm myself. First and foremost, I had to find out how I had come to this place, why that worm was still turning inside me, devouring any semblance of certainty. Drake was not God. He was simply a manipulator playing at being the demiurge, sowing chaos and destruction. But even so, I could yet be proved wrong.

# XXI

Liber LXXVII
"the law of
the strong:
this is our law
and the joy
of the world"
-AL. II.21.
"Do what thou wilt shall be the whole of the law"
-AL. I. 40.
"Thou hast no right but to do thy will. Do that, and
no other
shall say nay" -AL. I. 42.3.
"Every man and every woman is a star" -AL. I. 3.
**There is no god but man.**
1. Man has the right to live by his own law -
to do live in the way that he loves to do:
to work as he will: to lay as he will:
to rest as he will:
to die when and how he will.
2. Man has the right to eat what he will:
to drink what he will:
to dwell where he will:
to move as he will
on the face of the earth.
3. Man has the right to think what he will:
to speak what he will:
to write what he will:
to draw, paint, carve, etch, mould, build as he will:
to dress as he will.
4. Man has the right to love as he will:
"take your fill and will of love as ye will,
when, where, and with whom ye will" -AL. I. 51.
5. Man has the right to kill those who would thwart
these rights.

"the slaves shall serve" -AL. II. 58.
"Love is the law, love under will" -AL. I. 57.

Summary of the Thelemite Doctrine
Book LXXVII: Oz,
published in postcard form c. 1943
Aleister Crowley

Not knowing where the library was, I went to Hausen's bar. When I got there, I pushed on the door, but the place was shut. The lights were off but there still seemed to be one on in the back room. I knocked several times, and after a minute a figure appeared. The person walked slowly over, drew back the drape and undid the lock.

"I'm shut. I was just leaving."

"I just need you to tell me where the library is," I said wearily.

"That'll be shut too."

"Doesn't matter. Tell me where it is."

"Go up Leila Waddell Street, past Oz Street on the right, and you'll come to a square. The big building is the library. You can't miss it."

"Leila Waddell?" I said, turning to leave.

"That's the name of the street."

"That name…" I said in confusion.

"She was Crowley's wife," he said indifferently.

"God!" I said rubbing my forehead. "Someone would have to be stark raving to call a street that."

"It's a name like any other. What's wrong with it?

"The name of a she-devil, isn't that enough?"

Hausen shrugged.

"I suppose it's to stop us from forgetting the law," he said.

"What law?"

"The Book of The Law. This is the only law," he smiled, and it sounded like something he'd been taught in a song, the way schoolchildren are.

"Do what thou wilt." I said.

"Exactly," he said, pointing at me.

"Just in case they weren't nutty enough, right?" I spat.

Hausen said nothing, merely frowned at me. I left him by the door, I started towards the library, going along Leila Waddell Street, which threaded between rows of houses and came out onto a square. The library was housed in a majestic building, far larger and more elegant than the rest. A pair of columns thick as towers flanked a wide set of steps leading up to the main door. I almost ran there and, reaching the foot of the building, I glanced up and saw the clouds skittering by overhead, as though being pursued by something. I pushed open the door. The thud as it swung shut behind me resounded lugubriously against the walls. The air was cold and damp, drifting slowly down from the vaulted dome. The place lay in half-darkness, only the wan, purplish twilight to illuminate it.

I paused for a moment. The silence was broken intermittently by a metallic sound, something like the tick-tock of a wall clock. I made my way along a wide passageway with high bookshelves on either side. Thousands of books stacked high and out of reach. There were steps one could use, but they barely went as high as the fifth shelf, leaving the higher ones out of reach. At the centre of an oval-shaped chamber stood a circular wooden table bearing a faded sign on which the word 'Information' could just about be deciphered. I didn't know where to begin my search, I didn't even know the name of the man I was looking for. I noticed that the sound of the clock seemed to be slowing down. When I had come in, it had made a continuous noise, but now it seemed tired, as though the cord were about to break, to mark out its final seconds.

I went slowly on, trying to establish where the sound was coming from. My footsteps led me to a glass door beyond which was a dark, rather disorderly looking office. On the far side of a desk strewn with objects, feet knocked against a rocking chair which squeaked lethargically. The rocking chair was in turn knocked by the lifeless body of the man I'd met in the forest the night before. He was hanging by the neck from a gilt chandelier bowed under the weight of the years and accumulated dirt. He had gone a livid purple, with the bloated look of the recently hanged who have just yielded to asphyxiation after the vain struggle to stave off death. I felt dizzy and my vision went dark for a moment. I leaned against the desk to stop myself from falling.

"Another suicide," said a female voice behind me.

I spun round in surprise, giving an unwitting cry. A thin, unfriendly-looking woman stood leaning against the door. A kerchief covered her head and she had an apron on over her dress. Coming forward, she gave me a withering look before glancing at the bulging eyes of the hanged man stubbornly vigilant in the darkness. After a few seconds, the body stopped swinging back and forth. The tap-tap and squeak of the rocking chair disappeared. A profound quiet descended on the library.

"Who are you?" I asked the woman in fright. My chest was throbbing.

"Vahlemkamp."

"What's happened?" I said, feeling quite unnerved. My brow was covered in sweat. My legs felt weak, as though the bones had been removed and I was having to prop myself up on mere muscle.

"Who knows?" she shrugged.

"Who was he?"

"The librarian."

"Why do you think he did it?" I said, my stomach heaving.

"No idea. I just came to return a book," she said, holding out a small book with a dark cover. "It's a mystery." Going over to the body, she calmly considered it, as though by seeing the face close up she might establish the man's motives. "No, search me. What about you? Do you know what might have happened?"

"No," I said nervously. "I've only just found out who he is."

"Are you here to return a book as well?" she said, looking down at my hands.

"No, I… I saw him last night and wanted to talk to him."

"I thought you said you didn't know him."

"I didn't. It was fleeting. He came over to talk to me, and we exchanged a few words."

"That is strange," she said slowly.

"What do you mean?"

"Just that Emons was a man of exceedingly few words. I don't actually remember having heard more than monosyllables from him in the last ten years. That was when he said anything at all."

I didn't know what to say.

"Well," she said, turning back to the door, "I guess I'll need to bring the book back some other time."

"But!" I said, going after her. "Are we just going to leave him here?"

"What do you suggest? He'll be dealt with. Don't worry about it." Then, going to leave, she turned back and said offhandedly:

"By the way, isn't there a film you'd like to see?"

"Film?"

"There are some really interesting ones."

"Where?"

"At the hospital, of course. All you have to do is ask for them."

They knew what I was looking for. They knew I'd spoken to Emons that night, and that I was destined for the library. They knew everything.

"Who sent you to tell me this? Did you kill the librarian?"

"Me? No."

"Why are you telling me about the films?"

"Because everybody needs to see these films, sooner or later. You aren't the only one who needs answers, and they hold the only truth there is. Don't be afraid of going and asking for them. Anyone's allowed to see them."

"Where?"

"The first floor of the hospital. Ask for Schneider."

The woman went off down the hallway. I heard her footsteps grow fainter, then the dull thud of the main door shutting. Turning around again, I was presented with the unpleasant grimace on the librarian's face. His body looked as though it weighed several tons, as though weights were attached to his feet. A sudden feeling of tiredness and indifference took hold of me. I'm never going to get out of this place, I thought, whatever I do; they'll have second-guessed it, they'll be one step ahead of me. They'll do with me as they please. They'll try to make everything seem normal. They want to make me believe this woman was really here to return a book, that it's pure coincidence the librarian hanged himself, as though it were something he liked to do after work every day. But they killed him because he was going to help me. This man knew something, something I needed to know.

I left the library with a hole in my stomach. There was nobody on the street and it had started to rain, a drizzle so fine you hardly felt it.

I stopped in the middle of the empty square and for a moment had the feeling that nothing was actually happening, that the whole thing was a charade and I wasn't really there. But if I wasn't there, where was I? Was I really anywhere at all? The left side of my head was hurting. It was the rain. It always gave me a headache. That's it, I said to myself, none of this is real. It's just a nightmare, a bad dream. How could a place like this really exist? How could people like Drake really exist, or his assistants for that matter? I felt a certain relief at reaching this conclusion, but straightaway thought I must be fooling myself. No dream was like this. Dreams did not invade one's waking life, did not destroy one's capacity to reason. They were too brief to let us become lost in space and time to the point of forgetting who we even were… Why couldn't I get Max out of my head? Why couldn't I stop thinking about that word he'd said in that low, hesitant voice? A simple conjunction of sounds was all it was, spoken by a person whose mind was completely gone. Why was everything growing dark around me? It wasn't only the night. The light of hope was also growing weak inside me. I suddenly realised that I was alone, truly alone. I couldn't even rely on my own sense of truth. And that was solitude in the true sense. My situation wasn't very different to Max's. Each of us was wandering lost in our own inner worlds, horrified at the prospect of losing ourselves. I needed to see those tapes. To find out how it was I had got there.

I crossed the town in the rain and made my way through the forest to the hospital. On coming to the clearing bounded by the glass buildings, the same feeling of panic came over me that I'd felt the first time. Night had nearly fallen, and the glass surfaces reflected nothing but dark, indistinct blurs. Small, half-buried lights lined the earth paths. The lights gave the place the feeling of a country club, or some modern residential area. Lights were on in some of the rooms, and the glass walls gave a clear view of the interiors. By day they reflected the sun and the surrounding forest, but by night the artificial lights put everything inside on display, its true source. Like shop windows, one could see the people moving around inside. The tiny rooms in the first building, which were part of the hospital, contrasted with the cheerful tones of the illuminated rectangles in subsequent ones. Each of the rooms was a different colour. I moved in the direction of the path that led between the buildings. People came and went with an air of utter normality. A tranquil kind of motion, only reached when the everyday becomes invisible. They were just getting on with life. A group of people chatted animatedly in one of the rooms, each sitting on a bed; in another, on one of the higher floors, a couple was having rough sex up against the glass, their silhouettes jerking violently back and forth. Lower down, in a kind of seminar room with individual desks, another group listened attentively to a man in a white coat holding forth. I saw them laugh in unison at the man's words, before immediately taking notes in their respective notebooks. To the right, on the ground floor, was a dining hall. A number of men were having a heated discussion around a table covered with empty plates and cups of hot, steaming drinks. The exchanges were interspersed with enthusiastic puffs on cigars. The room was dense with smoke, like a nightclub. I backed away, thinking, how was it possible for these people to live so comfortably, so carefree, when on the other side of the forest in the town, two murders had so recently taken place? Didn't they know one of them might be next? Why were they smiling? Why did they seem to be enjoying their lives? Didn't they want to get out of there?

I made my way towards the hospital, feeling appalled. They seemed like everyday people, people content with their lives, integrated into the world, with opinions of their own. To look at them, nothing suggested they were spending their days in a psychiatric hospital, in this isolated place, miles from anywhere. It was the general air of contentment that so horrified me. They seemed not to have a care in the world, let alone any discernible mental illnesses. They acted like any group of men and women would in a holiday destination.

"Hey, Mr Bughin," I heard someone behind me say. Turning, I found Hausen before me, approaching with his awkward gait.

"Have they given you a room?"

"No," I said brusquely.

"Is something wrong?"

"Everything's wrong," I exclaimed.

"Why, what's the matter?" he said.

"What are you here for?" I said, eyeing him suspiciously.

"I'm off to bed."

"Off to bed?"

"Nobody sleeps in the town, nobody except Bezel, the doctor and Vahlenkamp. We all have to come back here at night. The town is just a place for daytime things."

"And what about those midnight processions? I said, remembering what I'd thought when following the lanterns through the forest.

"That's just for any stragglers – the night watchmen go and gather them up after lights out."

"Tell me, Hausen: don't you want to get out of this place?"

"Get out? And go where?"

"What do you mean, where? The outside world."

"But I'm already in the outside world," he said, breathing in the fresh mountain air. "Don't you think this place is sufficiently outside?"

"I'm not talking about fresh air, Hausen."

"The air's the same everywhere. Look," he said, gesturing at the clouds. "See, it's the same as any place in the world. The sky is the same, the moon, clouds, trees, the ground. Everything."

"No, it isn't the same."

"Oh? And how is it different?"

Turning towards the building, I looked up at the silhouettes of the people inside. They were going on with their lives, concerned with what concerned them, caught up in their conversations and relationships. They did the same as any person in any place. That was true. I myself had just been thinking how natural everything seemed.

"They can't leave," I said eventually. "That's the difference."

"Who told you that?" he laughed. "We're allowed to leave whenever we like."

"You're lying."

"Why would I lie?" he said, offended.

"Because they want me to stay, not to kick up a fuss. To fit in with their savage ways."

"What do you mean 'savage'?"

"Of course," I smiled. "You don't know. You don't know that Bezel has been brutally murdered, or that the librarian has been hanged from a chandelier."

"Murdered?" he said, taken aback.

"Yes. Max did it. Are you surprised?"

"To be honest, no."

"She's lying in a bloody bath as we speak, and the librarian is still hanging by the neck from a chandelier. Call that normal?"

"No, no, I don't. But," he said hesitantly, "are you trying to tell me that kind of thing doesn't happen in the outside world?"

I said nothing. I didn't know what to say.

"So, you see," he said nonchalantly, "this is a normal place, even in this regard it's like anywhere else. Everybody dies," he said, as though explaining the secret of life to a child.

"Of course they do, but where else would you get people watching a murder take place and not lifting a finger to help? Knowing that somebody is going to be brutally murdered, and not doing anything but watching it on camera?"

"Well, everywhere," he shrugged. "Don't you watch TV? Just yesterday, in Los Angeles, a tourist recorded some police beating a black guy to death. In Bosnia and Palestine, people die every day. I've seen it, nobody does anything. I don't know why you find it strange."

A great yawning chasm opened up in my stomach, a feeling of overwhelming reluctance that left me barely able to stand up. I dropped to my knees, unable to speak. Hausen crouched down next to me.

"What are you crying for, my friend? What's the matter?"

"This isn't the way things are," I said, utterly enervated. "It just isn't."

"What things?"

"You can't go around deceiving people like this. The whole lot of you, you're living a complete lie."

"Honestly, I beg to differ. This place suits me. I could leave, indeed, but what for? To spend the rest of my days up to my eyeballs in tranquillisers in some lunatic asylum? I chose to come here, Drake offered me the chance years ago, and I took it. What's so wrong with that?"

"Why are you here, Hausen?"

"I tried to kill two doctors," he said sadly. "I just lost it, that's all there was to it. My wife and I had a car accident on our honeymoon, and then a medical oversight led to her death. I was left half-paralysed," he said, pointing to his dead foot. "I was in a lunatic asylum for years, before Drake showed up to help me. He got me out of the despicable hole I found myself in and gave me a new life."

"I'm sorry."

"It was all a long time ago," he said, making a show of not being affected.

"You might be here of your own free will. But I was kidnapped. I don't want to stay."

"Where do you want to go?"

"Home. I want to go back to my life."

"Maybe it isn't as simple as all that."

"What do you mean?"

"Maybe there are things you are still forgetting. It happened to me. I had amnesia for a number of weeks. I didn't even remember trying to kill those two doctors. When my memory came back I thought the whole thing was made up, that my wife wasn't dead, that people were having me on. I still saw her, we'd talk. I thought everyone else was crazy, for not being able to see her. It took me a while to accept it. But something good came out of the whole thing. After the accident I realised I was able to communicate with the dead. Yes," he said, putting a hand on my arm. "Don't laugh, it's true. Well… The reality is, I'm not completely sure they are dead people, but I'm certain there is somebody who talks to me, and tells me really interesting things."

"That's what I'm talking about. This 'somebody who talks to me'. Do you see what I mean?"

"No."

"I mean, the dead don't talk to anybody."

"How do you know that?"

"You're right, I don't, but even you aren't sure that it's the dead."

"What does it matter who speaks? I listen, and the things I hear strike me as reasonable. More than that – they seem true."

"Nothing seems true to me anymore."

"That's what happens when we begin to understand other people. We stop being able to tell who is right because, in reality, everyone has their view of things. Isn't that true?"

"I feel frightened, Hausen. I'm old and I'm frightened, afraid of what might happen. Did you know I'm here to see some tapes?"

"That's good. The tapes don't lie. You'll feel calmer once you've found out the truth. The worst part about all of this is the uncertainty. Once your doubts are resolved, everything changes colour."

"I'm not so sure. Take Max – you saw him in your bar. He was out of it, it wasn't him. And then what's happened with Bezel. You can't imagine what he did to her," I said, rubbing my brow. "Nothing's going to be the same for him again, and I know it. Something tells me he didn't choose all of this: he's been manipulated."

"You love him, don't you?"

"Why do you say that?" I said, feeling suddenly defensive.

"No reason. It just struck me seeing the two of you in the bar. He feels affection for you as well."

I eyed Hausen. Suddenly everything he'd been saying seemed premeditated. Like he'd been sent to convince me that everything was rosy, and that some bond existed between Max and me.

"What are you up to?" I said, suddenly furious.

"As in?"

"Why did you come over and start talking to me?"

"I saw you and I came over. That's all."

"No, you're lying. Just like that woman in the library. She wasn't there just by chance, she'd gone specifically to tell me I could come and see the tapes, and that I didn't need to go on pretending to be somebody else. Because they know what I'm thinking."

"Now it's you talking like a madman."

"Yes, it might sound like madness, but what I'm saying is the truth."

"So is what I'm saying. You're telling me your experience and I am telling you mine."

He gave me a sympathetic look and patted me on the shoulder, just as an old friend would. That look calmed me.

"Know what, Hausen? Sometimes you don't seem crazy."

"Well, I am. I can assure you."

"If I were to see you," I said, struggling to my feet, "in the street somewhere, in a café, in an office, I wouldn't say you were any crazier than anybody else."

"If it's any use to you, I would say you don't seem crazy either."

"That's because I'm not!" I said, offended. "That's what nobody seems to understand."

"All I know is that people don't wind up in this place by accident. Did you see the way in?"

Looking at Hausen, I gave a weak smile. No, I hadn't seen the way in, or at least I didn't remember it. But I did remember Max's notebook.

"What's the matter with the way in?" I asked.

"There isn't one. That's what's the matter."

"Yes, there is. Max came into town over a bridge which collapsed."

"That bridge is just for show."

"Just for show?"

"It isn't really a bridge. It's pretend."

"But it is there?" I said, unsure now about what I'd read in Max's notes.

"Yes, I'm not saying it isn't," he said indifferently. "But they put it up and take it down at will. You see what I mean."

"Yes, I see."

"Why don't you go and take a look at those tapes? You might feel better afterwards."

"To be honest, I'm feeling increasingly afraid of what I might find on them."

"I'm not going to say it won't be traumatic. I myself spent several months like a vegetable. But you come out of it. When you're here, you come out of it, and out of everything else as well."

"But don't you feel like they've invented your life?"

"How would they go about doing that?" he smiled.

"Beats me. But have you never felt that this shouldn't be your life, that your past is not the one you remember?"

"Before, as I said, I couldn't remember anything. But when I faced up to the reality, everything changed. It was as simple as that. Drake was a great help as well, of course. The kind of therapy he provides can't be found just anywhere."

"And what about Crowley?"

"What about him?"

"Doesn't it seem awful to be following the ideas of a psycho like him?"

"Well, I don't know what you call a psycho. The Book of The Law was a great help to me. It's a wonderful piece of work. Have you read it?"

"No, just the odd paragraph. It's ridiculous you lot see Crowley as a guru."

"Nobody here treats him as their guru. You've got a very strange way of looking at things. We simply share some of his ideas."

"Don't you know that Drake thinks Max is Crowley reincarnated?"

"I don't," he said, shrugging his shoulders.

"What do you mean, you don't know?" I was irked by his indifference.

"I've heard something about it, but I wouldn't know what to tell you."

"Wouldn't, or don't want to."

"Simply, I don't have to answer your questions."

"Yes, you do. That's why they sent for, you right?"

"Nobody sent me to do anything. I was on my way back to my room and found you here. That's all."

"In that case, why don't you go? Why don't you go and leave me in peace? Why don't you get out of here, stop with the propaganda drive?" I said, convinced he wouldn't give up his mission.

"Do yourself a favour. Go and see those tapes."

Turning away, he left me with a stupid smile across on my face. A smile that said: I know your game. What are you going to come up with next? Hausen walked slowly away down the path, and I felt like calling him back, asking him to come and convince me how good life was in this place. There was no point watching those tapes. What if I actually turned out to be mad? How would I react? I couldn't go on without watching them, and perhaps if I did I wouldn't want to go on living.

I entered the building and padded down the stairs. Coming to the bottom floor, I stood and waited in the empty foyer until a young man came by.

"Can I help you?"

"I'm looking for Schneider."

"Some tapes you want to see?"

"Yes," I declared.

"This way, please."

He took me through into a white room with a large television screen and a big burgundy coloured sofa.

"Have a seat for a moment. I'll go and tell him."

Full of nerves, I made myself comfortable on the sofa. My hands brushed against something hanging from each of the sofa arms. There were leashes to tie people by the wrist, velvet-lined as a kind of camouflage. Looking down, I found leashes on the sofa legs as well. The big television screen shone black and brilliant before me. I saw myself reflected in it and began to sweat. I was here now. There was no way back. The door opened and a man in his early forties appeared, black hair and wire framed glasses.

"Are you… are you Simon?"

"Yes," I said, not at all conclusively. I was hardly sure either.

"What do you want to see?"

"I need to find out how it was I arrived in this place."

"I see. Wait here, I'll be right back."

As he was about to go out, I called to him:

"Tell me, Schneider. Do you know about Bezel and the librarian?"

"Yes, of course."

"It's been more than half an hour since I left Max in his room. Has anything been done?"

"No."

"And what are you waiting for?" I said in disgust.

"For you to watch the tapes," he said.

I once more felt distraught.

"Fine, I said. "Bring them in."

"Right away."

He soon returned, carrying a box labelled 'Gerald' on one side. A male nurse, standing well over six feet tall, came and positioned himself by the door like a guard dog.

"This is crazy," I smiled nervously.

"Try to stay calm. Would you like a sedative? It might be an idea. In your case, it's difficult to predict how you'll react, but it's very likely that when you see the reality, a violent side of yourself will emerge, and it might try to hurt you."

"A violent side of myself?" I said, unnerved.

He was speaking as though there was a chance some alien monster might come bursting out of my chest.

"I'm hardly one to be lecturing you, Dr Gerald, but considering your state, I think it's worth reminding you what happens when memories have been repressed by means of alternate personalities. When a person finally faces up to the truth," he said, slipping my hands into the leashes, "it's highly probable that person will react in a violent way. You've been blocking out your true personality by means of another with which you feel more at ease, safer, and the part of you keeping your damaged past from you will do anything it can to stop you from finding out the truth."

"I don't know what you're talking about. Is all of this necessary?"

"Yes. We don't know how you're going to react. Do you?"

Given that I didn't, I kept quiet. Glancing up at the ceiling, I saw a small camera pointing at me from the corner.

"Is this going to be filmed as well?"

"Everything. It's highly useful information."

"Let's get on with it then."

Schneider took a tape out of his box and put it in the player. The screen turned blue, then black again. After a couple of seconds, a title came up in white letters: Gerald's Transfer.

"Wait a second!" I said, my heart jumping out of my throat.

Schneider stopped the tape.

"What's going to happen to me?"

"Nothing. Nothing is going to happen to you. Would you like a sedative?"

"No," I said. "Get on with it then."

The screen changed colour. It was a windy night-time scene. A date blinked on and off in the bottom right-hand corner of the screen. At first, I couldn't tell what I was looking at, but then I realised that it was a heliport surrounded by a bank of trees. A helicopter started to descend, and its bright lights lit the whitened screen for a few seconds. The helicopter landed, and someone opened the rear door from inside. Two male nurses stepped out, reaching back in for a stretcher on which somebody lay. Drake appeared on the right, went over to the men and ordered them to stop for a moment. As he lifted the sheet that covered the body, I saw a head of grey-flecked dark hair. Leaning closer, Drake stroked the forehead of the man. Then covered him up to his neck with the sheet and stood back to let the nurses go by. As they came past the camera, I saw that it was me lying on the stretcher. My eyes were shut and my head lolled to one side, resting on the pillow.

"Stop a moment!" I said to Schneider.

He paused with my face filling the shot. I tried to cast my mind back, but nothing came to me. It was me, no doubt about it, but the image left me cold.

"What does this mean?" I asked.

"What does what mean?"

"Think I'm completely stupid? They could have sedated me on any of the nights since I've been here, and cooked this whole thing up."

"Look at the date though. It's the day you arrived."

"The date? Don't be ridiculous. Did they really think I would swallow this? That seeing myself being pulled out of a helicopter in a drugged-up state would turn me into Mr Hyde? Now, take these things off my wrists."

The feeling of panic evaporated: I felt an immense calm. It had been days since I had felt this calming sensation of safety. Relaxing on the sofa, I took a deep breath. I still didn't know how it was I'd got there, but there was no way these images were going to convince me that I was somebody else, that some monstrous thing was hidden inside me.

"I was so afraid," I said in a low voice.

A hesitant Schneider came over. But rather than untying me, he said:

"Maybe it's better you speak to Drake before seeing another tape."

"What other tape?"

"This one," he said, lifting another one from the box.

"From today?" I said, seeing the date on the side. "I don't

understand what could possibly be on it that's of any interest. My memory's been perfectly fine since I arrived."

"Let's wait a little while, until Drake calls you."

Just then somebody knocked on the door. Schneider went and opened it, and a white-haired young man appeared.

"You've got to come up, right now."

"Let's go," said Schneider. He quickly untied me and we hurried out of the room.

"Where?"

"There isn't time. Let's go up. You'll see."

We took a short flight of stairs and went through some double doors into a room full of screens. There were doctors grouped around the different screens, carefully studying the images before them.

"This way," said Schneider.

Making our way to the far end of the room, we came to a glass section, set apart from the rest of the apparatus. There was Drake, sitting in an armchair, and either side of him a row of men and women and white coats, among whom I saw Margaret. Seeing me come in, Drake got up and came towards me.

"This is important."

He motioned to the man sitting next to him, who gave up his seat. I tried to say something about my situation, about how they couldn't just do with me as they pleased, how I'd fight to the very end – but nobody was listening. They were all glued to the screens up in front of them. Not even Drake, who seemed tense, bothered to look at me. It was then that I noticed Max on one of the screens, and I too found myself immediately enrapt.

"He's just woken up," said Drake, keeping his eyes forward.

Straight ahead of us was a board bearing nine screens, though only four of them were turned on. Over to one side, a man stood at a control desk. One of the central screens showed the room with white walls and the burgundy sofa I'd just left. Two of the screens were dedicated to Max's bedroom, showing it from opposite angles, and a fourth was filming Max's bathroom. Bezel's body was still slumped against the tiled wall. Her eyes looked very white, in contrast to the near-black dark red of her face. The bath water had turned a murky, indeterminate colour. In the bedroom, Max was sitting on the bed looking vacant. He was still staring questioningly at the bloodstains, and his irrational, obstinate attempt to decipher them produced immense sadness in me. He got to his feet and began drifting around the room like a sleepwalker. He was naked and his body looked tiny and frail like the remnant of a life someone had abandoned in a ditch.

He tottered slowly over to the bathroom, peeking in through the door. On seeing Bezel, he let out a cry and covered his mouth. Backing away, he fell back down onto the bed once more.

"Now!" said Drake.

The young man at the control desk pressed a button, and Bing Crosby's silky tones started up in Max's room. Max looked at the ceiling in horror, letting out a cry while convulsively jerking his head from side to side. He grabbed a pillow and stuffed it down over his ears, before collapsing in a trembling heap on the bed. His shouts and moans could be heard through the music. He was convulsing as though possessed.

"Okay," said Drake. "Stop the music a moment."

The music halted and Max seemed to recover. He slowly lifted his head, frightened the music would start again, and dried his eyes on his arm. His face was red and he was having difficulty breathing, as though the room was airless, or the air had been poisoned. His wiry body looked shrivelled and defenceless. His chest was collapsed and his shoulders slumped low. He jumped to his feet and started rummaging around for something in the bed sheets. He frantically shook them and turned them over. He did the same with his clothes, before going into the bathroom. Spotting his notebook in one corner, he used his foot to bring it close, before shaking the blood-spattered pages and trying to clean them with a towel. But the blood wouldn't go away. He moved spasmodically, as though too overwrought to be able to move in a controlled fashion. He blew his nose on the towel, went out of the bathroom and locked the door behind him. Perhaps he was worried that Bezel would get up. He looked around for his pen but couldn't find it. Taking another from his bag he stood staring at it for a brief while, looking completely absent, as though the pen were somebody he was supposed to recognise. He took the lid off and began to write, head twisted down over the notebook. As he wrote, his posture became contorted and tense, with one of his shoulders almost up against his ear. He seemed to be trying to wring every last drop of something out of himself. He began to weep. A silent weeping, like that of a hungry puppy. I felt my stomach curdle.

"What are you doing to him?"

This won me looks of all-round disapproval from the people in the room. Only Drake nodded comprehendingly, before putting a finger to his lips and gesturing for me to go on watching. Max was writing in his notebook, his wailing growing louder and more desperate. Wiping his running nose and the tears with his forearm, he went on writing, writing, as though nothing could stop him.

"Again," said Drake.

The music began to play once more. Max gave a start and dropped the notebook. Crying out, he began running back and forth across the room. He tried the door, but it was locked. He banged on it with his fists, threw his body against it, shouting over and over. His face looked haggard. It looked like he was trying to escape some invisible thread that was about to catch up with him.

"Do something!" I shouted. "Can't you see he is suffering?"

"Shush," Drake said. "Be quiet! There's no avoiding it."

Max hared around the room, glancing at the walls and ceiling as though they were alive, as though seeing something we could barely begin to imagine. Going over to the window, he tried to open it.

"Careful now!" said Drake. "Someone needs to get down there immediately."

One of the men in the room issued orders over a telephone, before hanging up.

"Shall we stop the music?" said the man at the control desk.

"No, not yet," said Drake, though he was clearly worried. "How long before they get there?"

Max had taken a chair and was approaching the window. I felt my heart rate accelerate. Looking at Drake, I saw a bead of sweat rolling down his brow. We each held our breath. He threw the chair against the windowpane, though only managing to make a small crack.

"He's going to jump!" I shouted. "Do something!"

"Where the hell are they?" rasped Drake, looking at the man with the phone, who gave an apologetic shrug. Just then, two men burst into the room and wrestled the chair from Max's hands. Max ran at the window, but the crack he had made was too small. He put up a struggle, but to no avail. He was too weak, and it didn't take much for the pair to subdue him. Eventually he gave up, still sobbing silently. The men looked up at one of the cameras. With a sigh, Drake said:

"Bring him."

The man at the control desk repeated the order, and the two men disappeared from Max's room.

"Well, that's that," said Drake, with a satisfied sigh.

He turned and gave me a questioning smile. My heart was still pounding. For a few seconds I'd thought Max was going to jump, and despair had gripped me. I didn't know what to say, I felt confused and on edge.

"Why did you want me to see this?" I said.

Making himself comfortable in his armchair, as though he'd been expecting my question, he replied:

"Because Max has now remembered everything he needed to remember. He knows who he is now, and I wanted you to be here to see it. This was a unique moment. You can see everything that's happened in his life on our tapes, but this is the present moment. Now, he's going to be himself for the first time in his life. No one will ever make him forget what he is. Now," he said cautiously, "I have a proposal for you: before you see today's tape, the one Schneider here has, think for a moment – think carefully – about everything you know about Max. There's a room here with all his notebooks, and with all of the recordings since he arrived in Shimts, and all the other documents I have gathered over the years. Some of the reports are summaries, of course. Before you find out who you are, you ought to know who Max is. It might help you to make the right decisions. Only by analysing his life will you understand."

"Like you did?"

"Yes, like I did – for the good of Max. Now the spell is broken. No more Bing Crosby songs for Max."

"Bing Crosby," I said, smiling weakly.

Drake shrugged.

"Max is very sensitive to music," he said.

"Why did he try to throw himself out the window?" I said, glancing up at the empty room on the screens. "What was he trying to get away from?"

"I already told you. He's remembered everything."

"What was there still for him to remember?" I said, peering into Drake's face.

"The most important part."

I said nothing. Drake was searching my face as well, with those clear blue eyes of his. I could see he was about to come out with it, that he could barely hold back.

"Well, in a sense I know that you already know this, but... It was Max who killed his mother."

I felt something inside me crumble.

"Are you surprised?" Drake asked. "You've already seen what he did with Bezel."

"I don't believe it."

"You don't know how to listen, Gerald. You're out of practice, your ear's out of practice. Didn't you hear what Max said when you went into the bathroom? He said: 'She never let me be myself.' Obviously he didn't mean Bezel."

"I was far too keyed-up at that moment to hear anything at all."

"He killed her. I have the proof," he said, ever so slightly bashfully.

"Perhaps you'll find it grotesque, but we've also got that on film. You're free to watch it. I am a psychiatrist and it behoves me to use any means available," he said, semi-apologetically. "Max is my most important case, the one of greatest interest to me. But you already know this isn't merely a scientific question. I never abandoned them. I was always there for him. Maybe things could have turned out differently, unfortunately we'll never know. We have no choice but to stick to the facts. The relationship between Max and his mother is one of the most complex I have encountered."

I was struggling to understand Drake's tone. It was like he wanted my forgiveness, like my opinion mattered to him and he wanted me to know his reasoning. I waited for him to go on.

"What Max felt for his mother was more than love. He was utterly dependent on her gaze, needed her approval. In his eyes, she was more real than he was. The truth is that he never felt himself to be more than an extension of her, an object belonging to her."

"And yet he could bring himself to kill her. "

"Don't you see? The person he wanted to kill was himself. But even that was hard precisely because he knew how important he was to his mother. Killing himself was almost worse than killing her. He was nothing but a reflection, a projection. He felt that if her eyes disappeared, he would disappear too. In reality, it wasn't murder he committed, but suicide. In the eyes of the world he might be a murderer, but fundamentally he is nothing more than suicidal.

The strange thing was, I had come to the same conclusions as Drake. Perhaps he and I were not so unlike in mind – a thought that made me shudder.

"What about Bezel? You knew he'd end up killing her. I realised when it was already too late. You used her to bring Max to a frenzy. She was nothing but bait."

"Just as we all are. Think Bezel is less innocent than Max? Well, you're wrong. Very often the victim is more to blame for their death than the murderer. Being a victim does not mean being innocent. Sometimes it means being the author of a long, elaborate ritual leading to your own death, employing all the cunning and manipulation that's required to commit self-sacrifice. It was Bezel's fate to end up like this."

"From what I can see, it is you who decides the fates of all of us."

"That's where you're wrong. All I do is put things in motion, but I have no control over what might ensue. Someone has to put things in motion."

"But if Max isn't a murderer, what is he?"

"An enigma. In his own eyes, and in the eyes of the world. I have tried to understand him, to apply all the knowledge I've learned in books, in cases, in observations, but Max will always be a mystery, utterly indecipherable, a strange combination of circumstances, genes, coincidences and manipulations. Just like the rest of us, really."

Once more I felt a strange sense of communion with Drake's thoughts, difficult though it was to admit. I wanted nothing to do with him, not even in thought.

"In Max's case, all those 'impersonal' circumstances have a name of their own. There's never been any space for chance in his life. You and his mother made sure of that."

"And you, Aldo?" he smiled. "What right have you to exclude yourself from the trio?"

"The right to oblivion perhaps," I sighed. "I can't be sure of anything anymore. Perhaps after seeing the tapes I'll begin to draw conclusions, but even my own reality feels alien to me now."

"Max needs you. I heard him call you father and… that made me shiver. He knows you're his father, he can sense it. Aren't his notebooks astonishing? He has a photographic memory. Same as you. Your brain is just as efficient as these video cameras. There's something in it beyond rational comprehension."

"You can't seriously still believe there's something of Crowley in him. You're the psychiatrist. Don't you see that's absurd?"

"Absurd? There's no such thing as an absurd idea, only unimaginative thinking. What to you is absurd, to another person comprises the most solid of realities. We create the limits for things, dear Gerald. Each and every thought, once conceived, is part of our reality. However preposterous it may be, it comes from inside us. Its origin is irremediably linked to our own story. It is the fruit and at the same time the tree of our desires, of our obsessions, of all our experiences and dreams. You can't spend your life censuring people's thoughts, and your own. But," he said, giving me a disdainful nod, "what can one expect of someone who renounces their own life?"

"If all thoughts are valid, why are you so busy trying to convince me to accept the ideas I reject?"

"Because even chaos is subject to laws. Because it isn't honest to renounce your thoughts in exchange for social acceptance. That's what you've done. Renounced yourself so you could be one of the crowd. All we want for our patients here is that they renounce their self-destructive part. I have no desire to make model citizens of them, or sheep who can easily slot into the herd. This is a chance for them to live in a non-hostile environment. Away from here, they'd be sedated, and continually under pressure. You've seen them. Nobody here interferes in the decisions they make."

"But what do you think you've been doing for the entirety of Max's life, if not that? Who are you trying to fool?"

"Max has been observed, not manipulated. I've tried to make his suffering minimal, but sooner or later we have to pierce the darkness that prevents us from becoming our complete selves." Leaning closer, he gazed into my eyes: "Dive in, Gerald, the water may be cold, it may be dark, but immerse yourself and you will understand. All I ask of you is a week of your time. Study Max's case, take it all in, analyse it. All the material is available to you. If, after looking at it all and seeing your tape from today, you decide to stay on, you'll be very welcome. If not..."

I had splitting headache. Averting my gaze, I lay back in the armchair. Something in me was dissolving with his words. I knew what he was talking about – more than I would have wished to. I understood his point of view only too well, and that filled me with horror. I didn't want to understand him. I knew what this communion meant.

"Max has been stripped of all hope, and you know it..." I growled.

"He isn't my seed. He doesn't have my DNA. It wasn't me who forced him to be born with this mark on him. All I have done is show concern for him, for you and your wife," he said. "That's all I've done, all my life. I have dedicated myself to the three of you entirely. I haven't even had a family of my own. You've been my family: you, your son and Irene. I'm the one," he said jabbing a finger into his chest, "who's got you out of your problems, dealt with the mistakes you've made. Who stopped you from killing each other? Think I like seeing you like this? You've become a stranger, a figment of your own imagination. I'm just trying to help you remember, to bring you back to reality. You can't go on pretending any more, Gerald. You have to realise this whole thing is a charade. You can cure yourself if you stop all the self-censure. All sick minds are capable of doing it for themselves, and you know it. It's external pressures, morality, society that make us betray ourselves. Free yourself of all that. You don't need any of it here."

"This place is monstrous. Nothing in the world could make me stay on here."

"Not even your son."

"Enough of that," I said menacingly.

"He needs you, and you know it, you goddamned fraud. Stop playing at being somebody else, take responsibility for your mistakes – be a man. Your japes with the forbidden are over, because the forbidden doesn't exist here. You aren't alone anymore. I need you, and

Max needs you. Or would you rather spend the rest of your days in a lunatic asylum?"

"That's what you've got in mind for me, isn't it?"

"You won't believe me now if I tell you that I never planned your trajectory, but it's the truth. With Max, I just tried to protect him from himself, and in Irene's case, to protect her from you."

"You've made a psychopath of Max."

"Max was born marked, Gerald. And his mother did her bit to make it worse. She dominated his life, and for Max even living in her glass tower was hard, because she would say one thing and yet be feeling something completely different. Max could sense all of that. Haven't you read his notebooks? There lies the truth about Irene. She couldn't fool Max, far from it. He knew that his mother was afraid of him, of the chance he might one day end up like you. He lived with that his entire life. Again and again she told him he was a good boy, while always worrying what might end up happening. If anybody's to bear the blame, it's her. There was no way she could hide Max, I always told her that, and that the consequences of her attempting to do so would be dire. In symbiotic relationships like theirs, thoughts are more dangerous than words. Max always felt himself to be a monster but one he needed to hide from his mother, from whom all he ever heard was that he was a good boy, a little angel, the best thing that had ever happened to her. That just confused him, created a lack of security at an ontological level, unconsciously terrified as he was of disappointing her. It was this twisted sense of reality that prevented him from being able to love, and from feeling love. He thought himself undeserving. He killed Louis because he began to feel fond of him, to admire him, and then feared that Louis would find out what he was really like. Plus he felt guilty for loving someone other than his mother. That's the way we function. It might seem complicated, but this is just a verbal explanation: what we are able to observe is really very simple. The truth is more incredible still."

"The truth?" I repeated.

"A single truth does perhaps exist, or perhaps each person has their own individual truth, because we can never be anything other than ourselves. We can never see the world through anything but our own eyes, through the lens of our own experiences. Even the psychiatrist views everything via his or her own retina, coloured with that untransferable and unique colour. We are a mystery. Didn't somebody say that man is a mystery to man?" he mused, immersed in his disquisition.

"No," I said. "A wolf, I think. Man is wolf to man."

"All the same," he said wearily. "I too will die without knowing the true meaning of my obsession with the three of you. I will die without knowing if Max bears within himself a fragment of Crowley's soul. Perhaps in the end you will be proved right, and I am some lunatic trying to prise the divine spark from people who barely know who they are. As you can see, I'm not even sure about this, but I will go on dedicating myself to my obsessions. It is they that foster progress, they that change the world. Each and every one is an invisible motor. Who knows, perhaps the universe itself is nothing but the secret obsession of a being who does not know its meaning either."

I was shaken by the evident vulnerability of the look he then gave me; it felt like a jolt of electricity running through me from head to toe. I realised that he felt for me, that he was in fact the person he claimed to be and I was merely a lunatic refusing to accept myself.

"There's no more time to waste, Gerald. You know that, don't you? You have to remember. You have to do what's right for Max. We owe it to him, both of us."

I felt gripped by fear. A sensation of nausea and vertigo grew in my stomach, and for a moment I felt everything about me was underwater.

"And if you turn out to be right?" I said in a panic. "What will become of me? If I discover that I was who you say I was, and that inside me, like Max, a murderer is hidden?"

"You will have to accept yourself because all is not lost."

"But…" I returned to the feeling I'd had on seeing the woman in the library and Hausen in the gardens. "Who's to say I shouldn't resist? Put an end to all that you represent."

"Do I represent so much?"

"Everything's so overwhelming of late. It's been so intense. I've even started to doubt whether any of this is real."

"It is. It's real for you. Is anything more authentic? Your fantasy is more real than any of my realities because I am outside of you and you will never be outside of yourself. Your world, your universe, is in your mind."

I felt like I'd heard it all before. Hadn't I been thinking these same things moments earlier? What was he up to? Trying to show that he could read my mind?

"Why not leave it as it is, then? Why make the effort to uncover a reality that only wishes to remain hidden?" I said, my fear growing. "Who says reality has to prevail over fantasy, that it has to take its place?"

"Mutual understanding. Madness is an excess of subjectivity – or, as the ancients understood it, an excess of the humours. What we think

226

of as madness today was melancholy then. Aristotle put it down to too much black bile. He wasn't talking about just any kind of madness, though, but the kind that is intrinsic to a person's nature, that is born with a person and dies with them. A little like an invisible stigma that condemns us never to be understood by the common man."

"I can understand you. I can understand Max…"

"But we cannot understand you, and you go on causing damage."

"To whom?"

"Look at Max's case, study it, and after a week or a few days, however long you need, put today's tape in the player. Everything I can possible say now will go on sounding false to you. There's only one way to put an end to all of this."

"What's on the tape?"

"Irrefutable evidence of who you are."

"I feel so afraid… I feel like I might go mad even if I don't see it."

Coming close, he took my hands in his. At his touch, a feeling of security came over me, unjustifiable as it seemed. Only hours earlier I had been thinking of ways to kill him and make my escape. Now he was taking my hands in his, encouraging me to face up to an uncertain past upon which I was feeling increasingly dependent.

"Remember that it is only fear that prompts you to act like a madman. Everyone's boundaries are set by fear. I know that in your eyes I represent everything that needs destroying, that you've turned me into the justification of the personality you have taken on, but when this is all over, the self you invented will cease to exist. There's nothing more I can do for you. It's up to you now. If you accept that, we might be able to find a solution, if not, you can't stay on here. We only let people stay here who accept their real selves. You've already been a prisoner too long and it was no easy thing for me to bring you here. But I won't allow you to hurt Max. You don't need to worry because nobody will ever find out what's taken place here. My people will never breathe a word of it. So there's no need to worry."

"What are you talking about?"

"Trust. Facing up to it is the only solution, the only cure. After that, the passage of time, and some therapy, will help you get over it.

He gestured to a man standing by the door, who in turn signalled for me to follow him. I got up. Uncertainty had once more taken hold of me. I left the room immersed in an inner silence that I didn't dare to break. My own inner monologue seemed pointless in those moments. What could I think that would make any sense? What to do in the face of a reality that seemed to contain the definitive answer? Any thought was beside the point, any attempt to convince myself that the whole thing was made up would wither when presented with whatever I was about to see on the screen. If there really was something to it, something irrefutable in and of itself, my thoughts were going to be of no use to me. We entered a room full of folders organised by date, and a box containing Max's notebooks, a stack of videotapes to one side and then, straight ahead, a blank TV screen. Schneider and the towering nurse immediately reappeared.

"Max is under observation," said Schneider, warmly.

"How is he doing?" I said.

Schneider came nearer and I felt as though he was about to deliver the most awful news imaginable. I gave him a questioning, despairing look.

"He's in shock. The memories have stopped him from doing anything, he's catatonic."

I knew this was no offhand remark. It was a way of telling me that Max needed me, that I needed to fight, not only for myself but for him. That when I watched whatever it was I was about to be presented with, I should remember that someone other than me was involved, that my response had a bearing on more than just my life.

"You've got everything here you need. Through this door," he said, pointing to my left, "is a bedroom and a bathroom for you to use. If you need anything, you just press this button," he said, showing me a telephone on the table. "Food will be brought to you, anything you ask for. If you need to go outside you can, but it might be better for you to stay put until you have come to a decision. Until you are ready to see the tape, today's one."

Then Schneider went out, and I stood with Max's life before me. All his thoughts and feelings were there, days he had forgotten and others he had recently begun to remember. I was able to see his transformation from the night he arrived in Shimts, unaware of his own identity, through to the brutal murder of Bezel. It was all so awful. The cameras didn't miss a single look, sigh, or despairing grimace, not a single shudder. Max's notebooks were accompanied by Irene's diaries, organised according to date. There was even the tape showing her murder. I couldn't bring myself to watch it. I limited myself to reading Max's notebooks from the time when he'd been ignorant of his identity and to analysing the comments made about them by Drake and his team. I spent four days reading, watching and listening, until I knew more about him than he even did about himself. It was dreadful to see how little a life was, seen from the outside.

On the fifth day I decided I was ready to watch the tape. The last and definitive one.

Schneider led me to the room in which I'd watched the footage of my supposed arrival day. The towering nurse came over and placed a thick belt across my waist, hooking it into a pair of concealed hooks in the back of the sofa. My legs were trembling uncontrollably as I tried to get a grip. No thoughts, I said to myself. No thoughts until you've seen the tape. I nodded to Schneider and he pressed the button. The screen turned black and I was then presented with a small room I didn't recognise. There was a table with bookshelves around it lined with folders and, beyond, a rocking chair with a dark grey jacket draped over it. The sound of approaching voices made me jump. I saw two men enter the room. One of them went around the table, picked up the jacket and put it on. Then I was able to see his face. It was the librarian.

I suddenly felt I was going to vomit. My neck jerked, and my body tensed, rigid as stone. It all happened very quickly, as though the movements and the words were not unfolding inside time but all in one single instant, with no before or after. I saw myself from behind sitting at the table, but in reality I was jumping across it…

*I heard a ragged cry, words of harm, names I thought I knew and places I had visited. An enormous door opened in my mind and through it came an avalanche of images and voices, of days and nights, of men and women crowding my mind. All crowding into my soul. They jostled me, hounded me with their shouts and cries. A straight line began to bleed and it became a lacerated belly.*

The librarian's eyes bulged as I strangled him with my bare hands. This man knew something about me that even I didn't know and his words speared my soul. He spoke names that had been buried, laid to rest beneath layers of my intent.

*A baby's cry pierced the air. It was a cry of pain, marked by terrible incomprehension and despair. Then, a cackle pierced my left ear, fading as a procession of men in strange outfits welcomed me into what appeared to be a church, candles burning all around. The sight of a woman's face made me jump out of my seat, but I could hardly move. I cried out, trying to shake off the image of that face, Irene's face, her suspicious, accusing look as she shook her head from side to side. Drake was there, his face thirty years younger and free of wrinkles. I felt a force inside myself and was terrified by its unbridled cruelty.*

*White walls, hundreds of white shining walls, all of them blood-spattered. Hands and straps and coloured shirts, and a longing, a longing that made me dizzy. Crowley's painting and the image of a blue, smiling sun. The chase would never end because I always wanted more. Infinite, constant laughter, echo-less peals of laughter that seemed sincere, but seen from the other side were solitary and strident. A warm, ample bosom, and the moon as the only witness. An open expanse, surrounded by green fields and arms reaching out in supplication. The moon, solitary witness. A sweet, heavenly voice coming close, and an arm about me, a petrified cry. It's my sister. I try to hold her back, to kiss her, I tug at her clothes and find a man making love to her from underneath. I raise a knife in the air, but now the moon is not alone, they are watching me. They know who I am now. I go running along the street and inside the cars, which are being driven by babies, an enormous penis wearing a suit sits in the passenger's seat, reaching over and pulling on the arms of the baby, which refuses to drive any more. A dance full of red faces. Eyes shining white beneath the make-up, all looking at me.*

The librarian limply holds my arms. Once he faints, I pull off his belt and my voice makes my skin shudder. His dead weight rises and knocks against the back of the rocking chair. His face turns purple and I disappear from the screen.

*My sister, naked, crying before me; we both beg at once. I kneel down in front of her, but she doesn't understand, just whimpers, and then I have to slice her throat. A woman who has lost her child hits me on the chest, I spit in her face and hand back her child wrapped in a sheet. The child is Max and he looks up at me affectionately, no hint of any rancour. He hugs me and I feel something burning in my chest. There is a muddy hole in the centre; it burns as though made of wax. The lights go out and the library burns brightly. I drag myself out of the bed where I was lying with my sister. Turning around I see in her veins two dark clots of blood like worms, wriggling towards me. Drake helps me to stay on my feet, he's saying something in my ear but I can't hear him. I order him to get down on his knees and perform fellatio on me. He says he will, but instead slices off my penis and puts it in a woman's handbag. The moon has gone behind the clouds and it is raining. I am soaked through and cold to the bone.*

I reappear in the librarian's office, and as his body dangles before me I feel dizzy. Mrs Vahlenkamp talks to me from the other side of the room, a book in her hands. My head is going to explode.

*Max has just died and I fling a handful of muck into his grave. A prostitute dressed in Bezel's clothes calls out to me from the depths of the earth but all my attention is on Max, as he cries silently inside his coffin. I go scrabbling in the earth and my nails begin to bleed. Max cries out from some place, far, far down. It's him, I know it is. He's calling to me from down there, but I've got things to do. I have no childhood. I can't remember it. The years pass and nothing happens, all of my youth is a blur. There the secret lies. The moon has grown huge and spews out a white substance that makes me vomit. Then everything turns black. I can hear the silence. All around me, the void has triumphed.*

# XXII

## A DAY LIKE ANY OTHER

"If this morning and this encounter are dreams," I
replied, "then each of us does have to think that he alone is
the dreamer. Perhaps our dream will end, perhaps it won't.
Meanwhile, our clear obligation is to accept the
dream, as we have accepted the universe and our having
been brought into it and the fact that we see with our eyes
and that we breathe."
'The Other'
Jorge Luis Borges

Light enters gradually. I feel it through my eyelids. Something heavy and tense pounds inside my head. There is a sharp pain on the left side, just behind my ear. I try to move but cannot. My arms feel heavy. I can barely breathe. Everything goes black agai

I don't know how much time has passed. The light is strong, far stronger than me. I open my eyes and see a white ceiling made of square panels. I can feel my arms and legs but my head is still a dead weight.

Somebody comes into the room. A black man wearing a white coat.

"How are you feeling today?" he asks.

He prods around my eyes, my wrist, examines my neck, before giving me a smile.

"You'll be up and about within a few days, and strong enough to feed yourself again. It's all gone perfectly."

Then he goes out. I am tired. I close my eyes and pass out. When I wake again it's night. I attempt to move my head, but this produces a stabbing pain behind my ear. My head has been shaved and bandaged.

Outside the window of my room, through a cold curtain of mist, I see hundreds of flickering lights. Is it raining? I can't be sure. My neck hurts. Hundreds of ranked buildings grade away into the distance, buildings of glass and metal with tall windows, empty offices inside. I half-sit up and see two symmetrical towers in the distance. One of them, which I cannot say, is the reflection of the other. The towers seem familiar. I know where I am. It's the Twin Towers, I'm in New York. I begin to cry. I have the feeling that something's gone wrong. I shouldn't be here. I close my eyes and let myself drift away.

I hear a man's voice. I open my eyes. The man in the white coat is examining me once more. A woman is winding a clean bandage on my head.

"Where am I?" I say.

"In your room," says the man. "The operation was a success."

"What operation?"

"You had a tumour on the back of your head, we removed it."

"Where's Max?"

The female nurse presses a button and the back of the bed rises to vertical. Both of them smile.

"Where's Max? I repeat.

"Who's Max?"

"He's…" I hesitate, the words are hard to say. "He's my son," I say, holding back the tears.

"We weren't aware that you had a son. Your sister didn't say anything."

"So, she's alive?" I said, trying to think. I begin to remember.

"Well, yes," says the man, clearly confused.

"And Drake?"

"Mr Drake isn't present at the hospital, he had to go on a trip."

"When was I brought here?"

"Several weeks ago."

"I need to know what happened to Max."

"We don't know anybody by that name."

"He's catatonic, and I have to see him. He needs my help. Tell Drake that I'm ready to accept my mistakes. I've watched the tapes, and I know I killed the librarian. I've remembered everything. You have to let me see Max. Drake said that if I were to accept myself, I would be allowed to stay on in Shimts."

"Shimts?" said the nurse.

Frowning, the doctor came over to me. Examining me once more, he gave a look of consternation:

"Rest is what you need."

"Why was I operated on? Who said you could do that?"

"We did it with your authorisation, and that of your sister."

"You could have died if we hadn't removed the tumour," says the nurse, as though speaking to a child.

"I want to see Drake!"

"As we've said, he's out of town at the moment, but when he comes back you will be able to see him. Now, time for you to get some rest. You've already exerted yourself quite a bit."

"You don't understand. I left Max in Shimts and he needs me. I'm his father."

"Mr Verhaghe. We don't know anything about any relation of yours by that name, but I'm happy to give your sister a call… She lives a long way away, in Paris. Don't you remember?"

"What did you call me?"

Glancing at the doctor, the nurse turns back to me faking a smile. "Gerald Verhaghe."

"Gerald. Yes. That's me."

The pain in my head is unbearable. I begin to drift off. They give me painkillers, but it comes straight back. I can't think straight.

I know that the tapes showed me everything I needed to understand. I know who I am now, and who Max, Drake and Irene are. Drake was right, I am mad. I've spent years pretending to be someone I'm not. I know that all is not well in my mind, I'm a psychiatrist and I know that I need help. The answer was on those tapes. I can't think clearly but I remember having seen my soul and Max's on those tapes. It's all crammed in my head. I need some time to assimilate it all, to put it in order. I'm saturated with information, with feelings.

I don't know what I'm doing here. I should be in Shimts. Maybe Drake, realising I was ill, brought me back here to be operated on. I have a memory of something hurting at the back of my head the first time I went to the Shimts hospital to speak to Drake. But I don't remember the journey here or signing any kind of authorisation.

The light changes, days pass. My strength is returning, I can feed myself again. Every morning on waking I ask after Drake, but the answer is always the same: out of town. They won't say where. I ask if he's in Shimts, but nobody seems to recognize that name. Or at least they claim not to. I ask them to tell me how Max is, and again no answer. They keep saying I don't have a son, and I start to feel afraid. I don't know what they're up to.

The team of surgeons who performed the operation came to see me this morning. They asked me how I am: fine, I said, but I need to go to Shimts straight away, my son is in a catatonic state and he needs me. They seem not to understand. A nurse explains to them that I don't in fact have a son, but that since I woke up I've been insisting on seeing somebody named Max and going to a place called Shimts.

Now they've begun coming to see me on a daily basis, and they ask me questions about my life. I'm very forbearing in my answers: perhaps that will make them understand, and then they'll let me go. But they have another account of my life, what they claim to be the true version of events, though everything about it is quite alien to me. For some reason they're trying to make me forget who I really am. They're incapable of understanding how much it's taken for me to recover my sanity, to accept the mistakes I've made and face up to my true inner self.

Now I understand: they don't know anything about Max, my life or my relationship with Drake. Perhaps I'm better off not telling them anything. It could compromise us.

They come back every day to see how I'm getting on. They look me over. They examine me like an insect in a jar. I've been assigned a psychiatrist, and she tries, with utter ineptitude, to find out what I'm attempting to conceal with my story. I tell her that I know who I am, that I am mad, or was at least, but I am finally willing to get better. It's now that I'm ill, she says, before the operation I was perfectly normal, and the memories I've been talking about are the result of some childhood trauma. I insulted her, I practically pushed and shoved her out of the room. I don't know why Drake is doing this to me. It's beyond me. I want to get out of this place.

Now a pair of men has been sent to see me. The psychiatrist doesn't want to go on with the case. She seems to be afraid of me. I've started writing down the things I remember in a notebook. Everything that happened in Shimts, all that I know about Max and his mother, and about me and Drake. I remember it all in incredible detail. Drake is a real-life person, and he's coming here soon. I don't know if I ought to talk about Shimts now, but I need to show them it's all true. I try to order what we've been through, to render it in as much detail as I can, to show them I know what I'm talking about. This notebook is my life now. My memories are my life. I have described Max, his mother, Drake and even myself, as exhaustively as I can. I began at the beginning, at the moment when my awareness began to grow and an unconscious necessity for change took charge of my life. Before that, I thought I was someone else. A lawyer in Paris. I believed it in the same way you believe in your lives, with the same level of certainty. It's strange. I am far better acquainted with madness now that I know myself to be ill.

Every day, every week, the same. The doctors' questions go on and on. They say mine is a very unusual case. They say that perhaps some part of my brain was affected in the operation, and that's produced these delusions. They aren't delusions, I shout, they're my life. I feel my hope ebbing away. Nobody wants to listen to what I have to say.

I woke up this morning and went looking for my folder. All my notebooks have disappeared. They've taken them away, and now they'll be analysing the contents.

After a number of days with no word, a group of doctors came in accompanied by specialists from other hospitals. They asked me about the things in the notebooks. One of them said, conviction in his voice, that 'Perhaps this can happen'. I don't know what he means, what it is that can perhaps happen.

"When did you come up with the contents of these notebooks?" asks a very tanned, grey-haired doctor.

"I didn't, I've already said that. It all actually happened, just ask Drake."

One of the doctors comes forward and says firmly:

"We've spoken to Drake, and he says he's unaware of any of these events having taken place, whether in the distant past or, as you claim, only recently. Tell me, Gerald, in your capacity as a psychiatrist, can't you see that everything you've written on these pages is just too incredible for anyone to believe? Interesting though it may be, I'm afraid none of it actually happened. Your relationship with these sects," he said, half smiling, "and Mr Drake's participation… This place you describe… Are you unable to see how absurd an invention it is? Are you? Do you still believe that something as horrible as the murder of that woman… Bezel," he said, looking at his notes, "took place while a team of psychiatrists looked on? The way you describe her death it's almost as though you'd been present, or had experienced it yourself."

"I've already told you lot, thousand times, how things worked there. Everything was being filmed. I was given access to the information about Max and about everyone else, because everybody was allowed to see the tapes. There was no such thing as private life in that place, even people's feelings were on display. I am a psychiatrist and I've had no difficulty filling in the gaps. There are times when it doesn't take a genius to see that a person is suffering or that they are afraid. You people are psychiatrists. Presumably you can understand this. The average person in the street has the capacity to. If someone goes to the cinema, can't they tell what the main character is thinking by just looking at their face? This is like that."

"If he had seen all this in recordings, it would be understandable…"

said the youngest doctor in the group, looking at the rest of them. The one with the tan gave him a disapproving look.

"Don't you see that his whole tale lacks logic?"

"Logic?" I repeat.

"It is an interesting story, but the desire to believe that it really happened, this attempt to turn a fantasy into one's own life... We don't know where this chaos in your mind has originated, but the sooner you begin to accept that your thoughts are not real, the sooner you'll get better."

"What do you mean, not real? Don't be ridiculous. How can a thought be unreal?"

"What you have assimilated as the truth," says another of the doctors, "are a dream, a bad, nonsensical dream that cannot, and should not, affect your vision of reality."

"And what, according to you, is my reality? You're trying to impose a reality on me that I don't recognise. All you're doing," I cry, "is messing with my head!"

They look at me in silence.

"I can tell you where Shimts is on the map. Again I say, everything I've put in those notebooks is true. Everything I've written down is my life, my experiences. As strange as they may seem to you."

"Mr Verhaghe," says another of the doctors, seemingly the oldest in the group. "When you have made a complete recovery, we are going to administer some Sodium Amytal. As you know, it is what we call a truth serum. It will help sweep away all the obstacles that prevent you from seeing your true past..."

"I don't need any drugs. In a Scottish town, my son is waiting for me. He's most unwell, and I'm the only one who can help him. The feelings I have for him are not the result of a bodged operation, or a bad dream. For the love of God! Please believe me. You have no idea what it's taken for me to come round to accepting my true identity."

"We have spoken to your sister," says a female doctor, "and she knows nothing about you having a son"

"As I've said, I didn't know either. I found out about Max days ago, in Shimts. Drake can tell you."

"Mr Drake says he doesn't know anybody called Max."

"He's lying!" I shouted, beside myself. "He's betrayed me. He said that if I were to accept myself, I could stay on in Shimts. He took me there under sedation, ask him. I didn't remember that part, because I'd created another personality for myself in my mind. I am crazy. Can't you understand that? I need therapy to make a complete recovery. There are still parts of my life completely inaccessible to my memory.

But I do know that I tried to rape my sister, and afterwards to kill her. Didn't he tell you that? I need to go to Shimts!"

I shout at the top of my lungs and yet nobody seems to hear. Glancing at one another, the doctors turn and file out. I don't know if they understand what I'm trying to say. Drake betrayed me. If he were to speak up, if he told them the truth, everything would be solved. They think I'm crazy and yet now that I'm coming back to my right mind, I'm able to accept my mistakes now. I know I deserve to be locked up. I don't care about that, but I want to go to Shimts, where Max is. Little Max.

They've given me the Sodium Amytal. After the session a doctor said I'd told them the same story, but that none of what I claim to have been through is true, and that I ought to try to accept that. And yet I remember it all with a kind of clarity I have never before experienced. The softness of Bezel's skin – the smell of damp earth and the chimney smoke floating on the air in Shimts. If I shut my eyes, I see before me Hausen's twisted foot and his bar on the high street, the bruised face of the librarian and the bathroom tiles with Bezel's blood splashed all over them. I can recall Max's slight frame the day he called me father for the first time, and all those beautiful drawings filling his notebooks. How can all of that not be real? I know that I was crazy at one point, that I was a tangled mosaic of different personalities, a man divided, composed of scraps. But I have finally managed to free myself of the curse. I have forgiven myself. Drake was right, it really was as simple as that.

Nobody is telling me the truth. They're all lying. They won't let me speak to Drake, and as the days go by, they become increasingly insistent that there's no explanation for any of it. I'm able to think clearly now, and I am beginning to suspect that nothing has changed, I am still Drake's prisoner. Perhaps this is all part of Drake's plan and I am still under observation. Perhaps his idea was this: to make me believe that I am Gerald when in reality I am Simon and, thereby, learn the extent to which it is possible to manipulate a person's mind and enumerate the possible divisions within a life. Perhaps it is only now that my observation has in fact begun. There is a small camera in the ceiling and it is pointed right at me.

They won't let me leave the hospital. The doctors say I am soon to be transferred to a hospital in Texas where they specialise in cases of multiple personalities. My sister doesn't visit. The nurses say she is due to have a baby and can't fly. They say she's married now, and lives in Paris. I've asked why she doesn't call, but nobody seems to know. Nor do they want to give me her number. She must have asked them not to. I know she doesn't want to see me. She detests me.

I dreamt of Max last night. I saw him lying in a bed, in a white-walled room like my own. He lay very still. He was calling out to me from the depths of his soul and I awoke in tears. A nurse came in to give me a sedative, and she stood there listening to my dream. She has children as well. She says that the things I feel must be real, that my affection for Max cannot be due to some short-circuit in my brain, but that there's nothing she can do to help me.

I've been transferred to Texas. They say they'll do all that is possible to help me, that I am in the hands of the best specialists, but that I have to do my bit. But I've run out of patience now. I spend my time shouting at them that I have to go to Scotland as soon as possible, and all they do is feed me sedatives. The more I shout, the crazier they think I am. I've begun missing Drake's therapy, the freedom people had in Shimts, the mountains, the fresh air. Hausen was right.

There are days when I remember nothing. In my lucid moments, I shout at everybody to let me go, saying I want to talk to Drake, but nobody heeds the words of a madman. I attacked one of the doctors. I can't remember what happened now. In the afternoons I go out walking in the gardens with other patients. People who shuffle along, who babble on while staring into the empty air, who shout like I do, just as loudly. I am no different from any of them.

I've lost all energy for the fight. It's pointless. All it gets me is an injection which leaves me feeling sluggish. I feel my hopes fading. It's been too long. The days have turned warm. I don't know if Max will still be alive, or what might have become of him. I still see his face in my dreams. I know that he needs me. The months pass and I feel bone weary.

I now begin to seriously consider the possibility that I am mad: not everybody in the world can be Drake's accomplices. A doctor insists that, in spite of the incredible detail of the world I have created, my story about Shimts is a product of my imagination. And yet… I'm not the person they say I am, though I'm also not sure I am who I think I am. I feel afraid. There's nobody I can trust, I'm completely alone. My memories of Max are the only thing of beauty I have left. At night, when they turn off the lights, I try to imagine him as a child, and I think of all the years I wasted. I look at myself in the mirror and see how much he resembles me. I don't understand how it took me so long to realise.

Might the doctors be right and I've made it all up? It's difficult to accept because the love and the sadness I feel are more real than any other thing in my life. Nonetheless, they say they have proof that I've imagined the whole thing. Perhaps Drake is sitting in his burgundy armchair having a good old laugh.

The days grow longer, there is nothing to differentiate one from another and four years have now gone by. Life goes on only in my mind, but I don't tell them anything because I don't know what they want to hear. I feel myself growing weak. I cannot accept that what we think and feel are not real, in spite of what everybody says. I ask myself the same questions over and over: was I really involved in those satanic sects from which Drake tried to protect me? Did we really perform a ritual to try to bring Crowley's soul back? Did Max really kill Louis as a boy? What was he trying to work out as he stared at those bloodstains? Is it possible for a place like Shimts to exist, where the mad live together, freed of their consciences? Why does nobody know where Shimts is on the map? Is it possible for the mind to create a world as real as that of my experience? If none of my memories are true, where have all these people come from that I know more profoundly than anyone I have supposedly shared my life with? What's in my mind? How many worlds would I be capable of inventing if I didn't think I'd just be called crazy for it? How many people would I be able to love if I believed love merely to be a feeling that can come about at will? Why is Max's cry of despair so strong in me if they say he doesn't exist? Is there anything more real than our own feelings?

The world is crumbling around me. This hospital, the people I now share my life with, the demented souls present in my every day: are they suffering the same agony as I am? In their incoherent babblings, are there also children, husbands, wives and siblings who, like mine, await them somewhere in the world? Are our cries of despair interchangeable? A request to be heard? Those gazes turned inwards on their lonely selves: are they inventing people and places that never existed, and that will abide only in their minds? Will those universes perish with them, or go on in some place with the thousands of millions of thoughts that are generated day after day? Could I still be dreaming, as I thought I was when I left the Shimts library that day? Is this what people mean when they talk about being crazy?

If the doctors are right and I never had a child, how is it possible for me to love a non-existent person with all my soul? Is the love I feel a fallacy? Is love a fallacy? How can we be certain we have a past when the only thing we are left with is the memory of it?

I now know that I will die without any answers to these questions because the greatest secrets in the universe are hidden inside us and we are not everlasting, but mortals. We have sent people into outer space and yet the impalpable essence that sustains our bodies is *terra incognita*. After all, what is the true meaning of our obsessions?

I sometimes think that Drake hates me, but I can't understand why that might be. I can never get to the bottom of what it is that binds us. What he feels for me. He is the only proof that something in my life is real, but he's still to put in an appearance. I don't know why I am unable to forget something he said:

"Someone has to put things in motion." He has turned me into what I now am: an enigma. The question marks spread the length and breadth of the world. And at the same time, he has returned Max to me, and the love I feel for him helps me to keep going.

We will go for a walk outside again today. The sun is bright in the sky and I know that somewhere, in a place very far from where I am, and from where my mind is now, Max is still lying motionless in his bed. Silent. Waiting.

Samantha Devin
London, 22 December, 1998